A TEMPTING THREAT

"Hah," Isabelle spat angrily. "Were we to meet under normal circumstances, you would be begging for a small crumb of my affection. And I would pay you no more mind than a buzzing insect."

Sebastion advanced on her suddenly, and she realized what a fool she had been to taunt him further. Her back was already pressed to the wall, and now he barred her path forward. She was trapped.

Her captor stopped mere inches from her, so tall that he blocked the meager light in the foyer. "I could prove you a liar, mademoiselle," he said in a smooth tone that sent a shiver down her spine.

"You said you had never forced yourself on any woman," she reminded him breathlessly.

He leaned in close, bracketing her small frame with outstretched arms, his hands planted firmly on the wall on each side of her. "I wouldn't have to force myself on you," he promised. "You would want me." The heat of his body and his masculine scent surrounded her. His mouth was so close to hers that they were almost kissing.

She was rooted to the spot, mesmerized by the smoldering flames in his eyes. "Never," she whispered. Her throat had suddenly gone dry, and she licked her lips nervously. Sebastion's gaze fell to her mouth, and for one breathless moment she thought he would make good on his threat. And for one breathless moment she wanted him to.

A TREASURE TO HOLD

KATHLEEN MCCARTHY

LEISURE BOOKS NEW YORK CITY

A LEISURE BOOK®

February 2003

Published by

Dorchester Publishing Co., Inc.
276 Fifth Avenue
New York, NY 10001

ISBN 0-8439-5146-X

Visit us on the web at www.dorchesterpub.com.

To Patrick, for giving me the time and encouragement to write. I love you.

Special thanks to my parents for instilling in me a love of books, to my sister for her interest and support, and to my Grandmother Ring for teaching me by example how to be a lady.

Most of all, thank you, Lord, for your many gifts.

A TREASURE TO HOLD

Prologue

Bedfordshire, England
1827

As thieves went he was particularly inept, but since he had never before actually stolen anything, this was to be expected. Getting into the great manor had not been too difficult, but he had gotten lost amid the intricate layout of the mansion, and as a result was now several minutes off schedule. He had planned to be in and out of the building in less than a quarter of an hour but had already used up that time in locating his prize.

With a shaking hand he mopped the sweat from his brow, then clumsily replaced his sodden handkerchief. At last the treasure was before him. All he had to do was take it and get out of this house and out of this wretched country, so he could get on with his life. As silently as a cat he crept toward the marble pedestal where his salvation lay. After all the trouble he had gone to, he was almost disappointed at how ordinary it appeared. A simple chest, smaller than what his mother might keep her jewelry in, with an overlay of dull gold. Though its age and workmanship bespoke value, it certainly could not be worth his risking his life. And yet that's what he was doing, risking his very life to obtain it.

He scowled, cursing the bad luck that had deposited him here. Why, if he had been brought so low as to become a common thief, could he not steal something priceless? Like the crown jewels, for instance. Now there was a goal worthy of his attention. This house was filled with countless riches, yet he had been instructed to take only one small chest, the contents of which were unknown to him. His ignorance angered him greatly, but he had no time for such emotions. Later, when he was safely away from here, he would discover for himself the secrets of his plunder.

He reached for the small box, then froze. Had he heard a noise? His heart beat wildly, so loud to his own ears that he was certain the inhabitants of the house must surely hear. But after several minutes of silence, he convinced himself that he had imagined the sound.

The chest was heavy in his hands, more substantial than he had first thought. He was glad that he had had the presence of mind to bring a sack with him, and he quickly drew it open and carefully placed the treasure inside the enveloping burlap. As he did, something small fell from the chest, landing silently on the Axminster carpet. It was difficult to see in the blackness of the room, so he was forced to go to his hands and knees, feeling his way along the rug for whatever it was.

After a few moments he located the object, a small key, gold by the weight of it. Yes, he had been informed of its importance. There were two of them, and the box could not be opened without both. He hastily felt along the front of the chest, sighing with relief when he felt the other key still resting safely in its lock. With a smirk of triumph, he stood and turned to retrace his steps. A scream lodged in his throat as he saw a dim light coming toward the room, growing brighter until at last he could see it was a single candle, held in the hand of a wide-eyed young man.

The man was obviously surprised but appeared more perplexed than frightened. "Who are you? What on earth is going on here?" His accent marked him as a gentleman of the highest order, and the thief realized that this could be none other than the master of the house.

Terror, stark and debilitating, flooded through the intruder. He couldn't allow himself to be caught here, for it would mean his ruin. But he couldn't leave without the prize. Not pausing to think, he pulled out the pistol hidden in the waistband of his dark pantaloons. He had almost left the weapon behind but had decided at the last minute to bring it along. Now he was glad that he had. Though he would never actually fire it, he hoped that he could use it to bluff his way past the aristocrat.

He brandished the gun in what he hoped was a menacing manner. "Get out of my way or I'll use this," he rasped in his best English accent.

His threat seemed to have no effect on the man. He continued to move closer, and the thief could see that the Englishman was not much older than himself. "Here now, old man. No need for violence. Put that away before you hurt someone."

Angry that the other man did not seem in the least bit intimidated, the thief uttered a muffled curse and leapt forward, thinking to simply push past the Englishman and gain his freedom. He started to run, intent on knocking the other man out of his way, but the master of the house was too quick and grabbed him by the arm. In terror the thief turned toward the gentleman, coming up hard against his chest. There was a muffled bang, and the Englishman's face registered shock and disbelief.

And then the man fell to his knees, dropping the now extinguished candle as he went down, his hands slick with his own blood. The thief was horrified and dropped the smoking pistol, sickened at what he had done. With a cry he moved toward the man, thinking to help, unmindful for a moment that he had been the one to cause the damage. The dying man lunged forward and grabbed the intruder's hand, but the gentleman's strength was no match for the terrified thief. With a cry, the robber managed to disengage his fingers, and run from the room, toppling an unwary servant who appeared before him and racing through the house, then out into the night.

A mile from the manor, hidden in a copse of trees, the thief fell to his knees and was violently ill. When the fierce retching had stopped he buried his face in his hands and wept, the burlap sack on the ground at his side. After several minutes he was able to gain control of himself. With shaking hands he delved into the bag to extract his loot. The chest was heavy in his hands despite its small size, and he had to fight the impulse to hurl it into the dirt. No, he had come too far not to see this through. He would complete his task, and then try to go on with his life, to forget this terrible night ever happened.

As he started to put the treasure back in the sack, he made a horrible discovery. One of the two tiny keys was missing from its lock. He had been warned that without both keys, the chest was useless. Rage and fear boiled up inside him, and he bit his lip until he tasted blood to keep from screaming. He had become a common criminal, had killed a man, and for what? The prize was valueless without that key. He had been admonished to be careful, but fool that he was, he had bungled the job, and now he would pay. Not only would he be wanted by the authorities, but, more terrifying, by the man who had sent him on this ill-fated

4

mission. He wished mightily that he had been the one shot.

He might as well have been, for at this moment he was as good as dead.

Chapter One

Orleanais region, France
1827

It was a beautiful summer evening, and the magnificent ballroom at the Lanoux chateau was overflowing with richly dressed men and women. The painstakingly polished floors glistened under the light from two massive crystal chandeliers, while the musicians, discreetly hidden behind potted plants, played one enchanting song after another. Madame Berthe Lanoux was beside herself with happiness at the success, especially since she had worried so that the unusually warm weather they had been having would keep people away. Fortunately, Mother Nature had decided to be kind, and yesterday's brief shower had ushered in a most pleasant day. With a genuine smile on her face, she circled the room, managing to chat briefly with those who mattered most and still keep an eye on the servants and her last unmarried child, Henri.

After a few moments of circumspect scanning, she

located her son standing with a small group of young men and women, among them Isabelle Saint-Simon. Berthe laughed to herself, for if things continued to go well tonight, Henri would announce his engagement to the Saint-Simon girl, and Berthe could finally stop worrying about her only son and favorite child. Henri was thirty-five, and Berthe had despaired of his ever marrying. Until recently he had seemed content to live the bachelor's life, overseeing the family vineyards since his father's death eleven years before.

Apparently he had now decided that it was time he took a wife, and Isabelle Saint-Simon had been chosen, much to Berthe's delight. The girl possessed the three qualities that a wife of Henri's should have: an aristocratic family, beauty, and, most importantly, a handsome fortune free and clear. Yes, she would make a fine addition to the Lanoux family.

Now all that remained was for Henri to ask the girl. That she would say yes was a foregone conclusion to Berthe. After all, who could resist her beloved Henri? Besides, at three and twenty years, Isabelle was well past the time when she could afford to refuse any offer of marriage. Had she been living with her father and stepmother, rather than her indulgent grandmother, the girl would have certainly already been wed. But Delphine du Vallon had a soft spot for her grandchild, and had allowed the girl her own way. Berthe considered this a mistake, but one had to make allowances, considering that the poor child had lost her mother at such a young age.

The object of Madame Lanoux's regard was at that moment laughing politely at one of her cousin Diedre's silly stories. Isabelle slanted a look up at Henri and noted his displeasure, though she was sure no one else in the group did. She couldn't blame Henri really. He *was* quite a bit older than the others, and Diedre was a bit of a ninny. Still Isabelle had come to the ball with

7

her cousins, and she felt she should spend some time with them.

And, if she were honest with herself, she didn't want to be alone with Henri tonight. Of late his attentions were becoming more and more apparent. Henri wanted Isabelle for his wife, and she knew that he would not take no for an answer. For years everyone had assumed that she and Henri had an understanding. The truth was that they enjoyed each other's company, but both were content to let their relationship progress at a moderate pace. Recently, though, Henri's attentions had become more like those of a lover than a friend. And Isabelle wasn't quite sure what her feelings were. Perhaps she was being fanciful, but she had always imagined the man she would marry as someone who would sweep her off her feet. Henri was quite dashing, but she had never felt carried away by passionate emotions when she was with him. Indeed, the feelings Henri elicited were more of pleasant warmth than raging desire.

Henri had cornered her earlier, insisting they slip away to be alone. Perversely, Isabelle had done everything in her power since then to make sure friends and acquaintances constantly surrounded them. Though she couldn't say why, the thought that Henri might actually propose to her filled her with trepidation. Things had gone on between them so nicely for so long, she wasn't sure if she was truly ready to take such a drastic step. But since she was already here and had no way of gracefully departing, she was going to have to handle the situation in her own way. If Henri wanted to make his intentions clear tonight, Isabelle was going to make it difficult for him. Thankfully her two cousins were only too happy to oblige, albeit unwittingly. She simply kept them talking, the one thing at which both of them were quite adept.

"Don't you agree, Isabelle?" Her cousin looked at her

expectantly, and Isabelle belatedly realized she had allowed her thoughts to drift.

"I'm sorry, Therese. What were you saying?"

The younger girl giggled in response and rolled her eyes suggestively at her sister. "It seems Isabelle has her head in the clouds. I wonder what she's thinking of." The two laughed conspiratorially. It was a well-known fact that Isabelle and Henri were practically engaged, and only last week the girls' mother had predicted wedding bells for their older cousin.

"Oh, look Therese, isn't that Monsieur Dubois? You remember, we met him at Aunt Cecile's dinner party." Diedre's brown eyes followed the gentleman in question.

Therese was equally excited, all former conversations forgotten. "You're right, it's him." She patted her dark curls nervously. "Do you think he will remember us? Oh, I shall die if he does not."

Isabelle smiled to herself. At seventeen and eighteen, Diedre and Therese were quite dramatic. And quite intent on making brilliant matches. Isabelle took pity on them and turned to Henri with a mischievous grin. "You are acquainted with the gentleman, are you not, Henri?"

He narrowed his eyes at her in warning, but it was too late.

"Yes, Henri, you *must* know Monsieur Dubois. Why else would he be here?" Therese took his arm and gave him a beseeching look. "You simply have to introduce us again, Henri. You will, won't you?"

Diedre was equally adamant. "We'll be forever grateful, Henri. And after all, you're almost one of the family, aren't you? So it will be quite appropriate, won't it, Isabelle?"

Now it was Henri's turn to grin. "Since you put it that way, how can I resist?" Gallantly, he offered each woman an arm and turned to lead them away toward the unsuspecting Monsieur Dubois. "I shall return momentarily, my dear," he said to Isabelle. "And then you and I will finish our earlier discussion."

Isabelle watched them go, smiling at the boldness of the younger women. She felt sorry for poor Monsieur Dubois, for he would soon find himself overwhelmed by the two silk-encased whirlwinds. Still, they were quite pretty with their dark hair and eyes. Perhaps the gentleman would count himself lucky.

"Isabelle, darling. How lovely you look this evening."

Isabelle turned and smiled with genuine pleasure as she identified her new companion. "Marie-Claire, how good to see you. And may I return the compliment?" Of Henri's four sisters, Marie-Claire was her favorite, and by far the most outspoken. Tall and angular, with Henri's brown hair and hazel eyes, she was more accurately described as handsome rather than beautiful. Still, she was well read and intelligent and, most shocking of all, honest. No thinly veiled insults or double entendres from Marie-Claire. If she didn't like you, she told you up front, and if she did find favor with you, there was never a more loyal friend.

"I'm surprised that brother of mine left you unattended. The way you look tonight, it would serve him right if some handsome stranger carried you away." Her gaze swept admiringly over the younger woman's blue silk gown, its wide sleeves and low rounded neckline enhancing Isabelle's slender figure.

Isabelle laughed. "I fear the only handsome stranger has already been claimed by Diedre and Therese. And Henri went along to make the introductions."

Marie-Claire rolled her eyes in response. "Don't tell me those two are with you. Honestly, Isabelle, I know they are family, but how can you stand those chattering magpies?"

"They really aren't so awful, you know. And they can be fun at times."

"Yes, like when they aren't speaking," Marie-Claire

retorted sarcastically. "Now enough about those two. How is your dear grandmama? Mama was so disappointed that she could not join us."

"She is doing very well, but her maid wasn't feeling well and Grandmama said she couldn't make the trip without her. I'll be sure to give her your regards."

"Please do." Marie-Claire scanned the room casually, seemingly disinterested, but Isabelle knew her appraising eyes missed nothing. "Mama should be pleased with herself. Tonight seems to be quite the success." She turned her attention back to Isabelle. "Of course, she would want everything perfect for this special night."

"Is tonight a special occasion? I don't believe Henri mentioned anything out of the ordinary."

Marie-Claire smiled. "Come now, Isabelle. You don't have to pretend with me. Mama told me in strictest confidence, and I haven't breathed a word to anyone. Except Jacques, of course," she said, referring to her husband. "And he certainly wouldn't tell anyone."

"I really don't know what you're talking about, Claire," Isabelle said, perplexed.

The older woman was incredulous. "I'm talking about your engagement. Mama said that you and Henri were making the announcement this evening."

Isabelle was stunned into silence. To think that Henri would take for granted that she would marry him made her furious. Had he even planned to ask her, or just make the announcement, secure that her answer would be yes? She was dismayed at her own anger, having always prided herself on her decorum. With some effort she managed to speak calmly. "I don't know what announcement Henri thought he was going to make, but it isn't our engagement," Isabelle said as evenly as she could manage. "I believe it's customary for the man to actually *ask* the woman before planning the wedding."

"You mean he hasn't even asked you yet?" Marie-

Claire paled. "Oh, Isabelle, please forgive my foolishness. Henri will be furious with me." She grabbed Isabelle's hand beseechingly. "Please don't blame Henri for this. It's all my fault."

"No, nothing is your fault. In fact, I'm glad you told me." She pulled her hand away. "Please excuse me, Claire. I would like to get some air." She turned to walk away and nearly collided with Henri.

"Isabelle, is something wrong? You're as white as a sheet." Henri's concern only added to Isabelle's ire.

"Nothing is wrong," she bit out. "I would like to get some air, if you don't mind." She moved away before he could follow.

Once outside, Isabelle breathed deeply and tried to calm herself. Her grandmother would hear of it if she made a scene, and she hated to displease the older woman. Not that she didn't have good reason. Just the thought of Henri and his overbearing mama plotting and scheming about her future was enough to make her want to shout in frustration. But she was a Saint-Simon, and such behavior was unacceptable.

She sighed in annoyance, angry with herself for becoming so upset, and angry with Henri for putting her in this situation in the first place. It wasn't that she wasn't fond of Henri; in fact she preferred his company to that of any of the other men she knew. It was the fact that he had planned all this without even asking her, as if she were so desperate that she couldn't afford to turn him down. True, she was well past the age when girls of her acquaintance married. But she had never considered herself desperate. Selective, perhaps, but never desperate.

Her father had called her selfish when last she had seen him. He'd chided her for her unmarried state, saying that a girl of her breeding owed it to her family to marry well. Fortunately, Isabelle did not see her father often, so she had been able to put his hurtful words from her mind. Until now. Was she being selfish in not marrying? She didn't think so. Grandmama had never pushed her toward matrimony, but Isabelle knew that it would make the older woman happy to see her granddaughter settled.

"Isabelle." Henri's voice startled her from her reverie, though she had known he would follow. She turned to face him, silently holding her ground, waiting for him to address her.

"I know you are angry, dearest. Please let me explain." His voice was soothing, but his bright eyes belied his calm. He was annoyed that his plans had been upset, and Isabelle knew that Marie-Claire had probably borne the brunt of his anger.

"Yes, please do explain, Henri." Her voice dripped with sarcasm. "Explain to me how everyone knew about an engagement that does not even exist."

Henri's brows drew together in a frown. "*Everyone* did not know. I may have mentioned it to my mother . . ."

Isabelle cut him off. "How could you tell your mother when you hadn't even bothered to ask me? Were you so certain I would say yes?" She knew that her display of temper was upsetting to Henri, but she was too agitated to care.

Henri regarded her with silent satisfaction. Despite her present peevishness Isabelle was a magnificent sight in the moonlight, her pale blue gown glowing silver and her eyes flashing with suppressed anger. Henri couldn't help but appreciate the picture she presented, despite his annoyance with the evening's turn of events. He had remained a bachelor for many years before deciding that the woman before him would make a suitable wife. She was wealthy and genteel, intelligent without being too bookish about it. And she was beautiful enough that just the thought of taking her to bed was causing him to be aroused. Yes, Isabelle would make him a perfect mate, inside the boudoir and out. But right now he needed to placate her, at least until she agreed to his proposal.

"If you will remember, I tried to get you alone earlier this evening so that I could speak with you." His tone was soothing, but not enough so that she would consider it condescending. He smiled in his most charming manner, the kind of look that woman found endearing. "Is it my fault that you kept yourself surrounded by those two cackling hens?"

Isabelle said nothing, though most of her anger was dissipating. She had been avoiding him for no real reason, she thought guiltily. Perhaps things really had happened as he said.

Seeing that she was weakening, Henri moved in to press his advantage. "I should be upset with *you* my dear." He pulled her into his arms and gazed into her eyes with obvious ardor. "But I can forgive you." His lips sought hers.

Isabelle pushed him away, fighting a smile. It was very hard to stay mad at Henri, especially when he was so near. He really was a handsome man, with his dark brown hair and neatly trimmed mustache and goatee. The few embraces they had shared had been enjoyable. "Do not think that you can turn this around so easily, Henri Lanoux. Perhaps I have been avoiding the issue all evening, but that doesn't excuse what you've done."

He moved closer still, his voice husky. "And what have I done, dear girl, but tell my mother that I hoped you would do me the great honor of becoming my wife?" His dark head descended once again, more slowly this time, his lips barely grazing hers. "Will you, my darling girl? Will you become my wife?" His mouth claimed hers in a deep kiss, quite unlike anything she had felt before. His mustache tickled her skin, but she found the sensation rather pleasant.

After a moment Henri broke away and stared down at her, his hazel eyes flashing. "Say yes, Isabelle. Say that you will be my wife."

A Treasure to Hold

Isabelle swallowed hard. Now was the moment of truth. Did she tell him of her uncertainties and risk losing his companionship and falling from grace with her family? Or did she accept his proposal even though she was not certain that she loved him as a wife loves a husband? She was being foolish, she knew, for most of her friends had made marriages based more on convenience than any feelings of affection. Was she selfish to want more than that? Her father thought so, apparently. Perhaps he was right. Marrying Henri was the right thing to do, and she would be content in knowing that she had done her duty to her family.

"Yes," she said, before she could change her mind. "Yes, I will be your wife."

Chapter Two

Sebastion Merrick was in a killing mood, a fact that did not go unnoticed by his fellow mourners. He stood alone, inconsolable and unapproachable, as the vicar issued his solemn funeral message. Few among the darkly clad crowd could resist the temptation to peek at the solitary figure, though they did so as discreetly as possible. That he was an impressive sight none could deny, neither male nor female. With his imposing height, piercing blue eyes and jet black hair, he brought more to mind a warrior than a gentleman of title, which he was (though he used the title rarely, and only then when it suited). Most of those watching had known him since his childhood, but he had always had an air of aloofness about him, somehow setting him apart from others. He was an enigma, an oddity among the titled world he inhabited only infrequently.

Now he seemed, and in truth was, devastated by the death of his closest friend. News of the Marquis of Kensington's untimely demise had shocked the nobility. Jonathan Larrimore had been a well-liked member of

A Treasure to Hold

the peerage, and his murder had been met with genuine grief by more than a few. But none so much as his cousin Sebastion. Local gossip had it that Sebastion had vowed to track down the killer himself, without benefit of the authorities. And no one doubted that he would do just that.

From his position well apart from the rest of the funeral party, Sebastion was aware that he was the object of much speculation. He had seldom seen any of these people since reaching adulthood, and he knew that his comings and goings had always been cause for talk. Now, as then, he did not care what others thought or said about him. He was glad, however, that so many had come to pay their respects. Whatever his own feelings about funerals, he knew that it was important to the marquis's mother and widow to see that Jonathan would be missed.

Mercifully the service was soon over. Resigned to the performance of his duty, Sebastion strode to where the family gathered and offered his arm to the dowager. Looking older than her years, Henrietta Larrimore, Dowager Marchioness of Kensington, shook her head. "Please see to Melanie. I shall lean on Chester, here." She forced a wan smile as she took her son-in-law's arm.

Grimly, Sebastion turned to Jonathan's widow. Melanie Larrimore was a small woman, her flawless white skin and large brown eyes granting her the appearance of a precious china doll. She gave Sebastion a reassuring look, but he noted the dark smudges of exhaustion under her eyes and the slight trembling of her hand on his arm. As they made their way toward their waiting carriage, Sebastion supported most of her weight, fearful that she would collapse if he did not.

Once inside the carriage, Melanie still clung to his arm, forcing Sebastion to sit beside her. Something wet fell onto his hand, and Sebastion saw that Melanie was

17

crying. Wordlessly he offered her a snowy linen handkerchief.

"Thank you." Melanie sniffed, wiping her tear-stained cheeks. "I promised myself I would not cry in front of anyone. Especially you, since I know how you hate a woman's tears."

"Go ahead and cry." Sebastion's voice was rough, harsher than he intended. "I think he was worth your tears."

"And what of your tears, Sebastion? Have you cried for him?"

Sebastion tensed and turned away from her inquiring stare.

Instantly Melanie was contrite. "Forgive me, dear Sebastion. I don't mean to be cruel. I don't even know what I'm saying any more." She wiped away fresh tears. "I know you loved him well. As much as any of us."

More, he wanted to say but didn't. He was a private man, and even if he had wanted to share his feelings, he wouldn't have known how. Only with Jonathan had he felt free to be himself, and now his friend was gone. He felt the loss keenly, like a missing limb, but he kept it inside himself. He knew that Melanie meant well, but she was too caught up in her own grief to truly understand the extent of Sebastion's loss.

Melanie began to weep softly again, but this time Sebastion did not try to comfort her with words. Instead he pulled her to his side and provided physical solice. It was best for her to vent her tears now, in private, for when they returned to the house there would be the funeral luncheon to get through. And get through it they would. For Jonathan's sake.

The last guest had finally departed, and the servants were quietly reordering the house with their usual efficiency. Sebastion had closeted himself in the study halfway through the luncheon, an action that was met with silent relief by most of the guests. Sebastion's cold blue gaze had quelled the chatter of more than one unfortunate well-wisher, so that soon the guests had avoided him altogether. For Sebastion's part, he endured the murmured expressions of sympathy as long as he could, then escaped to the silent haven of the study. No one would bother him there, not only because this was where the murder had taken place but because no one dared incur his wrath.

Sebastion was sprawled in an upholstered chair, staring pensively out the window, a half-empty bottle of brandy on the table beside him. Jonathan had never been much of a drinker himself, but he had carried on his father's tradition of maintaining an impressive liquor cabinet. He raised his glass in a mock salute, then drained the contents with one toss of his head.

He had always favored this room, as well as the library. Of all the various spaces in the house, they held the fondest memories for him. He often thought he could still feel his uncle's presence here, that he had only to turn around to see the older man's thinning gray hair and laughing brown eyes. Though Richard Larrimore was in truth only a distant cousin, he had insisted that Sebastion refer to him as Uncle Richard. The study had been Richard's territory, then Jonathan's after his father's death. It was purely a man's room, decorated in deep greens and dark wood. And yet it had never seemed dark or oppressive to Sebastion. The rich, elaborately draped curtains were always open to let in the sun, and there had always been laughter and camaraderie and acceptance here. Now, however, the room was silent and seemed empty and cold despite the mild summer air outside.

Absently he turned over the miniature key in his hand. Fenwick, the Kensington butler, had entrusted it to him the day he arrived. "I found it beside my lord's body . . . beside my lord, and I just picked it up without thinking. After the constable came, I realized that I had forgotten to give it to him. Then I thought I should give it to you. Pardon my forthrightness, but I hoped you could use it to find the man who did this horrible thing." Sebastion grimaced at the thought that the ever so proper servant had breached etiquette and possibly broken the law to withhold evidence for him. He had warned Fenwick not to speak of this to anyone else, to which the butler had replied stiffly, "Certainly not, my lord."

He studied the small golden object, wondering not for the first time at its importance. His aunt had already explained to him that the only thing missing was Uncle Richard's golden chest. It was a strange piece, dating back to the Middle Ages. Ornately carved, it could only be opened by using two small golden keys simultaneously. Inside was a chalice made of solid gold, also old and intricately carved. Richard Larrimore had used it to entertain the young Jonathan and Sebastion on more than one occasion, telling them tales and legends of King Arthur and the search for the Holy Grail. For almost a year both boys had thought that their chalice *was* the Holy Grail.

Richard had broken the disappointing truth to them gently, but the chalice and its container had always been favorites of theirs. Sebastion knew the chest and chalice must surely be valuable, but the house was full of other equally valuable treasures. Yet nothing else had been disturbed. Had Jonathan known the thief, thus making it necessary to kill him? Or had his cousin simply had the bad fortune to stumble upon the robbery in progress? Sebastion's hand tightened on the key. One way or another, he would find all the answers he sought.

Behind him the door opened, and Sebastion discreetly slipped the key into a small pocket inside his coat. He had not told the family about the butler's finding, realizing that it would serve no purpose. "Sebastion, I thought I would find you here." Henrietta,

A Treasure to Hold

Dowager Marchioness of Kensington, entered the room and closed the door softly behind her. "I hope you will forgive the intrusion." She seated herself in a chair opposite his. "This was always a special place for him," she said, studying the room. "And for you as well."

Sebastion remained silent. The dowager looked smaller to him somehow, almost frail in her black gown. Funny that he should think so, as she had always appeared to be such a strong, imposing woman to him. She had intimidated him as a child, for she had seemed so remote and unattainable.

"I want to thank you for all that you have done for the family. I realize this has been a difficult time for you." She turned to gaze at one of the many family portraits covering the deep green walls, but not before Sebastion noted the gleam of moisture in her pale blue eyes. To the ton, Henrietta Larrimore was a force to be reckoned with, but in the end even she was not immune to the great tragedies of life. Jonathan had been her cherished child, her only surviving son, and heir to the Kensington estate. His death had diminished her, both in size and spirit.

"Do you remember when you came to live with us?" Henrietta asked, her expression wistful. "You were six years old, and so thin your little arms looked like matchsticks. I can still see you standing so solemnly, holding your mother's hand." She paused and searched his face.

"I remember," he said finally. "I thought this was a castle, and you and Uncle Richard the queen and king."

Henrietta smiled sadly. "Did you really? I never knew. You were such a serious little thing." A solitary tear slid down her pale cheek, sparkling like a jewel in the afternoon sunshine. "Were you happy here, Sebastion?"

The question, so out of character for his aunt, took him by surprise. "I've never really thought about it," he answered truthfully, "but, yes, I was happy here."

21

Tentatively, Henrietta reached out her hand and briefly squeezed Sebastion's. "Thank you for saying so. I have often regretted the fact that I was not more ... affectionate with you. And with my own children," she added in a ragged whisper. "When little James died, I thought my heart would break, and I never wanted to feel such pain again. Then you came to us, and I wouldn't let myself care for you."

"Aunt, please, do not do this. You will regret such rash speaking." It unnerved him to see her so emotional. For as long as he could remember, she had been cool and very proper. An example used by other members of the ton when discussing how a lady should behave. As a child he had longed for some small show of affection, some word of comfort, but she had paid him little mind. Never deliberately unkind, but somehow always vaguely disapproving. Her youngest son, James, had died shortly before Sebastion's arrival, and he had always secretly aspired to take the child's place in her heart. It had never happened. Now here she was, sharing her deepest thoughts with him. He knew that once in her right mind she would be horrified at her lack of decorum.

Henrietta shook her head, as if reading his mind. "No, I will not regret my words. For too many years I have kept my emotions in check, and it has brought me nothing but grief. I have lost two sons, and I would not have you leave here without knowing my feelings for you." She stood and walked toward the empty fireplace. "You have been a true son in this house, even though you were not born to it. Richard often said that God had sent you to us to make up for losing our own little James. I never really thought of it that way, but I believe he was right."

Sebastion did not speak, so the dowager continued. "And Jonathan simply adored you from the first. You were the older brother he never had, and you were always so patient with him, and protective, too. Oh, yes, I knew how you watched over him throughout the years." She breathed a ragged sigh, her eyes taking on a faraway look, as if seeing scenes from the past.

"I watched over him when it didn't matter. And when it did, I wasn't here for him," Sebastion said bitterly. "I should have visited more often. He always wanted me to."

Then Henrietta stood before him. "Please do not blame yourself. How could you have known that someone would come into our home and . . ." She stopped, unable to complete the sentence. "Jonathan loved you like a brother, and he would not want you to think for one minute that you were to blame."

"Mother is right, Sebastion. We shall drive ourselves mad if we think that." Melanie entered the room, followed closely by Sarah, Jonathan's older sister. Of an age with Sebastion, Sarah had inherited her father's hawkish nose and her mother's fair coloring. So much like Jonathan. She was tall and rather too thin, but pretty in her own way.

"Melanie, dear, you look so tired. I think this has all been too much for you." Concern and genuine affection shone in the dowager's eyes. She had grown very fond of her son's wife, looking on her as another daughter.

Melanie waved away her concern. "I know I must look a sight, but truly, I would rather stay and talk, if you do not mind." The thought of going to her lonely room, filled with so many memories, gave her a sinking feeling in the pit of her stomach. Only when she was too exhausted to think would she retire. "It is you I'm worried about."

"Yes, Mother. You should really take your own advice and lie down." Sarah offered a tired smile to Sebastion. "Melanie and I will keep Sebastion company."

Company was the last thing he wanted, but Sebastion knew that the women were looking for some comfort of their own. "Won't Chester be looking for you?"

he asked, referring to Sarah's husband, Hugh, the Earl of Chester.

"No, bless him; he's taken the boys on a walk." Sarah had brought two of her four boys, who were keeping Jonathan and Melanie's sons company. They had all been a little bewildered throughout the last several days, too young to fully understand all that was happening.

Sebastion straightened in his seat. "Well, since you are all here, I would like to tell you of my plans."

"You aren't leaving so soon, are you?"

"Not immediately. I will stay for a while to help you get things in order, but I have duties that call me away." He was deliberately evasive, hoping that they would not delve further into his reasons for going.

Melanie was the first to speak. "Sebastion, I know you are trying to shield us from what you think is too harsh for us, but I have an idea of your plans." Her gaze found his. "You are going to search for Jonathan's murderer."

He saw no reason to lie since it was now out in the open. "Yes," he said. "I know that the authorities are looking into the matter, but I have to do this thing for Jonathan. He would have done the same for me." None of them could deny his words.

"And what will you do if you find the person responsible?" As always, the dowager cut to the heart of the matter.

Sebastion almost smiled at her abruptness. It made things seem more normal, and it was almost comforting. "I don't know. I suppose I'll have to decide that when I find him."

Melanie moved to warm herself in front of the sun-filled window, hugging herself against the sudden chill that raced down her spine. "When you find the man, and I know that you will, I want you to ask him one thing for me. Why? Why did he have to kill my husband? I cannot believe that someone would murder him over an old cup, no matter how rare or valuable. But since that is all that is missing, what else am I to think?"

"Melanie, please," Sarah said plaintively. "Does it matter why he did it? The main thing is that the murderer be made to pay for his crime."

The younger woman whirled around, her fists clenched at her side. "It matters to me why he was killed. I can't stand the waste of it. I can't explain it to you, but I have to know."

"Please, dear, it isn't good for you to get so upset," Henrietta interrupted in a soothing voice. "I, too, would like to know why. It cannot be a simple theft, as the authorities would have us believe."

Melanie sighed in defeat. "I suppose you're right. It's useless for us to speculate. But I cannot stop wondering why that chest was taken. I know how highly Jonathan prized it, but I thought it was just for sentimental reasons. When he gave that lecture on it in London, I was surprised that anyone besides a family member would have any interest."

Sebastion's head came up sharply. "What lecture? Jonathan gave a lecture recently about the chalice?"

"Yes. About two months ago he gave a talk at some historical society meeting." She frowned. "You don't think that has anything to do with the murder, do you?"

Not wanting to excite the women, Sebastion didn't share his suspicions. "I'm not sure, Melanie. I don't see why it would, but I don't want you to worry about it. I will take care of everything."

"We know you will." All three women looking at him trustingly. Sebastion nodded gravely. Of its own volition his hand moved to the small key tucked into his coat pocket.

Chapter Three

Paris

It was raining, a brief afternoon shower that kept those
with sense inside to wait it out and those unfortunate
enough to be outside scurrying about, trying to keep
dry. Isabelle was glad for the weather, for it had cleared
the streets sufficiently that she felt she might not be
recognized. As a precautionary measure she pulled the
heavy lace from her hat down to cover her face; then,
with the help of the driver, she alit from the cabriolet.

"Please wait for me," she instructed him. "I do not
know how long I shall be."

The coachman, taking in her cultured accent and elegant attire, nodded curtly and settled in to wait. He
thought the young woman out of place in this section
of the city. The Marais was mostly inhabited by unfortunate members of the declining aristocracy, possessed
of derisively termed "half-fortunes." Yes, she was out
of place with her obviously expensive clothes and re-
fined manner. But a fare was a fare, and she looked as

though she would pay well. So he would linger.

Isabelle turned and quickly ascended the steps to the once elegant town house where her stepbrother, Reynaud Andrassy, lived. Isabelle's father had married Reynaud's mother when Isabelle was ten and Reynaud fourteen. The two had become fast friends, mostly due to the fact that Isabelle could always be counted on to help Reynaud out of whatever trouble he had gotten himself into. The unfortunate tendency toward disaster had stayed with Reynaud well into his adulthood and was the reason why Isabelle was presently standing on his doorstep in Paris, chilled and wet, waiting for him to answer the door.

Isabelle rapped smartly three times, then a fourth, but could still detect no movement from within. She was fast losing her patience; she had come all this way at the man's request and he wasn't even here to greet her. She knocked again, harder this time, yet not hard enough to call any unwanted attention to herself from the few passersby on the street. Reynaud's note, which had arrived three days prior, had begged for her assistance and complete discretion. Though she hated to lie to her grandmother about her reasons for this hastily planned trip to Paris, she felt she had no choice. Better for Delphine to think her granddaughter was looking at patterns for her wedding gown than bailing her wayward stepbrother out of yet another scrape. Delphine already disliked Reynaud, and his desperate note would only further that aversion.

From the corner of her eye she saw one of the curtains twitch in the window to her right. She knocked again. "Reynaud, open this door. It is Isabelle," she hissed to the closed portal.

From within she could hear the sounds of someone moving about, then the door opened slowly, just a fraction. "Who are you?" an unfamiliar male voice asked.

Frowning, Isabelle opened her reticule to extract the letter Reynaud had sent. She studied the address he had given, uncertain now as to whether she had come to the correct house. Reynaud had only lived here a few months, and she had not visited the city in all that time. "I am Isabelle Saint-Simon. Reynaud Andrassy is my stepbrother. Please, is he at home?"

"He isn't here." The door opened a fraction more, and a dark-haired man peeked around to look at her, his eyes wide and darting from side to side. "Were you followed?" he asked in a whisper, trying to peer around her onto the street.

Isabelle turned to look behind her but saw only the driver, waiting patiently as she had requested. She turned back to the man. "What in heaven's name are you talking about? Followed by whom?" She had had enough of this nonsense. With a snap she closed her black umbrella, pushed the door open and swept past the thin young man. The interior was dark and had a musty odor, which Isabelle did her best to ignore. The once elegant furnishings were in need of a good dusting and polish. Evidently Reynaud and his friend were more interested in dressing well than living well.

"Where is my stepbrother, monsieur? I have gone to considerable trouble to come here today, and I should like to see him now." Normally the soul of good manners and gentility, Isabelle was now too aggravated to be polite.

The young man at her side did not seem offended at her abruptness. Rather, he was regarding her with something close to awe. "I'm so glad you are here, mademoiselle. Reynaud said you would come, but I was not sure." He paused before stammering on. "I have been quite frantic with worry, but now that you are here . . ." His voice trailed off suggestively.

Isabelle paused to remove her hat and heavy veil, shaking the rain droplets onto the threadbare carpet. "Monsieur, I do not make it a habit to address strangers. I take it you are a friend of Reynaud's?" She eyed him critically, taking in his lanky frame and dark, overly long hair. His plum tailcoat, scarlet waistcoat and white pantaloons hugged his lean frame and, along with his elaborately tied cravat, gave him the look of a garishly dressed crane.

The young man had the grace to blush. "Pardon me, mademoiselle. Michel Perrault at your service." He executed a rakish bow and beamed at Isabelle. Clearly this was meant to be a charming gesture, but Isabelle was not amused.

"You must forgive me if I seem rude, but I am rather put out at the moment." She held up Reynaud's letter with a gloved hand. "Three days ago I received this letter from my stepbrother informing me that his life was in danger and begging me to help him. I, naturally, put all my plans on hold, lied to my family about where and why I was going, and sneaked into Paris to come to his aid." She advanced on her hapless victim. "And when I arrived here, in the pouring rain, I was left standing on his front steps and greeted by a stranger who told me my brother was not home and asked me if I'd been followed." She moved past him out of the narrow foyer and into a small room decorated in blue. The wall coverings were faded and water-stained in places, and the furniture was scarred and worn. It was so dusty that Isabelle had to hold a finger to her nose to stifle a sneeze. Michel followed obligingly at her heels, waiting for her to speak. "Now, I am sure there is an explanation for all this, and since you are here and Reynaud is not, you will kindly give it to me."

Michel hesitated, obviously taken aback at her forthrightness. "Well," he stammered, "it isn't really a story fit for a lady's ears."

Isabelle forced herself to be calm. "Monsieur Perrault, I am very concerned about my stepbrother, so if you have any information that might help him, I suggest you tell me."

Michel lowered his lanky frame into a worn velvet

Kathleen McCarthy

chair, sprawling elegantly in a gesture Isabelle could tell he had perfected through countless hours of practice. The dashing young rake, throwing civility to the wind. Only Michel's overly thin frame and overall lack of polish spoiled the desired affect. "Please call me Michel. As you know, when Reynaud lost his position at the bank, your father stopped paying the rent on his house, so he moved in with me. He had a little money put aside, but it soon ran out. His mother tried to help, but your father found out about it and put a stop to it." He shook his head. "Reynaud is not the most frugal of men, and his funds soon ran out. He owed several merchants, but he had no way to pay them."

"He could have asked me for money," Isabelle pointed out. He has many times before, she thought but did not say.

"He was too embarrassed to ask you again. He said that he couldn't take advantage of your kind nature. Anyway, he was desperate enough to try anything, so one night we went to several gaming halls to try to win some money. Reynaud somehow bluffed his way into a very high-stakes game." Michel straightened in his seat. "To make a long story short, he lost. Badly."

Isabelle groaned inwardly and lowered herself onto a faded brocade settee. This was news she thought she ought to be sitting down to hear, no matter how unappealing that seat might be. "How badly?" she asked, dreading the answer.

Michel shook his head. "He would not tell me, but I know it was a very large amount. Of course he could not pay, and for a moment I thought the winner was going to call him out. But strangely, he did not. He took Reynaud into a private room, and they stayed in there for almost an hour. When Reynaud came out, his face was as pale as death. We left immediately after that, but I could not get Reynaud to tell me what had happened. He would only say that the matter had been taken care of."

30

A Treasure to Hold

He leaned forward in his seat, his thin elbows resting on knobby knees. "A week later, Reynaud disappeared for several days. He returned late one night and woke me up to say that he was in trouble and had to go away. He said that he would contact me when he could, but that I was to trust no one. That was over a fortnight ago, and I have lived in fear ever since."

"That is all you know? Think; is there something you are forgetting?" Isabelle felt sick inside. How could she help Reynaud if this was all the information she had to go on? "Do you know the name of the man Reynaud lost to? Do you know where Reynaud could have gone? And why did he wait so long to contact me? There must be something more you can tell me."

"Well, he did send a note to me several days ago, saying that he was going to write to you for assistance."

"Yes," Isabelle said impatiently. "What else?"

"I am sorry, mademoiselle, but I have told you all I know." He stood and ran a hand nervously around his stiff collar. "Trust me; if I knew where Reynaud had gone I would go and fetch him back. Since he left I'm afraid to leave my own home. Especially since those men came here looking for him . . ."

Isabelle sprang from her seat, bearing down on the inept young man. "What men? Why didn't you tell me about this earlier?"

Michel fell back into his chair, clearly intimidated by her display of anger. "I . . . I forgot. I told you, my nerves are on edge from this whole . . ."

Once again Isabelle cut him off. "Enough about your nerves. Tell me about these men. When were they here? Did you let them in?"

"No," Michel answered, shaking his head. "I told them Reynaud was away and I did not know where he was or when he would be back. They were rough-looking fellows, I tell you. Oh, they were dressed quite

31

well, but they had an air of the street about them. I was certainly glad when they left."

"And how long ago was this?"

"Over a week. I'm not very good with keeping track of time." He stopped suddenly, his eyes alight. "Oh, yes, and then there was another man looking for him last week. A big, tall fellow, well dressed, with very expensive boots. You can tell a great deal about a man by his footwear, I always say."

"Michel," Isabelle said as patiently as she could manage, "I do not care about this man's boots. Tell me what he said."

"He asked if Reynaud lived here. I told him that he did but had gone away. For a moment I thought he might try to force his way in, but he, too, left me in peace."

"And you've had no more visitors since then?"

"Thankfully, no." Michel sighed dramatically. "This whole thing has been a dreadful experience. It's just like Reynaud to get himself into trouble and then leave someone else to clean up after him. When he comes back, I have a few things I'd like to say to him."

Realizing that giving in to her exasperation and yelling at Michel would get no results, Isabelle returned to the worn settee and tried another tactic. "Michel, his note to me said that his life was in danger. I am sorry if this has caused you any inconvenience, but I think Reynaud is really in trouble this time." She leaned back on the couch, pinching the bridge of her nose between her fingers. "Perhaps I should go to the police."

Michel was horrified. "Oh no, mademoiselle, you cannot do that. Reynaud could be thrown in debtor's prison, or worse."

"Well, then, I am at a loss. I do not know what help Reynaud thought I could give him. Especially if I have no idea how to contact him."

"Perhaps there is something in this letter he left for

you." He pulled a wrinkled missive from his coat, proudly proffering it to Isabelle.

She opened her mouth to give him another dressing down but thought better of it. He was obviously hopeless, so she might as well save her breath. Quickly she scanned the note, frowning in annoyance at its cryptic message. *Register at the Hotel d'Orleans under the name Lady Hastings-Gray. I will check the registry each day for you. I am sorry for the trouble. Be careful.*

She read her stepbrother's words over again. Usually Reynaud was quite loquacious. Now, when she would have appreciated some further explanation, he was curt. And mysterious. Isabelle sighed. She was tired and hungry, and her temples were throbbing from the stress of the last few days. As worried as she was for her stepbrother, she could not help but feel a flicker of doubt at the validity of his claim. Was his life really in danger, or was this another of his histrionic imaginings? For his sake, she hoped it was the latter, though she did not know if she could forgive him were that the case. She loved Reynaud dearly, but sometimes he was just too much to take. Well, at least his sense of humor was still intact. Lady Hastings-Gray was the name of an Englishwoman who had visited her father once when she and Reynaud were children. Isabelle had always been an excellent mimic and had entertained Reynaud for many weeks with her perfect imitation of the upper-class Englishwoman's speech and manners. That Reynaud would instruct her to use the name after all these years lightened her heart somewhat.

Through veiled lashes she studied Michel as he paced. He hadn't been able to enlighten her much, but what little he did know did not bode well for her stepbrother. She was still torn by indecision. The police might help her locate Reynaud, but as Michel had said, they might lock him up for debt. Perhaps she should go to her father for help. She dismissed that idea as quickly as it had come to her. Victor Saint-Simon was not a charitable man in the best of times, and she shuddered to think of his reaction to Reynaud's latest folly. She could not go to the authorities or to her father. What did that leave her? As much as she hated the thought, she would have to wait and hope that Reynaud contacted her.

With a sigh she stood and placed her hat upon her head. "Thank you for your help, Michel. I will be staying at the Hotel d'Orleans, registered under the name Lady Hastings-Gray. If you should hear from Reynaud or think of anything else that may be of use to me, you may contact me there."

"Ah, an alias. How very clandestine! And an English name, no less. But why are you staying there when your grandmother has a beautiful home in the Saint-Germain?"

"Because I told my grandmother that I was staying with my cousins. If I resided at Grandmama's, her staff would report my every move back to her, and that would not be good for Reynaud or me. I am very tired and I would like to get some rest. I must go; that poor driver has been waiting for me all this time. Good night, Michel."

She swept down the stairs and out into the damp evening. The rain now fell in a fine mist that turned the light from the street lamps gray and luminous. Hurrying toward the hackney, Isabelle failed to notice the dark carriage parked across the street, which followed at a discreet distance as her vehicle started up the wet streets.

Chapter Four

The next morning when Isabelle checked at the front desk, there was a letter waiting for Lady Hastings-Gray. Hastily she scanned the note, her brow creasing into a frown at the message.

> *Dear Isabelle,*
> *Meet me at Chez Molinaux at one o'clock. If I am not*
> *there when you arrive, wait for me. If I do not arrive*
> *by two, there is no hope for me. Trust no one, as they*
> *may already be following you.*
>
> > *Reynaud.*

Isabelle folded the note securely into her reticule, then went to her room to wait. She chafed at being confined to her room, but there were few places in the crowded city where a female could respectably—and safely—travel alone. That she was forced to do it for Reynaud was yet another of the many injuries that he had caused her. It wasn't his fault, she told herself, but he did have a knack for causing her grief. She prayed that none of her acquaintances would inadvertently come upon her, for if her grandmother or father found out about her little adventure, she would surely suffer the consequences. No one must know that she was here, especially if Reynaud was in as much trouble as it seemed. Thankfully, her stepbrother had chosen a small café near his town house, a place none of those in her social circle would deign to frequent.

At precisely one o'clock Isabelle alit from a sleek cabriolet at the entrance to the modest café that Reynaud had chosen for their meeting. As unobtrusively as possible she scanned the busy establishment, trying to locate her stepbrother. Disappointment swelled within her when she did not see his face among the many customers. She was aware that several people were staring at her, and she blushed under their scrutiny. While her lavender gown was one of her more simple frocks, it was still of a higher quality and more fashionable than those worn by the other female patrons. She decided to find a table, hoping that she would draw less attention to herself if she were seated. The note had instructed her to wait, but the café was so crowded that there were few empty places.

She frowned, then surveyed the room once again, hoping she had overlooked her stepbrother in the press of people. Her searching gaze swiftly took in the crowd, ultimately coming to rest on two men seated in the far corner. Both were well dressed but seemed out of place for all their finery. They were rough looking, with harsh peasant features and belligerent attitudes that no amount of expensive clothing could disguise. And they were staring intently at her with more than just common curiosity. These men seemed to have been searching for someone, and from their expressions it appeared that she was that unlucky someone.

Isabelle felt her knees go weak, but she managed to keep herself upright. Michel had said that two men had been looking for Reynaud, and his description matched these two perfectly. They must have followed her from the town house last night. But how had they known about the note? And how had they gotten here before her?

As she watched, horrified, one of the two men pushed back his chair and began to rise. Isabelle panicked. With eyes wide with fright, she searched the room again, until she saw an available seat. A quickly as she could, but without drawing undue attention to herself, she hurried to the unoccupied table and sat down. A quick glance over her shoulder showed her that the man had resumed his seat, though his eyes were still pinned on her. Breathing a sigh of relief, Isabelle turned to face forward and found herself staring into a pair of very blue, very intense eyes. The table was not unoccupied, as she had first thought. Indeed, it was very much occupied, by a handsome gentleman reading a newspaper. *Now what?* she thought anxiously.

"Pardon me, monsieur," she stammered. "I . . . did not realize anyone was sitting here. Please forgive me." Isabelle's face flushed hot with embarrassment. What this man must think of her, she did not even want to imagine. And how could she have missed seeing him? Truly, he was not an easy man to miss. His black hair was rather longer than the fashion, reaching past his high collar. He was elegantly attired in a black coat and cravat, the only color coming from his dark green waistcoat. His clothes were simple, though of excellent cut and quality. But it was his eyes that held Isabelle mesmerized. They were a brilliant blue, surrounded by thick black lashes, and startling in their intensity. She felt as though she could look into them forever. And perhaps she would have if another patron had not walked by and jostled her into awareness. Isabelle's cheeks flamed with mortification, and she could only sit in silent misery, too embarrassed to speak.

The object of her fascination merely nodded and

folded the paper he had been reading. Had Isabelle not been so flustered she might have noted the gleam of triumph that shone briefly in his eyes. But as it was she missed the small flash of emotion before it was quickly contained. "No need to apologize, mademoiselle. It isn't often I find myself sharing a table with such a lovely partner." His French, like everything else about him, was flawless. From his jet black hair to his finely cut coat, he was perfection. The sharp planes of his face were clean shaven, unlike Henri's, and she couldn't help thinking that her fiancé came up lacking in the comparison. It was such an absurd thought, considering her present situation, that she had to stifle a hysterical giggle behind a gloved hand.

Isabelle darted a glance at the two men. She knew that she should excuse herself and leave immediately, but both men were now openly studying her. Far better to have a stranger think her a wanton than to fall into the clutches of those two thugs. She returned her attention to her companion. "Please, monsieur, you will think me mad, but I need your help. I . . . I am being followed, and if you would just pretend that we . . . know each other . . . If you would just let me sit with you for a little while until they leave . . ." She trailed off, knowing that she sounded ridiculous. He would probably call the authorities on her, not that she would blame him. She must seem touched in the head.

The stranger regarded her closely for a moment before speaking. "Are you in any danger, mademoiselle?" His expression was unreadable.

She hadn't expected this show of concern. "Oh, no," she hastened to assure him. "Well, not really. At least I hope not." She knew she was rambling, but her nerves were so on edge that she was having trouble thinking clearly. If her grandmother or, heaven forbid, her father could see her now, they would die of mortification. Saint-Simons did not behave in such an irrational manner. She took a deep breath and struggled to regain her composure. "No, monsieur, I am not in any immediate danger. I should just like to sit here for a few moments until those two gentlemen in the corner have gone." She indicated their general direction with a nod of her head. "Then I will be on my way and trouble you no further."

He smiled then, a slow, lazy grin that did funny things to her insides. He really was quite handsome with his dark hair and bright blue eyes, and he seemed quite a gentleman. Isabelle always prided herself on being a rather good judge of character. Besides, she had no other choice but to trust him, at least for the time being.

"It is no trouble, mademoiselle. I am glad I could be of service to you." He leaned closer and whispered in a confidential tone, "Are you in trouble with the law?"

Isabelle gasped in shock but calmed herself when she saw the ghost of a smile on his well-shaped lips. He was actually flirting with her. "No, monsieur, I assure you I am not in trouble with the law. Contrary to my actions today, I am actually a well brought up lady from a very respectable family."

"And what family might that be?" he asked silkily.

She hesitated. "The Hastings-Grays of London. But I'm sure you would not have heard of us, being a Parisian yourself."

"Oh, but I'm as English as the Union Jack itself," he answered in his native tongue. "Your father must be Lord Alfred Hastings-Gray. I've heard of him."

Isabelle blanched. His French had been so perfect that she had been fooled. Suddenly Isabelle felt a chill run down her spine, and she took a calming breath to steady herself. She must be careful what she said. After all, Reynaud had told her to trust no one. This seemingly helpful man could be the worst kind of villain underneath his attractive veneer. Just because he was as handsome as sin didn't mean that he was a nice person. She would need to choose her words with more prudence.

She flashed a charming grin at her companion, hoping he had failed to notice her momentary upset. "Your French is quite wonderful, monsieur," she replied in patrician English that matched his own, more grateful for her skills as a mimic than she'd ever been before. "I just assumed you were French. How nice to find a fellow countryman." Silently she said a prayer of thanks for her father's obnoxious English friends, on whom she had based her accent.

"Indeed the pleasure is all mine, Lady Hastings-Gray. Allow me to introduce myself. Lord Fairfax at your service. But you may call me Sebastion." He frowned thoughtfully. "Funny, now that I think of it. I was under the impression that Lord Hastings-Gray had no children."

She gave a trill of uncomfortable laughter. "Your memory must be failing you. I assure you that my father does indeed have children." That at least was true. The fact that her father was not Lord Hastings-Gray she ignored. Inwardly Isabelle groaned. From one bad situation to the next. Fortunately she would never have to see this man again, so what did it matter what he thought? She spared a glance toward the corner table and almost cheered with glee. The two ruffians were gone. Her ruse had worked. Now all she had to do was quit this handsome gentleman's company and get to Reynaud's. Perhaps Michel had more news.

Pasting on her most charming smile, she turned back to the Englishman. "Thank you so much for your help, but I believe I will be perfectly fine on my own now. Those two men have gone, and I would not want to intrude on your hospitality any longer."

She started to rise, but he was too quick for her. With one gloved hand he grasped her elbow, startling Isabelle with the strength and heat of his grip. "I could not call myself a gentleman if I let you leave without an escort." He helped her to her feet with a gentle pressure on her arm. "What if you are still being followed?"

She tried to extricate her elbow from his grasp, but he held her fast. "Really, sir, I am sure that it is perfectly safe now. I couldn't take up any more of your valuable time." He was quite tall, she realized, and she had to refrain from taking a step back as she would have liked. Towering over her as he was, he seemed quite menacing.

And then he smiled. She felt foolish for having doubted him. A man with a smile like that could not possibly have evil intentions. Could he?

"Nonsense," he exclaimed in an affable manner. "What could be more important than helping a fellow Englishman or-woman, as the case may be. I shall see you home," he stated with finality.

Isabelle wanted to protest but could think of no reasonable excuse. She was being fanciful, letting her imagination run wild because of the intrigue surrounding her wayward stepbrother. Reynaud's town house was quite near by, and it could do no harm to have a polite gentleman escort her there, especially since he knew her only as Lady Hastings-Gray. Besides, those two men might very well be waiting to trail her again. "Thank you, sir. I am going to visit a friend, but I would be honored to have your company on the short journey there."

As they walked, Isabelle couldn't help but notice the admiring stares Lord Fairfax received from other women. Young or old, they all beamed at the Englishman, blushing when he tipped his hat to them. He was quite the charmer, and had the circumstances of their meeting been different, perhaps she might have enjoyed his companionship. As it was she was eager to reach Reynaud's and say good-bye to her handsome escort.

"You seem nervous, my lady." He was the picture of solicitous concern. "I don't think your friends are following us, if that's what you're worried about."

Isabelle couldn't help but glance behind her. When she looked back up at her partner, she had to grimace in chagrin. "I suppose you think I'm imagining things. Another flighty female."

"No," he said quickly. "If you tell me that you're being followed I believe you. I wonder, though, why you think that ruffians such as those would be interested in you."

She tried to make light of the situation, shrugging in bemusement. "Perhaps I was mistaken. I suppose I am rather nervous, walking about the city without my maid. You see, she was ill and I did so want to see Paris," she ended wistfully, hoping she sounded convincing.

Sebastion made a sympathetic sound in his throat. "You are right to be wary, my lady. The city is full of very real dangers to a young woman alone."

Reynaud's town house came into view and Isabelle breathed a sigh of relief. "Here we are, monsieur. This is where my friend lives. It was very kind of you to accompany me."

"It was my pleasure, mademoiselle. Perhaps you would repay my kindness by inviting me in." His expression was hard, and for a moment Isabelle was stunned into silence.

After a few strained seconds, she regained her composure and pinned him with her frostiest stare. "That will not be possible, sir." Her tone was clipped, almost to the point of rudeness. But after his last comment, she didn't think he deserved much civility. "I thank you again for your kindness, but I must bid you good day." She turned away and started up the stairs but was brought up short by the iron band that was Sebastion's grip.

"I'm afraid you will have to tolerate my company for a little while longer. I must insist upon coming inside with you." He, too, started up the stairs, pulling Isabelle along beside him.

"Let go of me," she hissed. "How dare you treat me in such a manner?" In her agitation she slipped back into French. Sebastion ignored her struggles, merely tightening his hold on her arm. Isabelle thought briefly of screaming, but Sebastion's next words effectively silenced her.

"If you scream, I shall make sure that your brother suffers for it."

That got her attention. "Reynaud? What do you know about Reynaud?" She stopped abruptly, cursing herself for her stupidity at mentioning his name.

Sebastion shot her a dark look. "Don't worry, Mademoiselle Saint-Simon. I already know who you are." He inclined his head toward the door. "I suggest that you come along quietly like a good girl. For your stepbrother's sake."

"I demand that you release me this instant, and tell me where my brother is." She tried once again to wrench her arm free, but Sebastion held her fast.

Ignoring her struggles, he rapped on the door. A moment later, Michel's dark head came timidly into view between the draperies in the front window. Seeing Isabelle, he hurried to open the door. Once he did, Sebastion pushed his way inside, dragging Isabelle with him.

Frightened and angry, Isabelle rounded on the Englishman the moment the door was closed. "What have you done with my brother, you ruffian? If you have harmed him in any way . . ."

He cut her off. "I have not harmed him . . . yet. And if you'll tell me where he is, I won't harm you either."

"I do not know where he is. And even if I did, I wouldn't tell you." She eyed him contemptuously, drawing herself up to her full height. "I suggest that you leave now, monsieur, or I will be forced to send for the authorities."

He was unimpressed. "I don't think you want to do that, especially since your stepbrother is wanted by the English authorities for murder." With that, he shouldered past the frightened Michel and strode into the dimly lit study.

Isabelle was forced to follow. "What lies are you telling?" she sputtered angrily. "Whatever else he may be, Reynaud is no murderer. He isn't capable of harming another person."

Sebastion spun around so quickly that Isabelle collided with the solid wall of his chest. Angrily he grabbed her arms, pulling her up on her toes and shaking her slightly for emphasis. "Perhaps you don't know your brother as well as you think, mademoiselle. Would it shock you if I told you that he murdered my cousin in cold blood and made off with a family heirloom that dates back to the Middle Ages?" His grip tightened painfully on her arms, long fingers digging into the soft flesh a few inches above her elbows. "Tell me where he is, damn you."

"I do not know, I tell you." She struggled to free herself. "Please, monsieur. You are hurting me," she whispered, her throat constricted with fear.

Sebastion studied her wide eyes, brimming with frightened tears. What was he doing? With a muffled oath he released Isabelle and turned from her, pacing the room in agitation. He hadn't meant to hurt the girl, but the frustration of the last weeks was getting to him. He had managed to track Reynaud Andrassy from England across the Channel, and then to Paris. But there he had simply lost the trail.

It had been easy enough to learn quite a bit about Reynaud's family and history, but of the man himself he could find no trace. Until yesterday, when his surveillance of Reynaud's town house had paid off. He had followed Isabelle to her hotel, then bribed the oily little clerk into letting him read her message this morning.

That the young woman had literally fallen into his lap had been a stroke of luck he could not have anticipated. But there his good fortune had ended. He had thought that Isabelle knew her stepbrother's whereabouts, but from the look of things, she, too, was in the dark. It was frustrating to be so close to his prey and yet not be able to lay hands on him. But whether she was willing or not, this girl could still be of some use to him, of that he was sure. Andrassy had turned to her in his hour of need, so that must mean that he trusted her. And Sebastion was not above using that trust for his own gain.

Isabelle had moved closer to the door, her arms wrapped tightly around her midsection. She was clearly upset, and Sebastion knew he would have to try a different approach. "I regret that I frightened you, mademoiselle." His tone was less harsh, as gentle as he could manage given his present state of mind. "But what I have told you is the truth."

"I don't believe you," Isabelle spat at him. "No matter how nicely you say the words, they are still vile lies. Reynaud is a gentleman. He could never have done such a horrible thing."

He tried to reason with her. "Why would I lie about something like this?"

Isabelle frowned in confusion. "I don't know. Perhaps you are trying to trick me into helping you find him. Perhaps he owes you money." Her eyes widened at the thought. "Yes, that is it. He owes you money." She looked around for Michel. "Michel, where are you?"

Michel appeared in the doorway, pausing just inside, his eyes peering fearfully at Sebastion every few seconds. "Here I am."

Isabelle pulled the unwilling man into the room. "Didn't you tell me that Reynaud owed a gambling debt to a gentleman? Tell me, is this the man?"

Michel shook his head, his eyes darting from Isabelle

to Sebastion and back again. "No, mademoiselle. The man I saw was much older."

"So you have never seen this man before today?"

He shook his head. "I did not say that. This is the man who came looking for Reynaud a fortnight ago." He took a shuffling step away from the Englishman. "I am glad he did not find Reynaud. He frightens me."

Sebastion moved so quickly that neither Isabelle nor Michel had time to react. In an instant he was upon the slender Frenchman, his hands gripping the bright folds of the younger man's canary yellow coat. "But I did find *you*," he said with quiet menace. "And you are wise to be frightened of me."

Michel's eyes widened almost comically and he looked as though he might faint. "Please, monsieur. Mercy."

Sebastion released him with a look of disgust. "Leave us." Michel raced out of the room, stumbling over himself in his haste to flee. When he had gone, Sebastion strode to the door through which the young man had just exited and closed it soundly. "Now," he said almost conversationally, "suppose you tell me about this gambling debt."

"I will not tell you anything." Her eyes narrowed in disgust. "You are a madman, and I am sending for the police, no matter what you say." Isabelle moved toward the door, but Sebastion blocked her path.

"I am afraid I cannot let you leave this house."

Chapter Five

Isabelle was appalled. "What do you mean, you cannot let me leave? You can't keep me prisoner here," she cried, all the while knowing that if he wanted to, he could indeed. Michel had already shown himself to be of no use; she doubted he could even be counted on to think to go for the authorities. "Perhaps you do not know with whom you are dealing, monsieur," she sniffed haughtily. "My father is a very influential man, and he would not look kindly on your treatment of me thus far."

Sebastion appeared unimpressed by her supercilious display. "Perhaps not, but I doubt he would be pleased with the damage I could do to your family name if I were to expose your brother's crimes."

"Crimes that only you accuse him of," Isabelle said acidly. "Where is your proof, monsieur?" She paused for a moment, giving him ample time to respond. "I thought as much. You have no proof to verify your hateful accusations." She shot him a triumphant look, her chin rising ever so slightly in a gesture of condescending superiority.

That was a mistake.

His next words sent a shiver of dread down her spine. "My proof lies rotting in a grave in England."

He impaled her with his scornful gaze, and she had the fleeting thought that this must be what a butterfly felt like once caught and mounted on a collector's card. Her momentary bravado fled, and fear and doubt once again assailed her. Could this man be telling the truth? Was her stepbrother capable of committing murder? It was too fantastic to believe. And yet this man quite obviously did.

His animosity, so evident and tangible, made some of her own ire dissipate. If she pushed him too far in his present agitation, she would have no one to protect her from his wrath. And she had no doubt that he could cause her great harm. She would have to try to refrain from losing her temper. "Monsieur, I do not mean to mock your pain, but I really believe that you are mistaken. Reynaud is just not capable of such an act. Isn't it possible that you have made an error in your assumptions?" She almost smiled then, pleased at her rationale. Surely he would see now that he had drawn the wrong conclusions. While she was certainly sympathetic to his loss, she could not allow him to labor under these misconceptions any longer. Reynaud was simply not the man he sought.

"There has been no error." He frowned down at her. "I have other proof."

When he made no move to elaborate, Isabelle questioned him. "I would like to see your proof." At his black look, she hastened to explain her reasons for wanting evidence. "These are serious accusations you make against Reynaud, and he is part of my family."

Wearily Sebastion ran a hand through his hair. He was tired and frustrated, and the last thing he wanted to do was prove his case to this young woman. No matter how beautiful she was. But perhaps if he convinced her, she might assist him in discovering Rey-

naud's whereabouts. And if he could not convince her
. . . well, he would see to it that she helped him anyway. Reynaud obviously relied on his sister. And if he
had contacted her once, he would more than likely try
to contact her again. Isabelle Saint-Simon was the key
to finding Reynaud Andrassy, of that he was certain.

"Reynaud was listed among the passengers sailing
from Calais on a packet that reached Dover five days
before my cousin was killed."

Isabelle's throat went a little dry at that. Reynaud
had not mentioned any trips to her. And if he were in
such financial difficulties, how would he have obtained
the fare? She shook herself mentally. Reynaud's name
on a passenger list was hardly proof that he committed
murder, and she told Sebastion so.

"True. But three days later a Frenchman registered
at an inn about two miles from my cousin's estate, using the name Simon Andrassy. The innkeeper recalls
this Frenchman asking several questions about my
cousin and his family. He left very early the morning
after my cousin was murdered." Sebastion's eyes glittered darkly, and Isabelle wisely held her tongue. "All
circumstantial, true. But a little too coincidental."

Isabelle felt slightly nauseated and had to sit down.
She moved to the large cherry desk strewn about with
papers and sat in the chair behind it. While she still
refused to believe such a fantastic tale, she couldn't
help having some doubts. Why had Reynaud gone to
England? Perhaps it was all a mistake. Maybe there
was another Reynaud Andrassy. But what about the
man registered at the inn? "Simon Andrassy" was too
close to Reynaud's and the Saint-Simon name to be
mere coincidence.

Idly she thumbed through a small leather volume
that had been collecting dust on the scarred desktop.
Her thoughts were so troubled that it took a moment
for her mind to register what she was holding. It was
a book on medieval legends, mostly Arthurian, a

strange choice for either Michel or Reynaud. She had almost put it aside when she came to a page that had been turned down at the corner. Someone had written in the margins and at the top, and she recognized Reynaud's handwriting immediately. The name *Kensington* was written in Reynaud's inelegant scrawl, as well as *Bedford* and *England*.

Surreptitiously she spared a glance at the Englishman, but he had turned his back to her, lost in his private thoughts. Quickly she scanned the page, hoping to understand its significance. It was mostly about a noted French poet named Chretien de Troyes, who had lived during the Middle Ages and written poetry about the quest for the Holy Grail. Isabelle frowned, wondering why Reynaud would take such an apparent interest in this subject. He had always performed quite poorly in his studies and, to Isabelle's knowledge, had never willingly read a book.

But she could not ignore the fact of his handwriting. She turned the page and stopped again as she found a folded piece of stationery. It was of fine quality, a thick and creamy vellum. The sort of thing Reynaud would use if he had the means. As unobtrusively as possible she unfolded the creased paper and scanned the contents. It was a marker in the amount of ten thousand francs. Owed to one Monsieur E. Broussard by one R. Andrassy. It was unsigned, but that only meant that Monsieur Broussard probably had the signed copy.

Isabelle felt sick. It was a great sum of money, and for Reynaud it might as well have been a hundred thousand. It was no wonder that he had not sought her help. She did not have access to such a sum, and even if she did, she was not quite sure she would have offered her assistance. Over the years she had given Reynaud quite a bit of money from her own private accounts, a fact that annoyed her grandmother and would have outraged her father had he known.

She dared another glance at Sebastion, then quietly

refolded the note and placed it back in the book. She did not want him to know about this discovery, at least not yet. She would take the volume with her and study the contents later. Perhaps it would give her some insight into Reynaud's predicament.

"What are you trying to hide there?"

Uttering a small gasp of dismay, Isabelle nearly jumped from her seat. She looked up and was horrified to see Sebastion reaching for the book she held. Before she could even think to react, Sebastion had taken the volume from her and was flipping through it curiously. She held her breath as he paused at the turned-down page, knowing that soon he would discover the marker and know the extent of Reynaud's debts. But he didn't continue his search. He simply stared at the book in front of him; his eyes riveted on the dog-eared page on which Reynaud had scribbled three random words.

When he finally looked up, Sebastion's face held such a horrible look that Isabelle actually felt the fine hairs on the back of her neck stand on end. Sebastion obviously had found some meaning in her stepbrother's scrawling. He turned his gaze to her. "Did you see this?" he ground out in a deceptively calm voice. "Did you see what is written in this book?"

Too intimidated to speak, Isabelle nodded her assent.

"Do you know what they mean?" he asked, referring to the handwritten words.

This time Isabelle gathered her courage and spoke. "No. I have heard, of course, of Bedford and England. But I am not familiar with the name Kensington. Perhaps you are . . ." She could see that she had made a mistake, though she wasn't sure what. Sebastion's face drained of color and became even harder. He took a step toward her, and Isabelle could not help but shrink back a little in her chair. She was not used to such an unpredictable temperament and had never in her life had to deal with someone so hostile. Her family and acquaintances all prided themselves on their remarkable composure. Here was raw emotion, and it frightened her to see it.

Sebastion stopped just in front of the desk. "Bedford is the location of the ancestral home of the Marquis of Kensington." His voice was strained. "The man your stepbrother murdered was the current Marquis of Kensington, my cousin Jonathan." His finger tightened around the slender book, and she could see in his icy blue eyes that he wanted to rip it apart. He did not, she was sure, only because he needed it.

Oh, Reynaud, Isabelle thought in despair. Could it all be true? Her father had predicted for years that the feckless Reynaud would come to no good end, but Isabelle knew that even he could never have imagined just how low the young man would fall. A murderer and a thief. It was too much to be borne. She shook her head, disgusted with herself. Had she no loyalty to her family? True, the evidence might point to Reynaud as the culprit, but she would not allow herself to believe it until she heard it from Reynaud's own lips. Only then would it be real to her. Until such a time, she would have faith in her stepbrother and believe him innocent, as she so wanted him to be.

Choosing her words with care lest she incur more of Sebastion's wrath, she spoke in what she hoped was a reasonable tone. "I am sure that you take this as further proof of my stepbrother's guilt, but I cannot be swayed so easily. He is my family, and I cannot believe such a thing about him until I hear it from Reynaud himself."

She feared for a moment that he might strike her, but he did not. He simply studied her with his glittering blue eyes, darkened now with anger. Most women, and many men for that matter, would have looked away under such intense scrutiny, but Isabelle held his gaze, stubbornly refusing to be cowed by him. Inside she might be shaking with fear and uncertainty, but she would not give him the satisfaction of knowing that.

"Your loyalty is very commendable, but in the end you will see that I am telling the truth."

He flipped idly to the next page of the book and removed the folded note from its hiding place. One silky brow arched as he read the contents. "Ah," he mocked, "the infamous gaming debt. Quite a large sum, is it not?"

"Yes, it is a large sum, monsieur. Not that it is any business of yours." Reynaud's humiliation should have been kept inside the family, and it bothered her to have this man know the full extent of her stepbrother's folly.

"Until Reynaud Andrassy is brought to justice for his crimes, everything that might help me find him is my business. I suggest you get used to that." He moved to the desk. "I think it would be helpful to search this room more thoroughly. Perhaps it might give me some clues as to his whereabouts." He put the book down and began leafing through a small sheaf of papers stacked haphazardly on one corner of the desk.

Isabelle fought the urge to snatch the papers from him. He was still an enigma to her, and his flashes of temper made her tread more carefully than she otherwise might. Though he might look the gentleman and have a title—or at least claim to—underneath he was a very dangerous man. Very well; she would refrain from voicing her true thoughts and speak in a calm, rational manner. "I do not think it is proper for you to look through my stepbrother's possessions. If you insist upon knowing the contents, I shall sort through these things and give you any information that might be of interest." That seemed like a reasonable enough solution to her.

"No." His voice was flat, but what incensed her most was that he didn't even pause in his ransacking of Reynaud's personal documents.

She tried again. "Perhaps you did not understand me . . ." she began, only to be cut off abruptly.

"I have a perfect grasp of both the English and

French languages, and I understood you perfectly. Your idea is ludicrous and does not even merit a response." He picked up another stack of correspondence. "Now, do *you* understand?"

That did it. Isabelle stood so abruptly that the heavy chair almost toppled over. "You are the most boorish man I have ever had the misfortune to meet. You cannot come into this house and take over as if you had some divine right. I will not stand for it any longer, monsieur . . . Whatever is your name anyway?"

"As I told you earlier, my name is Sebastion. Sebastion Merrick."

Her mouth twisted into a sneer of disbelief. "Is that your real name, or are you lying about that too? You also said that you were Lord Fairfax, and I find that very difficult to believe."

"You find many things difficult to believe, mademoiselle. Nevertheless all that I have told you is true."

She knew he meant more than just his name, but she chose to ignore his implication. "You mean that you are actually an English lord? Pardon my skepticism, but your actions thus far are hardly the actions of a gentleman." Her tone was accusatory.

Sebastion was unruffled by her obvious antipathy. "I could say that your actions have been less than ladylike, but what would be the point?"

Isabelle had the grace to flush, knowing he was right. No lady of breeding would travel the streets alone, much less throw herself on the mercy of a strange male. Her brow wrinkled in a frown as a thought occurred to her. How had the Englishman known that Isabelle would be at the café? It was surely no coincidence, but how could he have planned it so that she would seek his help, and not that of another patron?

"I am curious about something, Lord Fairfax. How did you know I would be at Chez Molinaux this afternoon?"

He slanted her a bored look. "Quite simple: I followed you from here last night and discovered your alias at the hotel. This morning I arrived early and asked if there were any messages for you." Here he leered. "I wasn't sure how to best approach you once you arrived, but you saved me the trouble of all that, didn't you?"

Isabelle scowled at him. "Yes; how accommodating of me. Unfortunately you will not find me so in the future." Her eyes narrowed to green slits of dislike. "I find your actions thus far reprehensible."

Sebastion seemed more amused than offended by her attempts to put him low. "I am not concerned about your opinion of me. I am merely trying to find your stepbrother, and if I have to use you to do it, then I will." He turned his attention back to the desk. "Now, you may help me look through this, or you may take yourself off to some other room and leave me in peace. The choice is yours."

"What I would like to do is return to my hotel. I am tired and I should like to rest." She frowned at him, annoyed at his high-handedness.

He sighed. "We have been through that. I cannot allow you to leave, so if you would like to rest, I suggest you retire upstairs."

"But that was before," she cried. "I've told you all I know. What harm could it possibly do for me to go back to the hotel?" She was incredulous. He actually meant to keep her here, even though she had given him all the information she had, had even unwittingly given him more than that. Slowly it dawned on her—he wasn't going to let her out of this house, tonight, or even tomorrow. He was going to keep her here until he found Reynaud. The thought made her ill.

"When will you let me leave, if not this evening?" She was surprised at how composed she sounded, but she would not show any weakness to this odious man.

Sebastion studied her in the fading light of day. She was truly a beautiful woman. Her skin was ivory and

Kathleen McCarthy

flawless, her eyes large and of a green so pure that it made him think of emeralds. The faint sunlight turned her hair to burnished gold, making her appear almost ethereal. In other circumstances he would have taken great pleasure in seducing her, but he would not let himself be distracted now. He had promised himself and his family that he would have his revenge, and nothing was going to stand in his way. "You may leave when I have located your stepbrother," he answered coldly. "When you're no longer of any use to me."

"Then let me go now, for I shall never willingly be of any use to you." She turned from him and crossed to the door, pausing with her hand on the knob. "And know this: You may have the upper hand now, but you cannot keep me prisoner for long. I will be missed, and when I am, my family will come for me."

"That is what I am counting on," he answered somberly.

Chapter Six

After Isabelle had departed, closing the door softly behind her, Sebastion allowed himself to sink into the lumpy cushion of the desk chair. He was angry; with himself for losing his temper, and with Isabelle for her unreasonable loyalty to her stepbrother. But most of all with Andrassy for causing the whole situation.

Back in England he had had no doubts as to whether he would be able to find Jonathan's murderer. He still had no doubts as to that, but now there were other things to consider. Isabelle for one. Now that she was here, it made things that much more complicated. He couldn't allow her to leave. Though he believed that she had no knowledge of Andrassy's whereabouts, he couldn't trust her not to interfere in his plans. And just what were his plans? To find Andrassy and see him punished. And then what? He could not go back to his life as if nothing had happened. Jonathan was gone, and his sons were still babies. Someone would have to look after Melanie and the dowager, and Sebastion knew that he was that someone.

Kathleen McCarthy

There was no use fighting it; his fate had been sealed long ago, when his mother and he had come to live with Jonathan's family. Richard Larrimore could have turned them away, and none would have censured him. But he had not. Instead he had taken his cousin and her small son into his home and made them part of the family, or so Sebastion had thought. Looking back, he could see that his mother had never felt quite that way, always so careful never to offend, always looking for ways to make herself useful.

Lady Grace Larrimore Merrick had been born the only daughter of the Earl of Huntington. Raised in a world of privilege, she had spent summers with her distant cousins, Richard and Louisa Larrimore. The three of them had been inseparable as children, but as the years passed they had grown apart as their lives took different paths. Richard, the Kensington heir, had gone off to school, then married an heiress of his parents' choosing and settled down to manage his vast estates and holdings. Louisa had married young but died two years later giving birth to her first child, a son whom his grieving father named Louis.

Grace, on the other hand, had chosen to remain unmarried after a broken engagement, and was considered by all her acquaintances to be firmly on the shelf. Then, when she was twenty-one and well past the hope of making a favorable match, she met Andrew Merrick at a ball and fell hopelessly in love. Andrew was the youngest son of a minor member of the peerage, a man with little to recommend him except for the fact that he was utterly, divinely handsome. With his wavy black hair and piercing blue eyes he caused more than one young woman of the ton to sigh. But from the first he only had eyes for Grace or, as most speculated, for her considerable dowry. Unfortunately Grace's father, the earl, strongly disapproved of Andrew, and forbade his daughter to have anything to do with him. Seeing no alternative, Grace and Andrew ran off to Gretna Green and were married.

When the couple returned to London, they were summarily informed that Grace had been disinherited. Grace was unconcerned, so full of love that she could not see beyond the moment. Andrew was devastated. He had greatly miscalculated in his plans, having relied on the notion that, though the family might have initial misgivings, they would eventually accept him into the fold. He had been wrong, and thus found himself as penniless as before, but now with a wife to support. To his credit, he did his best. Grace was a pretty little thing, and she loved him so much that he felt he owed it to her to make it work. And always in the back of his mind was the hope that one day her family would change their minds and allow Grace her dowry.

Andrew appealed to his older brother, who allowed them the use of one of his smaller estates in exchange for Andrew's overseeing of it. The first year went along rather well, and when Grace gave birth to a baby boy eleven months after their elopement, Andrew thought himself lucky. Sebastion was a beautiful baby and grew into a handsome boy. When he was four, however, disaster struck. Andrew's brother was killed in a hunting accident, and all his holdings were left to his ten-year-old son. The boy's mother quickly took over the running of things, and within a month had informed the Merricks that she was giving their small estate to her own brother to manage. They would have to leave.

Andrew decided they should return to London so that he might find employment, and though he tried, he could not support them. He began to gamble then, winning steadily at first, so that he developed a taste for it. Each night Grace begged him to stay home, but he refused, insisting that this was the only way he could make a living. After six months his luck had run out and he began to lose—badly.

In their dingy rented house, Grace did her best to

keep the family together, but it became increasingly more difficult. Andrew was rarely home now, and when he was, he took his frustrations out on his wife and young son, terrifying them with his black rages. Somehow Grace managed to put food on the table, though not much, and keep a roof over their heads. Too often Andrew would find where she had hidden her meager funds, and they would go hungry that night. When Sebastion was five he began stealing so that his mother might eat properly. Grace was horrified and demanded that he stop, but Sebastion persisted, driven by the need to help his mother.

When Sebastion was six his father was killed, and he and his mother were left alone. Grace became ill that winter with a hacking cough that took her breath away. Fearing that she would die and leave Sebastion on his own, she decided to swallow her pride and appeal to her family for help. Knowing that her father and mother would make her life unbearable, she turned to her childhood playmate, Richard, for assistance. With her mind made up, she took from its hiding place her one last valuable possession, the remnants of the strand of pearls she had worn on her wedding day. Over the years she had sold off the pearls one by one to buy food and pay the rent. Now she used the last of them to pay for their journey to Bedford.

It was raining the night they arrived, Sebastion remembered, stinging sheets of rain that made the roads almost impassable. He could still picture standing, tired and hungry, in threadbare clothes that dripped puddles on the floor beneath him. He had waited with his mother outside a tall set of closed doors, holding her hand as tightly as he could, not fully understanding what was happening. Finally the doors had been opened by one of the imposing servants, and a male voice had bid them enter. Sebastion's knees had shaken so badly that he feared he might not be able to walk, but even then his will had been an awesome thing, and he had made his body obey his mind.

His first thought was that the man sitting behind the great desk was a judge, or a king, like in the stories his mother used to tell him. Whoever he was, Sebastion could tell that he was quite important. He was dressed in fine clothes and had a regal bearing that quite intimidated the young boy. And then the important-looking man had opened his arms and said, "Welcome."

Twenty-four years later Sebastion found himself still trying to repay his debt of gratitude, even though his mother and Richard Larrimore were long dead. His mother had died nine years ago, succumbing to a fever of the lungs. Six years later Richard had suffered a stroke from which he had never awakened. Jonathan had inherited the title, and most of the estates and holdings entailed. Sebastion had been almost embarrassed to discover that Richard had left him two of the smaller but still profitable estates upon his passing. Even in death Richard had seen to it that Sebastion was made to feel a part of the family.

Now Jonathan was gone too, and it had fallen to Sebastion to look after the family until Jonathan's oldest son, James Sebastion, was old enough. As the boy was only four, it would be many years before he could manage, years that stretched before Sebastion bleakly. Since reaching manhood, he had gone where he chose and done as he liked, returning to Kensington House only occasionally. He traveled a great deal, never content to stay in one place for very long. And if sometimes on cold winter nights or starlight summer evenings he felt lonely, he could always find feminine companionship to ease his isolation.

All that was done with now, or would be once he caught up with Andrassy. Then he would return to Bedford and the Kensington estate. Where he was needed.

* * *

Upstairs Isabelle paced back and forth across the worn rug in one of the bedchambers. She was struggling to control her temper but failing miserably. How dare that insolent Englishman keep her here against her will? This was not the Middle Ages. She was not so much chattel to be kept at some man's pleasure. And she would certainly see to it that her presence brought Sebastion Merrick anything but pleasure.

"He is wrong about Reynaud," she said aloud to herself. "I know he is, and I cannot wait to see that arrogant face when he has to admit his mistake." She smirked, already picturing the scene. He would beg her forgiveness for his rough treatment, but she would be unmoved, offering him only contempt. A little voice in her head scolded her that she was being foolish with her petty plans of revenge, but she hated feeling powerless, and it cheered her somewhat to at least think that she might triumph in the end. When that end might be, she could only wonder.

How long would it be before Reynaud showed himself? This whole matter needed to be cleared up soon—especially if the Englishman really had no intention of letting her go until he had accomplished his mission. That was a sobering thought, and her daydreams of retribution were forgotten. Her grandmother would not miss her for a few days, but Sophie would. Sophie was the maid she had brought with her, then deposited at a sister's house on the outskirts of the city. She had sworn the girl to secrecy, promising her a paid visit with her sister in exchange for her silence. When she had dropped the girl off, she had said she would return in three days, thinking that surely that would be enough time to help Reynaud out of whatever mess he had gotten himself into. Unfortunately she had miscalculated.

What would the maid do when Isabelle did not come for her? Wait a few days, assuming that Isabelle had decided to stay for a longer visit. But what would she do after a week, or two, and still no Isabelle? Isabelle shuddered to think. This whole thing was utterly fantastic, too awful to be real. Her father would be furious if he found out, and he would probably cut Reynaud off completely. And what of Henri? He would be livid, she knew, at her as well as at the Englishman. Why, he might even call the younger man out and demand satisfaction. As much as Isabelle disliked the arrogant lord, she did not want to see him killed.

She paced for several more minutes, waging a silent debate with herself. Finally, her head aching from tension, she went to sit at the small writing desk that occupied the space between two tall, narrow windows. The weather had cleared up and the late afternoon sun shone into the room, reflecting warmly off the faded yellow wall coverings, washing the room in a soothing golden light.

Isabelle breathed deeply, savoring the quiet and solitude. She found herself thinking wistfully of home and her garden, and the beautiful little pond where the black swans lived. Had it only been a few days ago that she had been there, blissfully ignorant of her stepbrother's problems, dutifully planning her wedding? She smiled as she thought of her grandmother, probably even now preparing menus and deciding on flowers and guest lists. Dear Grandmama, so delighted that her Isabelle would finally become a wife. And Isabelle was happy, too, or had been before all this trouble began. Soon, she promised herself, soon she would return home and settle back into her comfortable life. And when she returned home she would show more enthusiasm for the preparations for the upcoming nuptials, as her grandmother had wanted her to.

The sun was sinking lower now, and soon it would be out of sight. This had always been her favorite time of day, when the setting sun turned the sky into a painter's palette of pink and blue and gold. She stared out at the view, trying to make sense of all that had happened in the last twenty-four hours. It was hard to believe that it was so short a time, yet it was only yesterday that she had arrived in the city. Now here she was, tired and hungry, and most resentful of the circumstances that had made her a virtual prisoner in her brother's home.

Her thoughts turned again to the man downstairs. He was certainly attractive; she would give him that. But the violent nature she sensed just below the gentleman's exterior gave her much cause for alarm. She found herself comparing him to Henri. How different they were. Henri was the epitome of the modern gentleman, Sebastion filled with black thoughts and passionate moods. Henri was much more to her liking, she told herself. And yet she couldn't help but be intrigued by the other man. She didn't understand the attraction he held for her, other than for his pleasing physical attributes. But she had never been one to base her opinions solely on the basis of looks. She didn't stop to analyze her feelings further, however, for after this misunderstanding had been cleared up she would never see Sebastion Merrick again.

The sun had almost completely disappeared now, and the room was cast in shadows. Isabelle shivered despite herself, and moved toward the door. Her stomach growled as she did so, a most unladylike sound, but she did not care. It was one thing to be kept prisoner, but even the ill-tempered Englishman downstairs could not mean to starve her.

She descended the stairs and walked into the gloomy study. A few of the lamps had been lit, but they only served to illuminate small sections of the room. Sebastion sat at the desk studying a sheaf of papers by the light of one of them. He had discarded his coat and rolled up the sleeves of his fine lawn shirt. He looked up as she approached, one black brow raised in question.

"I thought you had retired for the evening, mademoiselle."

Isabelle bit back a retort. Honestly, she had never met a man who could infuriate her with such small effort. But she refused to rise to his bait. She was a Saint-Simon, a well-bred lady, and she would behave accordingly. "No, Monsieur Merrick, I only wished to gather my thoughts for a while, but there are some things that I would like to discuss with you."

"Such as?"

"Such as the fact that my belongings are back at the hotel and I require them. Also, I have not dined since early this morning and I am quite hungry and should like something to eat."

Sebastion leaned back in his chair, regarding her with his glittering blue eyes. "Reasonable requests, those. I have made arrangements for your hotel bill to be paid and your things to be brought here. They should be delivered at any moment. As for your hunger, our supper is being prepared as we speak."

"By whom?"

"I have been staying with a friend, and I made arrangements to borrow a servant or two. Very discreetly, or course. If you prefer not to dine with me, you may eat in whichever chamber you have taken." His attention was once again focused on the papers in front of him. Apparently she had been dismissed. "I will probably be in here most of the evening if you should need me."

She blanched at his last statement. Until now she had been so upset by the thought of being trapped in this house that she had not realized all that that implied. It was one thing to keep her here against her will; it was quite another to think that he would set up housekeeping here as well. Surely she misunderstood his intentions. He wasn't really planning to stay here overnight. It was unthinkable.

"I am sure that you will want to return to . . . wherever it is that you're staying tonight," she said. "The papers will still be here tomorrow when you return."

Blue eyes stared mockingly back at her. "Yes, they will be here tomorrow, because I am not going anywhere tonight. I shall sleep here, in one of the empty chambers."

"I am aware that you seem to have little regard for propriety, but even you must realize that you are putting me in an untenable situation," she said through gritted teeth. "You simply cannot stay in this house with me tonight."

Sebastion's expression was stony. "I can and I will. End of discussion."

She groaned inwardly at his implacable response. Her reputation would be ruined, no matter that she was forced to remain against her will. Her father and Henri would never understand.

"Please, monsieur," she said desperately. "I beg you to reconsider. I cannot spend the night in this house with you, alone."

Sebastion did not look up from his studies. "We won't be alone. The boy, Michel, will also be here, as well as two servants."

"Two servants and my stepbrother's friend hardly constitute suitable chaperons. I might as well be in this house with only you. It couldn't be any worse."

It could be much worse, Sebastion thought ruefully, but now was not the time to get into such a conversation. Perhaps someday he would show her what could happen if the two of them were really left alone. To Isabelle he shrugged, seemingly unconcerned. "It cannot be helped."

Isabelle made one last plea. "Monsieur, I don't know if you are aware of this, but I am engaged to be married, and my fiancé will not understand this. Please do not do this to me." She swallowed against the bile rising in her throat. To plead with this man went against everything she stood for, but she could think of no other way to sway him.

Sebastion's dark head came up, and he looked at her coldly. "If your fiancé is the kind of man who would think the worst of you, then perhaps you are better off without him."

"Henri is something that you will never be, monsieur, a gentleman," she shot back derisively. "Just because you are uncivilized does not mean that all men think that way. And don't presume to tell me how to improve my life. My life was going along quite nicely before I had the misfortune to run into you."

He was unperturbed by her verbal assault. "If you will recall, it was you who sought me out, not the other way around." His voice dripped with sarcasm. "But perhaps you make it a habit to throw yourself at strange men."

"I wish I were a man right now," she said, her jaw clenched angrily. "Then I'd show you what I think of you."

Sebastion clicked his tongue in censure. "Such a violent temper. I begin to feel sorry for the unwitting Henri."

"You need to feel sorry for yourself, monsieur, because I will see that you are severely punished for your actions." She raised her chin in a haughty gesture of defiance. "And I wouldn't be at all surprised if Reynaud sues you for slandering his good name."

His eyes narrowed in warning. "I suggest you cease your prattling until you know of what you speak. It is not slander to voice the truth."

She ignored his admonition. "The truth as you see it. Why should I believe a word you say?"

Sebastion's limited patience was at an end. His eyes raked over her with cold disregard. "Apparently you have not been listening to me, mademoiselle. It doesn't matter to me whether you believe me or not. As long as I feel that you will be of some use to me, you will

Kathleen McCarthy

do as I say." The icy blue stare stopped at a point in-
sultingly below her face. "And I believe that you can
be very useful," he finished suggestively. "One way or
another."

Isabelle stood in shock for a moment, letting his
words sink in. Not only was he unmoved by her plight,
he was subjecting her to innuendo and trying to
frighten her. It dawned on her that she was in a very
precarious position here. No one knew where she was,
much less that they should be worried about her. She
was completely at this man's mercy. Physically she was
no match for him, and if he chose to follow through
with his lewd insinuations, she would be powerless to
stop him. If she had feared him before, she was terrified
now. He could do whatever he wanted to her, even
assault her.

What kind of man was he to threaten her so cal-
lously, all the while looking so nonchalant? The answer
came to her in a flash of fear; he was a monster. Something inside her snapped and she suddenly, desperately, had to escape from this place, no matter the
consequences. Turning sharply on her heel, she gathered up her skirts and raced from the room. Once in
the foyer, she turned left toward the front door, rather
than right toward the stairs. She grasped the knob in
her hand and pulled the door open, freedom only a
few steps away, but she was brought up short once
again by Sebastion's cruel grip on her arm.

Angrily he pulled her back into the house, slamming
the door closed again with a resounding crash. "What
the hell kind of stunt was that? Did you think to run
through the streets of the Marais at night, a lone
woman with no protection? You could have been
killed. Or worse."

"Nothing is worse than what you have planned."

He crossed his arms across his chest. "And just what
torture do you think I've devised that is worse than
being raped by some street urchin?" His words were

68

blunt, but he wanted to show her just how much better off she was in here with him.

"What does it matter whether I'm raped out there or in here?" she howled at him.

He was stunned. "What the devil are you talking about?" He looked at her as though she had lost her mind. "Do you think I'm going to rape you?"

Isabelle backed up against the far wall like an animal trapped in a cage. "You threatened me," she accused, her eyes wide with alarm. "You said I'd be useful one way or another, and you . . . you *leered* at me!"

Sebastion was completely taken aback by her accusations. He had meant to intimidate her into cooperating with him, but he never imagined that she would take his words as a threat of bodily harm. Exasperated, he ran his fingers through his hair. "I have never forced myself on a woman, and I don't intend to start with you." He waited to see what affect his reassurance had. "In other words, mademoiselle, your virtue is safe with me."

She still didn't trust him. "I've seen the way you look at me, monsieur. I know when a man finds me attractive."

His answering smirk was cold and insulting. "You overestimate your charms, love," he said snidely. "I prefer my women with a little more warmth and a lot less ego."

"Hah," she spat angrily. "Were we to meet under normal circumstances, you would be begging for a small crumb of my attention. And I would pay you no more mind than a buzzing insect." Her eyes shot flames of self-righteous anger. "You would be beneath my contempt."

He came toward her, and she realized what a fool she had been to taunt him further. Her back was already pressed to the wall, and he was close enough to bar her path should she try to escape him on either side. She was trapped.

Sebastion stopped mere inches from her, so tall that he blocked the meager light in the foyer. "I could prove you a liar, mademoiselle," he said in a smooth tone that sent gooseflesh down her arms.

"You said you had never forced yourself on any woman," she reminded him breathlessly, feeling like a rabbit caught in a hunter's snare.

He leaned in close, bracketing her body with outstretched arms, his hands planted firmly on the wall on either side of her. "I wouldn't have to force myself on you," he growled. "You would want me." She could feel the heat of his body and smell the masculine scent of him. His mouth was so close to hers that they were almost kissing.

She was rooted to the spot, mesmerized by the smoldering flames in his strange light eyes. "Never," she whispered. Her throat had suddenly gone dry, and she licked her lips nervously. Sebastion's eyes fell upon her mouth, and for one breathless moment she thought he would make good on his threat.

He pulled away from her abruptly, leaving her shaken and strangely disappointed. She was glad for the support of the wall at her back, for without it she feared she would have slumped to the floor. Shaken to the core of her being, she pushed herself away from the smooth plaster and turned on wobbly legs to ascend the stairs.

She had taken no more than a few steps when Sebastion's gruff voice rang out in the unnatural stillness of the town house. "Mademoiselle," he said, "I trust you will behave yourself for the rest of the evening. I'm too tired to go chasing you about the city, and I would be most displeased to disturb my rest for you. Do you understand?"

Isabelle turned to face him. "Why are you doing this to me? I've done nothing to you, and yet you have ruined me. I even felt sorry for you, for your cousin's death, but you don't deserve my pity. You are an odious man, without any feelings." Now that there was some distance between them she felt some of her confidence returning. Her chin rose defiantly. "And I'll never help you find my brother. Never."

Sebastion was unmoved by her impassioned speech. Perhaps he was unfeeling, but his first duty was to the Larrimores, not the stepsister of a murderer. Isabelle might not deserve what was happening to her, but it was too late to change his course now. She was his key to finding Reynaud, of that he was certain. And no amount of hysterics on her part could change that.

"You're tired, mademoiselle," he said evenly. "Perhaps you should go lie down. When your meal is ready, I will have Michel bring it up to you." It was as close to a peace offering as he could manage, and he silently urged her to take it. "If you will cooperate with me instead of fighting me at every turn, maybe this whole matter can be resolved quickly."

Isabelle looked at him scornfully, her face pale with anger. "And what if it is never finished? What if you cannot find Reynaud?"

Sebastion's face was grim. "I will find him. And when I do, you can go on with your life as before."

"Once again you are wrong, monsieur. Your actions here today ensure that my life will never be the same again."

"Tell me what I want to know, mademoiselle," he admonished. "Now, before it's too late."

She turned from him and started slowly up the stairs, her back stiff with pride. "I've told you all I know. I cannot make you believe me." Silently she prayed that her traitorous legs would not give out on her and further her humiliation. "Do not bother with a supper tray. I find I have quite lost my appetite."

Chapter Seven

Isabelle slept fitfully that night and awoke early the next morning with a dull ache at her temples. She looked around the small dusty room, momentarily confused as to where she was. Slowly it all came back to her, and she groaned aloud as her memory returned. She had spent the night, unchaperoned, in the company of two men not related to her. If anyone were ever to find out, her reputation would be in shreds. She didn't mind so much for herself, but for her grandmother. And her father. Victor Saint-Simon priced family honor above all else, and he would not understand why Isabelle had allowed this dreadful situation to happen. As if she had been given a choice.

Fully awake and thoroughly annoyed now, she sat up and surveyed her accommodations. The narrow room was sparsely furnished and had a high ceiling. The walls that had looked golden in the fading twilight now more closely resembled old straw. The velvet draperies where a shade darker, but they, too, had seen better days, as had the dirty windows they framed. Isabelle was not surprised at their condition considering the general state of disrepair of the entire house. It was really quite a shame, because she had noted that the furnishings were all of high quality, despite their present state. Michel's family must have at one time been well off, or at least comfortable. It was obvious to her now that Michel was one of the unfortunate members of the aristocracy whose fortunes over the years had declined to the point that they could no longer maintain their residences in the fashionable parts of the city and were forced to relocate to more modest surroundings.

She wondered if her father knew that Reynaud was living in such a place. Victor would undoubtedly deem the dwelling unfit for human habitation, but really he had left Reynaud no choice in the matter. When the younger man had lost his job at the bank, a job that Victor had gotten for him in the first place, her father had been furious. Despite the pleadings of his wife, Helene, Victor had thrown his stepson out of the house, telling him not to return until he had made something of himself. Helene had taken to her bed for several days after the incident, but Victor could not be moved. Finally Helene had given up and gone about the daily business of living. She did not bring up the subject of Reynaud again, but every month she sent him a small sum out of her personal funds. Reynaud had told his stepsister this in confidence, as all of them knew that it would not bode well for Helene if Victor were to find out about her furtive assistance. He would view her actions not as a mother trying to help her son, but as a wife disobeying her husband. And disobedience was one thing Victor Saint-Simon would not tolerate.

Such thoughts only increased the throbbing at her temples, so Isabelle resolved to get up and see what she could do to improve her situation. She rose from the lumpy bed, massaging her stiff neck and back. The few hours of sleep she had managed to get were definitely not enough. Isabelle had always needed a lot of rest, and she was not the most cheerful person in the morning under the best of circumstances. Smoothing out the counterpane, she wondered how she had slept at all, so uncomfortable was the mattress.

Once she had tidied the bed to her satisfaction, she turned to the silvered mirror on the wall above the dressing table. The image reflected there did nothing to lift her spirits. Her hair was hanging loose and tangled down her back, there were dark circles under her eyes, and her dress looked as though she had slept in it. Which she had.

Isabelle searched the table for something to make herself more presentable but could not find so much as a comb or a single hairpin. Her own pins had fallen out sometime during the night, so she set about searching for them. After several minutes she managed to find three of them, but they were useless to her until she found some way to untangle her hair. She tried using her fingers but soon gave up in frustration. It was no use; she simply had to have a brush. And the only way to get a brush was to demand her belongings from the hotel.

Unbidden, her wayward thoughts turned to the previous evening and her encounter with the callous Monsieur Merrick. Her stomach did a funny little somersault as she recalled the manly scent of him and the way his eyes flashed when he was angry. She attributed the sensation to lack of food, unwilling to admit that the feeling could more aptly be described as excitement. She would not acknowledge such a ridiculous notion. The man was a heartless brute, after all. And she couldn't possibly feel anything for him but contempt.

Squaring her shoulders resolutely, she unlocked the door and marched out into the hall. She studied the closed doors along the passageway, wondering briefly in which room the Englishman had slept. With a shake of her head, Isabelle silently chided herself for having such thoughts. What did it matter to her where that overbearing monster slept? For all she was concerned, he could bed down on the street.

She resolved that today she would not let him goad her into losing her temper. She was a lady and would behave as such, no matter how base his actions. Never in her life had anyone been able to get under her skin like Sebastion Merrick. Last night she had let him intimidate her with his overwhelming presence, but today she would show him that she would not be so easily cowed. Regardless of his titled status, the Englishman deserved to be treated no better than the lowliest servant. And she knew how to deal with recalcitrant servants. Her father had taught her well.

Quietly she made her way down the stairs and directly to the study, knowing somehow that she would find the Englishman there. He sensed her presence before she could even speak, and it startled her. The man seemed to have a knack for disconcerting her, and she was already grumpy enough without having him catch her off guard.

"Good morning, mademoiselle," he said, not bothering to divert his attention from the papers on the desk in front of him. "Did you sleep well?"

"No, I did not," Isabelle snapped, knowing that she sounded peevish but unable to stop herself.

He glanced up then, his dark brows lifting slightly. She resembled a wanton, with her honey gold hair hanging in tangles down her back and across her shoulders. To him she was infinitely desirable, but it was clear that she did not share his sentiments. No doubt she was most displeased by her disheveled appearance. "No, I can see that you did not. Perhaps you will feel better after you have had some breakfast."

Isabelle advanced on him, annoyed that he cut such a handsome figure while she looked worse than the lowliest washerwoman. "I will feel better once you have come to your senses and released me. But in lieu of that, I will settle for having my belongings brought here from the hotel so that I might have some clean clothes and freshen up." It wasn't fair that he should be so strikingly turned out in a dark blue waistcoat that deepened his eyes to a shade of brilliant sapphire, while she was forced to wear the same dirty gown she had slept in.

"As I promised last night, I have already taken care of that. Your things have been unpacked and your gowns pressed. I believe they are in the room next to yours. I would have had them placed in your room, but I did not want you disturbed." He explained it all in such a reasonable tone that Isabelle was almost embarrassed at her own rudeness. She sounded more like a fishwife than the cultured young woman she was.

"Thank you, Lord Fairfax," she said stiffly, the words sticking in her throat. "It was most kind of you to see to my needs." There was no reason to antagonize the man, after all. As long as he behaved in a civilized manner, she would respond accordingly. Even though she was feeling more in control of her emotions this morning, she reminded herself that for the time being she was still at this man's mercy. He had decided to be considerate of her this morning, but he could just as easily change his mind. And despite his gentleman's clothes and speech, she feared him on some elemental level. He was not like any of the men Isabelle had ever met, and she sensed a wildness in him that both attracted and repelled her at the same time.

"You are most welcome," he answered, equally gracious in his tone, but somehow she had the suspicion that he was mocking her. "But I would prefer that you call me Sebastion or Merrick."

"You introduced yourself as Lord Fairfax, so I believe that is the proper way for me to address you." Isabelle considered him a moment. "Or perhaps I was correct in my assumption that you really do not hold claim to such a title." Another thrust in their verbal fencing match.

"Perhaps you would like to look me up in *Debrett's Peerage* to assuage your concerns. I know that someone of your social standing would look unfavorably at dealing with a commoner." *Parry.*

"That won't be necessary," she said loftily. She felt foolish for her obvious snobbery, but refused to let him see it.

His expression was inscrutable, but she knew that underneath it all he was laughing at her expense. "Although I do hold a title, I prefer people use my Christian name."

"That would hardly be proper." She sniffed.

Sebastion smiled pleasantly. "Then I suppose you will have to call me 'my lord.'"

He said the words in such a way that she would feel subservient if she addressed him thus. On the other hand using his Christian name established an unwanted familiarity. Neither option was tenable. And he knew it, drat his devious mind. From the little that she understood of him, she could tell that he was enjoying her discomfort immensely.

"Very well, *Monsieur Merrick*," she said pointedly. "I shall leave you to your work for now. I would like to talk to you once I have eaten, though."

He nodded his head once in dismissal before turning his attention back to the sheaf of papers in front of him.

Isabelle bit back a retort at his lack of civility, wisely deciding to choose her battles with this man carefully. His pleasant disposition this morning did nothing to make her forget his threatening words and actions of the previous day. Sebastion Merrick was not a man to be underestimated, and she would do well to remember that.

Once upstairs Isabelle wasted no time in locating her belongings, which had been unpacked and neatly arranged for her by the still unseen servants Sebastion had mentioned. The room she now occupied was decorated in shades of blue, and had recently been cleaned. The furniture gleamed, despite its scarred and scratched veneers, and the cobwebs so prevalent in the other rooms had been swept away. Overall, it was a vast improvement.

Hastily she divested herself of her wrinkled gown, then went to the wardrobe to select a new one. She had packed lightly, bringing only a few day dresses and something a little more formal for evening. Smiling for the first time that day, Isabelle reached for a lovely gown of pale green cotton with a floral pattern throughout. It was one of her favorites and always made her feel pretty when she wore it. Henri had told her that it made her eyes even greener.

Humming softly, she took the garment out and laid it across the bed. As she bent over, the small key on a thin gold chain around her neck slipped out from beneath her chemise and glinted dully in the morning sun. In all the excitement Isabelle had completely forgotten about her strange necklace. Reynaud had enclosed the small gold key in the letter that had resulted in her trip to Paris. Not knowing what the key unlocked, Isabelle had placed it on a fine gold chain around her neck and hidden it under her dress. She still had no idea what it would open, but now that she was in Reynaud's home, she thought that she could figure it out.

Isabelle had just begun to unfasten her undergarments when there was a knock at the door. Before answering she grabbed her discarded dress from the floor and held it protectively in front of herself. "What do you want?" she asked nervously. Surely Monsieur Merrick would not dare to come in while she was dressing. She cursed herself silently for not having had the foresight to lock the door. With one deft movement she dropped the key back under her chemise so that only the chain was visible. That was certainly nothing to raise suspicion, and she would find a secure hiding place for it later.

"Mademoiselle," said a feminine voice, "my name is Jeannette and I have come to help you dress. My lord said that you might need my assistance."

Isabelle's shoulders sagged with relief. "Just a moment," she called. So here was one of the mysterious servants. Sebastion had said that he had been staying with a friend who was now loaning him a few staff members. She wondered anew at this anonymous associate, and decided that she would try to ply the maid for some answers. Perhaps she could even charm the girl into helping her escape. She smiled pleasantly as the young woman stepped into the room.

Jeannette was a pretty thing, younger than Isabelle from the look of her, with dark brown hair and eyes. She wore a simple gown of dove gray with a muslin cap covering most of her hair, tied with a ribbon beneath her chin. All in all, she presented a most attractive picture.

She curtsied slightly to Isabelle, then came and took the soiled dress from her. Spying the new gown laid out across the bed, Jeannette's expression said she approved of her temporary mistress's taste in clothing. Silently she set about helping Isabelle out of her worn undergarments and into fresh ones. Apparently she was not much of a talker, so Isabelle realized that she would have to make the first move.

"It's very kind of you to help me, Jeannette," she said, sliding a white silk stocking up one long leg. "I don't know how I could have managed without you."

"Yes, madame."

This was going to be harder than she thought. Isabelle tried again. "I'm sure your employer is missing you today. Do you think she is?" She emphasized the *she*, wanting to see if the maid would contradict her. She had thought that Sebastion's friend must surely be a man, but perhaps the person was a woman. For some reason the notion was displeasing to her. Silly, of course. What did she care of Sebastion Merrick's love life? Nothing at all, that's what.

Again the servant answered with a "Yes, madame."

Isabelle bit back a sigh of frustration and decided to give up for the time being. She turned her attention back to her toilette, relishing the feel of clean undergarments against her skin. Before putting on the dress, though, she would have to deal with the matter of her hair.

"Jeannette, I am going to need your help brushing out my hair. It's full of tangles, I fear, so it won't be pleasant." She lowered herself onto a small bench and faced the oval looking glass opposite her. It, too, had been newly polished, and Isabelle grimaced at her reflection.

Jeannette moved behind her and started to work, her face a mask of determination as she tried to untangle Isabelle's locks with a minimum of pain to the older girl. After several minutes it became obvious to Isabelle that the servant was not comfortable in her role. Clearly, the girl was not a lady's maid, or a mundane task such as brushing out her mistress's hair, no matter how snarled, would not cause such distress. And since the girl was not a lady's maid, that gave Isabelle the answer to one question. Merrick's friend was a man.

"I'm sorry my hair is in such a state," she apologized, then added slyly, "especially when you aren't used to doing hair."

The girl sighed wistfully. "I have always wanted to be a lady's maid, but monsieur has never married."

Isabelle smiled in satisfaction at having her suspicions confirmed. Jeannette saw her expression in the mirror and gasped in dismay. "You tricked me," she said in a hurt voice.

"Whatever do you mean?" Isabelle asked with exaggerated innocence. "I was merely making conversation. I only wanted to let you know that I understood your problem."

Jeannette's brow wrinkled in consternation. "I'm sorry, madame, you're right. I have never been a lady's maid before. But my lord asked me to come and help you, and I was told to do whatever he asked me." She stopped abruptly as it dawned on her that she was speaking too much.

"By whom were you told, Jeannette? Who is your employer?" Isabelle studied her reflection intently in the gilt-edged mirror.

Their eyes met in the looking glass. "I have been instructed not to tell you that, madame. I am sorry."

The time for play was over. If she could convince the girl to help her, she might be able to escape. Isabelle turned abruptly to face the servant. "Jeannette, I am being held here against my will. If you assist me, I will see that you are generously rewarded."

The younger woman swallowed audibly and lowered the brush in her hand. Now refusing to meet Isabelle's gaze, she stared straight ahead at the wall. "I was told that you would say things to me that were not true, and I was to ignore you. I was told that you are sick, and that your husband is only trying to help you get well."

"My husband?" Isabelle said incredulously. "I'm not married." Why would the maid think that she was married? And for that matter, who was she supposed to be married to? A flash of understanding prompted her to ask, "Did Lord Fairfax tell you that he is my husband?" Jeannette's face gave her the answer more eloquently than words. "That is ridiculous. I did not even know that man until yesterday," Isabelle cried. "I am not married, I am not sick, and I am not lying to you! If you would only help me, you would see that." She grasped the girl's hand, imploring her to believe.

The maid regarded her sadly, as one would regard an older person whose mind has gone. "Madame, I am sure that you believe these things, but if you would only let your husband help you, you would feel much better. I am sure he is only doing what is best for you." She patted Isabelle on the shoulder. "Now, why don't you let me finish your hair so that you'll be pretty for monsieur?"

Too shaken to argue further, Isabelle numbly let the younger woman arrange her hair and finish dressing her. Even the pretty green gown did little to raise her spirits. Sebastion Merrick thwarted her at every turn, demonstrating just how weak she really was. For a few treasured moments she had thought she might beat him at his own game, but that ploy, too, had failed. With his malicious fabrications he had neatly fixed it so that her last hope for assistance was gone. She was truly a prisoner with no prospect of escape.

Chapter Eight

When she had finished helping Isabelle dress, Jeannette gathered up the discarded clothes and let herself out of the room, closing the door softly behind her. Isabelle moved back to the dressing table and sat once again on the small stool, absently gazing into the mirror. Despite the fact that Jeannette was not a lady's maid, she had done a fine job on Isabelle's hair. At any other time Isabelle would have admired the simple topknot and the curls framing her face, but today she had more important things on her mind.

She sat for a long time, considering her options. She could storm downstairs and demand that Sebastion apologize for lying about her, or perhaps she could give him the slap he so richly deserved. But where would that get her? She wouldn't put it past him to strike her back. He had already shown that he would do whatever was necessary in order to accomplish his mission. And as she knew so well, he was not above using physical intimidation to bend her to his will.

She had to face the fact that fighting him was useless.

He was stronger than she, and at the moment he held all the cards in this particular game. She could rail against him all she wanted, but that would accomplish nothing. In point of fact, Isabelle was getting tired of being angry. Every time she got within speaking distance of Sebastion Merrick she either got mad or frightened and had to leave the room. This left the Englishman with ample time to search her stepbrother's belongings, and perhaps discover more damning evidence against him. Reynaud's interests would be better served if she could maintain her calm and try to work in tandem with Monsieur Merrick. True, she had been treated most grievously, but she was beginning to feel like a spoiled child throwing a tantrum for not getting her own way. Isabelle had never behaved this way in her life, raising her voice and carrying on, and it did not suit her purposes to start now.

Both she and Merrick wanted to find Reynaud, so instead of fighting him at every turn, what if she helped him? Once they located her stepbrother, Isabelle could prove that Reynaud was innocent, and this whole ordeal could end. It occurred to her that she didn't even know the full story concerning her stepbrother's alleged crime. She knew that it had to do with a family heirloom and Merrick's cousin being murdered, but that was all. Perhaps if she set aside her animosity and put her energies toward finding Reynaud she might be able to help solve this dilemma to everyone's satisfaction. And she must stop thinking of herself as a prisoner; by offering her assistance, she would become Merrick's partner rather than his captive.

It still rankled her that she had been forced to stay with him in the house, but she decided that if Henri truly loved her, he would understand. After all, it wasn't as if she were carrying on an affair with the tyrannical Englishman. He was very handsome, in a disreputable sort of way, but his presence was too unsettling to her equilibrium. All her life she had always preferred men such as her fiancé, who was the archetype of a proper gentleman. Sebastion Merrick was overwhelming, too blatantly masculine for any woman of delicate sensibilities. And she sensed a darkness in him that frightened her as much as it drew her. That was part of the problem. In addition to the fact that he had kidnapped her off the street and was holding her hostage in such a disreputable manner, she had to suffer the added indignity of finding herself attracted to him. When she was with him she felt more aware of herself as a woman, of every breath and every movement. He intrigued her as no other man before. She was angry with herself for feeling that way, and at him for causing such stirrings within her.

It was an impossible situation, but one she had to try and make bearable. If she continued arguing with him and provoking him at every turn, she wouldn't be in any position to help Reynaud. She would be better served to try to work with the Englishman. In that way she would be privy to any information he obtained and could use it to prove her stepbrother's innocence. She realized that Sebastion Merrick was not the kind of man she would normally choose to associate with, but she was left with little choice. It was either cooperate with him and have some influence in the matter, or fight him and remain a prisoner. Never one to take orders well, she decided on the former. Whether he wanted it or not, the Englishman now had a partner.

Calmer now, and feeling more empowered with a definite plan of action, Isabelle left her room and went to have her breakfast, late though it was. She had not eaten since the previous morning, which her rumbling stomach insistently reminded her.

After she had enjoyed a large breakfast served by a subdued Jeannette, Isabelle once again traced her steps to the study. It, too, had been tidied this morning, and looked slightly less shabby. Sebastion had moved from the desk and was now leafing through the meager collection of dusty books occupying a tall wooden bookcase. From the looks of things, neither Reynaud nor Michel was an avid reader.

"Hello," Isabelle greeted him cordially. She was determined to be pleasant, no matter how he provoked her.

Sebastion turned to regard her suspiciously, surprised at her peaceful demeanor. The maid, Jeannette, had dutifully reported this morning's confrontation, and he had expected Isabelle to launch into another diatribe against him. Instead she seemed calm and was actually being civil toward him. Clearly she was up to something, but regardless of her motives it was a pleasure to see her looking so well. He had thought her beautiful before, even wearing a badly wrinkled gown and with her hair in tangles. Now she was absolutely stunning, in a dress that brought out the color in her cheeks and made her eyes all the more green and luminous. Once again he couldn't help but wonder what it would have been like to meet her under different, more normal circumstances.

"Jeannette has told you about my little scene earlier this morning." It was not a question, but neither was it a complaint. She walked gracefully to the window and peered out onto the street. It was a lovely summer day, and the sidewalks were full of people going about their business. She felt a pang of envy at their freedom, but quickly stifled the sentiment. If all went well, she would be released soon enough.

Sebastion studied her for a moment before speaking. "She said that there was a minor incident."

Isabelle smiled wryly. "That is a nice way to put it, but, yes, I was rather upset, *husband.* It isn't every day a woman finds out that she's married and deranged all at the same time."

It was clear that she was teasing him, a fact that

made him all the more wary. Isabelle Saint-Simon had shown herself to be many things, but flirtatious was not one of them. "I was merely taking necessary precautions in case you decided to enlist the servant's aid, which you did." He closed the book in his hands and placed it back on the shelf. "Might I ask what has caused this sudden change in attitude, or is this another ploy to rid yourself of my presence?"

"You are not a very trusting man, monsieur," she observed in a slightly offended tone.

"No, I am not. Especially when you have given me no reason to trust you."

"That is true," Isabelle conceded, "but I could say the same of you." She moved to the desk and began idly arranging the papers spread on top. Her next words were chosen with care. "I would like to propose a truce. I have given the matter some thought, and I have come to the conclusion that we both want the same thing. For different reasons, of course."

"To locate Reynaud Andrassy." Sebastion had not moved from his position at the bookshelf, but continued to regard her speculatively.

"Yes, we both want to find Reynaud. What I am proposing is that we work together, so that perhaps we might expedite matters."

He was clearly skeptical. "And why would you want to help me find him? You know what will happen to him when I do."

"I have faith in my stepbrother, monsieur. I know that he did not kill anyone, and once we find him we can clear up this entire matter." Her gaze locked with his. "I know you will be honorable enough to admit your mistake at that time."

She smiled at him hopefully, but his next words, uttered with quiet menace, made her falter. "You don't know me at all, mademoiselle."

He was trying to frighten her, she thought, but she was not one to cower in the face of adversity. "Then why don't you tell me?" When he looked as though he would protest, she elaborated. "Not about you, exactly. I mean, why don't you tell me more about this family heirloom that you spoke of, and why you think my stepbrother is involved." She did not mention his cousin's murder but hoped that Sebastion would provide the information of his own volition. Moving to a decorative armchair covered in worn green velvet, Isabelle sat and looked up at him expectantly.

Sebastion did not speak immediately, and Isabelle feared that he would deny her request. After several minutes, however, he turned to address her. "Jonathan Larrimore, Marquis of Kensington, was shot to death in his country home three weeks ago. Nothing was out of place or missing in the entire house, except for a small chest covered in gold that had been in the family for generations. The very age of the piece would make it rare, but there were many other valuables on the premises that were much more accessible to a thief. So I must assume that your stepbrother was trying to steal the chest and, when Jonathan surprised him, Andrassy shot him."

Stifling the denial that sprang to her lips, Isabelle said instead, "Did anyone actually see Reynaud shoot your cousin?" A most reasonable question, she thought.

"The noise from the gun blast awakened the butler, who went to investigate. A man ran past him, nearly knocking him down, and the butler is certain he heard the man curse in French. And as I have already told you, when I began to investigate, Reynaud Andrassy's name turned up."

"That could merely be coincidence. Perhaps Reynaud was visiting friends in England." Even to her own ears the excuse sounded hollow. As far as she knew, Reynaud had no English acquaintances.

"Then he must have had a falling out with these friends, because the proprietor of the inn where he stayed told me that Simon Andrassy disappeared the morning after the murder, leaving behind a few coins to cover his bill." Sebastion glared at her. "I wonder why he decided to depart so abruptly, mademoiselle?"

Isabelle swallowed past a suddenly dry throat. "I don't know, monsieur. I also don't know why Reynaud would travel all the way to England to steal this antique chest. It doesn't make any sense. Reynaud knows nothing of such things. He is much more interested in current fashions than heirlooms." A frown marred her brow. "Did your cousin perhaps keep anything valuable in the chest?"

Sebastion shrugged. "That depends on what you consider valuable. To my knowledge, it contained an equally ancient chalice. Fashioned of solid gold, the drinking vessel is quite valuable. But, as I said, hardly the sort of thing your average thief would steal. It would be too conspicuous a piece to sell, and there would hardly be a great demand for it."

Isabelle agreed. "Was there anything special about this particular chalice?"

"Other than its age, no." Sebastion moved away from his position at the bookshelf and went to the desk. He picked up the small volume that contained Reynaud's handwriting. "This book is about Arthurian legends and Middle Age mythology. The chest that was stolen dates back to that same period, and was supposedly made for a famous French poet named Chretien de Troyes. If you will recall, Reynaud's notes in this book are on the first page of a chapter about that same poet." He handed the book to her.

She looked down at the incriminating evidence but would not let herself be swayed. "I don't pretend to have all the answers, but it is quite out of character for Reynaud to develop a sudden interest in history. Scholarship has never been his strong suit."

"I don't know what caused your stepbrother's fascination with medieval artifacts, but I intend to ask him once he is found." He rested a hip on the desk and picked up one of the disorganized stacks of paper. "I've looked through his personal papers, but nothing else besides that book gives me any clue as to his motive. There are a large number of bills here, but I do not believe that he would travel to another country and steal a well-known antique simply because he needed money. As soon as he tried to sell such a thing, the authorities would be on him." Sebastion shook his head. "It makes absolutely no sense."

"If Reynaud needed money so desperately he would have asked me, as he has done in the past," Isabelle said quietly.

Sebastion's black brows raised in disbelief. "There are bills here for thousands of francs, not including the gambling debt he owes. Would you have given him such a large amount?"

"I don't really know," she answered honestly. "I've given him so much in the past. My grandmother says that Reynaud takes advantage of my soft heart."

"And does he?" Sebastion asked.

She folded her hands primly across the desk, like a schoolteacher reciting to a pupil. "I love my stepbrother very much, and he loves me. He cannot help the way he is."

Sebastion regarded her speculatively. "Who are you trying to convince, mademoiselle, me or yourself?"

Isabelle looked away, uncomfortable under his probing scrutiny. "No one, monsieur. I am just trying to make you understand. Reynaud has always had difficulty following the dictates of society. My father is quite rigid in his principles, and it has not been easy for Reynaud to live up to his high standards."

"And that excuses the fact that he is a murderer and a thief?"

Isabelle whirled back around to face him. "Monsieur Merrick, if we are to have a truce, I must insist that you refrain from saying such hateful things. Nothing has been proven yet, and until it has, I will thank you to keep your prejudiced opinions to yourself." She stood and walked restlessly to the window, her back to him. "I am curious about something. Why haven't you gone to the authorities?"

"The English authorities are conducting their own investigation, but I saw no need to involve the French. I am more than capable of seeing that justice is served."

"Your idea of justice might be different from the rest of the world's. Tell me, when we find Reynaud, will you give him a chance to tell you the truth? Or will you arrogantly assume that you are right and sentence a man to his death?"

She heard Sebastion push away from the desk and come to stand a few feet behind her at the window. "Despite your low opinion of me, I am not a vigilante. If your stepbrother can prove his innocence, then I will listen." He moved nearer, so close that she could feel the heat of his body. "Isabelle, I made a promise to my family that I would find Jonathan's murderer. If that proves to be someone other than your stepbrother, then I will put all my efforts into searching for that person. But for now I have to follow my instincts, and they are telling me that Reynaud Andrassy has the answers I seek."

Isabelle shivered at his nearness and wrapped her arms protectively around her middle. He had used her name, and somehow the intimacy of that act unsettled her. "I have to follow my instincts as well. And they tell me to protect my brother."

"But who will protect you?" he questioned softly.

She turned to look up at him. "Who would want to hurt me?" Her voice sounded strange and throaty to her own ears.

He leaned toward her, and for one breathless moment she thought he might kiss her. Instead he whispered gently in her ear, "Who, indeed?"

Before Isabelle could regain her shattered senses, Sebastion turned and walked from the room. Isabelle waited until the door was closed before sinking slowly to the floor, her hand touching her ear where Sebastion's lips had grazed her skin. She wondered if he was deliberately trying to demonstrate his power over her, or whether he was merely trying to frighten her. Whatever his intention, it was working. She was more frightened than she had ever been in her life, and it wasn't just of him. She was frightened of herself and the dark passions stirring within that she had never known existed—until Sebastion Merrick had shown them to her.

Chapter Nine

Isabelle did not see Sebastion for the rest of the day. She spent the afternoon looking through Reynaud's personal effects to see what information she could find. As Sebastion had said, Reynaud had an enormous number of bills. It seemed that he owed money to half of Paris, and Isabelle was certain that if given the opportunity he would have been in debt to the other half as well. After a few hours of research, she found herself quite frustrated at her stepbrother's lack of discipline. Why did he insist on having all these things if he didn't have the means to pay for them? Finally, she gave up. Nothing in these papers had given her a clue as to where Reynaud might be, and looking at them only served to irritate her at her brother's profligate spending habits.

She decided to find Michel, who had been conspicuously absent all day, and see if he might have recalled anything that could be of use to her. She walked across the foyer to the large sitting room, but it was empty. Someone had cleaned up this room too, though not as

thoroughly as the study and bedchamber. Clearly Sebastion had given orders to make the place habitable,
but it was not the borrowed servants' task to give it a
thorough cleaning. Such a job would have taken several weeks for an army of servants.

Since Michel was not to be found here, she decided
to try his chamber. As she walked up the stairs, it occurred to her that she did not know which room was
his. Once in the narrow hallway, she saw that all the
doors were closed. She ignored the two doors immediately to her left, since she had slept in the first and
her belongings were now stored in the second. That left
the two doors to her right. She tapped on the first one
and called for the young man. When there was no answer, she opened the door and peered in. It was a very
masculine room. The dark green velvet curtains had
been drawn back to let in daylight, and Isabelle could
see that the furnishings were modeled on the Egyptian
style that had been popular in the last decade. Somehow she knew that this was Reynaud's chamber.

The walls were faded gold, adorned only by a large
frieze running along the upper portion and draped
with fabric underneath. Dark emerald draperies hung
around the bed, which was decorated with ornately
carved mythological creatures. Two side chairs stood
on either side of the bed, and in front of them were
brass flower stands with carvings of hieroglyphics
down the legs. Against the far left wall was a sofa, the
corners of which each held a placid bronze sphinx. On
the opposite wall was a rather simple commode, the
only sensible piece of furniture in the room.

Isabelle grimaced in distaste. How on earth could
anyone sleep with all those creatures staring? She was
thankful that her own chamber was more tastefully
decorated, if not as grandly furnished. She stifled a giggle as she thought of Reynaud sleeping in that silly bed,
and then she paused. Sebastion must have also slept in
that bed, because the other chambers were accounted

for. The thought of him sleeping in that monstrous bed did not make her laugh; in fact it gave her a funny feeling in the pit of her stomach. She quickly closed the door and hurried to what must be Michel's chamber.

Her knock was answered by a barely audible response to enter. After seeing Reynaud's room, Isabelle had no desire to see what aesthetic horrors might await her, so she called for the young man to come out into the hall. Inside she could hear rustling noises and a few thumps. Michel's thin face appeared a few moments later.

He looked fearfully up and down the hall, only his head emerging into the corridor. "Is *he* here?" he asked in an anxious whisper.

Isabelle had to bite back an amused chuckle. "No, he doesn't seem to be." There was no question as to whom he referred.

Michel relaxed visibly and opened his door fully so that Isabelle could see all of him. Today he was dressed more sedately in a bright blue coat, jonquil waistcoat and cream pantaloons. "I am at your service, mademoiselle." He bowed and would have taken her hand if she had let him. "Allow me to say how beautiful you look today. I have an evening coat that exact shade of green."

Knowing that he would continue the conversation in the same vein, Isabelle got right to the point. "Michel, I know you have heard some of what Monsieur Merrick has said about Reynaud. I was hoping that you had thought of some more information that might help me find my stepbrother." She finished and waited expectantly.

Michel shook his head sorrowfully. "Alas, mademoiselle, I have no more information than what I have already given you." He frowned. "*He* asked me the same thing earlier this morning, and I was glad that I couldn't help him."

"Anything that helps him will help me. We have decided to work together to find Reynaud."

Michel drew back from her as though stung. "Mademoiselle, how could you do such a thing? To agree to help that ruffian is an outrage! How can you turn on Reynaud like that?" He sounded like the lead in a melodrama.

"I am not turning on him," she explained patiently. "One way or another Sebastion Merrick is going to find Reynaud, and if I help him, I can be there when he does. Don't you think that will be better for Reynaud?"

He nodded slowly, clearly still unsure of her. "Although I don't see how you can help him after all he has done to you. I know that he made you stay here last night against your will. And I may not be in the same social class as the Saint-Simons, but I realize what that will do to your reputation."

Isabelle felt herself pale but tried to ignore his implication. "Unfortunately that cannot be helped. It's true I was forced into this, but I will do whatever it takes to assist my stepbrother." She wiped her damp palms down the front of her skirt, smoothing it unnecessarily. "Perhaps no one will find out what has happened here. I hope that I can count on you at least to be discreet, for Reynaud's sake if not mine."

Michel's chest puffed out in indignation. "Whatever else I may be, I am a gentleman. I would never impugn a lady's honor. Especially a lady such as yourself."

His earnest response offered some relief for her anxiety. "Thank you, Michel. That is very comforting to me." Since it didn't appear that Michel was going to be of any further assistance, she begged his pardon and returned to her own chamber. She had not been there long when Jeannette knocked on the door and informed her that supper was ready if she cared to dine. Dutifully she followed the younger woman down to the dining room.

She was both relieved and disappointed to find that Sebastion would not be joining her. Marie, a short, plump girl with rosy cheeks, served her meal and informed her that monsieur had gone out for the evening. She also made a point of mentioning that he had left a rather large manservant to watch out for Isabelle's safety. Isabelle clearly understood that this man would ensure she remained in the house. And when is the monsieur expected to return?" Isabelle asked.

The maid offered her a look of sympathy.

"I am sorry, madame, but he only said that we were not to wait up for him."

It was very late indeed when Sebastion finally returned to the once elegant town house. He stifled a yawn as he divested himself of his dark blue coat and loosened his cravat. A single lamp had been left burning in the foyer, and he used its light to guide his way into the study, where he immediately sought and located a crystal decanter and glass. The brandy was of an inferior quality, but he had had much worse. With efficient movements he poured and drank two small glasses in quick succession.

The alcohol burned warmly in his stomach, and Sebastion realized how very tired he was. He had slept no more than an hour the night before and it was almost dawn now. Two days without sleep were taking their toll. Damn, but he must be getting old.

He became aware of her before she spoke.

Isabelle stood in the doorway, wearing a pale cotton dressing gown. Her hair had been brushed out and braided into a single thick rope that was draped over her shoulder. She had her arms wrapped tightly about her midsection, though it was not chilly in the house. Beneath her robe he could see ten bare little toes peeping out, and he fleetingly thought that in her haste she must have forgotten to pack her slippers.

"It's very late," she said in a tone barely above a whisper.

"What are you doing up?" Didn't she know it was

dangerous to greet a man late at night wearing nothing but her nightclothes? Looking at her, he decided that she probably didn't. Probably she had no idea of the effect she was having on his overtired senses.

"I have been waiting for you." She walked farther into the room, still speaking in muted tones. "I assumed you went to find information on Reynaud. Did you have any luck?"

"I learned nothing new about your stepbrother." He paused at the disappointment evident on her face. "But I did discover a great deal about a certain Monsieur Broussard."

It took a moment for the name to register with Isabelle. " 'E. Broussard,' the name on the note!" she exclaimed excitedly. "Did you speak with him? Does he know where Reynaud might be?"

One corner of Sebastion's mouth curled up into a wry attempt at a smile. "No to both questions. The gentleman in question lives in a chateau on the outskirts of Troyes. He has quite a reputation, though, and I found several of his 'friends' who were most talkative after a few drinks. Purchased by me, of course."

"Of course," Isabelle repeated sarcastically. "What do we do now?"

Sebastion had imbibed quite a few of those drinks himself, and the combination of too much alcohol and too little sleep made him almost capricious. "If the mountain will not go to Mohammed, Mohammed will go to the mountain," he quipped.

Isabelle regarded him suspiciously, puzzled by his uncharacteristic flippancy. Her eyes widened a few seconds later and she gasped in righteous indignation. "You're drunk," she accused. "You've been out drinking all night when I thought you were getting something accomplished." She glowered at him in annoyance. "And to think I believed that you were truly grieving for your cousin, and serious about finding his murderer. You're nothing but a common drunkard. You probably didn't give the matter one serious thought."

Sebastion was upon her before she finished the last word, his affable nature gone, his fingers biting into the tender flesh of her upper arms as he lifted her almost off the ground. "Don't ever question the depth of my grief again or I'll make you wish you'd stayed safely hidden in your room. You cannot imagine the magnitude of my loss, so do not dare to judge my pain."

The beast was back and he frightened her. "I'm sorry," she whispered fearfully. "Please, I'm so sorry." Of its own volition, her hand crept up to caress his rough cheek. "I didn't mean to hurt you."

Sebastion made a noise deep in his throat. A terrible growl of sorrow and something else. Raw passion. He palmed his large hand around the back of her head, bringing her mouth to his. And he claimed a kiss of such intoxicating sweetness that he later thought he must have imagined it. He ravaged her with his lips, tongue and teeth. Tasting, stroking, sucking until he was almost mad with the sensation. Her lips were so luscious, so soft, that what started out as a release of tension turned into the greatest pleasure he had ever known.

Isabelle struggled ineffectually, trapped in his steely embrace. "Sebastion," she panted, out of breath from the fierceness of his kisses, "please." He trailed a line of fiery kisses down her throat before claiming her mouth once again. The pleasure was so great that all thoughts of escape were forgotten. With a cry of surrender, Isabelle wrapped her arms around him, instinctively pressing her body into his. Her fingers threaded through his hair, grasping the raven tresses in her fists. She wanted to pull him closer, closer.

He teased her with his tongue, playing with hers until she wanted to scream with the joy of it all. His teeth bit down ever so slightly on her swollen lips, as though he really would devour her. And his hands, at first clenched in her hair, began to move on her body. They seemed to be everywhere. Tracing the curve of her brow, her cheekbone, the column of her long neck. And then his hand moved lower, his palm massaging her breast through the thin layers of cotton. Isabelle whimpered with desire, unsure of the sensations that Sebastion evoked. Her body was on fire with a need that her mind was not experienced enough to understand.

Dimly she was aware of a rending sound, but she cared for nothing beyond the feel of the night air on her skin and the touch of Sebastion's hands and mouth. Later she would be concerned that the bodice of her dressing gown was in shreds, but now such thoughts were beyond her. She moaned in protest when Sebastion's lips left hers, but that was quickly replaced by gasps of excitement as his mouth found her breast. She felt as though a bolt of lightning had struck her, and she burned with the heat of it. As Sebastion suckled her breasts, her fingers tightened convulsively in his hair, pressing him closer, pulling him nearer. Wanting.

In her innocence she had thought that her arousal was complete, until Sebastion put his hand between her legs, cupping her intimately through the thin cotton of her gown. She thought she might die from the intensity of her reaction. Her entire body convulsed, a thousand relentless jolts of electricity coursing through her veins. She cried out then, unable to help herself, and would have woken the house if Sebastion had not muffled the sound with his mouth.

Over and over the sensations gripped her until at last she was spent. Slowly she became aware of her surroundings again. She was leaning against Sebastion, and she was weeping both from the pleasure of it all and in disbelief. Isabelle looked into Sebastion's fathomless eyes that were almost black with unspent passion. She tried to speak, but no words would come out. When she glanced down at herself, naked from the waist up and covered with the marks of Sebastion's desire, she wept even harder.

Sebastion pulled her closer into his arms, tenderly stroking her hair. "Isabelle, don't cry," he soothed. "I didn't mean to hurt you." He doubted the sincerity of his own words. If passion like this could ignite between them after such a brief acquaintance, he wondered what would happen if their forced intimacy were to continue. He had never in his life lost control like this, and he wondered what it was about this one woman that could make him do so. It was madness, and it had to stop. This chemistry between them could only lead to heartache, and he would have to be very careful in the future to remain in control of his desires.

Isabelle stiffened at his words. She had said the same thing to him. Had it only been a few minutes ago? So much had changed in those fleeting moments. Though she didn't fully understand what had happened, she was ashamed and wanted to get away from the all-knowing eyes of Sebastion Merrick. Dashing at her tears with a clenched fist, she pushed away from him and took a few steps on wobbly legs. Trying to restore her modesty, she pulled the torn edges of her dressing gown up to cover her naked breasts.

"Isabelle," Sebastion rasped in a voice she didn't recognize.

She held up a shaking hand to him. "Please, stay away from me. I want to go to my room." Even to her own ears she sounded like a child asking for her mother, but at this moment that was what she felt like. Her lips and breasts still tingled from the attentions of his mouth, and she was mortified to feel an uncomfortable dampness between her legs. She almost started to cry again, but years of self-discipline enabled her to walk out of the room and up the stairs unassisted. Once in her room she locked the door and then collapsed on the bed, finally crying herself into an exhausted sleep a few minutes later.

Kathleen McCarthy

Sebastion remained in the study, sprawled in one of the uncomfortable little chairs that dotted the room. His head was thrown back and he covered his eyes with one forearm. What in the hell had happened? He couldn't ever remember losing control like that, no better than a rutting animal. And the worst of it was that his body was still so aroused, he knew that he would do it again if given the chance. Damn, but this was a mess. Isabelle was a virgin, the stepsister of a man he planned to see hanged, and he had almost taken her right on the floor of that same man's home. She had accused him once of being a monster, and now he thought that she might have been right.

He sat in the gloom of the study for over an hour, willing himself to calm down. His tired mind and restless body warred with each other, until at last he was so fatigued that he thought he might sleep. Dawn was just breaking as he made his way wearily to his borrowed chamber. Briefly he paused outside Isabelle's door, but he could hear nothing. He took that as a good sign, hoping that she slept.

Closing and locking his chamber door behind him, he dropped onto the monstrous bed, fully clothed, and fell into an exhausted sleep.

Chapter Ten

Isabelle slept through the morning and well into the afternoon. She was disoriented as usual upon waking, so it was not until she had risen and caught a glimpse of herself in the looking glass that memory came flooding back to her. The delicate material of her bodice was split down the middle and hung open to reveal her bare breasts. Isabelle studied her reflection with horrified fascination. Small bruises and chafe marks dotted her delicate skin from her neck down to her ribs, and her lips were swollen and tender to the touch, also bruised from the intensity of Sebastion's passion. Her hair was a wild mane falling about her shoulders and down her back. It was the reflection, she thought, of a whore.

She bit back a hysterical laugh, holding her hand firmly over her tender mouth. Once started, she feared the laughter would turn to tears, and she did not want to cry again. Tears served no purpose, other than to make her appear weak. And Sebastion Merrick had enough power over her already.

How could she have abandoned a lifetime of self-discipline and proper breeding so easily? The moment Sebastion's mouth had so angrily claimed hers, she had thrown aside her own sense of morality and behaved like the lowest wanton. And she had reveled in it, moaning and clinging to him, kissing him back with equal ardor. Lightly she caressed her swollen mouth, assailed by memories of his lips upon hers. Henri's kisses had never affected her in such a manner. She let her hand fall to her side, ashamed of her disloyal thoughts. Henri, her fiancé, and the only man who had the right to kiss her, could not stir her like the enigmatic Englishman. She had betrayed Henri by responding to another man, welcoming a stranger's kisses and caresses. She could not even bear to think of that final, shattering burst of sensation.

A soft tapping at the door was a welcome distraction from her troubling thoughts. She hoped it was one of the maids, for surely Sebastion would not dare disturb her after what had happened.

"Madame, are you awake?" It was Jeannette.

Isabelle sagged in relief. "Yes, Jeannette. Just a moment." She unlocked the door and Jeannette entered, carrying a small silver tray.

"Monsieur said that we were to let you sleep," she said shyly. "He himself only rose an hour ago." Though she tried to hide it, Isabelle noted the tiny smirk on the girl's lips. Isabelle flushed, ready to try to explain, when it occurred to her that the little maid thought she and Sebastion were married. As far as the servant was concerned, the master and his wife had settled their differences and were tired from a night of "making up." Well, better for the girl to think that than to know the truth.

Mustering as much dignity as she could, she thanked Jeannette for the tray and asked for a bath. Jeannette's gaze strayed to Isabelle's bodice, the two pieces held together in Isabelle's clenched hand. "Yes, madame."

A Treasure to Hold

By the time she had eaten a small portion of the meal Jeannette had brought, the servants had managed to fill a small tub with warm water. Wanting to wash in private, Isabelle dismissed the grinning women and sank blissfully into the rather cramped hip bath.

Feeling more like her old self once she was clean and dry, Isabelle dressed as best she could before calling for Jeannette's assistance. Once properly fastened and coifed, she was suddenly at a loss as to what to do next. She did not relish staying in her chamber, and she certainly did not need a nap since she had slept most of the day. But she wasn't sure that she was ready to face Sebastion. While she did not consider herself a coward, she reasoned that it was sometimes better to err on the side of caution. The wisest course of action would be to avoid any confrontations until she was better able to comport herself.

Jeannette's parting words dashed any hope of evading Sebastion. "Monsieur asks if you would join him in the sitting room when you are ready."

"Of course," Isabelle murmured, and followed the maid out of the room before she could change her mind.

The sitting room was a large, formal space where any guests to the town house would be received. It was decorated in shades of blue and cream, and had once probably been quite lovely. In the center of one wall was a grand fireplace with an intricately carved mantelpiece. Opposite it were two large windows with elaborately draped curtains that reached to the floor. Tall glass-fronted cases filled with various knickknacks flanked these windows. The other two walls were filled with paintings, hung from long brass picture hangers. Various tables, cabinets and chairs were positioned throughout, mostly along the perimeter, leaving the faded floral design on the carpet as the centerpiece of the room.

Isabelle studied the furnishings, momentarily relieved to find herself alone. She walked across the rug, the rustling of her skirts the only sound as she went to the china cabinets and absently studied the delicate pieces displayed inside.

"Isabelle."

Sebastion's voice was loud in the silence of the house. Isabelle turned, startled to find him no more than three feet from her. She hadn't heard him enter the room, and his close proximity unnerved her. With his uncanny ability to sneak up on people, she thought that he might have made an excellent thief. An opinion she refrained from voicing.

"Isabelle," he repeated, more gently this time.

The intimacy of her name on his lips made the room seem smaller to her. His physical presence was so strong, so overwhelming. Her resolve weakened. She took a step away from him, hoping that the added distance would help calm her already frayed nerves.

Sebastion's expression turned grim as he mistook her reaction for one of fear. "You don't have to shrink from me like a scared rabbit. Do you think I would hurt you?"

"I'm not frightened of you." Without conscious thought she raised her hand to her swollen and bruised mouth, adding softly, "But I think you could hurt me without half trying."

She hadn't meant to say that, hadn't even been thinking such a thing, but the words had come out just the same. And she realized that it was true. Sebastion Merrick could hurt her, and not just physically. She had known him for less than three days, and look how much had happened. And yet she really wasn't frightened of him, though she knew that he had the power to change her life. In fact he already had, for when she looked in the mirror this morning a stranger had stared back at her.

Without conscious thought, Sebastion closed the distance between them. Unable to stop himself, he carefully raised his hand to her face, caressing her cheek with the backs of his fingers, then grazing his thumb across her abused mouth. "I'm sorry," he said. "For this, and for all the rest." He pulled his hand away and let it drop back to his side, angry with himself for still wanting her. For wanting to comfort her, touch her.

"It won't happen again," he said harshly. No matter how badly he wanted her.

"You're angry." She regarded him solemnly with her enticing green eyes. "What is it between us, Sebastion? You make me feel things I don't understand. When I'm with you I'm either yelling or crying or . . . or kissing you," she finished in a self-conscious whisper. "I've never behaved so shamefully in my life."

"You've done nothing to be ashamed of. I am to blame for what happened last night. I should have had more self-control." He didn't like the turn this conversation was taking. He had intended to apologize to her, then drop the subject altogether. What had happened between them was best forgotten. He was on a mission, and seducing Isabelle Saint-Simon was not part of his plan. It was bad enough that she was a virgin, an *engaged* virgin, but she was also the stepsister of the man he had sworn to see hanged. No matter how strong the attraction or how desperately he wanted her, Sebastion was going to leave Isabelle alone. They were lucky that nothing more had happened last night, and he intended to keep it that way. Isabelle would go to her wedding bed a proper virgin. He would see to that.

"I would like to apologize to you as well. I shouldn't have said those things to you, and I'm sorry." Her eyes were wide and earnest, unblinking. "We certainly seem to provoke each other."

"It's called lust," Sebastion said baldly.

Isabelle blushed to the roots of her hair. "Lust?" she murmured faintly.

"That's why we constantly get each other's back up.

There is a physical attraction between us." He knew he should just keep his mouth shut because he was giving her far too powerful a weapon against him if she ever wanted to use it. But she seemed so genuinely bewildered about the entire situation that he wanted to explain.

"Then don't you think it would be best if you let me go?" she asked after a moment's consideration. "We don't want it to happen again."

Sebastion's face hardened. "I've already told you that it won't." His expression softened somewhat. "And as far as my releasing you, I thought we had agreed to work together."

"We have," she agreed, "but I have an uneasy feeling about this whole situation." Her voice lowered to a whisper. "I wonder how it will end."

Sebastion had his own ideas about that, but he kept silent. If Isabelle was willing to cooperate with him, he would at least attempt to keep his opinions of her stepbrother's guilt to himself. He had stated his beliefs, and they each knew where the other stood. Now if they could only control their desire for one another, they might accomplish their goal: to find Reynaud Andrassy.

They were both silent for a few moments, lost in their own thoughts.

Finally Isabelle spoke. "This is very awkward. I think we both agree that we made a terrible mistake, and that it was an incident that won't be repeated. We were tired and on edge, and we acted irrationally. Let's just agree that enough has been said on the subject, and we won't discuss it anymore." She offered a tentative smile and her outstretched hand. "Truce, monsieur?"

Sebastion took her hand and shook it, thinking all the while that she was a truly amazing woman. "Truce," he said agreeably.

Isabelle's own smile widened. "Good. Now we can

get down to business. Tell me, what did you discover about the mysterious E. Broussard?"

They arrived in the city of Troyes just as dusk was descending two days later. Located in the Champagne province, Troyes had served as the medieval capital and was still its principal town. It was situated on the Seine in an area known as *la Champagne humide*, its damp clayey soil making it an unusually fertile place. Dairy cows and other livestock flourished, along with grapes for wine, although the famous sparkling wine known as *le champagne* was produced from vineyards to the east and northwest of the area, near the city of Reims.

Sebastion had informed Isabelle of his plans to go to Troyes to investigate Emil Broussard, the man to whom Reynaud was in debt. He believed it was no coincidence that both the stolen chest and Broussard had ties to the same city. Perhaps Monsieur Broussard could enlighten him as to the connection and tell him the whereabouts of Reynaud Andrassy.

Briefly he had thought of making the journey alone, thinking it better to avoid the temptation and distraction of Isabelle's company, but he had decided that he still needed her. Though Reynaud had not tried to contact Isabelle again, Sebastion still believed that she would be useful to him. In order to move as quickly and easily as possible, he had decided against bringing one of the maids for Isabelle, who assured him that she could take care of herself. Isabelle would travel by coach, with Sebastion following on horseback. Their coachman, another servant of Sebastion's Parisian friend, was a necessary addition, and one who could be relied upon for complete discretion.

They traveled rapidly and efficiently, stopping late the first night at a small inn where Isabelle barely finished her supper before Sebastion led her up to her room and she promptly fell asleep. Though the coach was of the finest quality, Isabelle was still bounced around a lot on the bumpy roads, besides being anxious about what they would discover at the end of their journey. In consequence, she greeted their arrival on the second evening with much pleasure and relief.

She opened the carriage door as soon as the vehicle rolled to a stop, and waited rather impatiently for Sebastion to come and help her alight. As she surreptitiously stretched her aching muscles, Isabelle studied the inn in the fading light of the sunset. It was larger than the one from the previous night, and seemed to be of higher quality. It was an old building, the half-timbered walls faded to a creamy yellow that contrasted charmingly with the faded red of the wooden shutters and gently sloping tiled roof. Cheerful pink flowers brightened window boxes or hung from planters, giving the place a most welcoming appearance.

They were on the outskirts of Troyes, and in the distance Isabelle could see the buildings that made up the town, as well as several large farms and a few elegant chateaux. In between were lush green fields, some dotted with grazing cows, some lined with rows of ripening grapes, wheat or sugar beets. Sections of forest were sprinkled throughout. Isabelle couldn't help wishing that she were a talented artist so that she might capture the beautiful landscape on canvas.

Isabelle felt her spirits lift as she climbed out of the carriage, and she smiled with pleasure as a cooling evening breeze ruffled her hair. She was glad to be out of the stuffy coach and looked forward to partaking of a light supper, washing up and going to sleep.

The proprietors of the inn, noting everything from the quality of the shiny black coach and superior horses to the costly traveling clothes of the young couple before them, rushed out to greet their latest guests. The inn was not very crowded and they were more than happy to have such well-to-do patrons. Claude and Josephine Duvall were a hard-working couple who did their best to run a comfortable establishment and make a nice profit while doing so. Claude was tall and lean, somewhat stooped at the shoulders, with thinning gray hair. Josephine was almost as tall and looked as though she could keep up with most men in matters of physical labor. Her dark hair was liberally streaked with gray, giving her a rather severe appearance that was softened by her kind blue eyes.

Sebastion and Isabelle followed Madame Duvall inside while her husband fetched in their few pieces of luggage. Sebastion had insisted upon traveling light, so Isabelle had brought only a few essential items with her.

Madame noted this deficiency, along with the lack of servants, but wisely said nothing. She had learned early on that people did not appreciate overly curious innkeepers, so she had trained herself to allow her guests their privacy. Josephine reasoned that as long as they paid their bill, her customers' circumstances were none of her business.

"How long will you be staying with us, monsieur?" madame asked pleasantly. Now that *was* her business.

Sebastion flashed a charming grin at her, winning the older woman's affections in spite of herself. "I'm not sure, madame." He leaned in closer, whispering conspiratorially, "My wife and I have just eloped, you see." He glanced back at Isabelle, who stood across the room absently studying some paintings of the local landscape. "Her family didn't approve of me." He offered a Gallic shrug and sighed. "Alas, I was forced to resort to drastic measures."

Madame Duvall, secretly a romantic despite her serious exterior, commiserated with him on his in-law difficulties and congratulated him on an excellent choice. "We are very happy to have you, monsieur . . ." She paused and glanced down at the register that Sebastion had just signed, "Jourdain. And I am sure the family will come around." She had always had a weakness for a handsome face.

Sebastion continued, expertly playing the role of a love-struck newlywed. "I am hoping that these few days away might give them time to accustom themselves to the idea. Besides, I have always been interested in medieval history, and Troyes seemed a good place to visit."

Josephine offered a smile at the winning young man, even more pleased with him. She had always been proud of her home's history and was happy at this attractive man's interest in it. "I will show you to your room. This way, if you please."

Sebastion and Isabelle followed her up a narrow flight of stairs and down a hallway lined with closed doors. Madame opened one of these and motioned for them to precede her. The room was not spacious, but not so small as to be cramped. A large bed topped by a creamy lace canopy dominated one wall. There was also a mahogany wardrobe for their clothes, a small writing desk, two chairs and a sofa. It was a simple room, but one that was warm and inviting.

"It's lovely, thank you," Isabelle told the proprietress sincerely. "Perhaps after we have eaten you might be so kind as to have a bath prepared for me."

"Of course, my lady." Having assured herself that the room was to their liking, madame excused herself. "There is a small private dining room downstairs where we will serve your supper. At your leisure, of course."

"Thank you, we will be down directly." Sebastion nodded to the older woman, who promptly closed the door behind her, leaving them alone.

Isabelle surveyed the accommodations once more. "It really is quite charming. Is your room close by?"

"Yes," he said. "In fact, it's very close."

She thought that he was acting rather peculiarly but shrugged it off. "Next door?" she asked as she untied the ribbons on her bonnet. Once it was off she placed it on the bed and turned back to him.

"Closer than that."

She laughed at his response. "Closer than next door; how is that possible . . . ?" Her voice trailed away into silence and she breathed in a fortifying breath, then released it before addressing him. "Are you trying to tell me that this is also your room? That we are *sharing* this one room?" She said the word sharing as though it was foreign to her.

Isabelle struggled to keep her voice at a normal level. Jumping to conclusions had gotten her into trouble before with this man, and she would not make the same mistake so readily.

"Yes, that is what I am telling you." He waited for the inevitable dispute, but when Isabelle held her tongue, he explained. "I have told Madame Duvall that we are a married couple, that we just eloped today because your family didn't approve of me. You are now Madame Jourdain."

She couldn't say that she was surprised at the alias, or at the fact that he could successfully pass himself off as French. He had fooled her, after all. She merely arched an eyebrow sardonically and asked, "And what is your first name, *dearest?*"

"Henri," he answered blandly.

"How original," she shot back sarcastically.

His expression was guileless. "I thought you would like it."

She chose to ignore that. "Why did you feel it necessary to make up such a story? We had separate rooms last night."

"We came here to get information from Emil Broussard. In order for me to do that properly I am going to have to meet with him, go to his home. A wealthy gentleman is not going to invite to his home a stranger who is traveling with an unmarried female, no matter that she is staying in a separate room."

"I could have posed as your sister," she pointed out reasonably.

"Yes, but then it would look rather strange that you have no maid and so little luggage." Before she could come up with a rebuttal he continued. "The easiest plan was to say that we had eloped, which accounts for the lack of suitcases and servants. I can also keep an eye on you better this way."

Isabelle was stung. "You don't have to keep an eye on me. We have a truce. We're working together. Do you think I'm so deceitful that I need to be watched like a common criminal?"

"Isabelle," he asked patiently, "if you had your own room and Reynaud found you alone in it and asked you to help him, would you inform me, or would you help your stepbrother?"

She considered the question. "I'm not sure what I would do," she admitted honestly. "But is this arrangement really necessary?" Their stormy encounter in Reynaud's study flashed in her mind and she had to seriously question the wisdom of Sebastion's fabrications. She could only hope that in truth Sebastion planned to spend the night elsewhere. Sharing separate chambers in the town house had been bad enough, but to actually occupy the same room for an entire night was unthinkable. She decided to give him the benefit of the doubt and not raise a fuss until she could determine his true intentions.

Sebastion nodded. "Once I have made my initial call on Broussard, he will want to know more about me. What he will find out is that we are newlyweds staying here for a few days to let your family accustom themselves to our marriage, and that I have an avid interest in medieval history."

Isabelle frowned and folded her arms across her chest sullenly. "This certainly isn't the way I thought to spend my honeymoon."

She blushed crimson at the look he gave her.

Sebastion slept hidden in the coach that night.

Chapter Eleven

The inhabitants of Champagne, known as Champenois, were a hard-working, serious people with a reputation for being reserved with strangers. During their first day in Troyes, Sebastion found this estimation to be well-deserved. After a large breakfast, he and his "bride" set out for the town, hoping to gather some useful information. A more tight-lipped collection of citizens he had never encountered. They were polite and respectful, but nobody volunteered much in the way of information. The couple even visited the Gothic cathedral of Saint Pierre et Saint Paul and the ancient church of Saint Urbain to affirm Sebastion's supposed interest in medieval history. Isabelle was pleasantly surprised to learn that he really was quite knowledgeable about the subject. Of course he brushed aside her admiration, saying that he possessed only the rudimentary facts. Even Isabelle could see that it was more than that, but she let the matter drop. Sebastion Merrick was a complicated man, and she felt that she hadn't even scratched the surface.

Fortunately for them both, the women of Troyes seemed more inclined to gossip. At a small millinery shop where Isabelle feigned interest in several hats and bonnets, she struck up a conversation with the proprietress. Mademoiselle Caron, the spinster owner of the shop, was delighted by the fictional romance of Isabelle and Sebastion, and happily chatted with the younger woman.

"My dear, I think it is too romantic, this elopement," Mademoiselle Caron cooed wistfully. "I hope that your family will not be very upset with you." She looked out the shop window to where Sebastion waited patiently. "Such a handsome gentleman, too. You are very lucky, madame."

Isabelle did her best impression of a blushing bride. "Thank you, mademoiselle. I am so happy, and I'm sure my family will come to love my husband as I do." She pretended to admire her reflection in the mirror as she tried on a pretty little bonnet trimmed in green satin. "My husband is pleased to stay here for a few days, though. He does so love history. We visited the cathedral this morning." She turned innocent eyes to the unsuspecting older woman. "Are there any other places to visit, perhaps? Or someone who could give tell him more about the local history?"

Mademoiselle Caron chewed her lower lip thoughtfully. "There are several buildings of historical interest, as you can see. As for more information about this region's past, I suppose that Monsieur Broussard is the most knowledgeable. His family is supposedly descended from Chretien himself." Her expression turned troubled. "He would not be of much help, though, I am afraid. The man is a bit of a recluse and has little to do with the rest of us."

"Oh, what a shame," Isabelle said, hoping to prompt the talkative woman into further conversation.

It worked. "Yes, it is," she said wistfully. "He lives all alone in a beautiful chateau a few miles west of town. Of course, he goes to Paris several times a year, but I often think he must be quite forlorn rambling about in the great big house all by himself." From the way she spoke, Isabelle could tell that Mademoiselle Caron wished *she* could be the one to ease the man's loneliness.

"He sounds quite intriguing. I'm sure my husband would like to meet him."

Mademoiselle Caron shook her head in resignation. "I wish him luck, but I doubt the man would grant him an invitation. Why, I hear he keeps a guard in his gate-house." Her voice dropped to a conspiratorial level. "They say he shot a man once for trespassing. Can you imagine?" Clearly she thought this the height of scandal, though it seemed to only add to Broussard's dangerous appeal in her estimation.

Just then the shop bell jingled, announcing another patron. It was Sebastion, who had apparently come to the end of his tolerance for hat shopping. "Are you ready, my dear?" he inquired solicitously.

"Yes, I suppose so," she answered, and started to take off the pretty green bonnet.

Mademoiselle Caron, fearing the loss of a sale, asked smoothly, "Shall I wrap this one for you, my dear?"

"No," Isabelle declined politely.

"Yes," Sebastion said at the same time. "Have it sent to the inn, please." When Isabelle would have protested he stopped her. "I want to buy you pretty things, love. Besides, it matches your beautiful green eyes."

After her customers had departed Mademoiselle Caron set about wrapping and boxing the purchase for delivery, all the while thinking how lucky some women were. It was hard not to be jealous of a young woman like that who possessed such obvious wealth and beauty. How unfair that she had to settle for selling hats to such women. She consoled herself with the fact that she made a handsome living doing just that—even if sometimes she wished for more out of life.

Outside the shop Sebastion tucked Isabelle's arm through his and escorted her down the street. "You didn't have to buy that bonnet for me, you know," Isabelle said as they strolled down the cobbled lane to where their carriage waited. "That woman already thought you were a most doting husband without your having to go to the expense of making a purchase."

His expression was inscrutable. "I told you in the shop why I bought it."

"But that was just an excuse for Mademoiselle Caron's benefit," she protested.

"Of course," he agreed amiably.

For some reason she couldn't let the matter drop. "Really, Sebastion, why did you buy that bonnet?" she asked again. "And don't tell me it's because it matches my eyes, because I'll know you're lying."

Sebastion halted in midstride and looked down at her. "I bought the hat for the same reason I do everything; because I wanted to." They resumed their walk.

Isabelle sighed in frustration. "You really are an impossible man, Monsieur *Jourdain*." She would not call him Henri no matter what he said.

"So I've been told," he said archly. "I don't suppose you got anything useful out of the milliner?"

Isabelle slanted him a pert glance. "She confirmed your suspicions about Broussard's interest in medieval history, and said that he didn't associate with the people in town." A faint frown creased her brow. "She also mentioned that he had guards around his property, and that he once shot a man for trespassing. He doesn't sound like a very agreeable person." She shuddered delicately. "I hate to think of Reynaud mixed up with such a man."

They reached the coach and Sebastion assisted Isabelle inside, then joined her. He was silent for most of the brief trip back to the inn, and Isabelle supposed he was digesting the little information they had been able to gather about the enigmatic Emil Broussard. The more Isabelle learned about the predicament her stepbrother was in, the worse it seemed. It was bad enough that Reynaud owed money to anyone, but it was even worse to find out that this man was a recluse taken to shooting at people. And it was too much of a coincidence that the very man Reynaud was in debt to was also a medieval scholar.

It looked more and more as though Sebastion was right about her stepbrother having been involved in the theft of Sebastion's cousin's property. But that still didn't mean Reynaud was a murderer. If this Broussard character could kill a man for merely stepping on his property, then surely he wouldn't hesitate to kill a man for possessing something that he wanted for himself. To her mind, Broussard was a more likely suspect than her stepbrother. She would have to delve more closely into that possibility, but for now she decided to keep her opinions to herself. Sebastion wouldn't believe her anyway without some kind of proof. And she didn't have any. Yet.

Later that afternoon, while they were having their dinner, Sebastion casually broached the subject of Broussard to Madame Duvall. She frowned at the mention of the older man's name. "I don't know why Estelle Caron would tell you about him. He doesn't socialize with the people here, and though he may know a bit about history and such, he is not someone I would recommend to visit."

"He sounds quite interesting to me," Sebastion remarked.

Madame snorted in derision. "That is a charitable way of putting it, monsieur," she said. "Now, why don't we change the subject to something pleasant? You should be enjoying yourself with your lovely bride, not worrying about a strange old man like Emil Broussard."

"It's all right, madame," Isabelle piped in. "My husband has many interests, and I don't want him to curtail his activities just because he has a wife now. In fact, I encourage him in his pursuits."

"That is most admirable of you, I'm sure, Madame Jourdain." It was clear that she thought nothing of the sort, but was too well mannered to say so.

"Perhaps you could present your card to him this afternoon, dear," Isabelle suggested to Sebastion, for madame's benefit. "Then if he wanted to see you he could send a note 'round."

Still in character, he gave her a look of such blatant adulation that Isabelle had to smother her resulting giggle with her linen napkin. "That sounds like a wonderful idea, dear. I think I will." He turned to Madame Duvall. "Perhaps you would be so kind as to give me directions to his home." Noting madame's frown, he tried to placate her. "I promise that after I pay my respects, I won't bring up his name again."

The older woman smiled benevolently at him. "I know you must think me a foolish old woman, monsieur, but you are only young once and you should take advantage of it." She poured him another glass of wine. "I hate to see you waste your time going all the way out there for nothing." She raised her hands in mock surrender. "But if it will make you happy, I will tell you after you finish eating." Taking an empty pitcher from the table, she walked back to the kitchen, humming softly under her breath.

"I think you missed your calling," Isabelle teased once the woman had gone. "You really should have been on the stage."

He eyed her coolly. "Remember that the next time you think you're beginning to know me." With that he dropped his cloth napkin on the table and walked away, leaving Isabelle to wonder at his abrupt change of mood. He had been almost lighthearted all morning, and now he had reverted back to that dark, brooding man she had so feared that first day in the house. What had she said to anger him? Funny that she should even care. Three days ago she would have been glad to have him upset, but now she found that it bothered her greatly.

Without stopping to examine her motives, she went in search of him. If she had done something to inadvertently provoke Sebastion, she wanted to know what it was. A quick peek in the common room told her that he was not in the building. She did not even bother to look in *their* room, for she knew he wouldn't be there.

The stables were located behind the inn, and so she hurried to see if she could catch him, thinking that he might have gone for a ride. A guess that proved correct as Sebastion's horse was gone, and their driver informed her that Sebastion had indeed taken his leave and would be back for supper. Must keep up appearances for their little charade, Isabelle thought bitterly.

Too restless to go back indoors, she decided to take a walk around the grounds. It was a perfect summer day, not too hot but full of sunshine. She meandered about the lawns, pondering her problems. There had been times in the last two days when she had almost forgotten why they had really come to Troyes, forgotten that they were merely acting out a foolish pretense. Perhaps Sebastion had as well, and that was why he had gotten upset. From what little she knew of him, she understood that he would be angry with himself for any imagined deviation in his plan. He was not a man who took his responsibilities lightly, and it might have seemed to him that they were making a jest of a matter he took very seriously.

Isabelle viewed their venture soberly as well. Her stepbrother's entire future was at stake, and she knew that it would be up to her to save him. Once they tracked Reynaud down, she was sure that the young man would be able to explain his actions to everyone's satisfaction. Sebastion would then see that Reynaud was innocent, as she had advised him throughout this entire ordeal. The Englishman was so sure of himself, so certain that he was pursuing the right man, that he wouldn't listen to reason. While it was true he had a fair amount of circumstantial evidence, Sebastion had to be wrong. She couldn't imagine what she would do if his accusations proved to be true. Reynaud would either rot in an English prison or be hanged for his crimes. It was too grim a notion to entertain.

She thought of the tiny key hidden among her belongings. Why had Reynaud sent it to her, and what did it unlock? There were no locks in the town house that were small enough for such a pass, and a thorough search of the chambers had turned up no jewelry boxes or anything else that might fit the diminutive piece. She had racked her brain for every possibility she could think of, but her traitorous mind kept settling on one conclusion. The key must unlock the chest that had been stolen from the Marquis of Kensington. For the last few days she had been avoiding the obvious. Sebastion would not have mentioned it because he had no way of knowing that the key was even missing. As far as he knew it was with the chest. So maybe Reynaud had stolen the chest. But that did not make him a murderer. And as she had vowed to Sebastion, she would never believe her stepbrother's guilt until she heard the words from Reynaud's own lips.

Reynaud, where are you? she wondered. Was he back in Paris, hiding in the shadows and waiting for Isabelle to return? Somehow she didn't think so. Her intuition told her that Reynaud has taken leave of the city, but where he had gone she could not guess. Trying to comprehend her stepbrother's thought processes was a pastime Isabelle had long ago abandoned. She loved him as a true brother, but she didn't always understand or agree with the choices he made in life. It had been hard for him to live under the critical eye of Victor Saint-Simon, and Isabelle sometimes thought that he might have turned out better if her father had been more understanding of his stepson. But the damage had already been done, and it was once again left to her to pick up the pieces if she could. She feared that this time Reynaud had made such a mess that even she could not straighten it out.

Still troubled and restless, she continued her aimless stroll until the sun began to set and she was forced to return to her room. Closeted in her chamber, she continued to worry about the two men who had so recently disrupted her life, Reynaud and Sebastion. Both of them had turned her orderly future upside down, each in their own fashion, and she wondered whether she would ever be able to set things right again.

As promised, Sebastion returned in time for their supper. He was charming and solicitous to her in front of the Duvalls, but coldly remote when they were alone. Isabelle spoke little and ate less, irritated that Sebastion's dark mood should affect her. When at last the meal was over, she excused herself before he could do likewise. Pride kept her from inquiring as to his whereabouts that afternoon, though she was curious. She had done nothing to deserve this frigid indifference, and she would not lower herself to his level. It was probably just as well that they put some distance between them. They were adversaries, after all, regardless of their present truce.

With no other choice, Isabelle retired for the evening. She lay in the large bed, unable to sleep despite her long afternoon walk. It wasn't that she was hurt by Sebastion's aloofness, but it peeved her enough that she found it difficult to relax. Frustrated, she rolled over and plumped up her pillows to try to find a more comfortable position.

Someone tapped on the door, and Isabelle sat bolt upright. Before she could inquire as to the visitor's identity, she heard the grating of a key turning in the lock, and the door swung open to reveal Sebastion. He carried a small lamp in one hand, holding it high in the air so that he might see better.

She pulled the bedcovers up to her chest to safeguard her modesty. "What are you doing in here?" she hissed.

Sebastion closed the door behind him. "I've come to sleep with my lovely bride, as would any good bridegroom." His tone was mocking, but his expression was hard.

"Well, now that you have completed your performance for appearance's sake, you may climb out the window and sleep in the coach again." She eyed him coldly. *"Good night,* Monsieur Merrick," she said pointedly when he made no move to comply.

He gave her a calculating look. "What if I've decided to sleep in here tonight, my love?" He had no intention of doing any such thing, but he felt like taunting her.

"You wouldn't dare," she shot back, ignoring the fluttering sensation in her stomach that his words inspired. Just the thought of him lying next to her was enough to send her senses reeling.

It was too much of a challenge to resist. He sauntered to the bed and sat down beside her. "I would dare anything, my sweet." Lazily he caressed her arm.

She pulled away abruptly, angry that he should so easily disconcert her. "If you touch me again I'll scream to bring the house down. You'll have a hard time explaining that to our unwitting audience." She started to get out of bed to put some distance between them but thought better of it. The last time he had seen her in her nightclothes had spelled disaster for them both. . Angry at his current intrusion and earlier boorish behavior, she turned on him. "I don't understand you at all. This morning we get along fine, then this afternoon you become angry with me for no apparent reason. You barely speak to me at supper, and now you come to my room and tell me you're going to sleep here." She held her arms akimbo, letting the protective shield of covers drop to her lap. "What kind of game are you playing? Are you trying to drive me mad, because I'll tell you something, it's working."

"You're right."

She was stunned. "What did you say?"

Sebastion stretched his legs out fully beside her, casually crossing one booted ankle over the other. Isabelle chose to ignore his lack of manners, concentrating instead on his apparent apology.

"I said that you are right. I behaved badly toward you today."

He constantly surprised her. The last thing she had expected was for him to agree with her. "Do you mind if I ask why? I don't remember saying anything to provoke you. In fact, I thought we were getting along quite well."

"We were," he muttered. "And that's the problem. I don't want you to think that you can change my mind about Reynaud. Just because we have been forced into an intimate situation, that doesn't mean any feelings of attraction I have toward you could sway me from my course." He sat up and swung his long legs over the side of the bed. "Make no mistake, I will find your stepbrother and I will see justice done."

Isabelle hit him with a pillow.

"You insufferable, egotistical peacock! How dare you think that I would try to seduce you into abandoning your search." She swung at him again, but he was ready this time and dodged her easily. "I have gone along with this ridiculous charade of yours, have done what I can to help find Reynaud as quickly as possible, and what do I get for it? Abuse, that's what." Modesty was forgotten as she flung herself out of bed and rounded on him once again. "You're the moodiest, most foul-tempered, hardheaded man I know. I can never guess from one moment to the next how you are going to react, and I'm tired of walking on eggshells around you. I've had it. I demand that you take me home first thing tomorrow. I won't help you any longer." She folded her arms defiantly across her chest. "You probably wouldn't have given Reynaud the chance to explain himself anyway."

Rather than being perturbed by her vehement speech, Sebastion seemed mildly amused. "You have quite a foul temper yourself, mademoiselle, and I would appreciate it if you could keep your voice down. The whole inn does not need to hear our 'marital' problems."

Isabelle groaned in exasperation and threw her hands up in a gesture of defeat. "Aargh. You're impossible. Did you hear one word I said? I am through with this entire masquerade, monsieur. I am going home."

His amusement faded rapidly. "I don't think so. You are going to help me find Reynaud, whether you are a willing participant or not. Of course, I would prefer you compliant, but you will assist me regardless."

"This isn't Reynaud's town house, where you can easily hold me prisoner. This is a public place, and I can call for assistance."

"I wouldn't do that if I were you," he warned.

"You are not me," she snapped and drew a breath to scream.

He was on her before she could utter a sound, his large hand clamped firmly over her mouth. "Don't be a fool, Isabelle," he growled in her ear. "I don't want to hurt you." He waited until he thought she might listen to reason. "Now, if I take my hand away, do you give me your word that you won't shout? If you try it, I'll be forced to gag you." Isabelle nodded. Slowly he lifted his hand from her lips, keeping it poised in case she should change her mind.

"You are a brute, attacking my person like that." She glared at him and flung herself into a nearby chair.

He snorted in disbelief. "You are the one who hit me, mademoiselle, not the other way around."

Her features were set in a moue of dislike. "You provoked me. And besides, I only abused you with a soft little pillow. You tried to smother me."

"I warned you not to scream," he said gruffly.

"What would you have me do?" she asked in exasperation. "Meekly accept the fact that I'm once again your prisoner? Unlike your simpering English misses," she said loftily, "we Frenchwomen have more spirit than that."

"I know several Englishwomen who would take exception to that remark," he replied.

"That isn't the point and you know it. We were getting along well, even making some progress, when you had to revert back to threatening me." She crossed her arms over her chest. "I wasn't trying to lure you into changing your mind, and for you to think so cheapens both of us. We agreed to a truce, and I have honored that pact. Just because you find yourself liking me as a person does not mean that you are betraying your cousin's memory."

Sebastion looked at her sharply. "You're talking nonsense. How do you know what I think of you? As you said, I'm quite an actor."

She rolled her eyes, a gesture that had gotten her in trouble with her father on many occasions. "You just don't want to admit that you like me, but I know that you do. We were on our way to becoming friends, as strange as that may seem, and it bothered you. You don't want to feel anything for me because it might make it harder to condemn my stepbrother."

"Listen to me," he warned, leaning menacingly over her. "Whatever small amount of affection I might bear you would never begin to compare with the depth of feeling I have for my family. Nothing you could do would ever change that."

"Nor would I want to," she answered softly. "If you've learned anything about me these past few days, you will know that I speak the truth." She rose from her seat and walked to the bed. "It's late and I would like to get some sleep." She pulled back the covers and slid underneath them. "You may stay in here if you like. As you have so ably shown me, I can't stop you." With that, she turned on her side, facing away from him, and was silent.

He stood still for a long time before Isabelle heard him move toward the bed. Two soft thuds told her that he had removed his boots, then she felt his weight next to her. He stretched out fully beside her on top of the covers. Neither of them spoke.

Isabelle tried her best to doze, but sleep eluded her. They lay quietly for a long while, their breathing the only sound in the darkness. Still resting with her back to him, Isabelle finally spoke. "Where did you go this afternoon?" Even though she was still miffed at him, her curiosity got the better of her.

Sebastion took a deep breath, then exhaled slowly. "I left a calling card at Broussard's chateau."

That got her attention, and she rolled over to look at him. "You did? Well why didn't you tell me that earlier? Did you get to see him?" In her excitement she cast aside their earlier animosity.

Sebastion shook his head. "No, I didn't see him. I merely left my card, or should I say Henri Jourdain left his card. The rest is up to Broussard."

It didn't surprise her that he had calling cards with his alias on them. Nothing that Sebastion did shocked her anymore. "So now we wait." She sighed. "But what if he doesn't respond?"

"I'll give him a day or two, and if he fails to reply, I'll move on to my next plan."

Isabelle considered this for a moment. "I don't think I want to know what your next plan is, do I?"

"No," he responded. "You probably don't."

It was a very long time before either of them slept.

Chapter Twelve

Madame Duvall had made up her mind that the young couple should have a picnic. She spent the morning preparing a veritable feast of chicken, stuffed trout, fresh bread and her specialty, *andouilettes*, pork sausage made of chitterlings. It was enough food to feed several couples for many days, but madame wanted everything to be perfect. With infinite care she wrapped each item and placed it in a large woven hamper, along with a nice bottle of wine, glasses and all the other items necessary for a romantic lunch.

The happy couple was less than enthusiastic when presented with madame's idea, but they feigned pleasure for the innkeeper's benefit.

"I know the perfect place for it, too," madame pronounced enthusiastically. "It's about two miles from here, but well worth the trouble. Madame Jourdain, I know your husband has his own mount, but you may borrow one of ours for the day. Babette is a sweet horse, and she'll give you no trouble." She beamed at the dumbfounded couple. "There now, it's all settled.

You will have a lovely day, and forget any little differences you might think you have."

Sebastion slanted a knowing look at Isabelle from the corner of his eye. Their argument had not gone unnoticed. Luckily the words had been muffled, though not the tone. He shrugged to himself. Madame Duvall simply thought they had engaged in a lover's quarrel, and he would do nothing to alter that opinion.

An hour later they embarked on their afternoon excursion, Sebastion carrying the large hamper on his mount, Isabelle bearing a borrowed quilt on hers. They set out at a sedate walk, Madame and Monsieur Duvall waving enthusiastically to them from the path that led to the stables. Mother Nature had once again provided them with a perfect day, as though she, too, had conspired with the inn's proprietress. They had little choice but to proceed with the planned festivities, so they both tacitly resolved to make the best of it.

In any other circumstances Isabelle would have enjoyed herself immensely. She liked to ride, and the little mare Babette was indeed a sweet animal. The sun was shining and the countryside was lush and green with growing things. She began to hum softly to herself, determined to ignore for a little while all the worries that plagued her.

For his part, Sebastion was doing his best to ignore the fetching picture Isabelle made. In her blue riding habit with a fitted jacket that was very flattering to her slender figure, she could have been a fashion illustration for the well-to-do equestrienne. A narrow brimmed hat completed the outfit, its upturned veil framing her face in a most becoming manner. She sat her horse well, showing herself to be an experienced horsewoman.

Sebastion nudged his horse into a trot and Isabelle smoothly followed suit. Neither of them spoke. It was as though they both knew that this lull in their ongoing battle would not last, but neither wanted to cause the next rift. Following madame's directions, they eventually came to a small pond near a thick stand of trees. It was truly a beautiful setting, and Isabelle grinned in spite of herself.

"It's charming," she said in a pleased tone. "Madame was right."

Sebastion scoffed at the notion, causing Isabelle to look at him beseechingly. "Please, Sebastion. Please don't spoil this. I know you didn't want to come here today, and frankly neither did I. But since we're both here and Madame went to such trouble, can't we just try to make it through one afternoon without arguing?"

Sebastion nodded in a small gesture of apology and began to secure their mounts while Isabelle spread out the quilt and began unpacking the overflowing hamper.

Isabelle laughed at the abundance of provisions. "Madame has given us enough food for a week of picnics. She must think that marriage gives one a great appetite." She continued to sort through the contents of the picnic basket. "Just look at all this. And wine, too." Isabelle held up the bottle to show him.

Sebastion was just returning to the blanket but stopped in his tracks when he looked at her. He had never seen a more beautiful sight than the one before him. Isabelle knelt on the outspread quilt, surrounded by their feast, holding up the wine and two glasses in her hands. The afternoon sunlight turned her hair to spun gold, the entire image framed by the green of the trees and grass and the blue of the pond and sky. It was a scene that no artist could have done justice to. She was more exquisite than he imagined a woman could be. And he wanted her so badly, he scarcely trusted himself to speak.

Isabelle was unaware of his inner turmoil. "Come on," she called gaily. "Help me open this bottle, and then we'll try to make a dent in this mountain of food."

Somehow he managed to get control of himself and

make his body obey his will. He quickly closed the distance between them and lowered himself down beside Isabelle. Within a few minutes he had uncorked the wine and poured them each a glass of the dark red liquid. He took a large swallow of his, then another in quick succession. The way he was feeling, he could have gladly imbibed the entire bottle and wanted more.

"We might have to give some of this food to the horses so that Madame will think we ate enough," Isabelle said mischievously. Sebastion didn't respond. "That was a joke, monsieur. You're supposed to laugh."

He attempted a wan smile, which Isabelle declared a pitiful effort.

"All right, I know when I'm beaten. Getting you to laugh is a feat beyond my limited capabilities."

She was teasing him, but there was an underlying grain of truth to her words. Sebastion was not now and never had been a jovial sort. His early life experiences had made him dark and introverted. Not to say that he didn't have a wicked sense of humor, for he did. He just didn't let it show very often. For her sake, though, he tried to lighten his mood. After all, it had been a long time since he had been with such a lovely, intelligent woman.

They ate companionably, chatting about nothing in particular, bantering good-naturedly about the amount of food consumed by the other. When they had both eaten their fill they collapsed upon the blanket, groaning and patting their full stomachs.

"I don't think we'll need to use the horses after all," Sebastion said. "We both ate enough to satisfy even Madame."

Isabelle giggled, giddy from too much food and wine. "Monsieur, didn't your mother teach you that it is ungentlemanly to mention a lady's appetite?"

Sebastion rolled onto his side and regarded her with

his head propped up on one hand. "I believe you are a bit tipsy, mademoiselle."

"What of it?" she answered back. "I feel wonderful." She stretched luxuriously and closed her eyes. "Tell me something about yourself, Sebastion. About when you were a boy."

"Isabelle," he warned in a low tone.

She opened her eyes and stared up at him with an earnest, if slightly muzzy, expression. "I'm not trying to pry. Just tell me one thing; then I'll tell you something about me."

He knew this would only lead to trouble, but it was so enjoyable lying here beside her, pleasantly sated by good food and drink, that he went against his better judgment. "Just one thing," he conceded.

"And I get to choose what it is," she added smugly.

He rolled his eyes at her impudence but agreed.

"Hmm," she said, considering her options. "Let me see." She closed her eyes in thought, and was still for so long that he thought she had fallen asleep.

"I know," she said finally, her eyes still closed. "Tell me about your mother. What is she like?"

He shocked himself by answering her. "My mother was a quiet woman, always careful not to offend anyone. I suppose she didn't have an easy life."

"You talk about her in the past tense. Is she gone?"

"She died several years ago." He answered flatly.

Isabelle opened her eyes. "I'm sorry. My mother died when I was five. I can hardly remember what she looked like, except for seeing portraits. It's not the same thing, though."

"But your father married again."

"Father married Helene when I was ten and Reynaud was fourteen." Her serene expression clouded slightly. "I had been living with my grandmother those five years, and it wasn't easy going back to my father's house."

"You don't get along with your Father." It was more statement than question.

"No. When I was sixteen Father briefly banished Reynaud from the house and I went to live with my grandmother." She frowned. "Enough about my family." She angled her head toward him. "What did your mother look like? Was she pretty?"

He didn't bother to point out that she had asked more than her self-imposed limit. "She was slender and had dark hair and eyes." His voice fell to a whisper. "I considered her beautiful." *You're beautiful,* he wanted to say but didn't. He groaned inwardly at the poetic turn of his thoughts. It must have been the wine that was making him so maudlin.

"I take it you got your blue eyes from your father," Isabelle murmured. "He must have been very handsome." Had she been sober she would have been horrified at her artless compliment, but her pleasantly fuzzy mind thought the observation appropriate. Sebastion was quite unquestionably the most attractive man she had ever seen, and she found herself longing to be closer to him.

He looked down at her. "Isabelle, if you want to know about my father, why don't you ask?"

"Because"—she grinned impishly at him—"I said I would ask just one thing. That would be two."

"You've already asked two things, so that would be three." When she would have argued he placed a silencing finger to her lips. "Hush. Don't quibble with me when I'm being so agreeable." He shifted and rolled onto his back, staring up at the azure sky. "My father was a fortune hunter who married my mother for her dowry. Unfortunately for him, my mother's family didn't approve of the match and disinherited her after they eloped. I came along within the year and made things worse. When I was six years old, my father was found dead in a back alley." He closed his eyes, remembering that fateful trip to the Kensington estate, how frightened he had been. "To make a long story short, my mother's cousin, the Marquis of Kensington, took us in and made us part of his family."

Green eyes filled with compassion stared unblinkingly up at him. "That must have been a traumatic time for such a little boy." She smiled. "It's hard to picture you as a child. I think you were born fully grown, like Athena springing from the head of Zeus."

He chuckled. "I imagine I was quite a headache, at least to my father."

Isabelle reached up to touch his face, caressing the harsh planes of his cheekbones with slender fingers. "Don't say such things," she said. "I didn't mean it that way. I'm sure you were a joy to your family."

Sebastion closed his eyes, unwilling to let her see how her words affected him. He had never felt like a source of happiness for anyone, but rather an obligation to be taken care of. His adopted family had cared for him, but he could never bring himself to accept their kindness for anything more than familial duty. And here was Isabelle, who for all intents and purposes should resent him, earnestly reassuring him of his worth.

"So you lived with the Kensingtons from then on?" Isabelle's curiosity was not yet satisfied.

"My mother lived there until her death, but I left a year later to 'see the world.' "

Her voice was gentle. "And did you see it all?"

He offered a wry smile. "Not quite the entire world, but yes, I've traveled quite a bit."

"Did your mother ever reconcile with her parents?" She held up her hands in surrender. "I know I've overstepped my question limit, but I'd like to know."

He snorted rudely. "Once her tyrant of a father died, her brother tried to make amends. That is how I received my illustrious title. They thought to placate my mother by making me a viscount."

"From your tone I gather that it didn't work," she observed.

"My mother missed her family. She gladly accepted their token apologies, but I refused. I use their bloody title only when it suits my purposes; otherwise they can go to the devil." He heard Isabelle's clothes rustle as she propped herself up on one elbow; then he felt the feather-light touch of her hand on his cheek. He looked up into eyes so green and fathomless he felt as though he could easily lose himself in their emerald depths.

She smiled down at him, and he felt his resolve begin to crumble. "Maybe the family regretted what they had done but didn't know how to mend the breach. I think stubbornness must run in your family." Her face was so close that he could feel the warmth radiating from her skin, and he knew that he had only to raise his head for their mouths to meet. She knew it, too.

Sebastion stared up at her. "You're playing with fire, little girl."

"I won't get burned," she murmured.

"Sebastion?" she whispered after several minutes.

He groaned. "What?"

Her voice was so low he had to strain to hear her. "Why did you kiss me the other night?"

Because you were so beautiful, because I wanted you. Because you make me forget who I am and what I came here for. "What does it matter?" he asked in an equally low tone.

"I think I'd like you to do it again," she answered dreamily.

He kissed her then, because he couldn't help himself. The need to possess her soft, smiling lips was too great for him to deny, and he took her mouth hungrily. She kissed him back with equal ardor, and soon they were reclined full length on the blanket, Sebastion half covering Isabelle with his hard body. Intoxicated by the scent and feel of her, he lost himself in sensation.

Isabelle reveled in the solid weight of him, the hard

texture of his muscles beneath the fine fabric of his shirt. She longed to strip away the garment and touch his naked flesh, run her hands through the dark mat of hair she imagined grew on his broad chest. Her longings were almost painful and she moaned softly in need. She knew that what they were doing was wrong but couldn't bring herself to pull away.

Sebastion did it for her. Almost roughly he drew away from her, rolling to a sitting position and leaving Isabelle lying dazed on the colorful quilt, still throbbing with desire. He was so hard that he thought the slightest touch might be his undoing, but he managed to keep from lifting up her skirts and getting between her soft white thighs.

"Why did you stop?" she asked in a breathless little voice. "Don't you want to kiss me?"

He laughed, a harsh bark of sound. "I want to do more than kiss you, little innocent. And if you weren't so naïve you'd see how much."

She didn't quite understand what he meant but was too embarrassed to ask. "Then show me," she ordered petulantly.

He groaned inwardly. She would be the death of him yet. "I think that's one task I'll leave to old Henri."

Isabelle blushed furiously at the mention of her fiancé. "You are no gentleman," she accused.

"That's what I've been trying to tell you," he said. If she only knew just how much of a gentleman he was being by putting an end to their lovemaking, she would be on her knees, thanking him. He doubted good old Henri would be so gallant given the same circumstances.

"You try to act so hard and unforgiving," she murmured. "But I know you have some softness left in you."

"Don't do this, Isabelle. You will regret it." His voice was raw with emotion.

"I see how much you loved your cousin, how dedi-

137

cated you are to his family. That shows me that there's more to you than anger and resentment."

Sebastion grabbed her wrists in one hand and moved to lean over her, nearly pinning Isabelle to the ground. "You have misjudged me once again. I don't feel anger or resentment. In fact, I don't feel much of anything." He pulled her to a sitting position, their faces only inches apart. "Don't try to find weaknesses in me that aren't there, and don't try to make me feel things I'm not capable of feeling. You'll only get hurt." He released her delicate wrists but remained where he was. "I'm not a cruel man, Isabelle, but neither am I the man you want me to be."

Isabelle rubbed absently at her reddened wrists. "I think you feel more than you want to admit to yourself, Sebastion. I'm sorry that I provoked you, though. It certainly wasn't my intention." She dropped her hands dejectedly in her lap.

"What was your intention?" he asked.

She shrugged. "I just wanted to know you better."

"You know all that you need to know," he informed her. "More, in fact."

"I know that in spite of everything I'm glad we had this day together," she said with unnerving openness.

Once again she had caught him off guard with her candor. He lived in a world where people did not express their emotions, especially when those feelings might be used against them. Isabelle was far too forthright for her own good, and Sebastion cursed himself inwardly, knowing that soon he might have to use that against her. He had warned her from the beginning that he could be ruthless, so why did her disingenuous declaration make him feel guilty? "You might not feel that way in the future," he pointed out, hoping to assuage his conscience.

"That may be true," she admitted, "but I can appreciate the good things until that time."

He recognized that it would be useless to argue with

her, so he wisely said nothing. When their quest was
over, Isabelle would be thankful for his circumspection.
Once Reynaud had met his fate, his stepsister would
not look kindly on the man responsible. She might suffer a little now from his reserve, but it would be better
for them both in the long run. Besides, if he let himself
get any closer to her, the consequences would be dis-
astrous for all concerned. He knew he was right, but
that didn't make it any easier to keep from responding
to her.

He pushed himself up to his knees, wanting to put
some physical distance between them. "It's getting
late."

She nodded and rose to her own knees, surveying
the remnants of their picnic. "I had better get this
cleaned up so we can start back." Her eyes searched
his face. "Sebastion?"

"Yes," he answered, wishing that the sound of his
name on her lips didn't make him want to take her in
his arms and never let her go.

"We almost made it, didn't we?" she asked, referring
to her earlier request that they make it through the day
without fighting.

"Yes, Isabelle, we almost did." He rose gracefully to
his feet and walked toward the horses. With his back
to her, Sebastion effectively hid the look of quiet desperation that crossed his face. She was getting to him,
and he wondered how much more he could take before
he gave in to the need building up inside him.

The couple spoke little upon their return that evening.
Madame Duvall was disappointed that her plan had
not worked, though they assured her that they'd had
a lovely time. The innkeeper's sharp gaze took in the
way they avoided each other's eyes and touched as little as possible. Isabelle retired early, claiming that she
was too full for dinner. She went up the stairs alone
while Sebastion stayed in the common room drinking

at his solitary table. Madame clucked her tongue but said nothing. Her own marriage had been more of a business transaction, and she often thought that such a union was preferable to a love match. She hoped that the young couple would settle their differences, whatever they were, but she decided against further involvement on her part. After all the work she had put in to make their picnic a success, the pair seemed more distant than ever.

Sebastion slept in the coach that night, while Isabelle lay wide awake in her lonely room. Neither of them got much rest, and as a result both were cranky the next morning. Sebastion ate an early breakfast and went for a ride before Isabelle made her appearance. When she finally did come down, she again refused food, content to sip a cup of chocolate.

Later that afternoon, a message came for Monsieur Jourdain from Emil Broussard. Since Sebastion was nowhere to be found, Monsieur Duvall delivered the note to Isabelle. She immediately went to her chamber and tore open the missive as soon as she was alone. Eagerly she scanned the brief note, smiling for the first time that day. Their patience had been rewarded: Sebastion had been invited to call on Monsieur Broussard the next day. It was a welcome stroke of good luck, and Isabelle anxiously awaited Sebastion's return so that she might share the news.

When he finally appeared just before supper, Sebastion's reaction was less effusive than Isabelle's had been, but he was pleased just the same. *Now*, he thought, *we move the game to its next level.* He would have to be careful in his handling of the Frenchman, but he had no doubt as to whom would emerge the victor in their battle of intellect. And whether Monsieur Broussard knew it or not, he was going to help Sebastion find Reynaud Andrassy.

Chapter Thirteen

Emil Broussard lived in an ancient chateau several miles west of Troyes. Set on a steeply rounded hill overlooking the Seine valley, the land was rich with well-established vines that had produced a generous living for generations of Broussards. The chateau itself was an imposing structure of pale brick covered in plaster, rectangular in shape with towers at each of the four corners. The dark tiled roof was steeply pitched in accordance with the spires that sat atop the towers. A low stone wall surrounded the house and a small portion of the grounds, ending in a black wrought-iron gate that stood closed, protected by a gatehouse.

The property was set well back from the main road, hidden from view by a small forest of oak, poplar and beech trees. Sebastion turned his horse onto the meandering drive that took him up to the main house, following another ancient stone wall that was overgrown in places with climbing vines. Row upon row of emerald grapevines were now visible, and it seemed to Sebastion that Monsieur Broussard was going to have a very good crop this year.

Kathleen McCarthy

Sebastion rode for about a mile before reaching the house. A uniformed servant stood in the door of the small gatehouse, eyeing him warily. He was a large, rough-looking man, not the sort of person one would normally see working in such a fine home.

"Monsieur Jourdain to see Monsieur Broussard," Sebastion said pleasantly.

The surly attendant grunted in response but opened the gate readily enough. Sebastion prodded his horse forward, nodding his thanks to the man. This time his response was a nod, followed by a terse, "You're to go up to the main house. Monsieur is expecting you."

Sebastion inclined his head in acknowledgment as he urged his horse up toward the courtyard. As he got closer to the dwelling, he noted that the edifice was in need of some minor repairs. Pieces of plaster had fallen away in places, revealing the brick underneath, and several of the wooden shutters had holes in them where slats had fallen out. The state of disrepair struck him as odd, considering the superior condition of the extensive vineyards. Evidently such minor cosmetic repairs were beneath the regard of the owner.

Once in the courtyard he reined his horse to a halt and dismounted. A man appeared at his side, this one dressed in the plain dark homespun clothes of a stableman. Like the servant before him he was burly, with the course features of a peasant. He was as taciturn as the gatekeeper, but Sebastion noted that he treated the horse with care. A bored-looking man dressed in full livery opened the front door. Sebastion strode purposefully across the courtyard and up the few steps to the entrance.

The interior of the great house was dark and slightly cool. Sebastion's sharp eyes quickly noted the opulence with which Monsieur Broussard surrounded himself. While the outer walls might have sported some signs of disrepair, the inside was as immaculate as any home he had ever seen. Clearly the gentleman preferred to remain indoors. Not that he could be faulted for that, because the interior of the chateau was truly stunning. The entryway floors were of the finest Italian marble, and exquisite silken tapestries covered the walls on either side of the grand staircase, the balustrades of which were pale oak and ebony.

"Good afternoon, monsieur," intoned the sour-faced butler. "If you care to follow me, I shall show you to the drawing room." Without waiting for a response he turned sharply on a well-polished heel and started up one side of the wide staircase. Sebastion followed sedately behind, trailing him up one flight of stairs and through several doorways until at last they came to the drawing room.

The high tiered ceiling was painted in shades of blue ranging from navy on the outer edge to robin's egg in the center, where a magnificent crystal chandelier glinted in the sunlight shining in from two large windows. A creamy white molding crowned the walls, papered in midnight blue. Numerous paintings depicting generations of Broussards adorned the walls, as did an immense tapestry similar to those displayed above the grand staircase. The floors were of gleaming parquet set in a diamond pattern, bare except for an Aubusson carpet laid out in front of a high-backed red sofa. The floral pattern of the rug was repeated in a band of material under the molding and also on two armchairs. Various objets d'art were exhibited on pedestals throughout the room.

Sebastion turned his attention to the tapestry, which depicted the knight Perceval kneeling before the Holy Grail. Sensing that he was not alone, he relied on his memory and quoted softly for the benefit of his concealed audience:

> *"The grail, which had been borne ahead,*
> *was made of purest, finest gold*
> *and set with gems; a manifold*

display of jewels of every kind,
the costliest that one could find."

"Very impressive, Monsieur Jourdain. There are not many men who can recite Chretien's *Perceval* from memory." Emil Broussard stood just inside the room, having entered through a doorway draped with red velvet curtains. Bookshelves in the room behind him indicated that it must be the library.

"Thank you, Monsieur Broussard. But you must forgive my rudeness. I thought myself alone," Sebastion lied smoothly. "And allow me to say that I'm equally impressed." With the sweep of an arm he indicated the displays. "You have quite a magnificent collection." He sized the man up as he spoke. Emil Broussard was rather small in stature, but he held himself with such an erect posture that he seemed taller. His hair was thinning at the crown and gray in color, as were his neatly trimmed sideburns and mustache. Perhaps in his late fifties, he was impeccably turned out in cream trousers, a brown tailcoat and yellow waistcoat. Everything about him bespoke the affable country gentleman—except his piercing black eyes. They were black chips of ice in an otherwise pleasant face, and his welcoming smile did nothing to warm them.

Broussard crossed the room and took Sebastion's hand. "Welcome to my home, Monsieur Jourdain," he said, shaking the proffered hand. "It was kind of you to accept my invitation."

Sebastion demurred. "I know it was rather forward of me to leave my card, but I did want to meet you. I don't often have a chance to talk to someone who shares my love of medieval history."

Broussard motioned him to a chair. "Please, won't you sit down?" He settled himself into a seat opposite Sebastion's. "I must confess I was intrigued when you left your card. I don't often receive visitors I have not invited myself." Condescension was clearly written on

144

the man's face. "One has to be particular about whom one associates with," he explained haughtily.

Sebastion nodded. "I quite understand, monsieur." He crossed one leg casually over the other. "I would never have thought of leaving my card if you were not a gentleman."

The Frenchman seemed unsure whether to take Sebastion's words as an insult or not and Sebastion knew a moment's satisfaction. However, he hadn't come here to antagonize the man, and he needed to remember to play his part. "As you may know, I am newly married, and my wife and I are taking a short wedding trip. I had never seen Troyes, so we decided to stay there."

"And how did you happen to call on me, monsieur?"

"You came very highly recommended in town as an expert on the Middle Ages, so my wife suggested I pay my respects."

Broussard seemed to accept this explanation. "And does your wife share your enthusiasm for history?"

Sebastion shook his head sadly. "Alas, she does not." He leaned forward in his seat. "But a man must have some things in his life that belong solely to him. Don't you agree?"

"I do indeed, monsieur. I do indeed." His look was calculating. "Did they also tell you in town that Chretien is my ancestor?" His posture was defensive, as if he had made the claim before and been doubted.

Sebastion's brow creased, as if he were trying to remember. "I don't believe that was mentioned," he said. "How fortuitous for me." Inwardly he saluted the older man for having the gall to make such an avowal. Of course, since little was known about the ancient poet, Broussard's assertion could not be conclusively disproved. Had he desired, Sebastion, too, could have claimed kinship with Chretien and none could have proved him wrong.

They remained in the drawing room for another quarter hour discussing local history. Sebastion asked to further admire the pieces on display in the room, and Broussard obliged, warming to his seemingly innocuous visitor. Several times during the course of their conversation, Broussard tried to test the younger man's knowledge. Apparently satisfied with his answers, Broussard then started to glean information under the guise of casually asked questions. Sebastion was ready for him, answering all his inquiries cheerfully, seemingly oblivious to their prying nature.

Broussard suggested they continue their discussion in the library so that "Henri" might see more of his private collection. This room contained even more pedestals, some holding small glass cases. Bookshelves ran along three walls, so filled with books that Sebastion doubted even one more would fit. The men stopped at a tall glass case, in which was displayed a yellowed illumination of King Arthur and his Knights of the Round Table.

"I don't believe I have seen an illumination in as fine condition as this," Sebastion enthused. "You must devote a great deal of time to finding such treasures. I'm surprised that this piece isn't in a museum." He knew full well that it should be. Broussard had probably stolen it.

"When I am gone my treasures will go to those who will appreciate them. But for now they give me such pleasure that I could not bear to part with them."

This gave Sebastion the opening he had been waiting for. He chuckled companionably. "You are not alone in your feelings. Not long ago, perhaps two months, I was in London visiting friends and happened to hear a lecture by an English noble who said the very same thing."

Broussard's expression hardened almost imperceptibly.

"Yes," Sebastion continued conversationally. "He had a chalice that had been in his family for generations, evidently a very fine piece. I remember he said that it held such fond memories for him that he was loath to give it up."

The Frenchman's face flushed with suppressed emotion, but he said nothing.

"Now, what was his name?" Sebastion continued, thinking aloud. "Kendal, Kelsey . . . something like that. I cannot seem to recall."

Broussard's entire body stiffened. "I am afraid I cannot be of assistance. I do not often venture outside my homeland."

"That's a pity," Sebastion replied wistfully. "I found this particular lecture quite fascinating, and I'm sure it would have been doubly so for you." He smiled companionably. "You see, the chalice in question was said to have been given to Chretien de Troyes by Philip, Count of Flanders, as a reward for versifying a book about the Holy Grail. I've forgotten the particulars, but I remember the cup quite vividly. A splendid example of medieval craftsmanship." He paused here, as if searching his memory for more details. "As I recall, he kept it in a chest that he said had been made especially for it. Most unusual."

"Well, there are many golden chalices floating about. I myself have several, as you have seen."

Sebastion's eyes narrowed slightly. He had not mentioned that the chalice was made of gold. It could have just as easily been fashioned of silver, as were many chalices in the Middle Ages. He knew that Broussard would not be foolish enough to display stolen items if in fact he possessed them, but Sebastion hoped to goad him into giving something further away.

"It does seem odd that an Englishman would have that particular piece, though. Chretien was *your* ancestor, not some Englishman's." His face was a mask of guileless puzzlement. "Strange that you've never heard of it."

A muscle worked in Broussard's jaw, and Sebastion knew his barb had hit its mark. "Not so strange, my friend, when you think that it was probably stolen from my family generations before I was born. Such things have been known to happen." His voice lowered in anger. "There are some men who have no honor. Who think nothing of taking something that rightfully belongs to another."

Sebastion could see that his remarks had upset Broussard more than he had planned, and he quickly adopted a friendly air of nonchalance about the entire matter. He waved his hand in the air, as if brushing the matter aside. "It's of no consequence, monsieur. Your own collection is far superior to those pieces anyway." He looked around, hoping to find something to distract the older man from his present mood. When he spied a large round table in the corner, he knew that luck was with him.

"Do you play, Monsieur Broussard?" he motioned toward the rectangular rosewood box that lay on the top of the table. He guessed that it held gaming cards. "I fear that is also one of my weaknesses." He paused before adding, "Though I am not very skilled. In fact, I shall have to give it up if my luck doesn't change soon. My new wife is quite put out with me over the funds I have lost." Based upon the Frenchman's reputation with games of chance, it was unlikely that he would pass up the opportunity to fleece what he thought to be an unsuspecting pigeon.

Broussard took the bait, his black eyes glittering with anticipated pleasure like a cat sitting before a birdcage. "Monsieur Jourdain, I must say that I'm impressed by the depth of your historical knowledge. Most young men today are not interested in such scholarship." His hand swept outward, indicating the gaming table. "And now I see we have something else in common. Could I perhaps interest you in a little supper and a friendly game?"

Sebastion was not fooled by this display of camaraderie, but "Henri" accepted readily. "I would be delighted, monsieur." Remembering his role as a newlywed, he let his expression fall. "But I am afraid that my wife would worry."

Broussard was not to be dissuaded. "That is easily solved," he pronounced smoothly. "One of the servants can take a note 'round to the inn."

"Henri" brightened at the suggestion. "An excellent idea." His eyes glittered in anticipation. "How can I refuse?"

Thunder rumbled distantly in the evening sky as a summer storm approached. Inside her chamber at the inn, Isabelle waited impatiently for Sebastion's return. A servant had arrived at dusk with a message from her "husband," stating that he would dine with his host and return later than expected. This was good news to Isabelle, who took it as an indication that all was going well. Surely Sebastion would be able to glean some information during the hours of his extended visit.

While she was glad about the invitation, it meant that she would have to wait that much longer to discover what, if anything, Sebastion had been able to find out about Reynaud. It also meant that she would have to spend the evening alone with no one to talk to, and nothing to occupy her mind.

She ate a delicious but solitary supper, chatting amiably with Madame whenever the woman came in to serve the next course. She lingered over her meal as long as possible, even having a second glass of wine. Finally, with no other recourse, she retired to her chamber. After she had changed into her nightclothes and brushed her hair, she found herself quite bored. She wished fervently that she had something to read, and it was then that she remembered the little book of Reynaud's that contained his scribbled notes and the copy of the promissory note to Broussard. It must surely be in with Sebastion's things, and she reasoned that since it was really her stepbrother's book she had every right to read it.

With a furtive glance at her closed chamber door, she went to the wardrobe and took out the small leather valise that held Sebastion's belongings. She found that she was quite nervous, and kept looking at the door, half expecting Sebastion to come bursting in and catch her going through his property. She justified this invasion of privacy by telling herself that she wasn't really snooping. She was just looking for a book to help her pass the time.

Sebastion hadn't packed much, and she soon located the volume. Her hands lingered momentarily on one of his fine linen shirts, and she couldn't resist bringing it close to her face so she might inhale the scent that clung to it. A roll of thunder startled her then, and she jumped up, dropping the garment to the floor. When she realized what had happened she laughed at her own foolishness, then repacked the valise with practical efficiency. A moment later she was comfortably curled up on the sofa, happily absorbed in the text.

Over the next two hours she read portions of medieval poems and legends, about the famous poets Chretien de Troyes and Marie de France, who wrote of courtly love, heroic knights and the search for the Holy Grail. Heroes such as Perceval, Lancelot and Erec filled the pages, and Isabelle found herself caught up in the romance and mystery of it all. After a long while, though, her eyelids began to feel heavy and she closed her eyes briefly to rest. A few seconds later she was asleep.

Sebastion found her that way not thirty minutes later when he silently entered the room. She was still nestled on the sofa, her head leaning to one side, a small book opened on her lap. Careful not to make a sound, he walked over to the sleeping girl, scooped her up in his arms and carried her to the bed. She stirred as he lay her down, her eyes fluttering briefly. When she saw him, she offered a sleepy smile and stretched luxuriously.

"Sebastion," she said in a voice made husky from sleep, "you're back." She stifled a yawn, covering her mouth with the back of one hand. "I tried to wait up for you, but I must have fallen asleep." Slowly she awoke more fully and pushed herself into a sitting position, pulling her legs up to her chest. With her arms resting on top of her bent knees, she stared up at him with an expression of anticipation.

"Well," she prompted somewhat impatiently, "tell me all about it. What happened? You were certainly there for a long time. What was Broussard like? Did he know anything about Reynaud?" The questions tumbled from her lips, one after the other.

"If you would stop chattering for a moment," he drawled in amusement, "I will tell you everything."

Isabelle pulled an indignant face at him. "I never chatter, monsieur. But I'll be quiet so that you may speak."

"Thank you," he said with mock solemnity, and began to tell her about his evening. As he spoke he removed his black broadcloth coat, buff waistcoat and, finally, his cravat. When all that remained were his breeches and shirt, he went to the sofa and sprawled comfortably across it, still recounting his exploits. Isabelle listened intently all the while, not speaking until he was finished.

"So what do you make of it?" she asked.

"My meeting with the mysterious Monsieur Broussard simply confirmed my suspicions. I think that he blackmailed your stepbrother into stealing the chalice as a way of repaying his debt." He sat up straighter in his seat. "Broussard became very angry when I mentioned Jonathan's lecture about the chalice. He is obsessed with all things pertaining to his so-called ancestor. I think that to his mind the chalice is rightfully his and the Kensingtons are the thieves, and I think that he's mad enough to try anything to get it back."

"Even murder?" Isabelle asked in a small voice.

He leveled her with his bright blue stare. "Perhaps, but there was no reason to kill Jonathan if he only planned to steal from him." He left unsaid that, regardless of whether Broussard had given the order to kill Jonathan or it had been an accident, Reynaud was still the one who had pulled the trigger.

As usual when dealing with the subject of her stepbrother's possible innocence, Isabelle was unable to let the matter go. "But if he is as deluded as you say, then he might very well have been the one who killed your cousin." Her expression became more animated as she spoke. "In fact," she said, warming to the subject, "he may have used Reynaud's name to book passage and gone himself to steal the chalice."

He shook his head. "No, Broussard is not the type to do his own dirty work. He would not want to sully his aristocratic hands with something so common as theft. Although it seems he isn't above cheating at cards to ensure that he wins."

"He cheated during your game? Are you sure?"

Sebastion's look left no doubt of his certainty. "I have played a few hands of cards in my time and know enough to tell when someone is dishonest. I will give him credit for being quite adept at it, though. It took me two full hands to be sure."

"If he cheated in a casual game with you, he must certainly have cheated poor Reynaud. That means the marker is worthless. Reynaud doesn't owe him anything."

He held up a hand to stop her increasing excitement. "Hold on there. In the first place we don't know that Broussard cheated in that particular game, and in the second you have no way to prove it even if he did."

"Oh," she said, disheartened. "I hadn't thought of it that way. I suppose you're right."

Join the Historical Romance Book Club — and GET 4 FREE* BOOKS NOW!

A $23.96 Value!

Yes! I want to subscribe to the Historical Romance Book Club.

Please send me my **4 FREE* BOOKS.** I have enclosed $2.00 for shipping/handling. Each month I'll receive the four newest Historical Romance selections to preview for 10 days. If I decide to keep them, I will pay the Special Members Only discounted price of just $4.24 each, a total of $16.96, plus $2.00 shipping/handling ($23.55 US in Canada). This is a **SAVINGS OF AT LEAST $5.00** off the bookstore price. There is no minimum number of books I must buy, and I may cancel the program at any time. In any case, the **4 FREE* BOOKS** are mine to keep.

*In Canada, add $5.00 shipping/handling per order for the first shipment. For all future shipments to Canada, the cost of membership is $23.55 US, which includes shipping and handling. (All payments must be made in US dollars.)

NAME: _____

ADDRESS: _____

CITY: _____ STATE: _____

COUNTRY: _____ ZIP: _____

TELEPHONE: _____

E-MAIL:_____

SIGNATURE: _____

If under 18, Parent or Guardian must sign. Terms, prices, and conditions subject to change. Subscription subject to acceptance. Dorchester Publishing reserves the right to reject any order or cancel any subscription.

"I'm right, for all the good it does me. My visit only served to substantiate my theories about motive. I still am no closer to finding Andrassy."

"Do you think Broussard knows where Reynaud is?" Her expression was hopeful.

Once again he shook his head. "I don't think so."

"But surely when Reynaud brought the chest and chalice to him . . ."

Sebastion interrupted her. "I don't believe Andrassy ever delivered the goods. And even if he did, Broussard would be displeased enough with your stepbrother to make it unhealthy for him to stay."

Isabelle frowned in confusion. "You aren't making sense. Why would Reynaud go to all the trouble of stealing the valuables and then not taken them to Broussard?"

"Because Andrassy made a mistake that only he and I know about," he explained darkly. "A mistake that makes it impossible for Broussard or anyone to open the chest."

"Would you care to elaborate on this mysterious error?" she asked in annoyance.

"He dropped the key to the chest at the scene of the crime."

Isabelle's mouth went suddenly dry. "The key," she murmured weakly. "What does it look like?" she asked, dreading the answer.

Sebastion regarded her oddly but answered the question. "It is made of solid gold, and it's quite small."

She swallowed against the lump in her throat. It had to be the same key Reynaud had sent to her. And if that was the case, then he really must have stolen the chest himself. If Broussard had taken it, as she had hoped, her stepbrother would never have been in possession of such a valuable piece. But she had never mentioned the key to anyone, so how had Sebastion discovered it? Indignation flooded through her as she realized the answer. Sebastion must have looked

153

through her things again. She had expected the initial intrusion when her personal effects had been brought from the hotel in Paris. But that was before they got to know each other, before their truce. If Sebastion knew about the key, he must have ransacked her belongings a second time. And to think, she had felt sheepish about reaching into his bag to get her stepbrother's book.

Completely disregarding her stepbrother's culpability in obtaining the key, she directed her wrath at Sebastion. Angrily she shot off the bed. "You wretch! You sneaky, conniving blackguard! You went through my things—not for the first time, I might add—and you took that key. How could you do such a low, common thing?" She stomped toward him, her hands gesturing angrily in the air. "And to think I had started to trust you!"

Sebastion had risen to his feet during her tirade. "I don't know what you're raving about, woman. Are you saying that you have a key matching the description I gave you?"

"You know very well that I don't have it anymore, because you took it," she shouted.

"Go get your key from wherever you're hidden it," he ordered in a terrible voice. When she hesitated, he took a threatening step toward her. "Now," he bit out harshly.

Isabelle hurried to comply, though she thought him mad. What was the point of looking for the key when Sebastion had already taken it? She rifled angrily through her things before finding the item she sought. Intending to show him how foolish she thought his instructions were, she snatched up the slipper that was her hiding place. And was horrified to discover that the key was still there, safely tucked away where she had left it. Numbly she pulled out the delicate gold chain and held it up in front of her, the small key dangling from its length.

A Treasure to Hold

"You didn't take it," she whispered.

Sebastion snatched the chain viciously from her hand. "No, I didn't take it." Isabelle watched in horrified fascination as he reached into a small pocket at his waist and extricated a small object, an exact duplicate of the key in his right hand. "You see, there are two keys to the chest, and this"—he indicated the one in his left hand—"is the one I was referring to. Both of them are needed to open the chest." With a look of disgust he flung both keys on the bed. "You are so quick to judge me and label me a thief, when all the time you have been lying to me."

"I haven't been lying. I wasn't certain what that key was for," she cried defensively.

He laughed, a harsh, mocking sound. "But you had an idea, didn't you?"

She couldn't lie. "At first I thought it opened something at Reynaud's town house, but I couldn't find a lock small enough to fit it." She looked at him pleadingly. "After a while I decided that it probably belonged to the chest, but I didn't want to say anything in case I was wrong. I know I should have told you about it, but I didn't trust you in the beginning, and then there never seemed to be a good time. And I still wasn't certain that I was right. Reynaud sent it to me in his initial letter, but he never told me what it was for." Her eyes beseeched him. "You must believe me."

"You've given me no reason to trust you. But that shouldn't surprise me, considering the fact that your brother is a murderer." His tone was insulting. "It must run in the family."

She raised her arm to slap him, but he was too quick, catching her wrist in a cruel grip. "I wouldn't do that if I were you, mademoiselle. In my present mood I just might strike you back." He pulled her roughly against his body, increasing the pressure on her arm until she feared the bones might break. Isabelle knew she should be afraid, but anger overrode all other emotion.

"Go ahead and hit me," she spat contemptuously. "You seem to enjoy abusing me."

His expression darkened further with rage, and for a moment Isabelle thought she had finally pushed him too far. "I ought to give you the spanking you so richly deserve. You are nothing but a spoiled, willful child who throws a tantrum the minute she doesn't get her way."

"You wouldn't dare to spank me. I am a Saint . . ."

He cut her off rudely. "If you tell me your surname one more time, I *will* turn you over my knee. Maybe then you'll behave like a woman instead of a selfish little girl."

She couldn't resist taunting him. "You didn't think I was so little when you forced your attentions on me at Reynaud's."

His expression turned murderous as he pulled her up so that her feet barely touched the floor. "I have never forced my attentions on any woman. You welcomed my advances," he accused in a biting tone.

"That's not true," she denied in a choked voice, her eyes wide with apprehension.

He leaned forward so that his lips were almost touching hers. "Shall I prove you a liar once again?" His voice was rough as he taunted her.

"No." It was a desperate plea, because she knew if he were to kiss her right now, as emotional as they both were, they wouldn't stop. "You said you wouldn't hurt me," she offered in a final attempt to restrain him.

Uttering a foul curse, Sebastion dropped her arm and brushed past her to put some distance between them. They stood regarding each other, two combatants now on opposite sides of the room. Isabelle cradled her abused wrist in her hand, and Sebastion uttered another oath at the sight.

Isabelle drew in a shuddering breath and let it out slowly, trying to calm herself. This was more than just another skirmish in their ongoing battle; they had almost done violence to one another. Never in her life had Isabelle raised a hand to another person, and it was a sobering thing to recognize the depths to which she had sunk. Something about Sebastion brought out the worst in her, an animalistic part of her nature she had never before seen. And she knew that she had just the same affect on him. She feared that if they continued on as they were, one of them would end up seriously hurting the other.

When she dared a glance at Sebastion she noted that his entire body was rigid with self-restraint. He was furious with her but had enough control at this time to keep his awesome anger in check. Next time he might not be able to rein in his fury.

"We can't go on like this," she declared faintly.

"We have no choice," he stated flatly, pinning her with his gaze.

She tried not to fidget under the intense scrutiny. "Yes, we do. You can send me home." *Before it's too late,* she added silently.

"No."

She had expected that response. "Then whatever happens is on your conscience."

His fathomless eyes bore into hers. "There are those who would tell you that I don't possess one." With that he scooped the tiny keys from the bed and left the room, leaving Isabelle standing bewildered and shaken in the shadowed room.

"Yes, you do," she said aloud when he had gone. "You just hide it well."

For the second time in her adult life, she cried herself to sleep. She wept for Reynaud, who with each passing day seemed guiltier, for Jonathan Larrimore who had not deserved to die so young. And she cried for herself because she was afraid, of the future and what it would bring. But most of all she was afraid of Sebastion Merrick and the feelings he inspired within her.

Chapter Fourteen

The sun had not yet risen when Isabelle awoke from a troubled sleep. She lay unmoving in the big bed, loath to get up and face another day with Sebastion. Their situation had become unbearable and she honestly didn't think she could endure another confrontation. It wasn't that she was blameless in all this, and she freely admitted her part. She was constantly jumping to the wrong conclusions about Sebastion, blaming him for things before hearing his side of it. But he was the one who refused to let her go home, when that would be the best course of action for all concerned. And he was constantly insulting Reynaud's character, flinging his accusations in her face. What was she to do when her family's honor was questioned? Sit back and take the abuse? No. She had too much pride in her lineage to allow that. It was her duty to take up for her step-brother, especially since the worst of the allegations had not been proven beyond the shadow of a doubt.

Her grandmother had always told her that she must not rely on anyone to take care of things for her. If she wanted something done, she must be independent and do it herself. As much as her lifestyle permitted, Isabelle had tried to abide by that motto. Of course, until now there had not been much call for such self-reliance, but perhaps this was the Lord's way of testing her mettle. She could either accept Sebastion's dictates as she had been trying to do, or she could strike out on her own in an attempt to solve the problem.

But what could she do?

She pushed aside the covers and stood, pacing the room as she racked her brain for a way to help her stepbrother. Finally she stopped and stood very still as an idea occurred to her. It was such a bold and daring plan that she could scarcely believe she was considering it. The more she thought about it, the more anxious she became, but she knew before she took that first step toward the wardrobe that she was going to do it. She was going to pay a visit to Monsieur Broussard.

It was Reynaud's debt to Broussard that had set this whole chain of events in motion; if she paid off the debt a big part of Reynaud's troubles would be solved. Broussard would be happy to get his money back and Reynaud could then come out of hiding without fear of going to debtor's prison. But there was still the robbery charges facing him in England. And the murder. Though she had accepted the fact that her stepbrother must have committed the robbery, Isabelle refused to believe that he had any part in killing Jonathan Larrimore. She couldn't allow herself to imagine such a thing might even be possible. As long as she could reasonably deny his guilt she would cling to her belief in his innocence.

Even though paying off the debt wouldn't completely absolve Reynaud of his misdeeds, at least it would help. Isabelle had felt helpless since this whole ordeal began. At least this was something that she could do. Reynaud had broken the law by stealing from Sebastion's family, and he would have to be held accountable for his actions. Isabelle had no power to save him from the English justice system, but at least she could help him in her own way.

With her mind made up, she dressed quickly in her blue riding habit, noting that the sun was now up and she would have to hurry if she wanted to avoid running into Sebastion. When she was finished, she scooped up the slim volume of medieval mythology and extracted the debt marker. Monsieur Broussard might not know of her connection to Reynaud, so she thought it best to bring proof with her. She wished she might actually give him the money as well, but she didn't have easy access to such a sum. He would have to take her word of honor that she would make good on the note.

She started to leave the room but paused. Broussard would probably not accept her word, or even a note. She would have to leave something of value as a gesture of good faith until she could gather the necessary funds. But what? A brief search of her belongings showed her that she had nothing with which to bargain. She hadn't thought to bring any jewelry with her, except for her engagement ring. Her engagement ring from Henri, a heavy band of gold encrusted with emeralds—to match her eyes, he had said. It was the only costly piece she had with her, but she couldn't leave that as collateral on a gambling debt. She searched through her things again, hoping that she had missed something the first time. After a few minutes she was forced to admit that she would indeed have to barter her betrothal ring. She would just have to repay the debt and reclaim the ring before anyone found out. Especially Henri, who most certainly would not understand.

She didn't even allow herself to contemplate what Sebastion's reaction would be to her morning's maneuvers. Her only hope was that once the debt was repaid and Reynaud felt safe to return, Sebastion would understand and see why she acted as she did.

Getting away from the inn proved more difficult than she had imagined. She had hoped to slip away unnoticed by anyone, but that was not to be. Upon reaching the bottom of the staircase, she nearly collided with a startled Madame Duvall, who was clearly shocked to see her up and about so early. Isabelle hastily explained that she wanted to take an early morning ride before breakfast, but she didn't want to disturb anyone at such an unseemly hour. Madame assured her that she would have Babette saddled for her, but the young woman declined, pronouncing that she would perform the task herself. The proprietress regarded her strangely, but shrugged at the eccentricities of the well-to-do.

Once outside, Isabelle wasted no time in reaching the stables. Here she was in luck, for the only person about was a young stablehand who obligingly helped her saddle Babette and asked no questions. As the pair worked with quiet efficiency Isabelle kept a constant surveillance of the barn and surrounding grounds, fearful of being spotted by Sebastion or their burly coachman. The coach was housed in a large barnlike building located directly behind the stables, which also provided a small chamber for the driver to sleep in. As far as Isabelle knew, Sebastion had been sleeping inside the coach, so she knew he could easily be lurking about.

Fortune smiled on her, though, and she was able to escape without detection. She kept her horse at a smart pace until she felt she was far enough away from the inn to relax a bit. She hoped to be almost to her destination before Sebastion noted her absence. By then it would be too late to stop her. She supposed that she ought to have left a note for him, explaining where she had gone and why, but last night's altercation was too fresh in her mind. Besides, if all went well, she would return to the inn within a few hours and most of their

161

problems would be solved. Sebastion would undoubtedly be upset with her at first, but when he realized what she had done, he would thank her for it.

Though she was feeling a little anxious, she tried to enjoy the scenery on the road to Broussard's. Last night's rain had given way to an idyllic morning, and the dew-laden foliage sparkled in the sunshine as though covered with diamonds. Birds sang cheerily in the trees and cows lowed in the distance, the perfect pastoral setting. The temperate mare trotted sedately over the narrow road, occasionally splashing through the small puddles that dotted the ground. Isabelle found herself lulled into a sense of well-being, soothed by the gentle rocking motion of the horse and the tranquillity of the early summer morning. All the worries she had felt in the dark of the night gave way in the brilliant light of day. Everything would work out for the best, she told herself soothingly. And in that moment, riding peacefully through the sun-dappled countryside, she believed it.

Using the directions Madame Duvall had given Sebastion, Isabelle easily found Broussard's chateau. Though not as large as Henri's, the estate was still a testament to the wealth and prestige of its owner. Following a rambling old stone wall, she came at last to the iron gate. After several minutes a hostile-looking servant stepped from the gatehouse. His clothes were rumpled and his dark hair stood nearly on end in places. He clearly had been sleeping and was none too pleased at being disturbed.

"What do you want, girl?" he growled irritably.

Isabelle was taken aback at his rudeness. No servant in her grandmother's employ would dare speak to anyone that way, no matter what the hour of day. All guests and members of the family were to be treated with the utmost respect. Clearly Broussard had given no such instructions to his own staff.

Not wanting to appear intimidated by his surly manner, Isabelle sat up straighter in her seat. "My name is Isabelle Saint-Simon and I am here to see Monsieur Broussard." When the man failed to respond, she added, "It is a matter of some importance or I would not have come at such a premature hour."

The guard considered this before answering. "Wait right here," he ordered gruffly, then turned on his heel and stomped off toward the main house.

Nearly twenty minutes passed before he reappeared, during which time Isabelle's enthusiasm for her plan had waned considerably. When at last she spied the rugged gatekeeper, she had to fight the urge to turn her horse around and flee. But the servant was already opening the gate, and Isabelle felt she had no choice but to continue on with her scheme.

Slowly she made her way up the drive and into the spare courtyard, where she was greeted by yet another dour-faced servant who silently took her mount. The house servants proved no more cheerful, judging by the haughty butler. He eyed her in a calculating manner that she found insulting, and for the second time since arriving here, she doubted the wisdom of her plan. Caught up in her determination to help Reynaud, she had clearly acted hastily. She was a lone woman in a single man's home, no one at the inn knew were she had gone and her host was most likely a murderer. If the butler had not instructed her to follow him at that moment, she might have lost her nerve.

Instead Isabelle followed doggedly at his heels as he led her through the cavernous house to a small sitting room. Shafts of morning sunlight streamed in through a single window that opened onto a balcony. Decorated in shades of yellow and green, it was a welcoming and attractive space. Cheered by her new surroundings, Isabelle resolved to have courage and accomplish the task she had set for herself.

She meandered about the room, admiring the elegant furnishings and lovely artwork. The minutes ticked slowly by, until Isabelle finally decided to sit and wait for her host, tired from her lack of sleep the night before. She perched on the edge of the sofa, ready at any moment to stand and face her adversary. After half an hour, the unpleasant butler appeared bearing a silver serving tray. Only when he had placed the tray on the table in front of her did he bother to address her. "Monsieur Broussard sends his regards but regrets that he will be delayed in receiving you. He asks that you enjoy some refreshments while you wait." With that he turned and stalked from the room.

She frowned after him, wondering anew how such an ill-mannered man could be employed as a high-ranking servant. Turning her attention to the offering before her, Isabelle was pleased to find a small pot of coffee, a pot of chocolate and an assortment of food, including thick slices of brown bread and several types of cheese. Until now she hadn't realized the extent of her hunger. Since it appeared she would be forced to bide her time, she reasoned that she might as well try to make the best of the situation.

An hour later she had eaten a good portion of the food and finished her second cup of chocolate, but Monsieur Broussard had yet to arrive. Aggravated to the point of leaving, the appearance of the condescending attendant only added to her ire.

"Monsieur Broussard will see you now, mademoiselle," he intoned. "If you would care to follow me." Without waiting for her to stand, he turned and exited the room, leaving Isabelle to scramble after him. Had she not been so anxious about meeting her host, she would have given the insolent servant a good tonguelashing. As it was she had more pressing matters on her mind.

Isabelle was shown to a stately drawing room, where the master of the house awaited her. Emil Broussard turned as she entered, a calculating smile on his face. Looking into his cold obsidian eyes, Isabelle knew she had made a terrible mistake. Despite his genteel clothing and the fineness of his surroundings, this man was a dangerous predator. And she had foolishly set herself up as his prey.

"Mademoiselle Saint-Simon," he greeted her formally, offering a courtly bow. "What an unexpected pleasure." He moved toward her. "Please, won't you join me? I trust Randolph has taken good care of you?" he inquired, indicating the silent butler.

"Yes, thank you," she murmured politely. Broussard took her arm, and even through the sturdy material of her riding habit she felt the coldness of his touch. She allowed him to lead her to a high-backed sofa, where she took a seat. He remained standing, a fact for which she was thankful.

"I am a man of few words, mademoiselle. I prefer to get to the heart of things rather than dance around a subject, so I will be blunt." His reptilian eyes caught and held her gaze. "To what do I owe the pleasure of your company?"

Isabelle cleared her throat discreetly before speaking. "I have come to speak with you about my stepbrother, Reynaud Andrassy. I apologize for the earliness of the hour, but I felt the matter warranted immediate attention."

"Go on," he instructed. "I am listening."

"As you say, it's best to get right to the point." She reached into one of the pockets in her skirt and pulled out Reynaud's note. "I found this marker at my stepbrother's town house. It seems that he owes you a large sum of money for a gaming debt."

Broussard took the note and studied it. "That is true, mademoiselle. But I am not sure what that has to do with you."

"I should like to pay off the debt for Reynaud."

Broussard was obviously surprised, and for a moment he didn't say anything. "That is quite a burden for you to assume. You are very generous." He studied

165

her intently. "Did you travel here alone with such a vast sum?"

Isabelle dipped her head sheepishly. "I am afraid that I don't have the money with me today. I do have funds available, though, but it will take several days to access them." She looked up at him. "I had hoped that you would take a promissory note from me."

Broussard shook his head sadly. "Alas, I am afraid I cannot do such a thing."

She had expected that response. "Then perhaps you would accept this as a token of my good faith," she said, and pulled the heavy band from her finger.

"You would give me your engagement ring?" Clearly he was shocked.

"Only until I can get the money to you, monsieur. I would leave this as collateral."

"Tell me, does Andrassy know that you are here today?"

She shook her head. "No." Something stopped her from admitting that she didn't know the young man's whereabouts.

"Does anyone know that you have come to see me?" he asked silkily.

Her eyes widened. "Of course," she lied. "My family knows all about it."

"I find that hard to believe," he responded pleasantly. "Your father would never have allowed you to come here on your own. Nor would he allow you to pawn your engagement ring." He shook his head at her, seemingly disappointed at her actions. "Do you know what I think, mademoiselle?"

"What?" she asked in a choked whisper.

"I don't think anyone knows where you are."

"You're wrong," she said as firmly as she could.

He shrugged off her response, confident in his assumption. "We could debate that point all day long, but what purpose would that serve? Let us move on to more important matters, such as how you found out about this debt in the first place."

Isabelle chose her words carefully, mindful of the fact that she trod on dangerous ground. "I received a letter from Reynaud asking me to come to Paris."

"Is that all the letter said?"

She nodded. "It was very brief. Reynaud intimated that he was in some sort of difficulty and asked for my assistance."

"And so you went to Paris," he prompted, "and you met with Andrassy."

"No. When I arrived at his home, Reynaud was not there. I spoke to a friend of his who told me of the debt."

"Michel Perrault," Broussard supplied smoothly, "the young man with whom Andrassy is staying."

"You seem to know quite a bit about my stepbrother," she pointed out acerbically.

He was unperturbed at her tone. "I make a point of familiarizing myself with those who owe me money." His tone was light, almost friendly, as he continued. "So you have not heard from Andrassy since that first note?"

Something about the way he said *first* note made Isabelle pause. Obviously he knew there had been a second note, or he would not have made a numerical reference when describing the letter. "He sent a second one to me at the Hotel d'Orleans, asking me to meet him at a café near his town house. I waited for him, but he never arrived." As she recalled that afternoon, it occurred to her that the two ruffians she had been trying to escape that day were probably Broussard's hirelings. That meant that he might know of her involvement with Sebastion, though she hoped he would not connect him to Henri Jourdain.

"Please continue with your story, mademoiselle. I am eager to learn how you progressed from this café in Paris all the way to my humble home."

"I have already explained that I found that note" —she indicated the paper in his hands—"so I decided to meet with you and offer to pay the debt. I had also hoped that you might know where I could reach my stepbrother, as I am eager to locate him."

Broussard regarded her coldly. "I fear that I will be unable to help you in that matter, mademoiselle. You see, I, too, am unaware of your stepbrother's whereabouts, and I am just as anxious to find him." He crumpled the paper in his hands, causing Isabelle to gasp. "My answer to your initial question is no, I will not accept your ring, nor would I accept the entire amount in cash. Reynaud Andrassy owes me something far more valuable than mere money, and I will not rest until I have it."

Isabelle paled at the maniacal look in the man's eyes. Sebastion had been right when he labeled Broussard a madman. If only she had listened to him.

"I am sorry to hear that, monsieur," Isabelle said, as if they were having a normal conversation. "Thank you for seeing me, but I have taken enough of your valuable time. I must be going now." She slipped the heavy band back onto her finger and stood, hoping that she could escape unscathed from this ill-advised encounter. "They are waiting for me," she added lamely.

"We both know that no one is waiting for you. Why don't you sit down like a good girl?" She obliged reluctantly, afraid that if she did not comply he would become more agitated. What a fool she had been to come here alone. At this very moment Sebastion was probably furiously scouring the countryside for her. The thought gave her hope, but not much. Even if he did search for her here, Broussard's henchmen would keep him away.

"I want you to look at this and tell me what it means, mademoiselle." He pulled a small envelope from his breast pocket. "And I must warn you that my equanimity has reached its limit."

168

A Treasure to Hold

Warily she took the missive from him. It was addressed to her, written in Reynaud's distinctive scrawl. She removed the single sheet inside and scanned the cryptic message. *I must leave the city before he finds me. Remember the golden path. I will wait for you.*

"Well," he said impatiently after a moment, "what does it mean?"

"I don't know," she replied in a hushed voice. "Where did you get this?"

He ignored her question. "Come now, mademoiselle, you are trying my patience. Andrassy would not have made such an obscure reference if he wasn't sure you would know what he meant." He stood looming over her as she sat on the sofa. "I will ask you once again: Where is Andrassy?" He stressed each word slowly and precisely, as if speaking to an uncomprehending child.

She knew he was close to losing control, but nothing would make her betray her stepbrother. Broussard had intercepted a letter meant for her eyes only. A letter that, had she received it, would have led her to Reynaud instead of the odious criminal standing before her. She resolved at that moment to keep her secret, no matter how badly he threatened her.

"I do not know," she answered, stressing each word in the same manner as he had done.

"Listen to me," he hissed, leaning down so that she could smell his fetid breath. "I want to know where that thieving coward is, and you're going to tell me. Do you understand? No one cheats me and gets away with it. No one!"

She tried to turn away from him, but he grabbed her face and forced her to look at him. "You will look at me when I'm speaking to you," he ordered savagely.

Isabelle glared at him with icy contempt. "Get your filthy hands off me."

Much to her astonishment, he released her. "You find it offensive to be touched by one so common as myself," he said. "Let's see how high and mighty you are when I have your stepbrother thrown in debtor's prison."

"That might be difficult," she jeered, "considering the fact that you're too incompetent to find him."

He struck her across the face so hard she feared he had broken her jaw. The force of the blow knocked her back against the sofa cushions, and she lay on her side, momentarily dazed. She pulled herself up on one elbow, cradling her aching cheek with the other hand. Not daring to speak, she stared up at him, pure hatred in her eyes. Inside she was terrified, but she refused to give him the satisfaction of seeing her fear.

"Now see what you made me do," he said, rubbing his hand absently. "I dislike marring beautiful things, and you are quite exquisite." He leaned over her again. "Lesson one, never insult the man who holds all the cards," he whispered, his voice a gentle caress. "Now, shall I ask you again where your stepbrother is?"

"The answer will be the same," she said defiantly, "no matter how many times you ask."

With a snarl, he grabbed a handful of her hair, forcing her head back down to the cushion. "You forget, my brave little fool, that you are at my mercy. Striking you is the least of what I could do, and no one here would try to interfere." His grip tightened painfully in her hair as he pulled her up into a sitting position. He released her then and moved a few steps away, smoothing down his wrinkled coat and patting his hair back into place. "You will do well to remember that."

"And you would do well to remember who I am," she shot back in a scathing tone. "My family has blood ties to the greatest houses in all of France, and they would not look kindly on any harm befalling me."

She thought he might strike her again, but apparently her words had some affect on him. He straightened to his full height and regarded her coldly, though his eyes still burned with the intense heat of his wrath.

His was truly the expression of a lunatic. "Since my presence seems to offend your delicate sensibilities, I shall depart. But I leave you with this thought: your family's retaliation is not much of a threat, considering the fact that they don't know you're here in the first place."

Without a backward glance, Emil Broussard left the room, calling for Randolph to remove Mademoiselle Saint-Simon to one of the guest chambers.

Chapter Fifteen

Once again Isabelle found herself held against her will, but this time her captor was not a grieving relative on a search for justice. This time her jailer was a criminal himself, a thief and most likely a murderer. He had shown himself to be ruthless and cruel, not above harming an innocent woman to get what he wanted. And he was clearly insane.

After their confrontation, Randolph had escorted her to a bedchamber and promptly locked her inside. Like all the other rooms in the chateau, it was lovely, decorated in shades of yellow. It was well furnished and comfortable but lacked any object Isabelle might use as a weapon. She had hoped to find something with which to protect herself, but a thorough search revealed nothing of practical use. There was a rather large vase that would do in case of extreme emergency, but it would be decidedly awkward to wield with any accuracy. She would have to rely on her wits, which until now she had not done. Coming here in the first place had been the most foolhardy act of her life, and she only hoped she would live to tell of it. It was too soon to be sure of Broussard's plans for her, but she surmised that he would not let her live. She knew too much about his involvement in the whole awful affair. Even if he thought she only knew about the debt.

Thankfully she was left alone for the rest of the day, and it was only when evening came that she was "requested" for dinner. Out of habit she checked her appearance in the ornate wall mirror before leaving her chamber. The livid bruise marring her cheek was a graphic reminder of her host's volatile temper, and she cautioned herself silently to try and placate the man as much as possible. With no real choice open to her, Isabelle followed the butler down to the immense dining room. She had decided to feign compliance, reasoning that she might have a better chance for escape if Broussard were lulled into lowering his guard.

An impossibly long table that could easily have accommodated thirty people ran the length of the room. Two elaborate place settings were arranged at the far end, with Broussard standing before one of them. Obviously she was expected to sit at the other, directly across from him. She slid obediently into the chair that a footman pulled out for her. Still wearing her riding habit, she knew she looked quite out of place amid the room's finery.

Broussard had dressed for the occasion in an elegant dark blue coat and sky-blue silk waistcoat. His snowy white cravat was artfully arranged high around his throat, the stiff points of his collar showing above. He greeted her politely enough, but there was a tightness to his mouth that Isabelle took as a warning. If she wanted to avoid further physical abuse, she would have to make sure not to anger the older man needlessly.

The meal was interminable. Two liveried footmen served seven courses, of which Isabelle had eaten two bites. Whatever appetite she might have possessed had vanished under her host's watchful eye. Broussard spoke not a word during the entire meal, and the silence served to further stretch Isabelle's already taut nerves. She kept waiting for him to speak, and each little sound made by a servant caused her to start.

When finally the elaborate affair ended, Broussard stood and offered her his arm. The last thing she wanted to do was touch him, but she knew her well-being depended on this man's moods. Meekly she took his arm and allowed him to escort her back to the drawing room. She purposefully avoided the sofa where Broussard had struck her earlier, choosing an embroidered armchair instead.

Broussard disappeared briefly into the next room, and when he returned he was enjoying an acrid cigar. This surprised Isabelle; the older man seemed to pride himself on being a gentleman, and no gentleman would ever smoke in the presence of a lady. Even if the lady gave her permission. It simply was not done.

"Do you mind?" he asked belatedly.

"Of course not, monsieur," she murmured politely. The cloud of smoke produced by the cheroot tickled her nose unpleasantly and she had to stifle the urge to cough, but she smiled pleasantly through it all.

Broussard puffed contentedly for a few moments before addressing his guest. "I see that you have decided to behave in a more cooperative manner, mademoiselle. To what do I owe this sudden change of heart?"

She met his gaze with a level stare of her own. "I realized that it serves no purpose to antagonize you."

He seemed pleased at her response, offering her a benign smile like that of a favored uncle regarding his young niece. "Then perhaps you might continue to oblige me by answering a few more questions, since our previous discussion ended so abruptly."

"I will do my best," she answered. Lying was something she detested, but she reasoned that this man deserved nothing better. She would stick to the truth as much as she could, but anything of real importance she would fabricate or claim ignorance about.

"Very well," he said, and took a seat on the sofa facing Isabelle. With his legs crossed casually in front of him, he relaxed on the couch, lazily puffing his cigar. "Explain to me again how you came to Troyes, and who accompanied you."

"A friend allowed me to borrow a coach and driver," she said vaguely.

"Did that *friend* accompany you?"

Isabelle nodded in response. "Yes." It was better for him to think that someone would note her absence.

Broussard took another deep draw on his cheroot, letting the smoke out in a cloud that circled his head like a halo. "Mademoiselle," he chided, "I thought we agreed that you would be more forthcoming from now on. I do not want to have to pull the information from you like so many grapes from an unripe vine."

"I am sorry if my answers do not please you, monsieur. It is not my intention to upset you." That at least was true.

He waved his hand negligently. "I was just trying to give you a chance to redeem yourself, my dear. I already know all about your traveling companion." Another puff and resulting cloud of smoke. "You see, I have just received correspondence from an associate in Paris. It seems that you were seen entering Andrassy's town house several days ago, in the company of a gentleman." He leaned forward. "A tall, well-dressed man with black hair. Does that sound familiar?"

"Yes," she admitted softly, knowing it would do no good to lie. Her only hope was that Broussard's associate had not been able to discover Sebastion's identity.

"That account is rather broad, though. Why, it could apply to any number of men. Take for example the young man who visited me yesterday, Monsieur Jourdain. He matches that description exactly."

Isabelle remained mute, looking away from the

man's unwavering stare. It had not taken him long to connect her presence to Sebastion's visit the previous day. She hoped that her folly would not endanger the Englishman, but realized that was probably a hollow wish.

Broussard took her silence for guilt. "So, Monsieur Jourdain is the friend you mentioned, yes?"

"Yes," she answered in what she hoped was a reluctant manner. She didn't want to appear too helpful.

"Where is he now, mademoiselle? I have already sent some men to the inn, but he is no longer a guest."

Isabelle's head snapped up at the news. As quickly as possible she tried to cover her shock, but the damage had already been done.

"I see that this surprises you. Why is that?" he asked in a condescending tone. "Could it be that your lover has abandoned you?"

"He is not my lover," she retorted sharply before she could stop herself. She had no idea where Sebastion could have gone. Surely he wouldn't have left her here. But since she had not bothered to tell him her plans, he might have assumed that she had returned to the city. After all, the last thing she had said to him was that she wanted to go home. He might even have been angry enough to abandon her, although she thought that prospect unlikely.

Emil took another puff on the cigar. "Why did he come here yesterday? What did he hope to accomplish?" His eyes glittered dangerously, and Isabelle chose her words with care.

"I asked him to come here, hoping that he might discover some clue as to Reynaud's whereabouts."

"Why didn't you just come yourself?"

She blushed. "Henri said that gaming debts and such are a man's business and I should let him handle the situation." Her fingers crossed furtively under the folds of her gown as she hoped that he would accept her rather lame explanation. If Broussard were like other men, his male vanity would demand that he readily believe such an excuse.

The older man nodded in agreement. "Then what made you come here today? And where is Jourdain?"

His earlier assumption that Jourdain was her lover had given her an idea, which she played out to the fullest. Her green eyes filled with crocodile tears. "We quarreled last evening about our next plan of action. Henri became angry with me and left, so I decided to come see you myself this morning." A lone tear trickled down her cheek. "I felt that I had no other choice. Reynaud is such a foolish boy and he needs me to take care of him. I'm sorry for the trouble he has caused."

For a moment she thought she had convinced him, but then he began to clap his hands deliberately and loudly together, applauding her performance. "Bravo, mademoiselle, bravo. I don't think I've seen better in the opera house. You are quite the little actress." The clapping ceased abruptly. "Unfortunately I do not believe this little act of yours. I am not sure where your partner has gone, but I will find him soon enough. Until such time as both Jourdain and Andrassy are located, you will remain here as my guest."

Irritated with his smug demeanor, she couldn't resist contradicting him. "I believe the correct term is prisoner."

His thin lips curled into an ugly smirk. "Prisoners can be tortured by their jailers, mademoiselle." He looked pointedly at the burning end of his cigar. "Is that what you want?"

Fear made her heart race. He had already struck her; what was to keep him from burning her as well? Absolutely nothing. "Forgive my lack of manners," she managed to choke out. "I accept your hospitality."

Broussard's evil smiled deepened, and he took another long draw on his cigar. "A wise choice, my dear."

Isabelle wanted to wipe the look of satisfaction from the man's face, but good sense prevailed. Instead she rose gracefully and asked to be escorted back to her chamber. She might have to endure imprisonment here, but she would not endure Broussard's odious company a moment longer than necessary.

The small sliver of moon visible in the night sky cast little light through Isabelle's window. She sat in the oppressive darkness of the room, afraid that Broussard or one of his minions might try to accost her. Once again she had been locked inside the chamber, but Broussard had the key and could easily let himself in. She had levered a high-backed chair under the door-knob, hoping to keep out any unwanted visitors, but she knew it was a feeble attempt at best.

Tired as she was, she did not want to sleep, so she paced back and forth across the room mulling over her latest predicament. For twenty-three years she had lived a sheltered and privileged life, content to stay within the confines of her well-ordered world. An existence that was defined by words such as reserve, restraint and duty. If someone had told her two weeks ago that she would be kidnapped and risk her life in an attempt to prove her stepbrother innocent of murder, she would have thought that person mad. And yet it had happened.

And if she were honest with herself, she would have to admit that through it all, instead of rising to the occasion, she had behaved like a spoiled child. True, she had done nothing to deserve Sebastion's initial imprisonment of her, but she had constantly challenged him and disregarded his advice at every turn. Instead of thinking of the pain he was experiencing over the loss of his cousin, she had only considered how the situation affected her. And while she had truly been concerned for her stepbrother, her focus had been more on what an imposition it was to her than how Reynaud must be feeling. To make matters worse, she had rushed headlong into a situation that might very well result in her death.

Alone in the darkness, frightened and unsure of her future, she somehow saw her past more clearly. For most of her life she had shut off her own desires in an attempt to be the person she thought her family wanted. Her father was a cold man who valued family honor above all else. She had always worked to please him but never quite measured up to his unrealistic standards. At sixteen she had fled to her maternal grandmother, hoping to find the love and acceptance lacking in her own home. Delphine Brasseur du Vallon had welcomed her with open arms, giving her the attention she so craved. But even with her beloved grandmama, Isabelle had never felt entirely comfortable. For years she had acted solely to please her grandmother and father, basing all her decisions on their expectations of her.

Her family, friends and acquaintances regarded her as a model of what a young lady of breeding should be, but Isabelle felt as though she were living a lie. Only she knew of her quick temper and sarcastic sense of humor; she would never dream of showing that side of herself to anyone. That was why she tossed out the Saint-Simon name so frequently. It served as a reminder to herself and others of the high standards expected of her.

She had hoped that when she met the man she would marry, she would not have to be so guarded. But Henri was just like everyone else, thinking she was so restrained and proper—expecting her to be that way. Perhaps that was why she had been content to keep their relationship on a friendly basis for so long. Perhaps subconsciously she knew that she would never be happy as Henri's wife, and that was why she had had such reservations about accepting his proposal. She wondered how he would feel to know that his respectable fiancée had tried to pawn his engagement ring to pay a gambling debt. Or worse yet, that she had spent not just one but several nights in the company of an unmarried man. She had slept in the same bed with him and kissed him on more than one occasion. Of course, he would not understand, nor would anyone she knew. Except maybe her young cousins Therese and Diedre. They would declare the whole episode terribly romantic, and pronounce Sebastion devastatingly handsome.

An image of Sebastion flashed through her mind, causing her to cease her pacing. Sebastion, too, would understand the things she had done, because in some ways he understood her better than those who had known her all her life. He had called her spoiled and selfish, accusing her of being more like a girl than a woman. She had discounted his insults at the time, but upon reflection she had to admit that there was some truth to his accusations. If only she could see him again, she would tell him so. She would do so many things differently if given the opportunity, but it looked as if she had used up all her chances. Emil Broussard was going to kill her, and the irony of it all was that she was only now beginning to understand how to live.

She thought of the note from Reynaud that Broussard had intercepted. Her host had asked her if she could decipher the cryptic message and she had denied any knowledge of it. But she did understand it, and now she knew where her brother was. She wondered how different things would have been if she had received the missive as intended back in Paris. Would she have shared the information with Sebastion? Not willingly, she admitted. But he probably would have found a way to get the truth from her. The question was, if she got the chance now, would she tell him where Reynaud was hiding? Yes, she would. Because she wanted this whole nightmare to be over, but also because she owed it to him to be honest. She still refused to believe her brother was a murderer, so she would have to trust Sebastion not to condemn an innocent man.

Not that it mattered anymore whether she would relay the information or not. She was never going to see Sebastion again, or anyone, for that matter. She wasn't going to live long enough to sort out her problems. Death would solve them for her.

Her overtired eyes strayed to the canopied bed that looked so inviting, but she resisted the temptation to lie down. She sat instead on a curved divan, where she could at least stretch out her legs and get moderately comfortable. The problem was that in her exhausted condition, comfort was her enemy. She desperately wanted to stay awake, but her eyelids kept fluttering shut, thwarting her attempts at vigilance. It had been a long and arduous day, and she was too weary to continue fighting. Her eyelids drifted shut once more, and this time she slept.

She awoke sometime later, stiff-necked and disoriented. The room was black as pitch, the moon having been obscured by dark clouds. Groping her way along the wall, she came to the door and felt the chair to make sure it was still in place. A slight scraping sound came from behind her and she felt the fine hairs on the back of her neck stand up. Someone was in the room with her.

Her heart thudded painfully in her chest and she whimpered softly in terror. Whoever it was had come in through the window, and that did not bode well for her. Isabelle crouched low beside the chair, hoping that the intruder could not see her in the darkness. She uttered a silent prayer of thanks that her dress was dark hued and could not easily be seen.

A breeze flowed through the open window, fluttering the fine curtains. In that same instant a figure emerged, a shadow disengaging itself from the gloom. Isabelle pressed her fist hard against her mouth to keep from crying out. Her breath came in short, labored gasps and she feared that she would faint for the first time in her life.

"Isabelle," the invader whispered throatily. "Don't be afraid."

She thought her heart might stop. "Sebastion," she said hoarsely. "Is it really you?"

Seconds later she felt strong hands grip her trembling hands. "In the flesh," he answered flippantly, then pulled her roughly into his arms. "I ought to wring your lovely neck, you little fool," he murmured against her hair. "Do you have any idea what could have happened to you?"

Wrapped in his fierce embrace, Isabelle nodded mutely, clinging to him. She had a very clear idea of what ills could have befallen her, and she had never been so thrilled to see anyone in her life. "Sebastion, Sebastion . . . don't let me go," she pleaded in a choked voice. She hung on to him with a fierceness born of panic. He hadn't abandoned her, as she had feared. He had risked his own life to save her. She wanted to weep from the bittersweet emotions that assailed her, but that was a luxury they could ill afford. They needed to get as far away from this place as possible. The limited control that Broussard exerted on his own mental stability would shatter if he were to discover them here, and she had no doubt that both she and Sebastion would forfeit their lives.

"Are you all right? Did he hurt you?" His voice was strangely gruff and insistent.

"No, I'm fine." He would see the evidence of Broussard's cruelty soon enough, but by then they would be well away from the man himself. "We must hurry," she whispered fearfully. "If he catches you here he'll kill us both."

Sebastion abruptly let her go and pushed her toward the window. "I know. I disabled two of the guards, but I don't know how long they'll stay that way." As he spoke he wrapped a thick cord around her middle. "I am going to lower you to the ground. All you need to do is hold on to the rope, all right?"

She nodded, though he could not see the movement in the inky darkness. All her life Isabelle had been afraid of heights, but she would have scaled the highest mountain peak to get away from the treacherous Monsieur Broussard. "I trust you," she said softly and climbed out the window.

She almost turned back around when she glanced downward; it was as though she were looking into a bottomless pit. Terror flooded through her, but she forced herself to step off the small balcony. She dangled helplessly for a few panic-stricken seconds before she began to descend slowly until at last her feet touched solid ground.

As instructed, she untied the heavy coil from around her waist and flattened her slim form against the house, effectively concealing her body in the shadows. Within seconds Sebastion was beside her. She assumed he had shimmied down the rope after tying it to the wrought-iron bars on the balcony. Noiselessly they slipped through the shadows, Sebastion holding Isabelle's hand and pulling her in his wake. The chateau grounds were extensive and she wondered how he could find his way so easily. She held her breath whenever they crossed an open expanse of lawn, but luckily the clouds still obscured any light and gave them the cover they needed.

After several minutes, it became clear to Isabelle that they were heading toward a small section of forest. They had almost reached it when Sebastion halted abruptly. Isabelle careened into him, nearly stumbling to her knees. "What . . ." she whispered harshly, then quieted when she saw his reason for stopping so suddenly. A man stood in front of them, his light-colored shirt and breeches a pale blur.

"What do we have here?" he said in a gravelly voice. "Trying to run away, eh? Well, old Luc is too smart for you." He chuckled evilly. "The boss will be very pleased with me, yes indeed," he chortled to himself, then raised a dark object in his hands. A rifle.

Sebastion sighed dramatically. "I hate to upset your plans, Luc, but we won't be able to stay." He drew out a pistol and aimed it at the other man.

The guard responded by firing in their direction. Isabelle stifled a scream as Sebastion shot back. With a cry, the other man fell to the ground. Sebastion wasted no time in grabbing Isabelle's wrist and propelling her forward. They raced toward the sheltering grove of trees.

Behind them, Isabelle could clearly hear the sounds of pursuit, but Sebastion did not pause. Once they reached the woods he led them with unerring accuracy to two horses who stood saddled and waiting. With rapid efficiency he loosened the tethers, then helped Isabelle mount before leaping onto the other horse. "Follow me," he ordered tersely and kicked his mount into a gallop. Isabelle did as she was told, crouching low in the flat saddle. She was grateful to be able to ride astride. She felt much more secure than if she'd been forced to use an awkward sidesaddle.

The horses were fast, well-trained animals, and soon they could no longer hear the search party behind them. They rode through the night, staying within the cover of trees as long as possible before coming out into the open. Sebastion avoided the main roads as much as he could, instead taking them via pastures, rolling plains and streams. Luckily the moon had reappeared from behind the clouds, helping to light the rougher terrain. After several miles they slowed to a canter, offering the laboring animals some relief from their headlong flight, but still covering the distance at a rapid pace. The sky was beginning to lighten as dawn approached, and it was then that Isabelle realized they were heading southwest. She wondered where they were headed, but didn't ask. Sebastion had not spoken for hours, though he did glance back occasionally to see that she followed.

The sun was just peeking over the horizon when they came upon a farmhouse. It was a large structure, and though it looked quite old it had an air of prosperity. The fields surrounding it were rich and glowing with the green of good health, and all the outbuildings were in good repair. Colorful flowers grew in profusion around the main house and filled several charming window boxes. Isabelle had no idea where they were, but it was apparent from Sebastion's behavior that this was their destination. They reined their tired mounts to a walk and headed toward the inviting home.

Chapter Sixteen

A man stood waiting for them at the end of the tree-lined path that led to the house. Isabelle was both amazed and pleased to see that it was their carriage driver, but she quickly realized with some embarrassment that she had not ever bothered to learn the servant's name. He was a large man, dark and handsome in a gruff way. She guessed his age to be about forty, or perhaps a few years younger. He held himself very erect, and she thought fleetingly that he looked more like a soldier than a coachman. The man doffed his cap in greeting and proceeded to help Isabelle down from her horse.

"Thank you . . ." she said, trailing the end of the sentence into a chagrined silence.

The driver nodded down at her. "I am called Georges, mademoiselle." His eyes lingered on her bruised cheek, but he refrained from commenting on it.

"Thank you, Georges." She looked around at the farmhouse in consternation. "Could you please tell me where we are and how you managed to get here?"

He offered an understanding smile. "This is the farm where I grew up, mademoiselle. My family would be pleased to have you as our guests.

Isabelle turned to Sebastion for further explanation, and she was alarmed to notice that he had not dismounted. Instead of sitting with his usual grace, he was nearly slumped forward in the saddle, his horse dancing nervously in uneasy circles. She moved forward and grabbed the trailing reins. "Sebastion," she said worriedly. "What's wrong?"

He roused at the sound of her voice and looked at her, his face drained of all color. Much to Isabelle's alarm, he began to fall out of the saddle. Georges caught him before he hit the ground, and it was then that Isabelle noticed the blood spattered all about the soil beneath his horse. With a cry of dismay she saw the huge red stain covering the entire left side of his shirt.

"Oh Sebastion," she said in horror, "why didn't you tell me you'd been shot?" Her voice caught on a sob. "You could have bled to death."

Sebastion's head rolled back listlessly. "I just might if you stand there chattering any longer," he said weakly.

The burly coachman pulled Sebastion close to his side, slinging the injured man's arm around his neck. "Jean," he called loudly, and a man appeared in the door of the house. Without uttering a word the second man hurried to Sebastion's other side, and the two men helped Sebastion inside. Isabelle followed, too worried about Sebastion to care that she was rushing into a stranger's house without so much as a word of greeting.

Georges and the man called Jean led Sebastion to a sun-filled room at the back of the house. While Jean stripped the coverlet from the bed, Georges laid him carefully on the spotless sheets. His ashen skin was so starkly white against his raven hair that he appeared to Isabelle like a corpse. Looking down at him, so still and pale, Isabelle felt real fear. Sebastion could die. And it would be all her fault.

She glanced helplessly at the two men beside the bed. "We need a doctor," she said breathlessly.

The men looked at each other in silent communication. The one called Jean seemed to be the one elected to fetch the physician, and he quickly exited the room. Just knowing that help would arrive soon lightened Isabelle's heavy heart, and she was filled with a sense of purpose. She would not just stand there wringing her hands in anxiety until the doctor arrived. Sebastion needed her now, and she resolved not to fail him.

"Georges, can you please help me? I will need some hot water, cloths and bandages." She stripped off her fitted jacket and began to roll up her sleeves. "Oh, yes, and something with which to clean the wounds. I believe my grandmother used brandy."

If Isabelle hadn't known better, she would have thought she saw a brief smile cross the driver's face. "I will see what I can do, mademoiselle." He strode past her, leaving them alone in the room.

Isabelle knelt beside Sebastion's prone body, tenderly taking his hand in her own. With the other hand, she gently smoothed the hair from his hot, damp brow. "I know you'll get through this," she whispered, "if only to scold me for my recklessness." She wasn't sure whom she was trying to reassure, Sebastion or herself.

A few minutes later she heard Georges's booted footsteps coming toward the room. She released Sebastion's hand and went to meet him. "Here, let me help you with these," she said, taking the stack of cloths from him.

Working together, they began to ease the sodden shirt from Sebastion's broad shoulders, but soon found that it was not so easy a task. Saturated with blood, the shirt was stuck to the wound and would be quite difficult to remove. In an effort to lessen the inevitable pain, Isabelle soaked a cloth in hot water, then laid it on the material so that the heat would help loosen the fibers from the abused area. With infinite care she and Georges managed to peel away the shirt and pull it up and over Sebastion's head.

She had purposefully not looked at the wound while removing the garment, but she could no longer avoid it. Taking a fortifying breath, she turned her attention to the injury. The bullet had hit Sebastion shallowly in the side, entering in the front along the bottom of his rib cage and exiting a few inches away. The holes left by the slug were raw and dark, oozing a stream of blood with every breath Sebastion took. There was so much blood that Isabelle wondered how he had managed to remain in the saddle for so long. It was a miracle that he hadn't bled to death already.

Determined not to break down, Isabelle set to work stanching the life-threatening flow. Using two thick folded pads, she pushed down on the wounds with as much pressure as she dared. When her arms began to tremble, she eased the pressure and tried to clean the livid area with the brandy Georges had supplied. Sebastion grimaced in pain as the alcohol burned into the tender flesh, turning his torso away from the searing pain. Georges immediately moved to hold the half-conscious man still, while Isabelle once again worked to stop the life blood that continued to leak from the ragged openings. She lost all track of time as she attended Sebastion, and when the physician arrived, she was exhausted and covered with blood.

Louis Boyer was a gruff, no-nonsense man of fifty with a full head of steel gray hair and bushy silver eyebrows that gave the misleading impression that he was constantly scowling. He had been the only doctor in the area since his return from Paris more than twenty years before, and the residents of the nearby town counted themselves lucky to have him. If he was overly blunt at times, people tended to overlook it in the face of his practical advice and competent caregiving.

The doctor set right to work upon entering the sickroom, shooing Isabelle out of the way so that he might examine his patient. He studied the wounds briefly, then placed a hand to Sebastion's sweating forehead. Muttering softly to himself, he opened the small leather case he had brought with him.

"I will need some fresh water," he said to no one in particular, shrugging out of his coat.

"Will he live?" Isabelle asked the foremost question on her mind, unable to wait.

Dr. Boyer seemed to notice her for the first time. "What happened to your face, madame? That is a very nasty bruise."

Isabelle's hand moved to her cheek, covering it in embarrassment. In all the excitement she had forgotten about the large purple welt. "I had an accident," she mumbled. "It's nothing." She pointed to Sebastion. "He is the one to be concerned about."

The doctor momentarily glowered at her impertinence, but then softened, as if sensing her genuine concern. "His wound itself is not life-threatening. It's not deep, and the bullet seems to have glanced off a rib, so it didn't hit any vital organs." He began to wash his hands in alcohol. "However, he has lost a great deal of blood, and there is a high risk of an infection, especially since he already has a fever."

Isabelle felt her knees go weak, but she managed to remain upright. "What can I do to help him?"

The older man sighed. "I will clean him up and bind the wound. You will need to keep him quiet and try to keep his fever down. And try to get some broth into him." He shrugged. "Other than that, it is up to the good Lord."

The answer was less than satisfactory. "Isn't there anything more you can do? Don't you have some herbs or a potion you could give him?"

Dr. Boyer snorted derisively. "I am not a quack to give out elixirs that do nothing but drain a man's pocket. The human body is a powerful mechanism that, if given the proper care, can heal itself in the most miraculous ways." He turned his attention once again to the patient. "Now, if you will leave us alone, please."

She was having none of that. "I want to help."

The doctor regarded her speculatively. "Madame, I am perfectly capable of cleaning a gunshot wound." He held up a hand to check her when she would have protested. "The best thing you can do for this young man is to clean yourself and get some rest. You look ready to collapse, and I don't want to have two patients on my hands."

From his position behind her, Georges spoke up. "He is right, mademoiselle. You won't be of much use to him if you are ill yourself." When Isabelle hesitated, he took her elbow and gently steered her from the room. "Come; I will take you to your room."

She allowed herself to be led from the chamber and through the house up to the second floor. The room allocated for her was small and neat, filled with serviceable but attractive furniture. Someone had been thoughtful enough to lay out her belongings, which she assumed Georges had retrieved from the inn at Troyes. She had many questions for the coachman, but she was too tired to voice them.

"I'll have the water for your bath brought up straightaway, mademoiselle." He indicated a folding screen in one corner of the cheery room. "There is a small hip bath there. If you need anything else, you have only to ask."

Disregarding years of what she had been taught as the proper way to deal with servants, Isabelle laid her hand on the driver's arm. "Thank you, Georges, for all your help. You have been very kind, I don't know what we would have done without you."

The tall man regarded her with respect, and she had

191

the feeling that she had passed some kind of unofficial test. "It is my pleasure, mademoiselle." He bowed slightly before turning to depart. "I will leave you to your rest."

When she was alone, Isabelle wasted no time in divesting herself of the soiled and bloodstained riding habit. It was ruined, but even if it had not been, she would never have worn the garment again because of all the bad memories associated with it. When this was all over, she would fling the hateful outfit in a roaring fire, simply for the pleasure of watching it burn. Wearily she kicked the dark material into a pile and stood in her undergarments, waiting for the bathwater.

A few minutes later two young women entered the chamber carrying two buckets each of water. They both offered shy smiles as they emptied the steaming liquid into the tub. When they were done, the shorter of the two offered to stay and attend Isabelle. She declined graciously, assuring them that she could manage alone. The water was invitingly warm, and Isabelle sank thankfully down into it. The women had provided a scented cake of soap and a washing cloth, which she put to immediate use, scrubbing her skin until it was nearly red. Next she turned her attention to her hair, vigorously lathering the long strands to remove the dust accumulated during their trek. They had thoughtfully left another bucket of clear water for rinsing, and she dumped the contents over her head, splashing a little on the floor.

Minutes later she was wrapped in a large towel and rubbing her hair with a smaller cloth to dry it. She wanted to get back to Sebastion as quickly as possible, despite the orders to rest, and she resented having to waste precious time on her snarled locks. Her toilette articles had been arranged on a small dressing table, and she sat at the matching bench set before it, impatiently trying to comb out the tangles. The doctor would leave soon and Sebastion would need her to take care of him, even though she had no experience dealing with sick people. At the very least, it would make her feel better to sit with him and hold his hand.

She struggled with her unruly hair for a few more minutes before giving up the fight and coiling the damp mass into an unfashionable but practical chignon. Hastily donning a gown, she slipped out of the room. The house was quiet as she retraced her steps to Sebastion's chamber. Though she found it strange that there was a bedroom on the lower floor, she was glad of the location because Sebastion had not been forced to try to make it up the stairs. He had exerted himself enough.

Dr. Boyer had departed by the time she returned to the sickroom. She found Georges sitting in a chair beside the bed, keeping a silent vigil over Sebastion. He looked up as she approached, clearly not surprised to see her. He offered a token, "You should be resting," but Isabelle got the impression that he secretly approved of her stubbornness.

"I wouldn't be able to sleep for all the worrying," she explained. "Besides, if I get too tired I can doze in one of the chairs."

One of the women who had brought up her bathwater entered the room carrying a tray bearing a large bowl of dark soup and some water. She placed the food on a table near the bed, offered another shy smile and a deferential curtsy and exited the room, leaving the door open behind her.

"The doctor says we should try to get him to take some broth," Georges said in a low voice. "He will need nourishment to regain his strength."

Isabelle nodded and picked up the bowl and a broad, shallow spoon. Taking Georges place beside the bed, she sat down and brought the spoon to Sebastion's mouth. She managed to get the tip of the utensil between his lips, but most of the watery stock dribbled onto the pillow beside him. She sighed in frustration and tried again, this time setting the bowl on the table so that she could hold his head upright with her free hand. On her second attempt she managed to get a few more drops into him, but not much. After a few more futile tries, the pillow was stained with broth and Sebastion had taken in no more than a mouthful.

She looked at Georges in mute appeal. "This isn't working. How am I supposed to feed someone who is unconscious?"

"Keep at it, mademoiselle," he encouraged. "Even a little broth is better than none."

"But I'm making a mess." She was so drained from the night's adventures that the sight of the soup-stained pillow actually made her want to cry. Try as she might, she couldn't seem to do anything right.

Georges was unperturbed. "It can easily be cleaned."

Isabelle's shoulders slumped. "You're right, Georges. Please forgive my bad humor." Her father would be horrified to hear her asking a servant's pardon, but she didn't care. Life was far too short and full of the unexpected to waste time worrying about trivial and meaningless social dictates.

She continued spooning the broth into Sebastion, a fruitless effort, but one that occupied her time if not her mind. From the corner of her eye she saw Georges move from his position by the window and walk toward the open door.

"Wait," she said, not pausing in her efforts to feed the patient. "Please don't go yet. I would like to speak to you, if you have a few moments."

He nodded and took a seat on the opposite side of the bed. "I am at your service," he said formally.

Isabelle had the grace to blush. Until today she had not even bothered to learn the man's name, much less ask to have a conversation with him. In his own way, he was letting her know that her lack of concern had been noted. "I suppose I deserve that," she murmured. "I have been rather rude to you, haven't I?"

Georges did not respond, nor had she really expected him to. "You said earlier that this was the house you grew up in," she prompted.

"Yes. My brother and his family live here now."

She paused in her feeding to wipe a stream of liquid from Sebastion's cheek. "Your brother; that would be Jean?"

He nodded in response.

"It is very kind of him to let us stay here."

"His wife Elise and their children are away visiting their oldest daughter."

"I hope Elise won't mind us imposing like this."

Georges shook his head. "You are with me; that is all they need to know."

Another thought occurred to her. "We aren't putting anyone out of their room, are we?"

"No." His gaze swept the orderly room. "This was my mother's room when she was ill. She passed away a few years ago."

"I'm sorry," she murmured with sincerity.

Georges smiled. "Don't be. She lived a good life."

Isabelle tilted her head, regarding him speculatively. "Georges, you work for this mysterious friend of Sebastion's, correct?"

Again his answer was a silent nod.

"I don't suppose you would tell me the man's name?"

He shook his head. "No, Mademoiselle. Monsieur Merrick will tell you that when he is ready."

She was quiet for a moment. "You are not a coachman, are you, Georges?"

His amusement was evident. "I have many duties, mademoiselle. I do whatever my employer asks of me."

Isabelle grimaced at his vague response. "Your answers are rather imprecise, monsieur." She leveled him with a mock serious look. "I don't suppose you are going to give me any information."

He fought back a smile. "That depends on the question, mademoiselle."

The bowl of broth had grown cold, so she decided Sebastion had had enough for the moment. Gently she removed the soup-stained pillow from beneath his head, replacing it with a fresh one. When she was satisfied with his comfort, she turned back to the reticent Georges. "Can you at least tell me your last name so that I might address you and your brother properly?"

"Dumont."

"Georges Dumont," she said, trying out the name. "A very nice name, Monsieur Dumont." She offered a friendly smile. "Now, that wasn't so hard, was it? I ask you a simple question, and you answer it. See how easy that is?"

His expression was unreadable, but she thought she could detect a little warmth in his eyes. Encouraged, Isabelle continued. "I'll try not to ask anything too personal, but I would like to know how we came to be here."

"That I can tell you. When Monsieur Sebastion discovered you missing, he soon realized where you must have gone. Guessing that there would be trouble, he instructed me to gather your things and take the coach."

"But how did he know to come here?"

He shrugged. "I offered the use of my family's house. I knew they would not mind."

"That is very kind of you all."

Georges stood to leave. "I believe that is enough questions for one day." He hesitated before continuing. "I do not wish to pry, but might I ask if Monsieur Broussard was the cause of that mark on your face?" His tone was low and somehow menacing.

"He struck me," she admitted with some shame. "But that is all." She wanted it understood that nothing worse had been done to her.

He let the subject drop. "Please let me know when

you wish to rest. I will be happy to sit with him." He indicated Sebastion's prone form.

Isabelle nodded. "I will. Thank you." But she had no intention of letting anyone else keep the bedside vigil; she would watch over Sebastion until he regained consciousness.

Chapter Seventeen

All through the day Isabelle sat with Sebastion, sponging his head and torso to cool his fever, coaxing a few drops of water and broth down his throat, but mostly just watching. She scrutinized each shallow breath, worrying when she thought too long a span had passed between the rise and fall of his chest. At some point she realized that he was completely nude under the covers. Though she was initially embarrassed, she soon got over it in the course of caring for him. Periodically she would nod off in her chair, always snapping back to wakefulness after a few minutes. Georges and the two women made brief visits to check on them, but for the most part Isabelle was left alone with her patient.

Leaning forward in her wooden chair, she propped her elbows on the mattress and held Sebastion's slack hand. In low, soothing tones she talked to him. She told him stories of her girlhood, of her likes and dislikes, her hopes and dreams. All the things she had never really shared with any one person she related to him, knowing that he couldn't understand her but thinking on some level that the sound of another person's voice would be comforting.

She fought off sleep as best she could because she wanted to be alert in case his fever grew worse or he woke. Eventually she lost the battle, though, and fell asleep with her head and arms resting on the mattress, scant inches from Sebastion's prone form. Georges found her that way some time later when he came to try to coax her into eating some supper. She had not eaten a bite all day. But when he saw her sleeping peacefully, he decided to leave her to her much-needed rest. As silently as he could manage, he closed the chamber door behind him so that the noise in the rest of the house would not reach here.

On the great bed, Sebastion came slowly and painfully to consciousness. He heard the muted *thunk* of the door closing, then nothing except for the hushed tones of someone breathing very near to him. With wakefulness came pain, and for several seconds he couldn't recall the cause of his discomfort. Then he remembered that he had been shot. Images flashed through his mind, but it was as if he were seeing it all in a dream.

If not for the ache in his side and the throbbing in his temples, he might still have thought he was sleeping. He opened his eyes, blinking to clear his clouded vision. Everything seemed strange to him, and even the waning light of the afternoon sun was too bright for his eyes. Cautiously he tried moving his head, looking first to his left toward the window. He didn't think that he recognized the room he was in, but his head hurt so badly, it was hard to be sure. Slowly he shifted to the right, and there he discovered the sleeping Isabelle, half in a chair and half on the bed. Her face was turned toward him, peaceful in repose.

Sebastion's fever-dulled brain registered pleasure at her presence, and he gazed upon her for several long minutes before trying to wake her. In a voice raw from disuse, he whispered her name. Long, light brown lashes fluttered briefly, and then Sebastion was staring into a pair of slumberous green eyes. A sleepy smile curled on her pink lips and briefly her lashes fluttered closed again before popping open moments later, wide and full of joyous amazement.

"Sebastion," she breathed, "you're awake." With cool and soothing hands she touched the heated skin of his face. "How do you feel?" she asked softly.

He didn't answer, but continued to stare at her with a strange brightness in his pale blue eyes that Isabelle attributed to fever. "You're running a high fever," she explained gently. "Do you think you can drink some water?"

Sebastion nodded and raised his head off the pillow. She quickly filled a small glass and held it to his parched lips, tilting the glass so that he could more easily drink. He took a few swallows before letting his head fall back onto the pillow. He still hadn't spoken, and she was beginning to grow concerned. "Do you remember what happened?" she asked.

"I rescued you," he answered finally.

Isabelle smiled at the response. "Yes, you did," she agreed. "And you were shot while doing it. Do you remember?"

"You're so beautiful," he said.

There was a dreamlike quality to his voice that Isabelle had never heard before. She realized then that he wasn't really himself. The fever was affecting his mind, and she was certain that he didn't know what he was saying. She decided to humor him. He probably wouldn't remember what was said anyway.

"And you're very handsome," she soothed. "Now, why don't you try to get some sleep?"

Hot, dry hands found hers and pulled her forward toward the bed. "Why did you run away, Isabelle? You know I wouldn't hurt you."

Even though she knew he was nearly delirious, his words still pierced her heart. "I know," she answered.

"I'm very sorry for all the trouble I've caused you." She smoothed back an errant strand of hair from his damp forehead. He was so hot that his skin was almost painful to touch. Gently she extricated her hands from his and went to the basin of cool water that she had been using to try to lower his fever. She took one of the rags and wet it, wringing it out again until it was merely damp. Back at his bedside, she stroked the cloth tenderly over his face.

Sebastion closed his eyes as she tended him, then opened them when she moved lower to his neck and collarbone. "My angel of mercy," he said throatily, "come down from heaven to care for me." His feverish gaze caught and held hers. "Do you care for me, my Isabelle?"

She felt flushed in spite of the fact that she knew delirium accounted for his words. Did she care for him? Yes, she cared more than she wanted to admit. She cared so much that it was breaking her heart to see him so ill. And to know that it was all her fault. If she hadn't been so headstrong, Sebastion would never have had to come chasing after her. He never would have been shot, and so would not have this raging fever that threatened his life.

"I care," she admitted. "But I want you to rest, Sebastion. You are very ill."

He grinned up at her, a boyish smile that turned her insides to jelly. As sick as he was, he could still wreak havoc with her senses. "Kiss me and I'll go to sleep."

Isabelle felt her own temperature begin to rise. One chaste kiss; what harm could that do? If it got him to rest, it would be worth it. After all, he was hardly in a position to do anything more. "All right," she said reluctantly. "But then you have to promise me you'll sleep."

His grin widened. "I promise."

She leaned forward and brushed her lips briefly against his cheek, thinking to satisfy his request that way. He had other ideas. Surprisingly strong hands pulled her down to the bed so that she was forced to lie across him. She thought briefly of struggling but didn't want to reopen the wound on his side. His body was warm beneath her, and she was reminded quite blatantly that he was naked beneath the thin covers. He groaned, whether from pain or pleasure she didn't know. Hot, seeking lips found hers in a kiss that fairly melted her skin. And because she couldn't help herself she kissed him back, putting all her longing and desperation in that burning embrace.

Sebastion groaned again, causing Isabelle to come to her senses. She was rolling around on the bed with a barely clothed man who had a gunshot wound and a raging fever. What in heaven's name had come over her? Gently but firmly she pushed him away and rolled off the bed. Sebastion reached for her once again, but she stepped neatly out of his grasp. "You've had your kiss," she said a little breathlessly. "Now you need to rest." She bent over and snatched up the damp cloth that had fallen onto the mattress, then turned and walked toward the basin.

"Don't leave me," Sebastion said plaintively.

She dropped the cloth and hurried back to his side, taking his hand in hers. "I won't leave you," she vowed softly. "I'll stay right here until you're better." They stared at each other for a few minutes before Sebastion's eyelids drifted shut and he fell into a feverish sleep.

Isabelle kept her promise, staying at his bedside long into the night. His fever seemed to worsen, until his skin was red and burning to the touch. Hour after hour Isabelle worked, bathing his skin with cool cloths and dribbling water onto his parched lips. She didn't even blink now when presented with the evidence of his maleness, all modesty forgotten in her struggle to save his life. Georges came in several times during her vigil to help her, but she resisted his attempts to convince her to take a break.

Finally, in the middle of the night, the strain of three days with very little sleep caught up to her. Thinking to rest for a few minutes, she stretched out on the edge of the bed next to Sebastion and sank gratefully into an exhausted slumber. Near dawn a concerned Georges found her still curled up peacefully beside her patient. He briefly entertained the idea of waking her and taking her to her room, but he decided that it would do no harm to let her remain.

She was having the most wonderful dream. In it she was standing in the middle of a vast field of wildflowers. The sky was so blue it almost hurt her eyes to look at it, and the sun was warm on her bare head. She laughed from sheer happiness and whirled around in a gleeful circle. In the distance someone called her name, and her heart filled with even greater joy. She ran toward the voice, hurrying through the sea of flowers toward a clearing up ahead. A man stood at the edge of the field with his back to her. He turned as she approached, opening his arms wide in welcome. She stepped into his embrace as if it were the most natural thing in the world, and offered her mouth to him.

"Wake up, sleeping beauty," the man said gently.

She thought it a strange thing to say, considering the fact that she was awake. Her arms twined around his neck. "Kiss me again," she murmured.

"Isabelle." The voice was more insistent this time. "You're dreaming."

Abruptly the man before her faded and Isabelle blinked her eyes open in drowsy confusion. She was lying on her side with her limbs draped around Sebastion, who was sprawled beside her wearing nothing but a thin sheet and a lopsided grin. "Good morning," he said with mock solemnity. "Would you still like that kiss?"

Color flooded her cheeks as she realized that she must have spoken her request aloud. She wondered what else she had done.

Quickly she scrambled out of the bed and stood for a moment with her back to it, her hands pressed against her stinging cheeks. It was mortifying enough that she had slept next to him, but to wake up draped on top of him was too much. Her befuddled brain could scarcely comprehend why she had been there in the first place.

Of course. The fever! She whirled back toward the bed. Sebastion was propped up on the pillows, regarding her with an expression of amusement that quickly faded as he caught sight of her face. "Sebastion," she breathed in excited relief, "you're awake." She sat down on the edge of the mattress and reached out a hand to check his fever.

Before she could place her hand on his forehead, he caught her wrist and held it. "What happened to your face?" he asked in a deceptively calm voice.

There was no way to evade the question. "Monsieur Broussard took offense to something I said."

"Obviously," Sebastion said between gritted teeth.

Self-consciously her other hand moved to cover her cheek. In her worry about Sebastion, she had completely forgotten about it. The last thing she wanted to do now was upset him. He had been so ill, and he needed to rest and regain his strength rather than worry about her. "It's nothing to be concerned about," she said lightly. "I can hardly feel it anymore."

He pulled her fingers away. "Don't try to hide it. I want to see it and remember what it looks like for the next time I see Monsieur Broussard."

Isabelle was alarmed at the dangerous gleam in his eyes. "What do you mean, next time?" she asked worriedly. "You don't mean that you're going back there?" The idea horrified her. Broussard's henchmen had almost killed him before, and the next time they might actually succeed. She took his hand in hers, pleading with her eyes. "Please don't endanger yourself again. Not for my sake."

"I have another reason for seeking the man out," he said, placing his other hand on top of hers. "But be assured that he will be paid back for any harm he caused you."

She shook her head. "No. I haven't cared for you all this time just so you could return to let him finish the job." Her eyes dropped to her lap. "I couldn't bear it if anything happened to you."

One of his hands moved up to tip her chin so that she was forced to look at him. "I have to do what I think is right, Isabelle. You can't ask me to change my principles for you."

She knew he was right, but that didn't make it any easier. No matter what happened and how she felt about him, they always came back to the issue of Sebastion's sense of honor. It was an invisible barrier that separated them at every turn. He wasn't going back to Broussard's because of her, but because the man had been instrumental in causing his cousin's death. The Frenchman had set in motion the whole chain of events that had resulted in tragedy, and now he, too, would have to pay for his sins. As would her stepbrother.

Reynaud, she thought with deepening dread, whom she now knew was definitely a thief and most likely a murderer. She also knew where he was. Should she share that information with Sebastion? Once she did, the Englishman would find her stepbrother and take him back to his homeland for punishment. Could she live with herself if she sentenced her brother to his doom? But could she live with herself if she lied to Sebastion, the man who had almost lost his life saving her from certain death? Either way she would be betraying someone she cared for. Her only hope was that the evidence was wrong and, though Reynaud was guilty of burglary, he was innocent of murder. That was the tiny thread of faith that she would cling to in the days to come.

Taking a deep breath, she uttered the words that would change their lives. "I have something to tell you. I believe I know where Reynaud is." She said it in a rush, afraid that the confession would become stuck in her throat if she didn't.

Sebastion didn't answer right away. He was still propped up on the stack of pillows, but his body was tense and rigid. "How long have you known?" he asked with deceptive calm.

She was stung by the implication that she had known all along, but she resolved not to jump to conclusions. "While I was a *guest* at Monsieur Broussard's home, he showed me a note that Reynaud had written to me in Paris. I don't know how he managed to intercept the letter, but I never received it. It was rather cryptic, and Broussard wanted me to explain it to him." She raised her chin in defiance. "I refused."

"What did it say?"

"Reynaud wrote that he had to leave the city before he was found. He then asked if I remembered the golden path, and that was where he would wait for me." She continued at his questioning look. "When Reynaud was a child, before his own father died, his family lived on a small farm near a village called Salmaise. His grandmother insisted that they have some sunflowers on the land, so his father planted them twenty feet deep on either side of the road leading up to their house. Reynaud always referred to it as the 'golden path.' "

He took the information in without expression, and Isabelle could not tell what he thought of her tale. "Does his family still own the property?"

She nodded in affirmation. "As far as I know, though no one has lived there for many years. Not since his grandparents died." A sigh escaped her. "I cannot imagine how he expected to get there with no money, but that is all we have to go on."

"Why did you tell me this?" Sebastion inquired. "You could have kept quiet and I would never have been the wiser." He was looking at her strangely, as if trying to discern her motives by sight alone.

"You risked your life to save me. I couldn't repay you by keeping such a secret." Isabelle could only answer him with the truth.

"So it's a debt of honor," he said. "I saved your life, so you owe me. Is that it?"

"Something like that."

"Well, then, I must owe you as well."

She frowned, not following his reasoning. "Why?"

"For all this." He made a sweeping gesture with his arm. "You've taken care of me this whole time, haven't you?" At her nod he continued. "Then I guess you could say that you've saved my life. I was pretty sick, wasn't I?"

"Yes, and it was all my fault," she declared contritely. "So you can hardly claim that I've saved your life. If it weren't for my foolhardy actions, you would never have gotten shot in the first place." She regarded him earnestly. "I want you to know how sorry I am. I hope you can forgive me."

Sebastion didn't know what to say. He had been furious with her the day he discovered her missing and had vowed all manner of severe retribution. But even more than being angry, and much more disconcerting, he had been afraid for her. A feeling of powerlessness had assailed him when he realized where she had gone, and that had made him even more furious. If he had known then that Broussard was physically abusing her, he probably would have killed the man without thinking twice. Luckily for the older man, Sebastion had been unaware of his actions and had focused solely on getting Isabelle out of harm's way.

Isabelle was the kind of woman he had always

avoided. Gently bred virgins had never held an attraction for him because of all the complications that came with them. He much preferred married women or, occasionally, a well-compensated mistress. Although even the latter had little appeal to him because they made him feel tied down. He cherished his freedom and therefore chose his brief liaisons with care, never getting involved with a woman who would expect too much from him. Women could certainly prove to be a pleasurable diversion, but lately even the promise of physical fulfillment had not been enough to entice him into an affair.

Until now. Here was this aristocratic French girl, the stepsister of his cousin's murderer, and he could think of little else but taking her to his bed. When he had awakened this morning and found her curled up beside him, it had been all he could do not to take what she was unwittingly offering. That he had not was a testament to his willpower. Here in the intimate setting of this room, with only the insubstantial bed linens covering him, he was hard pressed to contain himself. And if Isabelle continued to stare at him with those doleful, yearning green eyes, he wouldn't be responsible for his actions.

"There's nothing to forgive," he answered finally. "But you have to promise me that you won't do anything so foolish again. You could have been killed." Or worse, he thought. Then he really would have murdered the little Frenchman. Just the thought of him placing his hands on Isabelle was enough to fill him with renewed rage.

"Sebastion, what's wrong?" Isabelle asked worriedly. "Are you in pain? I'll send for the doctor."

He held up his hand. "No, I'm fine. I don't need a doctor." Noting her uncertainty, he added, "I could use something to eat, though. I'm starving."

"That's a good sign. I'll call for the maid." She stood to go. "I'm so thankful that you're better."

He smiled crookedly. "I would have thought you'd be happy to get rid of me. After all, I'm a wretch and a conniving blackguard, I believe you said."

She blushed. "You know I didn't mean any of that. I was angry." Her eyes were fixed on a point above his head. "When you were sick I realized I care for you a great deal."

Again he was left speechless, disarmed by her unnerving honesty. He wanted to warn her against wearing her heart on her sleeve, but strangely that was one of the things he admired most about her. True, she was naive to the ways of the world, but it was refreshing to meet someone who said what she meant. He had called her a liar for not telling him about the key, but deep down he knew why she had kept it from him. He owed her an apology; not only for that, but for all the other times he had wronged her. But now was not the time. Especially since he was so desperate for her that if she didn't leave soon, he was sure to do something he would regret.

"Thank you," he said for lack of anything better. "Now, what about some breakfast?"

She hurried out of the room, leaving him to lie on the great bed, hungry for much more than food. Isabelle did not return for the remainder of the day, having been given strict orders from Georges that she was to get some rest.

After an early breakfast the next morning, Isabelle decided to brave the sickroom again. She was not too startled to find Sebastion out of bed and nearly dressed. He was a stubborn man, and if he decided he was well enough to be up and about, nothing anyone said would deter him. Still, she felt as though she should offer some objection, no matter how futile the attempt.

"You know that it's too soon for you to be up and about," she scolded. "What if your wound begins to bleed?"

Sebastion offered her a condescending frown. "I've had worse injuries than this in my life. And I'll be damned if I'll spend another day in that bed."

"If you will recall, you were in that bed because of a bullet wound, not to mention a raging fever." She threw up her hands in surrender. "But if you want to traipse around and get sick again, far be it from me to offer some common sense."

He grinned rakishly at her. "You're nagging like an old fishwife."

"You're impossible," she said between gritted teeth. "And I have never nagged anyone a day in my life." She turned to exit the room, intending to leave him to his foolishness. His next words stopped her.

"Walk with me," he said. "That way you can make sure I don't overtax myself."

She rolled her eyes in exasperation but couldn't resist his invitation. When he put his mind to it, Sebastion Merrick could be utterly, devastatingly charming. And as much as she wished otherwise, she was not immune to his considerable appeal.

The morning sky was overcast, but it was still a mild day. Sebastion and Isabelle ambled sedately down the narrow drive, away from the farmhouse. Long moments of companionable silence passed before he finally spoke.

"I don't want to start an argument, but I need to know if Broussard hurt you in any other way." He said it brusquely and without inflection. Though Georges had assured him that Isabelle claimed no other injuries beside the bruise, Sebastion had to be sure. The question had been plaguing him since the previous day, and he would not be satisfied until he heard the answer from Isabelle's own lips.

"No," she answered truthfully. "He just scared me." She kicked a rock with the toe of her shoe, her eyes trained on the ground. "I still can't believe I was so reckless and foolish as to go visit him."

"Why did you?" he asked curiously. "Was it to get away from me?"

"No," she answered quickly, then paused. "Well, not really." Her eyes found his. "I was very angry with you and I wanted to go home. I thought that if I offered to pay Reynaud's note, Broussard would be satisfied and Reynaud could come out of hiding, and everything would turn out all right. Then Reynaud could tell you that it was really Broussard who committed that horrible crime."

"But Broussard wouldn't accept your offer?"

She shook her head. "No. He said that Reynaud had taken something more valuable than money from him and it was too late to just pay off the debt."

Sebastion did not comment.

"So it seems your theory was correct. Reynaud stole the chalice but never delivered it to Broussard." Her steps quickened in agitation. "That should make you happy."

Sebastion reached out and put a restraining hand on her upper arm, holding her with just enough pressure to make her stop. "It doesn't make me happy to see you upset, Isabelle. But I would be lying if I said I wasn't pleased to know that my assumptions have been correct." His grip slackened until he was just resting his hand on her arm, not holding her. "And no matter what happens, I want you to know that I regret any pain I've caused you."

"I wish things could have been different between us," she uttered wistfully. She looked up at him, longing clearly written on her face.

His insides twisted painfully at the sight. Before he could think better of it, Sebastion leaned down and kissed Isabelle's soft, inviting lips. It was a gentle kiss, unlike their previous encounters. Sebastion's mouth worshipped hers with a tenderness he hadn't known he was capable of.

She breathed his name like a plea. "Oh, Sebastion . . .

211

I wish we could stay here forever. Just the two of us. I wish . . ."

He put one long finger to her lips. "Sssh," he breathed. "All the wishing in the world won't change things, love." He kissed her one last time, then broke away and moved his chin to rest it against her forehead. He savored the feel of Isabelle's slender form against his chest, wanting to crush her to him and never let her go. But he was older and wiser than she in affairs of the heart, and it was up to him to keep a level head. Though it would have been easy to use his recuperation as an excuse to spend more time with Isabelle, he knew that the sooner they found Reynaud the better it would be for both of them. It would serve no purpose to prolong their strange partnership, and in fact would only cause harm. They came from two different worlds, worlds in which they each had obligations to other people. And no matter how much they might wish otherwise, they could never be together. He had to remember that his debt to his family came first, regardless of his personal desires.

"This whole ordeal has been very difficult for you," he offered reasonably. "It's only natural that you feel confused and unsettled." He was offering her an excuse for the feelings that she was experiencing, but he was also trying to convince himself. It had been easier when Isabelle openly disliked him. Now that her perceptions about him had changed, he was finding it difficult to keep her at arm's length. "When this is all over, you'll go back to your Henri and forget all about me."

Isabelle knew that she would never forget Sebastion, no matter how many years came between them or how many men she might meet. None of them would compare to him. He was trying to dismiss her attachment to him as the result of the many upsets she had endured. But regardless of his words Isabelle knew her true feelings, and she recognized that they would never disappear. She cared for Sebastion more than she had ever thought possible, and there was nothing either of them could do to change that. But she also knew that he wasn't able to return those feelings; not now, and probably never. Duty and family loyalty came first for him, and she would have to settle for being a distant second. It nearly broke her heart, but she had too much pride to let him see that.

"You're right, of course," she said with false enthusiasm. "So, what happens now?" It was best to change the subject.

"We leave tomorrow for Salmaise. I want to get an early start," he warned, "so be sure that you're all packed. I know how you are in the mornings, love."

She nodded, trying to smile at his teasing. It struck her then that he really did know how she was in the mornings. In fact, he knew a lot about her. More than any of her friends or even Henri. Funny how quickly they had gotten to know each other in such a short time. Perhaps that was why she felt so connected to him. Or perhaps it was because she had fallen in love with him. The thought was so disturbing that she didn't even bother to argue about his traveling so soon after his illness. He would do what he wanted, as always. "I'll be ready," she promised, wondering if either of them could ever truly be ready for what they would face at their journey's end.

Impulsively she hugged him tightly, brushing her lips lightly over his unshaven cheek. "I wish I were your love," she said, then turned and ran up the long drive to the farmhouse.

Sebastion stood rooted to the spot, watching her retreating form grow smaller and smaller. His eyes closed in a heartfelt if unfamiliar prayer as he fervently asked for strength.

Chapter Eighteen

They set out at dawn the next morning, Isabelle riding in the hated coach and Sebastion following on horseback. Isabelle objected to being confined in the coach, but Sebastion and Georges had insisted. They kept a moderate pace in deference to Sebastion's condition, but Isabelle still found the bumpy, dusty carriage uncomfortable. Despite their slow speed, by traveling all day without stopping they managed to reach a resting place well over halfway to their destination by the evening.

Sebastion procured rooms for them at a simple inn, where they ate a light supper and retired to their separate bedchambers. Sebastion and Isabelle's rooms were adjoining, and she could hear him pacing late into the night. Briefly she considered joining him so that they might keep each other company, but she decided against such an action. They were both tired and on edge from being so close to Reynaud, and she knew it would take very little for their smoldering emotions to ignite.

A Treasure to Hold

Sometimes when she was around Sebastion she felt like a child playing with matches, knowing that she would probably get burned but doing it in spite of that fact. Tonight, however, she let common sense guide her. If she went into his room, no matter how innocent her intentions, she feared that this time she would not come away unscathed. She knew she was unsophisticated when it came to passion, but she was woman enough to know that Sebastion wanted her. And she wanted him. A very dangerous combination. Trying to ignore the urgings of her body, she rolled over and placed a pillow over her head to drown out the muffled footsteps in the next room. After a long while, she slept.

It was still dark when she was awakened by a sharp knock at her door. She mumbled a grumpy response at the closed door and huddled deeper beneath the covers. Only when the lock began to rattle did she sit up and consider getting out of her comfortable bed. "I'm coming," she called peevishly. "It isn't even daylight yet, you tyrant," she muttered. Sebastion's answering bark of laughter told her that he had heard her.

She hurried through her morning toilette, putting on the same clothes from the previous day and securing her hair in a low knot. She ate a rushed breakfast and then sped to the coach, where Georges and Sebastion waited. Still cranky to be up at such an uncivilized hour, she made a childish face at Sebastion, which further amused him. Once inside the dark coach she tried her best to go back to sleep but found it impossible. With a sigh of resignation she settled in and tried to occupy her mind with pleasant thoughts of home.

At midday they stopped briefly to water the horses. Sebastion produced a hamper from its place beside Georges, offering bread and hard cheese to eat. He had also filled a wine bottle with water, which was welcome despite its tepid temperature. All too soon they

215

were once again on the road, and Isabelle's anxiety increased as they neared their destination.

When they halted a few hours later, she knew with dread that they had reached the end of their journey. She opened the door and looked around, curious as to why they were still on the road. The directions she had been able to give were vague at best, and she wondered if perhaps they were unable to find the farmhouse. "Are we lost?" she asked when Sebastion came to help her from the conveyance.

One eyebrow rose as though it were an outrageous suggestion, as though she questioned his masculine ability to lead. "No. According to your *excellent* directions" he gently mocked, "that should be the farmhouse over there." He pointed to a building some quarter mile away.

"Then why are we stopping here?"

"I thought Andrassy might grow nervous if he saw an unfamiliar carriage. You will ride in front of me on the horse, so your stepbrother can clearly see you if he's watching the road."

With little effort he grasped her waist and lifted her high into the saddle. She was not wearing a riding habit, so she was forced to sit with both legs hanging off the side. A most precarious position, even for an experienced horsewoman such as herself. Sebastion quickly mounted behind her, taking the reins in one hand and holding her securely with the other. They left Georges waiting by the side of the road and started off down the overgrown path that led to Reynaud's childhood home.

It was obvious that no one had worked the land for years. The fields lay fallow, except for a few straggling sunflowers that had managed to survive. Like withered scarecrows they lined the drive, choked with weeds and brown from lack of care. It saddened Isabelle to think that this was what had become of Reynaud's golden path, and she wondered what his thoughts had been upon first seeing them. As they got closer, Isabelle could see that the house was in a similar state of disrepair. Tiles were missing from the roof, nearly all of the shutters were broken or missing and most of the outside walls were covered with some prolific creeping vine that was visible through holes in the ceiling as well. The smaller outbuildings were in even worse shape, and Isabelle wondered how they managed to remain standing. Only the barn seemed to be structurally sound, and that, too, was in need of restoration.

Sebastion reined his mount to a halt several yards from the dilapidated house. Wordlessly he dismounted, then helped Isabelle down. "Call him," he said flatly, and Isabelle complied.

Cupping a hand to her mouth she shouted, "Reynaud, it's Isabelle. You can come out." She waited for a response, but none was forthcoming. "Where are you, Reynaud? Please answer me. I've come all this way to find you." Again there was only silence. She turned to Sebastion in dismay. "He's not here."

"We don't know that yet. I'm going to look around." He started toward the house. "Stay here," he warned.

The front door of the farmhouse was warped with age and nearly devoid of the reddish paint that had once adorned it. It was also unlocked. Pushing it open, Sebastion cautiously entered the musty building. A few pieces of broken furniture littered floors that were covered in dirt and the remnants of animal visitors. After a quick but thorough search of the premises, he gratefully returned to the fresh air outdoors.

"If he's living in that house, I don't see any evidence of it."

Isabelle reached up as he spoke and removed a silky cobweb that had attached itself to Sebastion's dark hair. "I hope nothing happened to prevent him from getting here."

"Let's make sure he's not here before we start worrying about that. I'm going to check the barn and out-buildings."

He started away and Isabelle followed. "I want to go with you," she said in answer to his inquiring look. He didn't argue with her, and they walked together to the large, drafty barn. Inside the building was dark, except for shafts of light spilling in from the high square windows. Motes of dust danced in the air, giving the still space a surreal quality. In a flash of intuition, Isabelle knew immediately that Reynaud was there.

She began looking behind bales of ancient hay and old barrels. Sebastion took his search higher, climbing the wobbly ladder that led to the loft. When he reached the top Isabelle heard a rustling, followed by a high-pitched squeal of alarm. Reynaud.

With a cry, she ran toward the ladder. She could no longer see either man, but her stepbrother's words rang out clearly. "Get away from me or I'll run you through," he threatened.

"Put that thing down before you hurt yourself, Andrassy." Sebastion's voice was hard as steel.

"Reynaud, Sebastion, what's happening?" she called anxiously as she ascended the ladder, hampered considerably by her skirts. When she reached the top she nearly fell off at the sight that met her eyes. Her stepbrother was standing in the far corner of the loft, brandishing the business end of a large, rusty pitchfork at Sebastion.

"Reynaud," she cried again, "stop it this instant. Sebastion is a friend."

The young man seemed to hear her for the first time. He turned abruptly at the sound of her voice, dropping his makeshift weapon at the sight of her. "Isabelle," he said in disbelief. "Can it really be you?"

"Yes," she cried happily. She scrambled somewhat clumsily up the last few rungs of the ladder and ran to her brother. The two embraced warmly, leaving Sebastion to watch from the side. Reynaud began to weep in great gasping sobs, and Isabelle tried to soothe the trembling man.

"I thought you'd never come, Belle," he whimpered piteously, calling her by her childhood nickname. "I thought I would die here all alone." His slender form shook with the force of his grief, and Isabelle held him like a mother comforting her child.

"I'm here now," she soothed. "You're not alone anymore."

The storm of tears soon abated, and Reynaud once again turned his attention to Sebastion. "Who is he?" he asked Isabelle, wiping the remnants of moisture from his eyes. Eyes that darted distrustfully back and forth between them.

"This is Sebastion. Why don't we get down from here and I'll explain everything?"

Reynaud descended the shaky ladder first, followed by Isabelle and then Sebastion. Once on the ground, the trio made their way out of the gloomy barn and into the late afternoon sunshine.

Isabelle studied her stepbrother more closely in the light of day and found him sadly lacking. His frame had wasted away from being merely slender to looking as though he'd been starved. The clothes he wore were dirty and hung on his too thin frame, looking as though they belonged to a larger man. His sandy hair was overly long and in need of washing. He presented an altogether pitiful appearance.

"Isabelle," Reynaud gasped in horror as the sunlight illuminated her bruised face. "What happened to you? Did someone strike you?"

Isabelle waved away his concern impatiently. "It's nothing, really. I'll tell you all about it later." She was getting awfully tired of having to explain the mark on her face; it served as a continual reminder of how much she had underestimated Broussard.

They walked to a crumbling stone wall, and Reynaud sat down gingerly on an intact portion. "Now," he said to Isabelle, eyeing Sebastion distrustfully, "Who is this man? Is he responsible for marking your beautiful face?"

Before she could respond, Sebastion cut in. "I am the cousin of the man you robbed and killed in England. The man who struck your stepsister was Emil Broussard."

Reynaud's already pale skin blanched to a chalky white. "I don't know what you're talking about," he stuttered nervously. "Who . . . ?"

Sebastion began to advance on him, but Isabelle rushed to put her body between the men. Reynaud cowered on the low wall, shrinking into himself as though preparing for a blow. Isabelle pushed firmly against Sebastion's rock-hard chest, and he reluctantly allowed her to block him. She was thankful for his self-restraint, for she knew that if he wanted to, he could easily push her aside and get to the other man.

"Don't lie to me, Reynaud," she ordered. You know who Emil Broussard is, don't you?"

For several tense moments she feared that he would not answer. Beneath the layers of his clothing, she could feel Sebastion's muscles begin to tense as they waited. Finally Reynaud nodded. "I owe him a great deal of money."

"And what else?" Sebastion ground out impatiently.

"Nothing," Reynaud said petulantly. "I have nothing else to say."

"Reynaud," she pleaded. "Please. You need to tell us the truth." She turned imploringly toward him, searching his face for answers. "We know all about Broussard and the chest you stole."

He still was not ready to confess. Completely ignoring Sebastion, he addressed Isabelle. "How do you know what this stranger says is true? Are you going to take his word over mine, Belle?"

She sensed that both men were waiting to hear her response. "I have spoken to Broussard."

"You didn't cover your tracks very well, Andrassy." Sebastion's voice was devoid of emotion.

Reynaud's eyes filled with tears as he looked beseechingly at his sister. "I couldn't pay my marker. He said if I went to England and stole the chest for him, he would forgive the debt." He squeezed his eyes shut in pain. "I was desperate, Isabelle. I didn't know what else to do."

"You could have come to me," she said. "Why didn't you? I would have helped you."

He shook his head. "I couldn't come to you again, and for such a large sum. Father would have found out about it and stopped you, anyway."

Isabelle didn't argue; he was right. Victor would have heard if she tried to remove such a sum from her accounts, and he would have never allowed her to give it to Reynaud. She took a calming breath. "So you took the chest. What happened then?"

"Nothing," he muttered.

"Reynaud," Isabelle said in warning, knowing that Sebastion would not stand for much more of his evasiveness. "There's something you're not telling me."

"What do you want me to say?" he asked defensively.

"What I would like you to tell me, what I need you to tell me, is whether you did what Sebastion claims. Did you kill Jonathan Larrimore, the man who owned the chest?"

Brother and sister stared at each other for a tense moment before Reynaud looked away. He began to weep again, softly this time. "It was an accident. I was just supposed to take the chest and leave, but he caught me." He used the back of one bony hand to swipe at the tears. "I was trying to scare him with the gun. Somehow it went off."

Isabelle's hands fell away from Sebastion's chest. The slender thread of hope she had held on to for so long had broken, and she felt sick with remorse and disbe-

221

lief. "Oh, Reynaud," she whispered brokenly. "How could you?"

As though to escape his stepsister's censure, he hid his face in his hands and sobbed. "I'm sorry," he wailed. "I'm sorry." He raised his tearstained face to hers. "I've caused you nothing but trouble from the start. Broussard did that to you because of me, didn't he?" A fresh bout of weeping followed.

Sebastion had remained quiet throughout the scene. Now that he had gotten a confession, he felt as if the vise of grief in his chest had loosened. He had tracked down Jonathan's murderer, and in doing so had repaid in some small way the kindness that Jonathan's family had shown to him over the years. His obligations were far from over, for he still had to convey the criminal back to England. But for the first time, he saw an end to this horrible ordeal in sight.

He watched as Andrassy broke down before him. The man was obviously remorseful for what he had done, but nothing could soften Sebastion's attitude concerning punishment. Reynaud Andrassy was a thief and a murderer, and he would have to face up to his crimes. Isabelle was the one he felt compassion for. She had turned away from her stepbrother's weeping, walking to a spot some forty yards down the crumbling stone wall, where she now stood alone with her thoughts. Against his better judgment, Sebastion went to her.

She was not crying as he had expected. Instead she stared blankly ahead, gazing with unseeing eyes at the barren fields before her. Sebastion came up beside her and joined her in staring at the landscape. He did not speak immediately, waiting for her to talk to him if she wished.

"Have you come to gloat?" she asked bitterly, unable to stop the anger that welled up inside her.

"No," he answered calmly. "But I think you already know that."

A Treasure to Hold

Isabelle closed her eyes tightly, pressing her closed fist to her forehead. "I do know," she admitted, "but that doesn't make this any easier." Her gaze trailed back to the spot where Reynaud still sat. "Look at him. Does he look like a cold-blooded killer to you? He's more like a child."

Sebastion agreed with her assessment. Although he knew his view differed somewhat from Isabelle's. He couldn't help thinking that like a child might, the younger man cried because he had been caught, not because of what he had done. In deference to Isabelle, he refrained from speaking the thought aloud. "What do you want me to do, Isabelle? Let him go now that I know for certain he killed my cousin?"

She shook her head sadly. "I don't expect you to do that. And I'm sure it was very painful for you to hear his confession."

"You didn't answer my question. What do you want me to do?"

Isabelle turned to face him. "Why do you even ask? If I said 'Let him go,' would you do it? Of course not."

"You've never asked me," he pointed out, his expression carefully neutral.

"I wouldn't ask that of you."

"Why?"

"Because you once told me that what you felt for me couldn't begin to compare to what you felt for your family." She regarded him intently, searching his face. "That hasn't changed, has it?"

He shook his head, wondering as he did whether he was telling the truth. His feelings for her were something he couldn't put a name to, but he knew that he owed loyalty foremost to his family. Even if she did get on her knees and plead for the man's life, Sebastion would have to deny her. "No," he said. "Nothing has changed."

She took a deep breath. "So what happens now?"

"We return to Paris. Georges can take you home

223

from there." He left unsaid that he and Reynaud would travel on to Calais, then across the Channel to England. And to certain death for the Frenchman. Even if the man confessed that it was an accident and threw himself on the mercy of the court, a foreigner who had killed a peer of the Realm would be executed. That knowledge stood between them, as real as any wall.

"Georges isn't just a coachman, is he?" she asked, finally understanding the man's role. "He came to help you with Reynaud."

"Yes." There was no point in denying it now.

"Who is his employer?" When he hesitated, she pressed on. "I think I deserve to know."

Sebastion made an impatient motion with his hands. "Not that it makes any difference, but he works for the Duc d'Amboise," he said blandly, naming an infamous and fabulously wealthy aristocrat. The man had one of the worst reputations as a womanizer and libertine in all of France, and everyone had heard of his exploits. Somehow given what she knew of Sebastion, she was not at all surprised that the nefarious rake was Sebastion's mysterious Parisian *friend*.

"I've known him for years," Sebastion said almost defensively. "I knew I could count on him to offer whatever help I might need with no questions asked."

Isabelle sniffed derisively. "Of course he wouldn't ask any questions. He probably kidnaps innocent young women every day of the week. In fact, he probably gave you some advice on how to keep me in line!" She looked away from him, offering her profile. "I'm tired and I don't want to talk any more about you, your disreputable friends, or their henchmen."

"Georges is hardly a *henchman*," Sebastion chided. "He's been a good friend to both of us."

Isabelle's mouth hardened into a grim line. "I thought so too until I realized he was only here to help you apprehend my brother." She tried to walk away but he held her back.

"Isabelle, don't be angry. I know this is hard for you."

She shot him an angry look. "Do you? Do you really know how hard it is for me to blithely hand my step-brother over to you so that you can take him to his death? I hardly think so." Angrily she pulled her arm away. "Throughout this entire ordeal you have thought only of yourself and your family's grief. What about *my* grief? My brother is already lost to me, and you expect me to act as if nothing is wrong." She turned her back to him. "You once called me selfish and spoiled, and maybe you were right at the time, but I've changed. I can look outside my own feelings to consider how my actions affect others. Can you say the same?"

He studied her slender back, held so proudly and painfully erect. She was right, of course, but hearing the truth did not make him want to change. His actions were born of necessity, and he made no excuses for his single-mindedness. From the very beginning he had stated his intentions, and just because he could not be swayed from his course did not mean that he should apologize. Yes, he imagined that he seemed very selfish to Isabelle, but if he had it to do all over again, he would behave in a similar manner.

Isabelle was also right that she had changed. The spoiled, haughty girl he had met at the café in Paris was a far cry from the woman who stood before him now. He had played a large part in that transformation, but he wasn't so sure that the change was all for the good. Looking at her now, so forlorn and confused, he wondered how this new creature would be able to function in her old surroundings. He wanted to take her in his arms and ease her pain, but he held back. He had caused most of her sadness by forcing her to help him find Andrassy, and she would feel even guiltier if she took comfort from him.

Sebastion put both hands on her shoulders and gent

225

ly turned her to face him. There were unshed tears glistening in her eyes, but he knew she was too stubborn to cry in front of him. "I have treated you badly," he conceded. He did not say out loud that he was sorry for hurting her, but his eyes offered the apology.

"I wish I still hated you," she said. "That would make things much easier."

"Remember what I said about wishes." He patted her arm reassuringly, a poor comfort at best. Her brother was going to die no matter what Sebastion said, and they both knew it. It was there between them, and always would be. Decisions had been made and there was no turning back.

Chapter Nineteen

When Isabelle had regained her composure she returned to the spot where Reynaud sat slumped on the low wall. Sebastion remained at a distance. Reynaud had finally stopped crying, but his mottled red face still bore the evidence of his grief. He looked up at her approach, his expression one of derision. "You seem awfully friendly with that fellow," he said peevishly. "What is he to you, *sister*?" he spat contemptuously, emphasizing their familial connection.

Isabelle was taken aback at his vehemence. "What do you mean?"

"Are you lovers?"

She let out a shocked gasp. "No. What would make you say such a thing?"

His hands clenched into fists in his lap and he sneered at her. "You're quite familiar with him." His scowl intensified. "Do you know what I think? I think you're his whore and you betrayed me by bringing him here."

Her hand itched to slap him, but she held her formidable temper in check. "You have no right to say such vile and untrue things to me." She would have said more, but Sebastion stopped her.

He had moved up behind them, and before she could prevent it, he grabbed Reynaud by the coat front and hauled him to his feet. Sebastion was at least a head taller than the Frenchman and quite a bit heavier. One blow from his powerful fist would be fatal to the younger man. "I should kill you right now, Andrassy, and save us all a lot of trouble."

Reynaud and Isabelle both screamed at the same time, Reynaud from fear and Isabelle in warning.

"No, Sebastion," she cried. "Please don't hurt him. He doesn't know what he's saying."

Sebastion shook the smaller man once more for emphasis, then let him fall to the ground. "It would be so easy to end your miserable life. Don't tempt me." He loomed over Reynaud's cowering figure. "Apologize to your sister." His voice was as hard as iron.

"I'm sorry," Reynaud mumbled shakily. Awkwardly he pulled himself to his feet and shot Sebastion a look of pure hatred. "You have no right to treat me this way," he whined plaintively. When Sebastion's eyes fixed unwaveringly on him, Reynaud moved so that Isabelle was between the two of them.

"You are wrong about me, Reynaud," Isabelle said with a calmness she did not feel.

"Then why did you bring him here? He's related to the man I killed, for pity's sake. Don't you know what that means for me?"

Isabelle nodded. "I had no choice, Reynaud." She didn't say that Sebastion had forced her to help him.

Sebastion did it for her. "I made her help me, Andrassy. All along she was trying to prove your innocence." It galled him to offer any explanations to the younger man, but he did it for Isabelle's sake. He knew that she already blamed herself enough for her part in finding Andrassy. She certainly didn't need her step-brother accusing her.

Isabelle expanded on his terse offering. "I could not believe that you had committed murder. It was so unlike you, and I thought that if I helped him find you, you could explain what really happened." She took his hand in hers. "You are my brother, Reynaud. I love you." Her voice fell to a whisper. "Please don't make this any harder than it already is."

Reynaud bowed his head in shame. " "Forgive me. I know that you love me, and once again I've let you down." With the toe of one booted foot he drew circles in the dirt. "Does Father know any of this?" he asked in a choked voice.

"No. I thought it best to tell no one in the family." Isabelle's voice was kind.

Reynaud sniffed. "They'll know soon enough, I suppose." He laughed, a mirthless bark of sound. "Father always said I'd come to no good in the end. How right he was. A murderer and a thief; that's what I am."

Isabelle wanted to deny his self-incriminating claims but couldn't. Reynaud had spoken the truth about himself, and she couldn't change the facts.

"Speaking of thievery, where is the chest you took from my cousin's house?" Sebastion's voice held not a trace of sympathy.

Reynaud's head came up at the question. "What if I told you that I don't have it?"

"I'd call you a liar."

The younger man's shoulders sagged. "You're right, I still have it." He indicated the area behind him with a toss of his head. "It's in the barn." Clearly he expected Sebastion to retrieve the article.

"Then go get it," Sebastion said in a low, menacing tone.

Reynaud hesitated momentarily, then turned to comply.

When he was out of earshot, Sebastion addressed his

companion. "Your foolhardy stepbrother is trying my patience."

"I know," she said. "But please don't hurt him. I'll make sure he behaves from now on."

A few moments later the object of their discussion returned carrying a straw-covered burlap sack. Reaching into the dusty bag, he pulled out a small closed chest and handed it to Sebastion. Isabelle regarded the antique with distaste, for it was the acquisition of this little prize that had caused her stepbrother's downfall and irrevocably changed all their lives. She had to admit that it was beautiful, with its intricate designs and exquisite craftsmanship. Still she would have gladly seen it destroyed for the damage its existence had caused.

"It won't do you any good to have it," Reynaud said snidely. "The keys have been lost."

Sebastion pulled the objects in question from a small pocket in his coat. "And I have found them," he said coldly.

Reynaud gasped and looked at Isabelle accusingly. "You gave him the key, too?" He frowned at Sebastion. "But where did you get the other one? I thought I had lost it."

Sebastion's eyes turned to the younger man, boring into him with blue fire. "It was found beside my cousin's corpse."

The Frenchman blanched and said nothing, watching intently as the older man inserted both keys into their locks and opened the chest.

"That's it?" he asked in disbelief when a dull gold cup was revealed. "That is the *treasure* I've ruined my life for? A cup?"

"It is called a chalice, Andrassy," Sebastion answered derisively. "And no one forced you to steal it."

"Yes, someone did," Reynaud said defensively. "Emil Broussard forced me to steal it. I had no choice."

Sebastion said coldly, "You had a choice. You just took the coward's way out."

Reynaud started to respond, but Isabelle stopped him before he could utter the words that would surely antagonize Sebastion. "Please, no more arguing." She appealed to Sebastion. "Can we just put that away?" She indicated the chest. "I can't bear to look at it any longer."

"Very well," he said and went to where his horse was tethered and slid the chest inside a dark leather pouch hanging from the saddle. When he returned he addressed Isabelle briefly. "We need to start back now." Without sparing a glance at Reynaud, he ordered, "Get your things together, Andrassy. We're leaving." And with that he turned on his heel and walked away.

Since the better part of the day was already gone, they only traveled a few hours that evening, a fact for which Isabelle was exceedingly grateful. Inside the coach, Reynaud alternated between fits of crying and long, sullen silences. Isabelle was sympathetic to her brother's plight, but found her patience with him wearing thin. When they finally stopped at an inn, Isabelle wasted no time in getting out of the carriage and keeping as far away from her stepbrother as possible.

Much to Reynaud's indignation, he found himself forced to share a room with Georges. The burly driver was no more satisfied with the arrangement than the younger man, but Sebastion did not trust the boy and wanted him watched. He had come too far to allow Andrassy to get away. He offered to take turns with the coachman, but Georges declined. Part of his job was to make certain they reached Paris with Reynaud Andrassy in tow. And if the smaller man gave them any trouble, he pointed out casually, he'd simply truss him up and drag him across the country.

The night passed uneventfully and the next morning

they continued on their journey to Paris. Reynaud and Isabelle were once again relegated to the carriage, but Isabelle was pleased to see that her stepbrother had gotten over his earlier moodiness. They traveled through the French countryside at a rapid pace, stopping only when necessary. Isabelle and Reynaud spoke little to each other, but Isabelle wanted to believe it was a more companionable silence than the day before.

When the sky at last began to grow dark, she estimated that they were somewhere between Troyes and the Dumont family farm. It was hard to tell traveling in the confines of the coach, but it seemed that they were traveling faster on their return trip than they had coming here.

It was very late when they arrived at a nondescript inn. As usual Sebastion secured their accommodations while Isabelle stretched her legs in the courtyard. Reynaud leaned negligently against the coach, his arms crossed in a gesture of belligerence. He was clearly not looking forward to another night in captivity.

Sebastion emerged from the low doorway and walked purposefully toward her. "Come on; our rooms are ready."

Isabelle turned to Reynaud, who obligingly pushed his lanky frame away from the carriage and ambled toward them. There was something about the way he looked at her that she didn't quite like, but she attributed it to his ill humor. She was too tired to ponder what he might be thinking, so she let the matter drop. Stifling a yawn with one gloved hand, she followed the innkeeper to her assigned chamber. It was much like all the others she had inhabited the last several days, and she didn't give it more than a cursory glance.

Sebastion's room was directly across from hers, with Georges and Reynaud relegated to an area more suitable for servants. Isabelle thought it best not to ask where those accommodations might be. Reynaud had doviously reverted back to his sulky mood, and Isabelle was glad to be away from his accusing eyes. It was apparent to her that, rather than blaming himself for his ill fortune, he was increasingly laying the blame on her shoulders.

Rather than facing the ordeal of dining in the strained atmosphere of Reynaud and Sebastion's presence, she asked that a supper tray be brought to her room. Sebastion seemed relieved at her request, and saw to it with all due haste. When she had finished the rather poorly prepared fare, she donned her nightclothes and crawled into bed, pulling the covers up over her shoulders and promptly falling asleep.

Chapter Twenty

It was sometime later in the night when she awakened, struggling through the silken webs of sleep to lie wide-eyed and alert in the unfamiliar bed. The hairs on the back of her neck stood on end as she sensed someone else was in the room. Had she locked the door when she retired? She couldn't remember.

Cautiously, she shifted her head to try to detect what was amiss. Her eyes had not yet become accustomed to the gloom, and she saw only blackness. A rustling sound came from one side of the room; then Isabelle felt a weight on the bed. "Sebastion?" she whispered in a shaky voice.

A hand clamped roughly over her mouth and a low voice hissed in her ear. "Sorry to disappoint you, but it's not your lover."

Reynaud. She struggled to rise, but he held her down. Despite his thin frame, he was still stronger than she was.

"Promise me you won't scream," he insisted.

She nodded her head and he released her. "What are

you doing in here, Reynaud?" she said angrily. "You frightened me half to death."

"I need your help." His voice was urgent. "I'm going to escape."

She sat up to face him but was unable to see his expression in the dark room. "You can't be serious, Reynaud. Sebastion and Georges will catch you before you set one foot outside the building."

Something cold and hard rested briefly on her neck, and she recognized instantly that it was the flat edge of a knife. "Not if I have a hostage," he said coolly. He was actually holding a knife to her throat, she thought in disbelief. "Don't try to yell for help or I'll be forced to use this," he warned. "Now, you're going to get out of this bed."

Not wanting to anger him into doing something rash, Isabelle slowly peeled back the bedcovers and slipped out of bed. Reynaud rolled across the mattress and stood beside her.

"What do you think you're doing?" Isabelle demanded in a low voice. He might have had a blade in his hand, but he was still her brother, and she couldn't believe he would use it to harm her. She pushed his outstretched hand away from her body. "Get that awful thing away from me. Someone could get hurt."

Reynaud's answering chuckle was full of malice. "I hope that it won't come to that, sister dear. But since you were so eager to see me dead, I find that any family loyalty I may have had has vanished."

"I'm not eager to see you dead, Reynaud. You know that." Her voice rose slightly in agitation. "I've already explained all that to you."

He snorted his contempt. "Forgive me if I don't believe you. I think that English Adonis across the hall has you so hot for him that you'll do whatever he says. Even betray your own brother."

Isabelle gritted her teeth in anger. "I should slap your

face for that, you wretch. I've told you that he's not my lover."

"Then why did you whisper his name ever so tenderly a moment ago?" he taunted. When she didn't respond immediately, he answered his own question. "Because he's been in your bed so often that you assumed it was him."

"No," she cried. "That's not true."

"Enough," Reynaud hissed sharply. "We're wasting precious time. I don't want that hulk of a driver waking up and sounding the alarm. That is, if he's still alive."

She couldn't believe what she was hearing. "What have you done with Georges?"

"It's so touching, the way you're concerned for everyone but me, Isabelle. You don't seem to care that you're escorting me to my death." He pushed her toward the armoire that held her belongings. "Now, get dressed. You're going to help me get out of here."

She stumbled forward, striking her shoulder painfully against the wooden wardrobe. "You must be mad to think that I'll go with you now. You come in here brandishing a knife, telling me you may have killed a man, and you expect me to blithely follow you?" She folded her arms defiantly across her chest. "I won't do it, Reynaud."

"Then I'll go across the hall and shoot your paramour right between the eyes," he said calmly. "I also have a pistol with me, courtesy of your driver."

Isabelle felt her heart sink at his words. Sebastion had asked her once if she would assist Reynaud in this very same situation. At the time her answer had been yes, but now she knew she couldn't do it. She loved Reynaud as her brother and always would, but he had to be responsible for his actions. He needed to face the fact that he had committed a terrible crime. She had no desire to help him run away.

But he had threatened to shoot Sebastion in cold blood, and this time the Englishman might not survive.

She knew that in a fair contest Sebastion could easily defeat her stepbrother, but she was also aware that Reynaud would not give the other man a chance. He would raise his gun and pull the trigger while Sebastion slept.

"Don't hurt him," she said softly. "I'll do as you say, but you must promise me that you'll leave Sebastion alone."

"Shall I give my word as a gentleman, Mademoiselle Saint-Simon?" he asked sarcastically.

"If you give me your word, I'll believe you."

Reynaud laughed mockingly at her. "Then you're a bigger fool than I thought." He moved toward her. "Now, are you going to get dressed or wear what you have on?"

Isabelle stiffened. "I won't disrobe in front of you." She waited for his response, fully prepared to fight him physically if need be.

He grabbed her arm in a cruel grip, catching her off guard. "Very well; then you'll go in your nightgown. It makes no difference to me."

She balled up her fists ineffectually at her sides. "I'm getting awfully tired of men thinking they can just take me along with them like some prized possession. You will not find me a willing hostage, that I swear to you."

"I'm warning you right now," he growled, "if you do anything to endanger my escape I'll shoot you and your lover. You would do well to be more agreeable and assist me."

"And what happens to me once you're safely away?"

His grip tightened on her arm, bruising the tender flesh. "We'll discuss that when the time comes, sister dear." He pulled her up flush with his body. "Listen to me. I need to get that chest back from our English friend. And you're going to get it for me."

"That chest belongs to Sebastion's family. What could you possibly want with it?" She was confused by his intentions. If he had wanted to make an escape he could have already been a few miles away by now on a fast horse. Instead he was still in dangerous territory, worrying about a chest that had brought him nothing but grief.

"But Emil Broussard does want it, and I'm going to give it to him."

She tried to dissuade him, playing on his fear. "Broussard is very angry with you, Reynaud. I doubt you would make it past his gatekeeper."

Reynaud shook her angrily. "Shut up. You're just trying to distract me. Once Broussard has his precious box, he'll call off his hounds and I'll be free."

Isabelle shook her head, though he could not see the gesture. "No, you won't," she said tonelessly. Sebastion would hunt him down like a rabid animal. Nothing would stop the Englishman from finding and killing her stepbrother. But she did not say these things to Reynaud for fear that he would kill Sebastion in his sleep just to prevent the older man from following him.

"Isabelle," he warned in a low voice, "you're wearing on my patience. We need to go."

She tried one last desperate tactic to foil his reckless plan. "Reynaud, I accepted you as my true brother the day your mother married my father. I have loved you, and cared for you, and helped you whenever I could. And I know you loved me, too." She laid her hand on his chest in appeal. "Don't do this terrible thing. Be the older brother I've always adored. Please, Reynaud."

He wavered for a moment, and she could feel his indecision. "I'm sorry, Isabelle," he said at last. "I've never been strong, as your father was always quick to point out." He brushed her hand away from his body. "If I let your Englishman have his way, I'll be sentenced to death. How can you expect me to willingly go to my own execution?" His fingers tightened around her arm. "No, Isabelle. I won't do it. I can't."

"You are making a horrible mistake," she said with conviction.

He pushed her toward the door. "That may be, but at least it's my decision to make." He opened the door cautiously. "Remember, do as I tell you and your lover won't get hurt."

Isabelle took the few steps that led to Sebastion's closed door. The wooden floor was cool beneath her bare feet, but she pushed her mind from such a minor consideration. From behind her, Reynaud reached around and carefully tried the door knob. Much to Isabelle's dismay, it turned easily beneath his hand. Why hadn't Sebastion locked his door? she thought in agitation. Why hadn't she, for that matter? Then she would still be safely asleep, and Reynaud would have been forced to leave without the chalice.

The door swung open on squeaky hinges, and Isabelle knew before she entered the room that Sebastion was awake and alert to their presence. Reynaud pushed her into the room, following quickly behind her so that only a few scant inches separated them. When they had progressed no more than a few feet, he pulled Isabelle to a halt and pushed the door closed behind him.

"I know you're awake, English," Reynaud sneered. "Why don't you light the lamp so that we can chat more comfortably?"

The small lamp beside Sebastion's bed flared to life, and Isabelle could see that he was sitting on the bed, fully dressed down to his boots. This caused Reynaud to hesitate, but he regained his composure quickly.

"To what do I owe the pleasure?" Sebastion drawled mockingly. His face was devoid of all expression, but Isabelle clearly saw the warning glint in his eyes. He would kill Reynaud if given half a chance.

In response to the other man's flippancy, Reynaud twisted Isabelle's arm up behind her back, forcing her to step back against his wiry frame. The long knife appeared in his hand, its deadly blade shining in the light from the lamp, and he held it menacingly against Isabelle's unprotected neck. "Don't try anything," he said harshly, "or I'll slit her throat." To emphasize his seriousness, he pressed the tip of the blade into her soft flesh, until Isabelle felt a small prick of pain.

She stifled a whimper of fear, telling herself to be brave. "Don't listen to him, Sebastion. He's already done something awful to Georges."

Reynaud yanked on her wrist savagely, causing her to groan in pain. "Shut up," he ordered tersely.

Sebastion's voice was as cold and hard as the blade Reynaud held. "That's enough. What do you want, Andrassy?" He was still sitting on the bed, but Isabelle knew it would only take a few of his long strides to reach them.

"I want Broussard's chest," he said.

"No."

Reynaud clearly hadn't expected that response. "What do you mean, no?" he hissed. "Do you care so little for your whore that you'd let me torture her before your eyes?"

Sebastion's features might as well have been carved of stone. "Go ahead," he taunted.

The Frenchman snarled viciously and jerked Isabelle's arm so tightly that she feared he would dislocate it from her shoulder. "Just remember this was his choice," Reynaud said against her hair. And then he reached across with one hand and drew the razorsharp blade along her free arm, slicing through the fine cotton of her nightgown and her delicate skin. She gasped in stunned anguish. Reynaud had released her other arm momentarily, and she instinctively bent forward in an attempt to shield her body from further attacks. The wound was not deep, but it began to bleed profusely.

"Enough," Sebastion growled from across the room. A murderous rage pumped through his body. "I'll give you the damned chest." He didn't trust himself to say more. The sight of Isabelle writhing in pain had been enough to make him feel as though he, too, had been cut. He forced himself to stay calm, knowing that the young man was desperate enough to do great harm if he felt threatened.

"All I want is the chest," Reynaud said, breathing hard.

Sebastion's eyes gleamed in challenge. "Then come and get it," he said softly. "No, you'll bring it to me," Reynaud countered. "And for every second you take, I'll slice a little piece of dear Isabelle off for you." He grabbed her uninjured arm and pulled her up to shield his body.

Isabelle's hands were now covered with blood, as was her once white gown. And when Reynaud once again raised the deadly weapon to her throat, she was sickened to see that it, too, was coated in red. She felt the sting of the blade against her neck, and then a burning sensation as he pressed the tip more firmly against her delicate flesh.

She closed her eyes against the pain, fighting the waves of nausea that assailed her. She had not believed that Reynaud would actually harm her, but now she knew him capable of anything. The gawky fourteen-year-old brother of her memories was gone, replaced by the murderous man who was so cruelly hurting her. Finally, blessedly, the terrible pressure on her neck eased, and Isabelle opened her eyes to see that Sebastion had placed the chest in its pouch at her feet.

Chapter Twenty-one

"Pick it up," Reynaud instructed her, motioning toward the bag with his head.

He loosened his hold on her arm so that she might comply, but he bent down with her and held the knife to her throat as she performed the task. When she had the pouch in her hands, Reynaud forced her to her feet. She looked at Sebastion then, and saw the barely controlled rage in his expression. It was frightening to see such hatred, and at that moment she knew that Reynaud would never be safe as long as Sebastion lived.

"We'll be going now," Reynaud said. "And don't try to stop me or I'll kill her and anyone else unfortunate enough to get in my way."

Sebastion would have liked nothing better than to launch himself at the young man and choke the life from him. But he couldn't risk having Isabelle hurt further. "You don't need her, Andrassy. I'll let you go."

The young man laughed derisively. "You think I'm such a fool!" He opened the door at his back. "No, I believe I'll keep her with me. For a little while, anyway."

"Andrassy, I'm warning you," Sebastion snarled, near the end of his endurance. In a moment he would snap and go after the young man, regardless of the consequences.

Reynaud sheathed the knife in his boot and reached behind himself to pull a pistol from the waist of his trousers. He cocked it with a loud click. "And I'm warning you, English. Come any closer and I'll blow your head off; then I'll kill her anyway."

"Do as he says. Please." Isabelle begged for his compliance with pain-filled eyes.

Sebastion took a step back.

"Very wise," Reynaud mocked. He backed through the door, pulling Isabelle in his wake. Once in the hallway, he turned and dragged her along with him, racing down the stairs as if pursued by demons. Isabelle's arm throbbed painfully, but Reynaud was merciless.

She was disconcerted to see that Sebastion's stallion had been saddled and stood ready in the courtyard. Reynaud tossed Isabelle with surprising strength onto the animal's back before leaping up behind her and spurring the mount away from the inn. Isabelle's seat was precarious at best and she leaned low in an effort to remain balanced. Reynaud was not a natural horseman, and the horse, already nervous from the scent of blood on Isabelle and Reynaud's rough handling, responded badly to his clumsy directions.

"Faster, you filthy beast, faster," Reynaud urged angrily, kicking impatiently at the horse's sides. The stallion lengthened his stride until they careened along the darkened road at a dangerous pace. Isabelle knew that the farther they got from the inn, the less hope she had of being rescued. It would take Sebastion time to follow, and he would have to ride one of the carriage horses, which were far slower than the mount Reynaud had stolen.

If she wanted to stay alive, she would have to act quickly. Summoning all her courage, she raised her el-

bow and landed a crushing blow to Reynaud's nose.
He howled in pain and instinctively put up his hands
to his injured face, giving Isabelle the opportunity to
throw herself from the galloping steed. She landed on
her side, badly bruising her hip and shoulder and
knocking the wind out of her, but she somehow managed to roll away from the horse's deadly hooves, turning her body over and over until she was off the road.

Reynaud howled in outrage, and in the moonlight
Isabelle could see him holding his nose with one hand
and trying to grasp the reins with the other. His attempts were in vain, for the stallion had gotten the bit
between his teeth and was now racing full-speed ahead
with no thought of his hapless rider. In a moment man
and animal were out of sight, swallowed by the shadows of the night. Isabelle rose unsteadily to her feet,
intending to put as much distance between herself and
Reynaud as possible. If her luck held, he would not be
able to gain control of his wayward mount for a while,
giving her time to get out of harm's way.

Her entire body ached, and she bled not only from
the wounds that Reynaud had inflicted but also from
a hundred little cuts and scrapes sustained in her fall.
Pushing aside her pain, she turned back in the direction
of the inn. She decided to stay off the main road, and
instead cut a path through an adjacent field. The ra-
zorlike edges of a thousand ears of corn cut into her as
she ran, slicing mercilessly into her tender flesh. She
sped through the rows, her ears pricked for sounds of
pursuit, but she was relieved to hear none.

She ran until a stitch in her side pulled her up
sharply and made her slow down. Her feet hurt so
badly that she wondered how much farther she could
go, and she looked with longing at the dirt road no
more than twenty feet away. She decided that it would
be worth it to brave discovery on the packed earth. If
she heard Reynaud, she would simply slip back in between the sheltering rows.

On the flat surface she tried to quicken her pace to a jogging shuffle. In the distance she became aware of the distinct sounds of hoofbeats, but they were coming from the direction of the inn. Taking no chances, she darted back into the field and stood watching the road. In the moonlight she could just make out the rider, and as he came closer she knew without a doubt it was Sebastion. Even in the dark she recognized the way he sat his mount, the easy grace with which he rode.

She pushed aside the enveloping stalks. "Sebastion," she yelled. "Sebastion, I'm here."

Immediately Sebastion reined in his mount and turned back toward her. In a moment he was upon her, dismounting before his horse had fully stopped and pulling her tightly against his chest. "Isabelle, thank God," he said fervently. "Are you hurt?"

She shook her head, dizzy with relief at having escaped. "No, I got away before he could do anything." She began to tremble as the shock of the evening's events took hold. "I think he might really have killed me," she whispered.

Sebastion scooped her up in his arms. "You're safe now. Let me take you back to the inn." He lifted her onto the horse, which she recognized as one of the team animals. "Georges is waiting for you." He mounted deftly behind her and urged the horse to a gallop.

"Is he all right? I was afraid Reynaud had killed him."

"He has a rather nasty lump on his head, but he'll live. Your stepbrother evidently pulled a gun on him and then bashed him over the head with it when his back was turned."

Isabelle said nothing further, not wanting to hear any more about Reynaud's evil deeds. She still could scarcely credit that he had held her at knifepoint and threatened to kill her. Had her image of him as a sweet young boy been just a product of her own wishful thinking? Had he always been bad at heart, and she

245

too blind to see it? She wanted to believe that that boy had existed, that desperation had changed him, forced him to turn to a life of crime. She wanted to believe he was not a bad person, only misguided. Misguided— and dangerous in his present state of mind.

The inn came into view and Georges emerged, holding a wet rag to his head. He looked relieved to see them.

Sebastion helped her down from the horse and carried her inside and up to her room. He placed her gently on the bed and lit the small lamp on a nearby table. When he saw the full extent of Isabelle's injuries, he cursed softly under his breath. Her exposed skin was bruised and scratched, and many of the paper-thin cuts were bleeding. Torn, dirty and stained with blood, her nightgown resembled a rag, and peeking out from beneath its shredded hem, her feet were equally damaged, bruised and swollen.

Sebastion felt his gut twist with guilt. He should never have forced her to come with him on this ill-fated trip. She had been abused at every turn, and tonight her own stepbrother had almost killed her. The entire situation was his fault, and he cursed himself for a fool for putting her in danger. He was going to kill Reynaud Andrassy, not only for murdering Jonathan but also for what he had done to Isabelle.

Dropping down on one knee, he knelt beside the bed and took her hands in his. "You gave me quite a scare," he said gruffly.

"I told you Frenchwomen were strong," she said, giving him a watery smile.

He couldn't believe that she was trying to lighten the moment. "You were right. But tell me, how did you manage to get away?"

She grimaced in remembrance. "I hit him in the face as hard as I could, then threw myself off the horse."

His mouth tightened in anger. "You could have been killed."

"I know, but I had to take the chance. I couldn't let him harm me without putting up a fight."

A strange expression crossed Sebastion's face, and if Isabelle hadn't known better, she would have called it admiration. But Sebastion quickly erased all emotion from his features, and she was left to wonder if she had imagined it.

He drew her hands up to his mouth and kissed the injured areas tenderly. "I have to go after him."

"I know," she said. It took all her self-restraint not to plead with him to stay.

Sebastion leaned forward and pressed his lips to hers. When he would have drawn away, she slid her hands from between his and used them to pull him closer. She kissed him back with desire, taking his mouth as he had taken hers. He responded with passion, making Isabelle ache for all that could be, then he pulled away, a stunned look in his eyes.

"Georges will take care of you, love." He smoothed her tangled locks from her brow. "Do as he says," he ordered gently and started to rise.

Isabelle sat up on the bed, gripping his hand tightly in her own. "Sebastion, I . . ." There were so many things she wanted to say, so many things she wanted to tell him: how she had come to care for him, and respect him for his strength and sense of honor; how she couldn't imagine living in this world without him; how she loved him more than she had loved anyone in her life. But the words wouldn't come. Instead she whispered only, "Please be careful."

He nodded, a small, tight smile upon his lips. For a moment she thought he was going to say something else, but he turned abruptly and was gone. She heard the echo of his footsteps disappearing down the hallway, and she felt as though her heart was breaking in two. In spirit she had already lost Reynaud. She didn't think she could bear to lose Sebastion as well. And she knew if he tracked Reynaud to Broussard's, there was a good chance she would lose him.

When she looked up again Georges stood in the doorway. With a strength she did not know she possessed, she pushed herself from the bed and stood shakily beside it. Her abused feet screamed in protest, but she ignored the discomfort. She had no time for pain. "Georges," she said firmly, "we are going after them."

"Monsieur Merrick will be most displeased," he said, and then he gave her a cracked smile. "But I think you're right. He will need our help. Understand this, though, I'm in charge. At no time are you to put yourself in harm's way. Monsieur Merrick would surely have my head then."

Isabelle agreed with a nod of her head.

"Good. Now, let me see to your wounds and we'll be on our way."

When she started to protest, he shot her a warning look that effectively silenced her. As docile as a lamb, she allowed him to clean the shallow knife wounds, as well as her various other cuts and abrasions. He worked silently and efficiently, cleansing the affected areas and bandaging her arm where Reynaud's blade had torn the tender flesh.

A half hour after Sebastion's departure, Isabelle was cleaned, dressed and ready to go. Georges had settled their account with money Sebastion had left him, purchased a new carriage horse to replace the one Sebastion had taken and had the coach ready and waiting.

As they set out along the road that Reynaud and Sebastion had taken before them, Isabelle prayed that they were not too late to save the man she loved.

Chapter Twenty-two

It was not yet light when Reynaud Andrassy arrived at Broussard's chateau. Galloping up to the wrought-iron gate, he called out loudly to rouse the gatekeeper from his slumber. The servant was none too pleased at being awakened at such an hour.

"Who the hell are you?" he snarled as he stumbled sleepily from his post. His hair stood in wild tufts about his head, giving him the look of an inmate in an asylum, and his course shirt hung open to reveal a thick padding of muscle on his large frame. Clearly he was not a man to displease.

Reynaud hastened to explain his presence. "I'm sorry to come at such an hour, but I urgently need to speak with Monsieur Broussard. It's a matter of life and death." He didn't add that it was *his* life that would end in death if the servant didn't open the gates and let him in. Sebastion wouldn't be too far behind him and he wanted to be safely surrounded by Broussard's guards and an iron gate before the man arrived.

"What's your name?"

"Reynaud Andrassy."

This caught the retainer's attention, and he stomped over and opened the gate with only a few grunts of displeasure. "I'll have to go up with you," he said, indicating the chateau with one meaty hand. "Give me your pistol."

Reynaud obligingly handed over his gun but said nothing about the knife hidden in his boot. The larger man accepted the weapon without comment, then turned toward the house, plodding along with shuffling steps. Reynaud followed sedately behind, still on his stolen mount. When they reached the main house, the gatekeeper ordered him to wait while he went around to the kitchen. After several long moments, another servant opened the front door, and Reynaud was ushered into the hushed and shadow-filled residence.

The stone-faced attendant led him through the house to a room that Reynaud assumed was the study. It was difficult to see his surroundings in the pre-dawn darkness, but he was too nervous to pay much attention anyway. Left alone with only a small lamp to dispel the gloom, Reynaud paced the room, waiting for his host to make an appearance.

Less than a quarter of an hour later, Emil Broussard entered the room. One look at his face and Reynaud's resolve vanished, leaving him to wonder at the wisdom of his plan. The older man, though smaller of stature than himself, was somehow menacing. His usually impeccable clothes appeared to have been haphazardly donned, and his thinning gray hair was in need of brushing. But his face might have been carved from marble for all its hardness.

"So, Andrassy, you have come to face me like a man," he said coldly. "I must say I am astonished. I didn't suspect you had that much courage."

Reynaud swallowed uneasily, his mouth suddenly gone dry. "Let me first apologize for the unsuitable hour. I am sorry to have disturbed you." He offered a timid smile. "But I think when you hear why I have come, you will forgive my rudeness."

Broussard sauntered farther into the room, selected a chair and lowered himself onto it. He said nothing, but raised one gray eyebrow to indicate his interest.

Now that he was finally here and had the man's full attention, Reynaud was at a loss as to how to begin. He could just present the chest to him, but he wanted the older man to know all that he had been through in his quest to deliver the prized object. "As you know," he began hesitantly, "I had some difficulty in completing the task you asked me to perform."

"That is an interesting way to describe murder," Broussard observed wryly.

Reynaud blushed. "Yes, well . . . that was an accident, I assure you." He was beginning to sweat, beads of perspiration forming a nervous mustache above his lip. "But I did manage to obtain the item you wanted."

"Indeed?" he questioned with polite interest. "Then why, may I ask, did you not deliver it to me as promised?" His tone turned hard. "I was most distressed when you did not meet me as planned."

Reynaud stuttered in his haste to explain. "The key— keys, I mean. Th . . . there was a problem with the keys." He felt as though he was a young boy again, called before his unforgiving stepfather to answer for some transgression. A wave of nausea swept over him, and he feared he might be ill.

"You lost them," Broussard said flatly.

"Yes," Reynaud admitted. "But I managed to retrieve them both," he added quickly. "I've brought them to you. Along with the chest and the golden cup, of course." He held up the pouch proudly for inspection.

Broussard was unimpressed. With a withering look, he accepted the proffered bag. Carefully, almost reverently, he placed it on the table nearest him. After a brief pause, he unfastened the bindings and removed the contents. Sublime satisfaction spread across his face as he regarded the diminutive chest, an expression of such supreme pleasure that Reynaud felt himself begin to relax. Broussard was happy, and Reynaud felt sure that boded well for his own future.

Tenderly, as though caressing a lover, the older man ran his hands over the ornate surface of the box. "At last," he said, addressing the inanimate object, "you've finally come home. I've been waiting for you for so long, and at last you are mine."

Broussard's voice was dreamy, almost otherworldly, and the sound caused chills to run down Reynaud's spine. His brief feeling of well-being vanished, replaced once again by unease. He had known Broussard to be dangerous, but he hadn't guessed at the extent of the man's mental deficiency. It was apparent to him now that Emil Broussard was insane. He spoke to the chest as he would a person, even going so far as to caress the thing as he would a woman. And the maniacal gleam in his eyes made Reynaud want to get as far away from him as possible.

"I hope that you enjoy your … er … possession," Reynaud said lamely. "You'll forgive me rushing off, but I do have to be going." He took a few tentative steps toward the door. "If you would be so kind as to give me my marker, I'll be on my way and trouble you no further." He bobbed his head in a bowing motion, backing away with what he hoped was a pleasant smile on his face. It would not do for Broussard to see how agitated and frightened he truly was.

The smile of elation faded from the older man's face as he turned his attention to his guest. "There's no need to rush off, Andrassy," he said pleasantly enough, but with an underlying hint of a threat.

"I'm afraid I must, monsieur. Besides, I've taken up enough of your valuable time." He took another step back toward the closed door, his shoulders thudding silently against the solid wood.

"You will stay," Broussard declared and turned his attention back to the chest.

Reynaud took his distraction as an opportunity to flee. He got no farther than the hallway before literally running into a hulking servant, who silently directed him back to the study. Left with no alternative, he returned to face his host.

Broussard was still fondling the chest and didn't even bother to look up when the servant ushered Reynaud inside and closed the door behind him, leaving the two men alone again. "You wound me with your reluctance to share my hospitality," Broussard said from across the room. "What am I to think other than that you don't care for my company?"

"Nothing could be further from the truth," Reynaud assured him. "I simply have some pressing business to attend to. But I would be very happy to be your guest for as long as you like."

Broussard smiled. "A very wise choice, young man." He indicated the chair opposite his own. "Sit down," he invited, "and I'll show you the prize you've worked so hard to bring me."

Reynaud almost blurted out that he'd already seen the chalice inside but bit his tongue instead. The less he said, the less chance he had of antagonizing Broussard. He settled himself on the proffered chair and directed his attention to his host. His stomach pitched nervously as he noted the fierce scowl on the man's face. What could possibly have caused such displeasure?

Broussard raised his eyes from the chest in front of him, pinning Reynaud with a look so black that the young man shrank back in alarm. "Where are the keys?" he asked in a dangerous voice.

Reynaud swallowed against the lump of dread in his throat. "In the locks," he said stupidly.

"No, they aren't," Broussard answered with rising impatience. "Don't you think I checked there first, you imbecile?" He pounded on the table with a white-knuckled fist. "Where are they?"

"Perhaps they're still in the pouch," Reynaud said, rising. "I'll check for you."

Broussard snatched the sack away before Reynaud could lay hands on it. "Stay away, you incompetent fool. I shall find them." He opened the bag and peered inside, then reached in and felt around with his hand. "They aren't here," he said angrily. "You mentioned earlier that you'd had some trouble with the keys. Is this your idea of a little trouble, losing the keys?"

"I saw them with my own eyes," Reynaud bleated pitifully. "They must be here." He reached once again for the pouch, but the older man brushed him aside.

"Well, they aren't," Broussard snapped. "Which means I cannot open the chest." He stood and snarled at the younger man. "And that means you are going to be very sorry."

Reynaud backed fearfully away. "Wait, please. If you'll just let me think, I know I'll be able to find them." He tried to gather his scattered thoughts, racking his brain to remember where he had last seen the keys. The Englishman had used them at the farm to show them the chalice that lay inside. And after that he had placed all the items in the pouch. But later he must have taken the keys out again.

"I know where they are," Reynaud stammered. "I can get them for you in a few hours if you'll let me go."

Broussard advanced on him with murder in his mad black eyes. "Liar," he shouted. "You lost the keys and you're trying to deceive me again." He bore down on the hapless man with outstretched hands. "I offer you an honorable way to satisfy a debt and you repay my kindness with lies and betrayal." He grasped Reynaud's lapels with both hands and shook him roughly.

"No, no," Reynaud cried, trying to extricate himself from the older man's grasp. "I made a mistake, as I told you, but I did try to honor our agreement."

"By keeping my possessions from me, and then bringing them to me without all the pieces?"

"I thought I had found the keys, or else I never would have come here," he whimpered.

Broussard pushed him away in contempt.

"Please," Reynaud cried. "I can get the keys for you if you'll only listen."

"You were a fool to come here, Andrassy." Broussard's voice was calmer now, but somehow that only increased the threat. "It would have been better not to have the chest at all than to possess it and not be able to open it. I have waited all my life to hold the contents in my hands, and you have cheated me of that."

Reynaud couldn't hold back his opinion. "It's only a cup," he said. "What is so special about an old cup?"

"You've seen the chalice?" Broussard hissed.

Reynaud knew then that he'd made another costly mistake. "Yes," he said cautiously.

"How could you open the chest when you've lost the keys?"

Reynaud's gaze fell to the floor. "I told you that I lost the keys, but I was able to locate them."

Broussard's anger was rising. "Then where are they now?" he said through gritted teeth.

"I don't know," Reynaud said. "The Englishman must still have them." Another mistake.

The older man's face paled. "What Englishman? What nonsense are you talking, Andrassy?" His eyes narrowed. "Does this have anything to do with your stepsister?"

"Isabelle," Reynaud said stupidly. He had forgotten about Isabelle's run-in with Broussard. Though he knew little of the details, he was certain he had just made another grave error in judgment.

"Isabelle Saint-Simon, your stepsister," Broussard said in a derogatory tone. "She was my guest several days ago, but apparently she, too, found my hospitality lacking. She disappeared in the middle of the night. With a man." He paused here for emphasis. "They killed one of my guards."

Silently Reynaud cursed his sister and her lover but held his tongue. He had already gotten himself into enough trouble without volunteering more. If Broussard wanted the information, he would have to work for it.

"Who is this Englishman you spoke of? Your sister was with a Frenchman."

Reynaud shook his head. "I know nothing of a Frenchman. The man Isabelle was with when I last saw her was English."

"What was his name?"

"I only know him as Sebastion," he answered truthfully. Neither Isabelle nor the man himself had even had the common decency to make a complete introduction. He knew only that Sebastion was the cousin of the murdered man.

Broussard frowned in annoyance. "I will have to look into this matter once I have taken care of . . . present concerns." He turned away from Reynaud and paced about the room with small, precise steps. "Where are they now?"

Reynaud shrugged. "I don't know. We didn't part on the best of terms." Both honest answers.

"You are trying my limited patience," Broussard warned. "I need those keys, Andrassy. I must get inside that chest."

"Couldn't you try to pry it open?" He was desperate to find a solution that would appease his host.

Broussard glowered at him. "That chest was fashioned by a master craftsman. There is no way to open it without causing irreparable damage, and that I will not do." He sighed. "I grow weary of this conversation. You cannot get the keys for me, so you are as useless to me as that locked chest."

A frisson of alarm raced up Reynaud's spine. If he

were no longer useful to the man, he knew his life was in jeopardy. "I can get the keys," he blurted out.

"How?"

"I can find the Englishman. As I told you, he has the keys."

"I can do that for myself," Broussard answered. "Just tell me where he and your stepsister are. I have some unfinished business with them as well."

Reynaud considered revealing where Isabelle and Sebastion could be found, but for some reason he held his tongue. He had already harmed his sister far more than she deserved, and he shuddered at the thought of her in Broussard's grasp. He remembered with revulsion the livid bruise on her cheek; surely even his own violence toward Isabelle paled in comparison. No, Reynaud thought, he would not give up their location to pacify his host. He doubted they were still where he had left them anyway. Sebastion did not strike him as the kind of man who sat around and waited for things to happen. He was the kind of man Reynaud had always wanted to be, a man who made his own destiny.

He would make his own destiny now. "No," Reynaud said softly, knowing that Broussard would likely kill him for his insolence.

This caught the man's attention. "No?" Broussard said incredulously. "You dare to tell me no?" He crossed to a mahogany writing desk and opened one of the drawers. In the next instant he was pointing a slender pistol at Reynaud. "You realize that I could easily kill you right now and no one would be the wiser."

"That's true," Reynaud conceded, "but then you might never find the keys. And you'd never be able to retrieve the chalice." He hoped fervently that the older man would agree with his reasoning.

Broussard laughed mockingly. "Do you think I would go to such trouble for a chalice? That cup is only part of the chest's value." He stepped from behind the desk, the gun in his hand still trained on Reynaud.

"Since you have sacrificed so much for my treasure, let me tell you a little story." As though this was an ordinary social visit, Broussard moved to a chair and took a seat, crossing his legs casually at the ankle. "My ancestor, Chretien, was a famous poet in the latter part of the twelfth century. One of his patrons, Philip of Flanders, asked him to put to verse a book about the Holy Grail. Chretian did so, and as a reward for his excellent work, Philip had a solid gold chalice made for him. It was an exquisite piece, and Chretian treasured it. He had a chest made especially for it that could only be opened using two keys simultaneously. After his death, the family kept the chest in a place of honor, and it was passed down to the eldest son of each generation."

"How did it end up in England?" Reynaud asked.

Broussard shot him a quelling look and continued. "Late in the sixteenth century one of the elder sons decided to leave Troyes and explore the world. He took the chalice with him and disappeared for many years. When he was a very old man he returned to what was left of his family, bringing the chest with him. He had no children of his own, so he passed the treasure on to the eldest son of his brother. On his deathbed he told his nephew that he had altered the chest by adding a small hollow compartment in which he had hidden a fortune in precious stones. The boy kept his uncle's secret, intending to tell his own son when the time was right. Unfortunately he waited too long. His son was a wastrel, given to gaming and drinking. Not knowing the real value of the heirloom, he wagered the chest and its contents in a game of chance, which he lost. When he returned home and confessed to his father what he had done, the man became enraged and told his son the secret. The boy tried to get the chest back, but the man who had won it was gone and could not be found. The boy killed himself that very day, but the family has never forgotten about the treasure. The story has been passed down to each generation in the hope that someday we might reclaim our prize." He smiled malevolently at Reynaud. "And after hundreds of years, I'm finally close to restoring the family's honor."

"I was glad to help the first time," Reynaud lied. "Now perhaps you'll allow me to assist you further by obtaining the keys for you."

Broussard shook his head. "Alas, my young friend, I am afraid I cannot do that. I am quite confident that I can get the keys myself; so you see, you have outlived your usefulness to me." He rose slowly.

Reynaud looked into the man's hard black eyes and saw only madness. Broussard was going to kill him in cold blood; he would die here, alone and without the comfort of a loved one. He closed his eyes and made a last desperate prayer for mercy; then he opened them to face his assassin.

"Good-bye, Reynaud," Broussard said softly and pulled the trigger with a smile on his face.

The bullet tore into Reynaud's chest, knocking him into the sofa behind him. He lay sprawled, half on the floor, half propped up against a striped satin cushion. His mind seemed to be working too slowly to comprehend what had happened. With a trembling hand he touched the spreading flower of blood that now decorated his coat. His fingers came away shiny with his own blood, and he stared at it in fascination.

Dimly he was aware of a disturbance outside the room, but the roaring in his own ears blocked out most sound. He had been shot and was dying. His stunned mind could scarcely process this realization, so abhorrent was it to him. His life would end in the home of a madman.

Reynaud closed his eyes and thought of his mother.

Chapter Twenty-three

In the east, the sky was beginning to lighten with the coming dawn. Sebastion recognized that he had reached Broussard's property. Skirting the main drive, he instead took the path that he and Isabelle had used to escape several days before. When he was safely hidden in the sheltering stand of trees, he dismounted and tethered the tired animal to a tree. Pulling his pistol from his waistband, he made his way stealthily toward the chateau.

He came upon the first guard at the edge of the copse. The man was standing with his back to Sebastion and did not hear him approach until it was almost too late. Not wanting to alert the rest of the henchmen with the noise of a shot, Sebastion was forced to disable his opponent with his fists.

A few minutes later he was standing at the kitchen entrance, his shirt splattered with blood from the unfortunate guard's broken nose. Brandishing his pistol he burst into the house and quickly scanned the room for adversaries. The kitchen staff stood rooted in their places, fear evident on every face. No guards were present here, just the cook and two scullery maids. Discounting the wide-eyed women as threats, he raised a finger to his lips and said, "Ssshh." One of the maids dropped to the floor in a dead faint.

Sebastion hurried through the now-silent kitchen and out into the rest of the house, making his way quickly but cautiously through the many rooms and passageways.

As he rounded yet another corner, a shot rang out. Sebastion cursed foully and ran to the closed set of doors where the sound had come from. Before he could open them, a guard, alerted by the shot, came running down the opposite passage. He raised his own weapon and fired at Sebastion. The bullet whizzed by Sebastion's ear, so close he could feel the heat of it. He fired back and hit the running guard squarely in the chest, killing him instantly.

With a howl of rage, Sebastion kicked open the heavy wooden door and bounded into the study. He saw Reynaud first, propped against the sofa legs, sprawled in a pool of his own blood. His eyes were closed, but they opened at the noise of Sebastion's entry. The dying man offered a wan smile. "You're too late," he said weakly, "he's already done the job for you."

"Monsieur Jourdain," Broussard sneered. "What a surprise to see you again."

Sebastion turned to address the older man. "A surprise," he conceded, "but not a pleasant one, I can promise you."

Broussard seemed to falter for a moment, then regained his superior attitude.

"What is your real name?" he almost purred. "I would like to know before I kill you."

Sebastion let his mouth curl into a hard smile. "You're very confident in your abilities, aren't you? Or do you plan to have one of your minions do the job?"

"Shut up," Broussard snapped angrily. "I asked you a question, now answer me."

Sebastion spoke slowly, clearly enunciating each word. "Sebastion Merrick. The Marquis of Kensington was my cousin."

Broussard paled but said nothing.

Sebastion continued. "You are familiar with the name, of course. He's the man you had murdered." He moved to the table that held the chest. "And the rightful owner of this pretty piece."

"That's a lie," Broussard shouted. "I'm the rightful owner. I merely reclaimed what was mine."

"By killing the legal owner?" Sebastion raised one eyebrow in challenge.

Broussard's hand shook with rage, and Sebastion feared he might pull the trigger in his agitation. "That was Andrassy's doing. I told him to take the chest, not to kill anyone."

"And if I don't believe you?"

"I don't care if you believe me or not," Broussard said defensively. "You will be dead soon anyway. You were foolish to come into my own home and threaten me."

Sebastion took a step toward him. "I've already killed two of your men and disabled another. Do you think I would hesitate to kill you as well?"

Broussard began to sweat visibly. Pulling his pistol closer to his body, he moved toward the door. "Randolph," he screamed, calling in vain for his manservant. "Randolph, where are you?" There was no response.

"Apparently your servants are not as loyal as you thought. You must not pay them enough to sacrifice their lives for yours."

This enraged the older man. With a cry of fury, he turned and leveled his weapon at Sebastion. "Then I'll kill you myself," he snarled and cocked the pistol. Just as he fired, Reynaud launched himself at Broussard from behind and buried his knife deep in his back. The shot went wide, easily missing its intended target. Broussard screamed in agony, clutching at his back in an anguished attempt to remove the protruding blade. Gasping for breath, he fell to his knees and then forward onto his chest. After a moment he was quiet.

Reynaud sank wearily to the ground beside the dead man. He was covered in blood and so weak that Sebastion wondered where he had found the strength to stand, let alone stab the other man. His breathing was labored, and Sebastion knew that his end was near.

"Why did you do it, Andrassy?" Sebastion asked.

Reynaud coughed feebly. "Not for you, English," he answered. "For Isabelle. To say I'm sorry." His pain-glazed eyes sought Sebastion's. "She loves you, you know."

Before he could respond, there was a commotion in the outer hallway, and a moment later Isabelle and a pistol-wielding Georges raced into the room. Isabelle came to a skidding halt just inside the doorway, gasping as she took in Sebastion's blood-spattered clothes. From where she stood she could not see the two bodies on the floor.

"Sebastion, you're hurt."

He held up a hand when she would have come to him. "It isn't my blood," he explained. "He is the one who needs you."

Isabelle turned then and saw Reynaud. A cry of horror rose in her throat at the sight of her stepbrother. It was obvious he was dying. She ran to him, dropping to her knees beside him, carefully averting her eyes from Broussard's prone form. "Reynaud, what happened?" she said with tears in her eyes. "We must get you to a doctor."

"It's too late for that," he answered. "Broussard shot me. I fear I'm done for." The effort to sit up was now too much for him, and he fell backward onto the blood-soaked carpet.

Isabelle pulled him up against her, cradling his head against her chest. "Don't say such things, Reynaud. We'll get you a doctor and you'll be as good as new." She rocked him gently as she spoke, tears sliding silently down her cheeks.

"I'm sorry for hurting you, Belle," he said. "I love you."

"I love you, too," she answered, her voice breaking. "Don't give up," she urged. "Please be strong just a little while longer."

Reynaud raised a trembling hand to touch her face. "You were always the strong one, not me." His hand dropped back to his side. "It's better this way."

"You're wrong," she whispered urgently. "Think of your mother, Reynaud. She needs you. I need you."

"You never were a very good liar, Belle." He struggled for breath. "English," he gasped.

"What about Sebastion?" she said.

His answer was so soft that she had to place her ear next to his mouth to make out the words. "Jewels . . . hidden in bottom of chest. That's what Broussard wanted. Tell him."

"I will," she assured him. "I promise."

Reynaud smiled then, and for a moment he was a little boy again. "Belle," he whispered softly, "tell my mother I love her." Then his eyelids fluttered closed and he was gone.

Isabelle shook him slightly. "Reynaud?" she said. "Reynaud, wake up. Please." She shook him again and his head dropped lifelessly backward. Without uttering a sound, Isabelle pulled him tightly against her chest and bowed her head, her body racked with silent sobs of grief. She sat that way for a long while, clutching her stepbrother's lifeless body to her own and weeping noiselessly. She wept for the boy he had been, always trying to please his distant stepfather and never succeeding, and for the man he'd grown into, who was always just one scheme away from prosperity. And she cried for the guilt she felt at her own part in his untimely end.

"I'm sorry," she whispered brokenly against his temple.

"Isabelle." Sebastion's voice broke gently into her mourning. "We need to get you away from here."

She looked up at him. "I won't leave him here alone," she vowed.

Reynaud was past caring about where he was, but Sebastion refrained from pointing that out. "I'll take care of him," he assured her, "but you need to go with Georges now." He held out a hand to her.

She studied his hand mutely for a moment, considering her course of action. Looking down at her sleeping brother, she gently brushed aside a stray lock of hair from his now placid forehead and placed a kiss against his brow. Reverently she laid him down upon the carpet and allowed Sebastion to help her to her feet. She took a few tentative steps, then glanced down at herself. Her pale dress was covered with Reynaud's blood, and she nearly fainted at the sight. She swayed unsteadily on her feet, and Sebastion was instantly at her side to support her.

Numbly she allowed herself to be led from the bloody scene. She was dimly aware of voices around her, but nothing penetrated the thick fog of grief that enveloped her. Except the comforting warmth of Sebastion's arms around her. She leaned heavily on him as he all but carried her from the house. The black coach was sitting where Georges had left it only a few moments before, and Sebastion helped her inside.

"Georges will take care of you," he explained, as though speaking to a child. "And I'll join you as soon as I can."

Isabelle did not respond. Her green eyes were tear-reddened and glazed with pain, and they seemed to stare right through him. She was a terrible sight, white with shock and covered with blood. Sebastion knew it was a picture that would haunt him for the rest of his life.

Chapter Twenty-four

The rest of the day passed in a blur for Isabelle. She was aware of all that went on around her, but she was strangely detached from it, as though she was watching a play. It was the character Isabelle who sat so forlornly in the coach while Georges drove her away from the Broussard chateau. It was this other Isabelle who allowed herself to be ushered inside the familiar inn of Madame Duvall, and who went to her room without speaking. It was this strange girl who lay on the bed staring into the air. She was very docile, this strange Isabelle, and she allowed Madame to bathe and change her. Afterward, she lay back down on the bed and was silent.

Sebastion found her that way many hours later when he stepped into the room. He was freshly bathed and shaven, and had changed from his bloodstained garments into clean ones. Georges had apprised him of Isabelle's nearly frozen state, so he was prepared for the vacant-eyed creature who greeted him. She lay stiff and straight on the bed, her hands folded neatly across her abdomen. It was rather disconcerting to note that she looked for all the world like a corpse laid out for burial. The last rays of the afternoon sun shone through the window, adding to the otherworldly feel of the room.

Sebastion sat on the bed beside her and took one of her cold hands in his. "Wake up, Sleeping Beauty," he teased softly.

It took a few minutes for his words to sink in, but finally she turned her wide green eyes to his. "Sebastion," she said faintly. "Tell me this is a bad dream."

He wished for her sake that he could, but it was better that she faced reality now. "No, I'm afraid it isn't." He stroked her hand idly with one thumb. "Do you remember what happened?"

She nodded dully. "Reynaud is dead. Broussard shot him."

"That's right," he said soothingly. "I'm sorry."

"I'm glad it wasn't you," she said in a choked voice. "I'm glad you weren't the one who did it." Her eyes found his. "Were you the one who killed Broussard?"

He shook his head. "No. Reynaud stabbed him just as he was about to shoot me." He tilted up her chin with one long finger. "Whatever else he was, he was brave at the end."

Isabelle's eyes welled with tears, but she did not cry. "Thank you for that," she whispered brokenly. She closed her eyes against the pain. "Will you please hold me?"

Sebastion raised his booted feet so that he was reclining fully on the bed; then he pulled her into the sheltering curve of his arms. She rested her head against the solid warmth of his chest, taking comfort in the steady thrum of his heart. Her arms wound tightly around his lean waist and she held him as if she'd never let him go.

She felt strangely empty inside, as though she was a hollow shell instead of a real person. In a way that was true. Isabelle Saint-Simon had effectively died on this day, and the person who lay here now was a new creation. She would never be able to return to her former way of life. Reynaud's death had shown her that. He had spent his entire life trying to live up to an impossible standard, and it had ultimately killed him. But she still had time to change her life. She didn't have to end up like that.

With a sigh she buried her head in the soft fabric of Sebastion's shirt, finding comfort in the very scent of him. She was exhausted from all her crying and worrying, and she just wanted to lie here safe in Sebastion's arms and not think of anything.

Sebastion began to idly rub a lock of Isabelle's hair between his thumb and forefinger, his thoughts revisiting the events of the last several days. Though he was not one given to examining his own feelings too closely, he did so now. All along he had wanted one thing, to find Jonathan's murderer and see him punished. In one respect he should be happy that he had been successful in tracking the man down. On the other hand, he had been denied the privilege of seeing the guilty party tried and convicted. Emil Broussard had acted as both judge and jury for the unfortunate Reynaud, taking the decision out of Sebastion's hands.

Sebastion should probably have felt cheated of his rightful day in court. Strangely, though, he found himself almost relieved that he had not been the one to cause the young man's demise. If he had succeeded in taking Reynaud back to England for trial, the Frenchman would have surely been sentenced to death for murdering a Peer of the Realm. Isabelle would have held Sebastion responsible for the outcome, no matter that Reynaud was guilty as charged. Yes, in a way Broussard had taken a burden off of him, although Sebastion would have given anything to spare Isabelle the grizzly sight of Reynaud dying in her arms.

As if sensing her place in his thoughts, Isabelle

shifted against him, her soft voice stirring him from his silent reverie. "I'm sorry," she said, her voice slightly muffled against the wall of his chest.

"For what?"

She raised her head and looked up at him, and Sebastion was relieved to see that vacant look gone from her eyes. "You were right about Reynaud all along, and I wouldn't believe you. I'm sorry for that, and for your loss. I hope you can forgive me and my family for all the harm we have done to you and yours."

Sebastion tipped her chin up with one long finger. "Thank you for that, but you don't ever need to apologize to me. You and your family were not responsible for Reynaud's actions."

Isabelle closed her eyes briefly, seeing once again her stepbrother's face and hearing his dying words.

His mother would be beside herself with grief, that much she knew. For all her faults, Helene Saint-Simon had loved her only son. His death would be a harsh blow to her. She wondered if her father would even care that his stepson was dead.

"What did you do with the body?" she asked abruptly.

"Isabelle . . ." Sebastion began, his voice wary.

"Don't try to spare my feelings. I want to know where he is because I owe it to his mother to take him home for a proper burial."

"I've made arrangements for that."

"What about Broussard?" she asked.

Sebastion sighed. "That's all been taken care of. The authorities have been notified and everything is all right." He offered a reassuring smile. "You don't need to worry about a thing."

"I can't help it," she admitted. "That is all I've been doing for days and days." Her voice caught on a sob as she was assaulted by a fresh wave of grief. "I don't know how I'll occupy my time from now on."

Sebastion wiped a tear from her cheek and stroked

her hair tenderly back from her forehead. "You can go home now," he said, wishing he had never subjected her to this pain. If he had let her leave when she wanted to her stepbrother might still be alive and she would be at home with her fiancé, where she belonged. But the thought of Isabelle pledging her life to another man filled him with dispair. He knew that he didn't have the right to feel that way, but he couldn't help it. Isabelle was his, whether he gave her his name or not. She was his, but he could never truly have her because he had a responsibility to his family. After all the things he had done to her, he couldn't very well ask her to give up her life, leave her homeland and follow him to an uncertain future. It would be many years until either of Jonathan's sons could take over the running of the estates. How could he ask Isabelle to live in someone else's house, not even to be mistress of her own home? No, he wouldn't ask her to give up so much for so little. He felt that he had so little to offer those he cared for, but at least he could pay his debt to the Larrimore family. And if that meant giving up his own happiness, that was a sacrifice he would have to make.

Her next words weakened his resolve. "What if I told you that I didn't want to go home?" she queried softly.

"I wouldn't believe you," he answered. "You've been begging me to take you home since that first day." He didn't like the tone of her question and he prayed that she would let the matter drop. She might feel that way now, when she was upset and not herself, but one day she would certainly regret giving up her home for him.

She didn't. "I've changed my mind. I want to stay with you."

He refused to look at her, knowing that if he did, he wouldn't be able to resist what she was unconsciously offering. "You're upset right now," he said in what he hoped was a reasonable tone. "That's understandable, but you don't know what you're saying."

She placed her hands on either side of his face and

forced him to look at her. He knew what she was going to say even before her lips moved, saw the truth of it shining in her bright eyes. "I'm saying that I love you," she whispered. "I didn't want to, but I do."

I love you. Such simple words, but such powerful ones. Sebastion's first impulse was to deny them, to fling them back in her face and make her recant them. She couldn't love him. He had kidnapped her and dragged her across the countryside on a quest that had ended in her brother's death. How could she love him?

"You don't love me," he said before he could stop himself.

Isabelle would not be dissuaded. "Yes, I do," she answered with resignation. "And I understand that you don't share my feelings."

Irrational anger flooded through him. She was making him yearn for what he could never have, and part of him wanted to hurt her as she was unknowingly hurting him. Sebastion grabbed her wrists and forced her hands away from his face. "I don't want your love," he ground out savagely. "I don't need it." He felt as though he were fighting a battle with her and he couldn't let her win. Because no matter how she felt, no matter how he felt, they could not be together.

"Everyone needs to be loved, Sebastion. Even you." She smiled tenderly at him. "I'm not asking for anything in return. I just wanted you to know."

He grabbed her upper arms and shook her once for emphasis. "You look at me with those yearning green eyes and tell me you're not asking for anything. You're asking for everything," he said fiercely, "and I can't give it to you."

"I don't know how to feel what you want me to. You have a life here and I took you away from it. The only honorable thing I can do is give it back now."

Isabelle shook her head mutely, tears making silent tracks on her pale cheeks. *I have nothing without you,* she wanted to say, but did not. She couldn't make him love her, though she felt in her heart that he *must* have feelings for her, he must love her in *some* way. "It isn't yours to give back," she told him sadly.

With a growl he pulled her roughly to him. "Then this is all I can give you." He captured her mouth in a passionate kiss.

She tried to speak, but his tongue delved between her teeth, effectively silencing her. He didn't want her to talk anymore, to tell him of her love. He wanted only to possess her in the one way he could—by taking her lovely body and claiming it as his own.

Isabelle reveled in the feel of his lips on hers. She offered a little moan of surrender, of her heart as well as her body. It frightened her, this laying bare of her feelings, but she wanted him too much to deny herself. She wanted to give herself to him. Where she should have felt shame at her actions she felt only a deep sense of rightness. Whatever else happened in her life, she knew that for this one night she and Sebastion belonged together.

Sebastion's mouth pulled reluctantly away from Isabelle's. As much as he might want her, he needed to be sure she understood that this time there would be no turning back. Once he started loving her he wasn't sure he would be able to pull away. "Tell me that you want me," he said. "Give me the right to take you." His eyes caught and held hers. If she turned him away, he would stop. Though it might kill him, he would let her go.

Isabelle was almost frightened by the intensity of his gaze, but she could no more have denied him than she could have stopped breathing. He was angry with her for declaring her love. He had even thrown her offering back in her face, but whatever their past had been and whatever their future might be, she would always have this to remember. "Yes," she answered, knowing that she was sealing her fate. "I want you."

He kissed her again, so sweetly that she thought she

might weep from it. With his mouth and hands he told her what his mind could not. He poured out his emotions for her in every touch, every stroke, every caress. *With my body, I thee worship.* The line came unbidden into her mind, but she realized that that was how to describe his actions. He was worshiping her with his body. And that more than any spoken words told her of his true feelings.

She felt his weight shift, and then he was no longer kissing her. She whimpered in protest, eager to feel his lips once again on hers. Dazed with passion, she opened her eyes to find him staring down at her.

"I want to see you," he rasped. "Will you undress for me?"

Her heart began to hammer wildly in her breast, and she felt a warmth spread from her stomach to the tips of her toes. She knew that she should be embarrassed, but only desire coursed through her at his request. She couldn't imagine anything more erotic than stripping in front of this man. She rose on unsteady feet and began to unfasten her dress.

"Take down your hair," he ordered in a low voice. She complied, letting the long golden locks free from their confining pins. With visibly trembling fingers she continued to disrobe, slipping off her thin summer dress to reveal the fine white linen undergarments beneath. Sebastion sucked in his breath at the sight. She was more beautiful than he had dared dream, with a narrow waist and long, slender legs. The light corset she wore further enhanced her figure, lifting her breasts provocatively. He had to restrain himself from tearing the remaining clothes from her.

Suddenly self-conscious under his intense scrutiny, Isabelle fumbled with the ties of her corset for a few seconds before the knots would come undone. Once the binding material was off, she quickly shed her other garments, glad that Madame had not made her put on stockings. When she was completely nude, she stood uncertainly before him, refusing to meet his gaze.

Immediately Sebastion went to her, tipping her head up so that she was forced to look at him. "You are truly beautiful," he whispered. He took her hand and placed it against his chest. "Feel what you do to me." Beneath her hand his heart beat in a frantic tattoo, telling her that he was just as affected as she. She smiled then, a shy, uncertain grin that went straight to his heart. That this perfect, beautiful woman had given him her heart and was now willing to give him her body was almost beyond comprehension. Nothing he had ever done in his life was good enough to deserve this.

Sebastion reached out tentatively and touched her breast, and Isabelle caught her breath at the sensation. Gently he cupped the delicate mound in his palm, kneading it lightly while pulling her to him with his other hand. The sensation of his clothes abrading her naked flesh was strange to her, but she soon forgot everything but the feeling of his hands on her breasts and his lips on her mouth.

Bending low, Sebastion scooped her up in his arms and carried her to the bed, placing her gently on the counterpane. With hooded eyes she watched as he undressed. She did not look away, too curious and eager for the sight of him. When he was naked, he stood before her, a magnificent creature she could scarcely believe was real. She had seen him unclothed while he was ill, but that was a far cry from his present condition. Even in her most secret dreams she could not have imagined such a glorious sight as the man before her. He was powerfully built and sleekly muscled, from his broad shoulders to his lean waist to his long, corded legs. Her eyes strayed to the raven nest of hair surrounding his swollen manhood. She felt a moment's uncertainty at the sight. His aroused male body was so different from her own, and its very strangeness frightened her.

Slowly he walked toward the bed, and Isabelle

looked up at him with a mixture of yearning and apprehension. He sank onto the bed beside her, stretching out on his side, his head propped up on one hand. He smiled reassuringly at her, but she could see the fire of his need burning brightly in his ghostly blue eyes. "Isabelle," he said softly, "do you remember that night at the town house? How you felt when I touched you?"

Her body grew flushed at the memory his words triggered. She nodded.

"It felt good, didn't it?" he asked even more softly. She nodded again, not certain that she could speak. His low-timbered voice was doing strange things to her insides. "It will feel even better this time," he promised, a slow, sexy grin spreading across his face.

"How can it?" she asked breathlessly, remembering the explosion of sensation that had ripped through her body. Sebastion rolled his upper torso onto hers. "I'll show you," he promised. And he did.

He began slowly, tracing her features with his fingers. Her eyebrow, her cheekbone, her lips. His mouth brushed tenderly against the fading bruise that she knew still marred her cheek. Then his hands moved lower to caress her swollen breasts. He teased the delicate rose-colored nipples with his thumbs, massaging them in slow, sensuous circles. He shifted lower and began to trace a path down her body with his moist, seeking mouth. He missed nothing in his downward journey, kissing and touching every cut, scrape and bruise that marked her delicate flesh as though trying to heal them with his touch. Isabelle moaned in pleasure and threaded her hands through his midnight-hued locks. She breathed his name like a plea, turning her head from side to side in mindless abandon.

When his mouth began to descend even lower, she thought her heart might burst in her breast. Before she could utter a protest, his lips had found the most intimate part of her, and he kissed her there as well. Her body responded instantly, gripping her in a paroxysm of such intensity she thought she might die. She writhed beneath him, making animal sounds of pleasure deep in her throat. When at last it was over, she lay panting and flushed beneath him.

"You were right," she said faintly.

Sebastion grinned wickedly at her. "We haven't even started yet," he said, sliding back up her damp body. She groaned. He captured her mouth in another breathtaking kiss, and she tasted the musky flavor of her passion on his lips. He moved his body more fully over hers, and she could feel the hard, hot length of him pressing against her thigh. With one seeking hand, he reached down to tease the damp blond curls between her legs. Her body arched instinctively toward his hand as he caressed her more intimately. Long fingers stroked the tender flesh hidden there, and she twisted beneath his hand, her hands gripping the tangled counterpane beneath her. Ever so slowly, Sebastion slid one finger into her welcoming warmth, then another, moving them in and out in a rhythm that caused the now familiar tension to build within her.

He increased the rhythm, sliding erotically across the sensitive flesh until she was nearly mindless with the pleasure of it all. And then he shifted, and settled between her thighs, the tip of his manhood nudging her moist curls. Her eyes met his as he began to lower himself into her, filling her throbbing flesh with his own. She felt a strange pressure as her body stretched and expanded to accommodate his length, and she was startled to feel pain. Instinctively she tensed and tried to move away from the source of her discomfort.

"Ssh," he soothed. "Just trust me." He stilled his movements, letting her body become accustomed to the size of him. Then he eased out of her, almost to the tip, before thrusting once again into her tight sheath. Sebastion tried to go slowly for her benefit, but his need was so great that he couldn't stop himself from increasing the rhythm and intensity of his thrusts. Isabelle was so tight and wet around him that it was all he could do not to find the release he so urgently sought.

Beneath him Isabelle once again felt the all-encompassing pressure begin to mount. Sebastion filled her so fully that it took her breath away. Without realizing that she did so, she wrapped her legs tightly around him, forcing him even deeper within her. Her fingers curled into claws and she scratched and pawed at his back with frantic movements. Once again her body convulsed with the ultimate satisfaction and she screamed with the pleasure and pain. Sebastion's hoarse cry mingled with her own as he drove into her one last time, convulsing in a spasm that shook his entire body.

They lay together for a long while, their bodies still intimately joined. Finally, Sebastion rolled onto his back and pulled Isabelle securely into the crook of his arm. She draped one arm and leg languidly across his body and rested her head atop his chest. Sebastion's heart thrummed solidly beneath her ear, reassuring in its steady rhythm. Drained from the day's events and her glorious introduction to lovemaking, Isabelle was lulled to sleep by the comforting cadence. As she drifted off, she murmured softly, "I love you."

Sebastion stared up at the ceiling with troubled eyes. He should have felt satisfaction at finally sating his lust for the sleeping woman in his arms, but instead he felt strangely bereft. Isabelle had declared her love for him, had given herself unreservedly to him; why did he feel so empty inside? Why did his future stretch before him so bleakly?

Because no matter what she might feel toward him, Isabelle could never be his. It wouldn't be fair to ask Isabelle to leave her home for life as a guest in someone else's house. She deserved a home of her own where she was its mistress. Sebastion couldn't imagine Isabelle sitting idly by as the Dowager and Melanie ran the household. No, Isabelle would hate that.

A Treasure to Hold

And even if they could live away from the manor, what did he really have to offer her as a husband? His parents' ill-fated union had certainly been a poor example of what a marriage should be, and it had showed him that love had the power to wound. Love made a person vulnerable, and he never wanted to feel that way again in his life. No, it was better to end this with Isabelle right now, while he could still find the strength to leave her. She would be better off without him, anyway. She would marry and have a family, and he would pay back his Uncle Richard's kindness by taking care of the remaining Larrimores.

His fate had been sealed the night Jonathan Larrimore died, and probably even before that. He owed a debt to the family that he could never truly repay, but he would do all in his power to try. Jonathan's widow would need him to look after her and her two small sons, at least until they were old enough to assume the responsibilities of the estate. Sebastion would have to take care of them all, just as Jonathan's father had taken care of him when his mother had been unable to. Richard Larrimore could have turned his back on them and none would have faulted him for it. But he hadn't, and for that reason Sebastion was forever indebted to the Marquis of Kensington.

Beside him, Isabelle stirred in her sleep, snuggling even closer to him. He looked down at her, so young and beautiful in repose. And he felt a weight settle painfully on his chest. He had taken her body in need and want, and she had given herself freely. She had given him her love, but that was a gift he could not keep. He had made a promise that he would look after Jonathan's family, and he would fulfill that promise. Even if it meant he would lose the greatest joy he had ever known.

It was a long time before he slept, and when he did he dreamt of all those he had lost. His parents. Uncle Richard. Jonathan. Isabelle. And the last was the greatest loss of all.

Chapter Twenty-five

The street lamps glowed dully in the evening gloom as night descended on Paris two days later. A pair of travel-weary horses led a dark, dust-covered carriage through the almost deserted streets. Inside the conveyance Isabelle sat beside Sebastion, her head resting on his shoulder as she dozed fitfully. They had spoken little on this last leg of their journey, neither one wanting to disturb the false calm that had descended upon them after their one night together. For the rest of the trip they had slept in separate rooms.

The coach pulled to a stop. Sebastion gently shook his companion. "Wake up, love. We're here."

Isabelle raised her head, blinking tiredly in the dimness. She stifled a yawn behind a slender gloved hand and lifted the shade to peer out the window. Her grandmother's house stood before her, nearly every window in the residence lit. She felt a sinking sensation in her stomach at the thought of facing the people within. There was no doubt in her mind that her grandmother had come to the city as soon as Isabelle disappeared, and her father and stepmother might have joined the older woman in her vigil. Letting the cloth fall back into place, Isabelle leaned back in the seat but made no move to exit the coach.

She admitted to herself that she didn't want to leave the shadowy confines of the carriage. Once outside the vehicle she would have to face questions and accusations and tears. And she would have to face her old life and the fact that she no longer could live that way. She wasn't the same girl who had come to the city a little more than a fortnight ago. It amazed her to think of all that had happened in such a short span of time. She had been kidnapped, threatened and abused, rescued and redeemed. And she had given herself body and soul to a man who had promised her nothing in return.

It would be easy to blame Sebastion for all of her troubles, but she knew he had been honest with her from the start. He had always planned to return to England and his family; it wasn't his fault that she had fallen in love with him. And she couldn't blame him for taking her virginity, for she had given it to him as a gift. How could she regret something that had given her so much pleasure? She couldn't. She would remember that night for the rest of her life, and comfort herself with the knowledge that for a few hours Sebastion had truly been hers.

Still, she couldn't help the feeling of bitterness that rose in her when she thought of never seeing him again. They had been together almost constantly and he was now such a part of her life that she could scarcely imagine how she had existed before she met him.

"Isabelle," Sebastion prompted gently.

She glared up at him, hurt that he was so eager to see her go. "I didn't realize you were in such a hurry to see the last of me," she bit out. Tears of anger and hurt glittered on her lashes. Despite her resolve to part amicably, she was letting her emotions get the better of her.

Sebastion took her hand in his, pulling her toward him. "You know that's not true."

"Do I?" she countered, blinking furiously at the hated tears. She had always disliked crying in front of others, but lately that was all she seemed to do. Unbidden, two salty tracks ran down her cheeks.

Sebastion reached out and wiped away the evidence of her sadness with his thumbs, his fingers bracketing her face on either side. "Don't cry, my beauty," he whispered. He felt faintly ill at the sight of her tears, and he closed his eyes in desperation, wanting to hide from the raw pain he knew he had caused. It was all he could do not to take her away from this brightly lit house, from this city, and claim her as his own forever. He felt as though his heart were being ripped from his chest. He wasn't sure if he was strong enough to let her go. He wished that he could say the words she longed to hear, but they lodged in his throat, sticking there like a bitter pill.

Isabelle's tears flowed freely now, silent and heartrending. She was so full of hurt that she couldn't have stopped them if she tried, and she was beyond the point of caring. Sebastion was leaving her, and she felt as if her heart must surely be breaking. She wanted to beg him to stay with her, to forget his obligations in England and make a new home with her. To love her as she so desperately loved him. She looked up at him, so still and silent beside her, and her breath caught in her throat at the longing and desire she saw reflected in his startling blue eyes. At least she could be comforted by the fact that he wanted her as much as she wanted him. Though she knew that nothing had changed. He was bound by his honor and nothing, not even her love for him, would alter that.

She had always known that his family came first; why did it hurt so much to see the proof? Because deep down she had hoped that he might love her enough to change his mind. If only he had said he loved her, she would have done anything for him. He said that he was giving her life back, but she would gladly leave it all behind again to start a new life with him. He could have her and his family too. If only he had asked. The fact that he didn't wounded her more than any blow ever could. He simply didn't love her enough, and she would have to carry that knowledge with her for the rest of her life. For she knew as she looked into his handsome face she would never forget him. And never stop loving him. As long as she lived.

"I have to go," she said, suddenly anxious to distance herself from him. Delaying the inevitable would only cause her more grief. She placed an unsteady hand on the door.

Sebastion reached out and covered the hand with his own. "Isabelle," he said bleakly. He stopped then, unable to speak the words that would bring her back to him. It would be so easy for him to show her how he felt, take her in his arms and claim her, as he wanted to. But he was not free to have her, and it would be unfair to both of them to make false promises. Whatever else he had done to her, he had never lied. There was nothing for it but that he would have to let her go.

She placed her other hand over his, cradling his fingers between her own. Slowly she brought them up to her face and placed his palm against her cheek. "You are a very special man, Sebastion Merrick, don't ever forget that," she said tenderly. "And when you're old and gray, remember that there was once someone who loved you dearly." She leaned forward and brushed her trembling lips across his. "Good-bye," she whispered and opened the coach door.

He pulled it shut again. "I'm going in with you," he said evenly.

Isabelle shook her head. "No. It will be easier if I go alone." The last thing she wanted was for her family to see Sebastion. One look at the two of them together and surely her relatives would be able to see the feelings she had for him. "My family can be quite difficult."

Sebastion held firm. "Nevertheless, I will accompany you. I won't let you face this alone."

Seeing that he was adamant, Isabelle acquiesced and allowed him to leave the carriage first so that he could help her down. Georges was waiting for them beside the coach, Isabelle's small trunk at his feet.

The next few minutes were a blur of activity as Isabelle and Sebastion were admitted to the stately Parisian home of Delphine du Vallon, amid much excitement and uproar. As Isabelle had expected, her grandmother had made the trip into the city from her country estate. Victor and Helene Saint-Simon were also present, having come for the evening from their own home, which was located a little over a mile away. Unlike the overcrowded center of the city, this section of Paris, inhabited by the aristocracy, was sparsely populated and consisted of many great open fields. Only the oldest and most wealthy of families could afford to live here, a stark contrast to the cramped and narrow quarters of the less fortunate Parisians.

Sebastion paid little attention to the opulence of his surroundings, focusing instead on the occupants of the house and their reactions to Isabelle. Isabelle's grandmother was the first to greet her. She was a slender woman of small stature, but her proud carriage gave her the illusion of greater height. Her hair was silver and pulled back in a modest chignon, the simple style an attractive foil to her bright green eyes, so like Isabelle's. She rushed to her granddaughter the moment she stepped into the room.

"Isabelle, thank the Lord you are here," she said. "We have been so worried about you! Where have you been?" She moved to embrace the younger woman, but stopped as she drew close enough to get a clear view of her. "What happened to your lovely face? It looks as though someone struck you." Gently she reached up to touch the yellowed bruise. "And you're covered with scratches," she said in dismay, placing a comforting arm around the girl's shoulders.

"I'm all right, Grandmama," Isabelle murmured, suddenly tired. "I'll explain it all later."

"You'll explain it now," said a stern voice.

Isabelle and Sebastion both looked up. Delphine stiffened but did not turn toward the person who spoke.

"Father," Isabelle said faintly.

Delphine bristled. "Victor, leave my granddaughter alone. Can't you see that she has been through an ordeal?" She frowned and pursed her lips in displeasure.

Victor was not to be deterred. "Who are you?" he demanded baldly of Sebastion as he strode across the room. A slender middle-aged woman followed meekly in his wake.

Sebastion regarded the man coldly, instantly disliking his haughty demeanor. Victor Saint-Simon was of average height and build. His dark hair was cut short in the current style and his face was clean-shaven. Dark eyes peered out from beneath heavy brows that were drawn into what seemed to be a perpetual scowl.

"My name is Sebastion Merrick," he answered coldly, his manner bordering on condescension.

Victor's scowl deepened at the response, but before he could reply his wife spoke up timidly. "Victor, perhaps we should let them sit down before we start questioning them."

Victor nodded curtly to his wife, obviously only acquiescing for the moment.

Delphine led Isabelle to a richly upholstered sofa where the two women sat down side by side. Victor and Helene followed suit, choosing a matching pair of chairs that faced the sofa. Sebastion remained standing.

"Now, suppose you tell us where you've been, young lady," Victor began. "Your unexpected and unexplained absence has caused us all a great deal of distress. I hope you have a good excuse for all the trouble you've caused."

Isabelle had to bite her tongue to keep from making a sarcastic comment to her father. He hadn't been concerned about her, just about how her actions might affect the Saint-Simon name. In deference to her grandmother and stepmother she was respectful.

"It is a long story," she said, "but let me first start by apologizing to Grandmama for lying." She turned to address her grandmother. "I didn't come to the city to look at patterns for my wedding gown," she confessed. "I came because I received a note from Reynaud telling me that he was in trouble and asking me to help."

Delphine patted the young woman comfortingly on her clasped hands. "I understand, my dear."

Victor's voice cut harshly into the conversation. "I should have known Reynaud was involved in this. What has that feckless boy done now? And why were you and this Englishman involved?"

Isabelle's fingers clenched into fists on her lap. "How dare you . . ." she began, but Sebastion cut her off.

"Your son was involved in some trouble that concerned one of my relatives," he explained. "When I went to find Reynaud, I met Isabelle, and I rather insisted that she help me locate her stepbrother."

Isabelle stared up at Sebastion in surprise. He was glossing over the entire story to spare her family. He hadn't mentioned the theft or the murder, or even the gambling debt that her stepbrother had incurred. And he was doing it all for her, she knew. But it wasn't right. As little as she wanted to cause her stepmother additional suffering, she knew that her family needed to know the whole truth. As painful as it might be.

"Sebastion is kindly trying to spare your feelings," she said. "The truth is not so pleasant as he has made it seem."

Beside her Delphine squeezed her hands. "What is the truth, my dear? It's better that we know."

As dispassionately as possible, Isabelle told them the story. When she got to the part about how Reynaud had threatened to kill her and tried to kidnap her, she didn't have the heart to tell them. She merely said that he had escaped. Her eyes filled with tears as she recounted her stepbrother's attempts to satisfy his debt and how he had ultimately saved Sebastion's life. Her voice broke on a sob as she looked into her stepmother's eyes and told her that Reynaud was dead.

"He asked me to tell you that he loved you, Helene," she said in a strangled voice. "Those were his last words. I'm so sorry."

Her stepmother's eyes had widened with each word, and they were now glazed over in shock. A low, keening sound came from her throat that was almost too terrible to bear. Suddenly her face crumbled as the full impact of the words hit her. She doubled over and began to cry, great racking sobs that shook her entire body. Victor sat not more than three feet away from her, regarding her strangely, as though he couldn't quite believe what he was seeing.

When Victor made no move to comfort his wife, Delphine went to the weeping woman and placed a consoling arm around her. Uttering kind words of sympathy, she led the younger woman out of the room. After a few minutes the sound of Helene's anguish faded away into silence.

Isabelle regarded her father through tear-spiked lashes, waiting to see if he would eventually go after his wife. She doubted it, for he found all emotional displays to be distasteful. The object of her scrutiny turned to address Sebastion. "I would like to know of your intentions concerning this matter," he said stiffly. "Do you intend to name my stepson as a thief and murderer? Or can I persuade you to be discreet?" He cleared his throat. "I don't need to tell you that it would be extremely embarrassing for my family to have such personal matters become public knowledge."

Sebastion's face hardened into a mask of dislike. "I won't honor that remark with a response. Perhaps you should be more concerned about your wife and the fact that she has lost her son than about saving face. As far as I can see, you do more damage to your own good name than your stepson could have done in a lifetime."

Victor shot out of the chair, outraged. His face was so red that Isabelle feared he might have an attack of some kind. "How dare you speak to me in such a manner?" he sputtered. "My family is one of the oldest and most respected in all of France. I should call you out for such an insult."

"Stop it, Father," Isabelle cried. "You've done enough harm already."

Victor was obviously stunned at his daughter's outburst. "Isabelle," he said in bewilderment. "What has gotten into you? You cannot speak that way to your father."

Isabelle stood and faced him squarely. "I can speak to you any way I choose. And right now I choose to tell you that I am ashamed of you. You have spent your whole life bullying people and using the Saint-Simon name as a club to beat people into submission. I didn't realize until recently that I had been taught to do the same thing, but someone showed me how wrong I was. It isn't what your name is that counts, it's what you do and how you treat others." She pointed a finger accusingly at him. "If you hadn't made Reynaud feel so unworthy, perhaps he might still be alive today. Nothing that he ever did was good enough for you. All he wanted was your love and acceptance, but you denied him even that."

"Are you trying to hold me responsible for his disgraceful behavior? Well, I won't have it!" her father shouted. "And you are certainly in no position to place blame on others. Your actions have been reprehensible, traipsing about the countryside with a strange man. And it was you who led him to Reynaud, may I remind you. Before you start pointing your finger at others you'd best remember that." He lowered his voice, suddenly mindful that he was shouting. "You have behaved shamefully. If this gets out, Henri Lanoux will never marry you."

Isabelle wrapped her arms around her middle. "That is a good thing, because I no longer want to marry him," she said in a raw voice.

Victor regarded her coldly for the space of several heartbeats. "I never thought I would live to see the day that a daughter of mine would show such disrespect. I have nothing more to say to you," he said harshly and walked out of the room.

"I'm sorry you had to witness that," Isabelle said softly to Sebastion. "I did try to warn you, though." Her knees started to wobble beneath her and she thought fleetingly that she might collapse. She managed to lower herself back onto the sofa. Sebastion came and sat down beside her, taking her now cold hands in his own.

"I've seen worse," he said.

She almost smiled at that. "How is it that you can make me laugh when I want to cry? And why is it that I want to cry all the time lately?"

Sebastion smiled gently down at her, smoothing an errant gold lock with one hand. "It must be my charming personality," he answered, pulling her into a comforting embrace. "I'm sure you'll be glad to be rid of me."

She shook her head sadly. "No, I won't." She sniffed slightly. "But I do think you should go now." Her arms tightened around his waist briefly before she released him. "I think it would be best."

Sebastion rose to his feet. "I'll come back in the morning to see you."

She nodded, though she had no intention of being

here. She had said her farewell to this man and she couldn't bear to say another one. It would be too painful. "Good-bye," she said, offering a tender smile.

"I'll see you tomorrow," he said before turning toward the door.

"Tomorrow," she echoed. And wished fervently that the hateful day would never come.

Chapter Twenty-six

It was autumn, and one of those rare days when the sky was so blue it hurt the eyes to look at it. The air was crisp and clear, just cool enough to hint at winter winds that were not far behind. A beautiful day. Sebastion reined his horse to a halt at the top of a rolling hill and stared at the picturesque landscape below. From this vantage point he could easily survey the Kensington lands and the village farther off in the distance. It should have given him a sense of pride to see how well the estate had been maintained. Instead he felt only the weight of obligation.

How quickly he had settled into the role of overseeing the lands since his return almost three months earlier. He had been welcomed warmly upon his arrival, and praised for finding the answers that had plagued the family since Jonathan's murder. The Kensington women had been sympathetic to Reynaud's ultimate plight, but they were also quietly satisfied to have been vindicated. Sebastion had mentioned Isabelle only briefly, greatly downplaying her role in the affair. He hadn't wanted to tell his family about her, afraid that he might give away his feelings for her if he so much as spoke her name.

After discussing the subject at great length with Henrietta and Melanie, Sebastion had decided to donate the chest and chalice to a museum. He did not mention the concealed jewels Isabelle had told him about. It was best to leave them where they had been for so many years. It was for want of them that Broussard had ordered the chest stolen, and Sebastion thought that they had caused enough trouble for one lifetime. Someday perhaps their hiding place would be discovered, though he doubted it. Having them in the museum, where they should have been all along, seemed a fitting end to the story.

As for Sebastion's responsibilities to the family, Henrietta and Melanie had been only too glad to hand over control to him, letting him make all the decisions and take care of them. He told himself that this was what he wanted; to be able to repay the family in some way for the debt he felt he owed. And if he knew that something elemental was missing from his existence, he hid it well. He played his role to perfection, always politely solicitous and kind to the women, patient and watchful of Jonathan's young sons.

He didn't know how much longer he could keep up the facade. Each evening during his first month back, he sat up drinking after the women had retired until he dulled the sharp pain left by his separation from Isabelle. When that stopped working, he took to riding late into the night so that he didn't have to sleep and dream of a golden-haired French girl. The strain of too many sleepless nights was starting to tell on him, and he wondered how much more he could take.

Part of him wanted to tell Melanie that he couldn't stay, that he loved another and had to be with her. But then he would pass by a portrait of Richard or Jonathan, and he would be reminded all over again of why

A Treasure to Hold

he remained. He owed a debt of honor, and if repaying it meant sacrificing his own happiness, he supposed that was the price he had to pay.

Behind him he heard the sound of a rider approaching, and he turned to see Melanie hail him smilingly. He returned the smile with genuine affection, for he really did care about her. But he feared that his feelings of friendship would lessen as resentment built. It wasn't her fault that he had to stay, but sometimes it felt that way.

Melanie cantered up to him on her pretty chestnut mare. She was a vision of English beauty, even in the somber black of widowhood. Her riding habit was plain, with no hint of adornment, as befit deep mourning. She had loved her husband dearly and wore her widow's weeds with true devotion.

Today her mood was light, matching the glorious autumn day. Sebastion helped her dismount; then they both returned to his chosen spot. Melanie looked out at all the land that her son now owned and smiled. "It's lovely, isn't it?" she said. "You've done a wonderful job managing things."

Sebastion made a gruff sound deep in his throat but didn't respond. She hadn't really expected that he would. Melanie peered up at him through veiled lashes, studying his handsome but stern profile. He was truly beautiful, if such a thing could be said of a man. And it wasn't just his outer self that made him so attractive. Inside he was a good human being, though at times she wondered if he himself was aware of that fact.

He was also desperately unhappy. Oh, he hid it quite well, but she could tell. Several times she had glimpsed his face when he was unaware of being watched, and the sadness there had nearly broken her heart. He was a proud man, though, and she was loath to bring up the subject. If she were to be honest with herself, she would have to admit that she hadn't wanted to discuss

293

it. Somehow she knew that whatever it was would take Sebastion away from them, and she was selfish enough to not want that to happen. It was nice having a man to take care of business matters and all the other hundreds of things the Marquis of Kensington had to oversee. Jonathan had never bothered her with the details, but she knew that it was a full-time concern, even with competent advisers. James Sebastion, her oldest son, was now the marquis, but he was only four and years away from being able to fulfil his obligations.

That left Sebastion. He was intelligent and shrewd at business, fair and honest, and with him around she didn't have to concern herself with anything more challenging than planning the dinner menus with Henrietta. Lately she had begun to realize how unfair it all was to him. It really wasn't his responsibility to take care of them. Why should he have to give up his own life for them? He shouldn't. Henrietta had said as much to her the previous week. At the time Melanie had been quite put out with her mother-in-law, but she had started thinking that perhaps the older woman was right. She was allowing him to forfeit his happiness to serve her comfort. That didn't sit well with her, and she had been struggling with her conscience for days now. Finally, this morning, she had decided that she would confront him with her suspicions. And if she discovered that he truly wanted to leave, she would have to be brave and let him go.

She continued staring out over the landscape, not bold enough to look him in the eye. "If I asked you something, would you be honest with me?" she queried hesitantly.

Sebastion was startled at her request. "I'm always honest with you," he said, a little irritated that she would question his integrity.

Melanie forged ahead. "Are you happy here?" She turned to gaze at him. "And I don't want you to tell me some nice little fib to spare my feelings."

He searched for the right words. "I'm glad that I can be of help to you and the dowager," he said carefully.

She sighed in frustration. "That is not an acceptable answer. Let me put it another way. If you could be anywhere in the world right now, where would you be?"

"With Isabelle," he said before he could stop himself.

Melanie smiled with satisfaction. "Ah, now we're getting somewhere. Who is Isabelle?" A few moments ago she would have been afraid to hear the answer, but now that she had seen his expression when he said the unknown woman's name, she couldn't deny him any longer. Jonathan wouldn't have wanted his cousin and greatest friend to sacrifice his happiness for them, and Melanie could offer him no less. In memory of her husband she would have to be strong and let Sebastion go to this Isabelle, whom he obviously loved so much.

"It doesn't matter," Sebastion said gruffly. What a liar he was.

Melanie placed a hand on his arm. "I think it does." She smiled somewhat sadly at him. "I think you're in love with this Isabelle, but you're staying here because you think you owe something to Jonathan's family. Am I right?"

He looked at her, letting all the pain and longing show in his flashing eyes. "Yes, you're right. But I owe the Larrimores a great debt, and I will pay it," he vowed roughly.

"Even at the expense of your own happiness?"

"Let it go, Melanie," he ground out. "You and the boys need me."

She nodded in agreement. "Yes, we do need you. How long do you plan to stay?"

His face was grim. "Until James Sebastion is old enough to run things." He felt sick just saying it. Years and years of his life, and by the time he was free to return to Isabelle, she would probably have children of her own ready to marry.

"Do you love her, your Isabelle?" Melanie asked softly.

"With all that I am," came the taut reply. Now that he had finally spoken the words aloud, he suddenly knew that he had to be with her, debts and obligations be damned. Life without her was only existing, not truly living. But he looked at the fragile young woman before him and wondered how she could manage without him.

Melanie saw his indecision and tapped his chest angrily with one gloved finger. "No," she said. "I won't let you do it. I have been selfish long enough, letting you stay here and take care of me, but no longer." She drew herself up to her full height, her head coming just to Sebastion's chin. "I won't be the one to ruin your life." There, she had done it. Her knees where trembling and her heart was pounding, but she had done it. And despite her fear she felt wonderful.

He stared down at her. "You don't know what you're saying, Melanie." He turned away from her with a rough jerk of his shoulder. "How will you survive without me? You know nothing of running an estate this size. Not to mention all of the other Kensington affairs. I owe it to them to stay here," he said, referring to Richard and Jonathan. "You don't understand."

"I understand more than you know," she said. "Jonathan told me all about when you were a little boy, how Richard and Henrietta took you in."

Sebastion rounded on her. "Then you should know why I have to stay."

"Do you think they took you in so you would be indebted to them?" she asked in exasperation. "No. They took you in because they wanted to, plain and simple." Her voice rose with each word until she was nearly shouting. "And as far as Jonathan was concerned, you owed him nothing. Your friendship was the most precious thing in his life outside of our marriage. You insult his memory to think that he would want you to give up a chance at finding the kind of love he and I shared." She stopped then, aware that she was yelling. Taking a deep breath to calm herself, she continued. "All that Richard or Jonathan or any of us would want is that you live your own life, doing whatever it is that gives you joy."

Sebastion was quiet for a long while, considering all Melanie had said. He had been tormented for weeks with thoughts of Isabelle, of their one night together and their bittersweet good-bye. When he had visited her grandmother's Paris house the morning after their return, it was to find that Isabelle and her grandmother had departed. He had been more disappointed than he cared to recall, but a part of him had understood why she had flown. Saying good-bye was painful, and she had already told him what was in her heart. Having to go through it all again would have been too much.

The words Isabelle had uttered so softly in the coach returned to haunt him: *Remember that someone loved you dearly.* She loved him, and though he had not said the words, he loved her. It was simple once he thought of it. It was a choice between love and duty. So which one would he choose? He looked out once again over the estate and all its holdings, then down at the pale young woman beside him. But all he could see was the smiling face and adoring green eyes of the woman he loved. He would find some way to help Melanie run things, but for now he knew that he had to be with Isabelle.

If she would still have him.

"I suppose you'll have to get along without me for a while," he said slowly. "At least until after the honeymoon."

A slow smile began to spread across his face, and he looked down at Melanie, who was also smiling, and crying at the same time. "Oh, Sebastion," she breathed. "I'm so glad." Impulsively, she threw her arms around him, and he surprised them both by hugging her back, lifting her off her feet in the process. When he put her back down, she grinned a watery little grin and said, "Go on, now. You mustn't keep a woman waiting, you know."

Sebastion kissed her chastely on the forehead, feeling lighter and more hopeful than ever before in his life. He was going to find Isabelle. He was going to claim his life.

A cheerful fire burned in the hearth of Delphine du Vallon's sitting room, but it did nothing to lift the spirits of the room's lone occupant. Delphine herself reclined on a satin divan, her shoulders comfortably warmed by a woolen shawl. She stared pensively into the flames, her mind filled with troubling thoughts concerning her favorite grandchild. Oh, she loved her other grandchildren, but Isabelle had always been special to her, just as her mother had before her.

Delphine had always felt as though she failed Isabelle's mother, Marie-Elise, somewhere along the way, and she had vowed not to make the same mistake with her daughter. And yet she was afraid that she had done exactly that. Marie-Elise had been a rather timid girl, sweet and gentle, stunningly beautiful. Delphine had never wanted her to marry Victor Saint-Simon, but the young woman had been adamant, and finally Delphine had given her consent. Victor was too harsh and cold for such a delicate creature, and secretly Delphine had always blamed him for her child's untimely death.

When Marie-Elise's daughter had asked to come live with her, she'd felt as though she had been given a second chance. Isabelle was as genteel and beautiful as her mother, but she had something else, too, something her mother had sadly lacked: strength. Delphine had nurtured that strength, molding her granddaughter into her version of the perfect woman. And therein lay the problem. She had been so focused on making Isabelle what she wanted her to be that she hadn't let the

girl be her own person. And Victor was even worse.
Between the two of them they had stifled whatever natural inclinations the girl had, influencing them to suit
their own needs. They had done Isabelle a great dis-
service, and Delphine was only now realizing just how
great.

Since their return from Paris more than three months
before Isabelle had been a changed woman. Gone was
the confident, somewhat spoiled girl Delphine had
helped raise. In her place was a quiet, introspective,
melancholy young woman. She spoke little and ate
even less, and spent her time taking long walks or solitary rides through the countryside. Friends and relatives had given up calling, for she would see none of
them. Even Henri Lanoux had finally admitted defeat
after two months of constant refusals. Isabelle had
given back his ring and Henri had accepted it.

Isabelle would not speak of her troubles. At first Delphine had thought her despondent over her stepbrother's death, but soon she began to suspect that
there was more to it. She had tried to discuss the matter, but her granddaughter stubbornly refused to talk.
The girl would claim that she was fine, and then find
some excuse to leave the house, fleeing the older
woman's prying questions. Delphine was no expert in
matters of the heart, but it seemed to her that the girl
was pining for someone.

It wasn't as if she moped around the house, though.
Far from it. She was very solicitous of her grandmother, and more kind to the servants than she had
ever been. But she would not speak of anything that
was of a personal nature, and Delphine was worried.
It wasn't good for her to keep all her feelings inside,
no matter what foolishness her father had taught her.
Delphine feared that Isabelle would cut herself off so
completely from the rest of the world that she would
end up a lonely old woman, living on faded memories.

"Madame." The butler's voice broke into her thoughts.

Delphine angled in her chair to peer up at him. "Yes, what is it?" A note of annoyance crept into her tone. She didn't like to be disturbed when she was thinking.

"A gentleman is here to see Mademoiselle Isabelle," he intoned gravely. "I informed him that she was not at home, but he is most insistent."

From the way he stressed *most insistent*, Delphine could tell that the caller was not a patient man. "Did the gentleman give a name?"

The butler raised his chin a notch. "Lord Fairfax, madame."

Delphine frowned in puzzlement. The name sounded familiar, but she didn't think she knew anyone by that name. What would an English lord want with Isabelle? She started to wave the servant away, then paused. *Lord Fairfax.* Sebastion Merrick. Isabelle's Englishman. Perhaps he could shed some light on her granddaughter's strange behavior. "Show him in," Delphine instructed.

"In here?" The retainer was clearly startled. Only family and very close acquaintances were received in the private sitting room.

"Yes," Delphine snapped.

The servant recovered his usual impassive expression. "Very well, madame."

A few moments later Sebastion Merrick was shown into the room. Delphine had risen from her position on the divan and stood with her back to the door warming her hands by the fire.

"Madame du Vallon," he said in greeting. "Forgive my intrusion, but I have come a long way to see your granddaughter. Is she here?"

Delphine turned to regard him, pinning him with a speculative glare. "Good afternoon, young man." She indicated a chair. "Won't you sit down?" He did so reluctantly, obviously impatient to see Isabelle. Delphine decided to be kind and get to the point. "What brings you so far from home, monsieur?"

His expression was one of serious intent. "I have come to ask Isabelle to be my wife."

The older woman gave no outward indication that she was at all surprised, but inwardly she had to admit she hadn't counted on this. Of course, if Isabelle was in love with this man, it would explain why she had been so unhappy without him. "Has my granddaughter given you any indication that she would accept such a proposal?"

"Yes, she has."

She pursed her lips at his brevity. Lord Fairfax wasn't much of a talker, apparently. "May I ask why you did not make this offer sooner? It has been more than three months since we last saw you." She wasn't going to make this too easy on the young man. If he wanted her blessing, she would have to get some answers.

His face darkened. "I had family obligations that I have only recently met." His eyes glittered with feeling. "Believe me when I say that I would have come for her sooner if I had been able."

"Do you love her?" she asked bluntly, throwing decorum and manners to the wind. Her granddaughter's future happiness was at stake.

"I do," he answered gravely. "And I believe that she loves me."

Delphine's lips twitched as she fought the urge to smile. She had always been a good judge of character, and she could tell that this handsome suitor was sincere. She actually found herself liking him. But it wouldn't do to let him know that too soon. "Very well, young man," she said imperiously. "Isabelle is down by the pond. Just follow the gardens all the way to the end and you'll see it."

His expression brightened. "Thank you, madame." He rose swiftly to his feet and turned to go. "Wish me luck," he said with such impertinence that Delphine couldn't help but laugh.

Chapter Twenty-seven

Sebastion found Isabelle by the pond, just as Delphine had said. She sat on a low stone bench several feet from the water's edge, staring at a pair of black swans that swam languidly across the dark water. Her head was bare and the afternoon sun caught the gold and silver highlights of her curls. She was dressed for warmth in a bottle green woolen coat, and he knew without seeing that it would make her eyes appear even greener.

The closely clipped grass muffled his steps and he was almost upon her before she sensed his presence. Slowly she turned, her face draining of all color when she saw who it was. How many times had he come to her just like this in her dreams? After all the terrible days and nights she had endured since he had left, she could scarcely believe he was actually here. She wanted to run to him and throw her arms around him, but pride held her back. She had offered her love once and been refused. It was up to him this time. He would have to say the words, if that was indeed why he had come. Isabelle wouldn't let herself even imagine such a thing. It would be too cruel to have her hopes dashed once again.

"Hello, Isabelle," he greeted in a voice made rough with emotion.

"Sebastion," she acknowledged, her expression stoic.

He moved closer to the bench but did not sit down. "How have you been?" he asked politely. Unsure of his welcome, he ruthlessly resisted the urge to take her in his arms. Instead he adopted his best gentleman's manner.

"Fine," she answered automatically. It wouldn't do to tell him how she had really been.

He indicated her coat. "I see you aren't in mourning."

She shook her head. "I grieve for Reynaud in my own way. It's no one's concern what colors I choose to wear."

"True," he agreed amiably. "I missed you that day in Paris when I came to say good-bye. You and your grandmother had already departed by the time I arrived."

Isabelle's heart fluttered painfully in her chest. "Yes, well, we had to leave rather suddenly." Her throat worked reflexively as she tried to swallow the lump that had formed there. "We had already said our good-byes."

"You may have said yours, but I never had the chance to say mine."

"It wouldn't have changed anything," she pointed out resignedly. "I thought it best to spare us both the trial."

His voice was low and earnest. "I didn't consider it a trial. I would have liked to visit with you one last time." He paused. "But perhaps you didn't wish to talk to me."

She sighed wearily, not up to engaging in a verbal sparring match with him. "I simply wanted to go home," she answered. "I'm sure you quickly got over whatever disappointment you may have felt at not finding me there. Besides, you were needed more by your family." She didn't try to hide the note of bitterness that crept into her voice. He had forsaken her, leaving her in misery for months, and now here he was making small talk as if nothing had ever happened.

"Duty calls and all that, hmm?" he said wryly.

Isabelle didn't want to discuss that particular subject, so she asked him the question foremost on her mind. "What are you doing here?"

He came around the side of the bench and sat down next to her. She turned to look at the pond in front of her, offering him her cameolike profile.

"I came to see how you were," he answered.

She still refused to meet his gaze. "As you can see, I'm fine."

"If that's true, then I'm glad," he answered.

Isabelle didn't trust herself to respond. At her silence, he continued. "I also wanted to tell you about the chalice. I donated it to a museum in London."

This surprised her. "I thought it was a family heirloom. Won't your cousin's children want it?"

Sebastion shook his head. "It's proper place is in a museum. Besides, it holds some rather bad memories now." He sighed. "It's better this way."

"I suppose," she said dully. Had he made such a long trip just to tell her that? He could have simply written her a letter and saved them both the trouble.

His next words answered her unspoken question. "I also came to tell you that I'm getting married," he said carefully.

Isabelle felt her stomach clench into knots and she feared that she might be ill. Why was he doing this to her? Didn't he know it would break her heart? She continued to stare dry-eyed at the swans, too hurt to even cry. "I suppose I should offer my congratulations," she said numbly, "but you'll forgive me if I cannot."

"I thought you would be happy," he remarked.

It was too much for her, she had to get away. She stood and began to walk blindly away, wanting to put as much distance between them as possible. She couldn't bear to see him so happy about marrying someone else. It was too much to ask of her. Sebastion caught her before she had taken a dozen steps. Strong hands held her shoulders while his body blocked her path.

"Please let me go," she said in a strained little voice.

Sebastion's voice was gentle. "Isabelle," he said, tipping up her chin with one long finger. "Look at me."

She raised her eyes to his, the aching sadness inside her almost crippling. "I want you to be happy," she whispered. "And if marrying Jonathan's widow will make that happen, then I will try to be glad."

Sebastion smiled tenderly at her. He was such a fool to have underestimated this wonderful woman. Even in the midst of her own sadness, she only wanted the best for him. "Who said I was marrying Melanie?"

She frowned. "You did."

He shook his head. "I said I was getting married. I never said to whom."

"Don't play games with me, Sebastion. I don't think I can bear it."

"Ask me, Isabelle," he said, suddenly insistent. "Ask me who it is I love."

Something in the tone of his voice made her pause. Gone was the polite stranger of a few moments before. In his place was the Englishman who had captured her heart. She looked up unto his eyes, so intent upon her. And she *knew*. He had come back for her. "Who do you love?" she asked, her voice thick with emotion.

"She's a French girl I met a few months ago." His well-shaped lips curled up at the edges into an endearing smile. "She's very smart and quite beautiful. Her temper sometimes gets the best of her, but we'll work on that." He lowered his head so that his forehead rested at her crown. "She's funny and warm-hearted, and when she looks at me I feel as though anything is possible." His voice dropped to a whisper. "She once told me that she loved me dearly. I haven't asked her to be my wife yet, but I'm hoping that she'll agree because I don't think I can make it through another day without her."

Isabelle reached up to touch the harsh planes of his face. "It certainly took you long enough to realize that, you silly man," she said, laughing and crying at the same time.

Sebastion brushed his lips across her cheeks, kissing the tears away. "I love you," he said huskily, "I was lost without you." He wrapped his arms around her waist. "Will you marry me and save me from myself, Isabelle Saint-Simon?"

"What about your family?" she asked tentatively, almost afraid of the answer. But if they were to have a life together, she wanted to be sure before she gave her answer.

Sebastion frowned slightly at her unexpected response. "I haven't worked out all the details yet, but my family understands that you come first. I know it isn't fair to ask you to leave your home, but maybe we could live half the year in England and . . ."

Isabelle stopped him with a kiss. "I'll go wherever you want me to and be blissfully happy as long as we're together." She couldn't help but chide him a little. "If only you had asked, I would have told you the same thing months ago. My home is wherever you are, and I will love your family simply because they're yours."

Sebastion pulled her into an embrace. "I don't deserve you," he vowed, "but I'll spend the rest of my life trying to prove I do."

Isabelle smiled. "Then, yes," she answered joyfully. "Yes, I will marry you." She offered him her mouth, and he took it greedily in a kiss that was so sweet it brought fresh tears to her eyes.

Kathleen McCarthy

All around them the leaves were falling like rose petals thrown at a wedding by well-wishers.

"When all this started," Sebastion said finally, "I came looking for revenge. What I found was a treasure to hold."

The Rogue and the Hellion

CONNIE MASON

When an audacious highwayman holds up his coach and points a pistol at a rather crucial part of his anatomy, the Marquis of Bathurst has a critical choice to make—give up his dead brother's ring or lose the family jewels. Gabriel decides to part with the memento, but he will track down the green-eyed thief if it is the last thing he does.

When the most infamous member of the Rogues of London takes her in his arms, Olivia Fairfax knows his intentions are far from honorable. Gabriel's hot pursuit makes her pulse race, but is he after a lover or the hellion who dared to rob him at gunpoint? Either way, Olivia knows it is her turn to hand over the goods, and she is ready to give him both her body and her heart.

Belle
Melanie Jackson

With the letter breaking his engagement, Stephan Kirton's hopes for respectability go up in smoke. Inevitably, his "interaction with the lower classes" and the fact that he is a bastard have put him beyond the scope of polite society. He finds consolation at Ormstead Park; a place for dancing, drinking and gambling . . . a place where he can find a woman for the night.

He doesn't recognize her at first; ladies don't come to Lord Duncan's masked balls. This beauty's descent into the netherworld has brought her within reach, yet she is no girl of the day. Annabelle Winston is sublime. And if he has to trick her, bribe her, protect her, whatever—one way or another he will make her an honest woman. And she will make him a happy man.

___4975-9 $5.99 US/$7.99 CAN

Rules For A Lady

Katherine Greyle

A lady does not attempt to come out in London society disguised as her deceased half-sister. A lady does not become enamored of her guardian, even though his masterful kisses and whispered words of affection tempt her beyond all endurance. A lady may not climb barefoot from her bedroom on a rose trellis, nor engage in fisticuffs with riffraff in order to rescue street urchins. No matter how impossible the odds, a lady always gives her hand and her heart–though not necessarily in that order–to the one man who sees her as she truly is and loves her despite her flagrant disobedience of every one of the rules for a lady.

___4818-3 $4.99 US/$5.99 CAN